Secrets of the Serpent's Heart

N. S. WIKARSKI

Secrets of the Serpent's Heart
Book Six of Seven – Arkana Archaeology Adventure Series

http://www.mythofhistory.com

This is a work of fiction. Names, characters, places, and incidents either are the product of the author's imagination or are used fictitiously, and any resemblance to any persons, living or dead, business establishments, events, or locales is entirely coincidental.

ISBN: 1519419139
ISBN-13: 978-1519419132

AUTHOR'S NOTE

NAMES YOU SHOULD KNOW
(Through the End of Volume 5 in the Series)

Key to books in the series:
GK – The Granite Key
MM – The Mountain Mother Cipher
DW – The Dragon's Wing Enigma
DD – Riddle of the Diamond Dove
JL – Into the Jaws of the Lion

Abraham Metcalf – Prophet and autocratic leader of the Blessed Nephilim. In his seventies.

Annabeth – Third wife of Daniel. Nervous and high-strung. Wants to improve her position in the Nephilim hierarchy by birthing more children.

Archwarden – Leader of a Nephilim satellite compound.

Arkana – Secret organization whose mission is to retrieve and protect the artifacts of lost pre-patriarchal civilizations around the globe.

Blessed Nephilim – Fundamentalist religious cult which traces its lineage to the Nephilim of the Bible. They practice polygamy, live in isolated compounds, and maintain a strict separation from the rest of the world.

Bones of the Mother – Collection of Minoan artifacts which have been hidden among the ruins of forgotten civilizations on every continent. Each artifact provides clues to the location of the next relic. Collectively, they will lead to the location of the Sage Stone.

Cassie Forsythe – Psychic with the ability to touch an artifact and relive scenes from its past. She succeeds to the title of pythia within the Arkana after the murder of her sister. Nineteen-year-old college freshman at the beginning of the story.

Central Catalog – Abandoned rural schoolhouse outside the Chicago metro area which contains the records of Arkana troves throughout the world. Also known as "the Vault."

Chatelaine – Arkana honorary title meaning "castle protector and keeper of the keys." Rank conferred on Maddie in recognition of distinguished service (DD). This title carries with it voting privileges within the Circle.

Chief Scrivener – Person responsible for managing the records of the Arkana Central Catalog. The title is currently held by Griffin. His rank was elevated to Right Honorable Chief Scrivener in recognition of distinguished service (DD). This title carries with it voting privileges within the Circle.

Chopper (Orvis) Bowdeen – Mercenary and friend of Leroy Hunt. Hired by Abraham Metcalf to provide weapons training to the Nephilim and set up surveillance systems at all Nephilim compounds around the world.

Chris (David Christian) – Librarian at the Chicago Public Library who assists Daniel with his research and becomes his friend.

Circle – Governing body of the Arkana.

Concordance – General Council of the Arkana.

Consecrated Bride – Nephilim term for married women within the cult.

Daniel Metcalf – Lesser son of Abraham whose skill with ancient languages has made him an unwilling participant in the quest to find the Bones of the Mother.

Diviner – Title given to the prophet of the Nephilim. A role currently occupied by Abraham Metcalf.

Dr. Rafi Aboud – Foreign doctor with a mysterious past who has been hired by Abraham to perform experiments at a secret laboratory. The purpose of his experiments is known only to the diviner.

Erik – Martial arts and weapons expert, in his mid-twenties. His job is to protect the pythia on field assignments and arrange for the safe transportation of artifacts. His title is security coordinator.

Fallen – Term used by the Nephilim to describe inhabitants of the outer world. Anyone who doesn't belong to the cult.

Faye – Elderly leader of the Arkana. She holds the title of memory guardian. Her age is unknown, but it may exceed normal human limits.

Field Agent – Operatives of the Arkana deployed around the globe who handle artifact retrievals. Individuals tasked with assisting in the retrieval of Bones of the Mother. In order of appearance: Fred (Turkey-MM), Rabten and Rinchen (Tibet-JL).

Griffin – Chief Scrivener. He is responsible for cataloguing all artifacts collected in troves around the world. British and in his early twenties, he has an eidetic memory.

Hannah Curtis – Teenage bride of Daniel Metcalf who is subsequently reassigned to marry his father Abraham. Runaway who has found shelter with Faye.

Joshua Metcalf – Daniel's biological brother and competitor for Abraham's favor. Appointed by the diviner as head of the Order of Argus.

Leroy Hunt – Mercenary currently on the payroll of the Nephilim. His job is to protect Daniel as they attempt to retrieve the Bones of the Mother. He has no conscience and a taste for violence.

Maddie – Short-tempered, chain-smoking Operations director of the Arkana. She manages day-to-day global affairs.

Matristic Civilizations – Arkana term for ancient goddess-worshipping societies which thrived without military fortifications, rigid social hierarchies, male dominance, or career warfare.

Memory Guardian – Faye's title as head of the Arkana.

Mother Rachel – Principal wife of the diviner. Highest ranking consecrated bride of the Blessed Nephilim.

Operations Director – Maddie's title as manager of global operations for the Arkana.

Operatives – Members of Blessed Nephilim satellite communities assigned to help Daniel in the field. In order of appearance: Nikos (Crete-GK), Ilhami (Turkey-MM), Sergio (Spain-DW), Mohammed (Egypt and Sudan, DD).

Order of Argus – Secret intelligence organization within the Nephilim. Abraham's eyes and ears among the congregation.

Overlord Cultures – Arkana term for male-dominated warrior cultures fixated on territorial expansion through conquest and exploitation of indigenous inhabitants.

Paladin - Arkana honorary title meaning "the pythia's defender." Rank conferred on Erik in recognition of distinguished service (DD). This title carries with it voting privileges within the Circle.

Pythia – Title currently held by Cassie. The official seer of the Arkana. Her rank was elevated to Right Honorable Pythia in recognition of distinguished service (DD). This title carries with it voting privileges within the Circle.

Rhonda – Antique store owner and Sybil's former business partner. Surrogate big sister to Cassie.

Sage Stone – Mythical Minoan relic which is reputed to possess great power. Nephilim prophecy reveals that this relic must be acquired by Abraham if his secret plan to orchestrate a global apocalypse is to succeed.

Scion – Nephilim title given to the diviner's successor and heir-apparent. Daniel currently holds the position.

Scouts – Operatives of the Arkana deployed around the world to ferret out undiscovered matristic civilizations and potential new trove sites. In order of appearance: Bobbye Johnson (Botswana-DD), Oluoma Okoli (Nigeria-DD).

Security Coordinator – Title originally held by Erik. He reports to the operations director.

Sentinel – Watchers posted by the ancient Minoans to guard the location of each artifact until the arrival of the Arkana team. In order of appearance: Iker Mendiluze (Spain-DW).

Sybil Forsythe – Cassie's sister. Late pythia of the Arkana.

Trove – Arkana collection point for artifacts related to a specific geographic region or culture.

Trove Keeper – Person appointed to manage the collection of artifacts at a particular location or trove. In order of appearance: Xenia Katsouros (Minoan-GK), Aydin Ozgur (Anatolian-MM), Stefan Kasprzyk (Kurgan-MM), Thea Xara (Maltese-DW), Ortzi Exteberri (Basque-DW), Ochanda Exteberri (Basque-DW), Grace Littlefield (Haudenosaunee-DW), Michel

Khatabi (Berber-DD), Sophie Khatabi (assistant, Berber-DD), Dee Pandala (Malabar-JL).

Tyro – Title which refers to an apprentice agent of the Arkana. In order of appearance: John (Sudan-DD), Zachary (Vault-JL).

Vault – Another name for the Central Catalog.

Vlad – Broker for shady arms deals. Aboud's ally in finding a buyer for weaponized pneumonic plague.

Zachary – Faye's teenage descendent—often referred to as her "great-great-something-or-other grandson." He has joined the Arkana as a tyro.

TABLE OF CONTENTS

1 – HOW A GOLDEN AGE TURNS BRONZE

Gansu Province, Northern China, 2650 BCE

During the age of Shen-Nung, people rested at ease and acted with vigor. They knew their mothers but not their fathers. They lived among deer. They ate what they cultivated and wore what they wove. They did not think of harming one another. –Zhuangzi

The woman stood upright and stretched to ease the stiffness in her back. She'd been cultivating around the roots of a row of millet plants. She paused to study the feathery seed heads drooping above their tall stalks—still green though the weather had been fair and promised to ripen them in a few more weeks. Her youngest son, barely more than a toddler, was attempting to help her by attacking weed clumps with a sharp stick.

Out of the corner of her eye, she noticed movement in the distance. Several dozen figures were descending from the mountains that surrounded the river valley where she and her clan lived. They were moving at a leisurely pace down the slopes. Curious, she dropped her hoe and, taking her son by the hand, threaded her way through the millet field. Several others of her clan, also working in the fields, had noticed the approach of the strangers. The farm folk wandered toward the river bank and gathered in a small group to watch their descent.

As the band loomed ever nearer, a collective murmur of surprise rose from residents. The woman gasped audibly at the spectacle. The strangers numbered about fifty men, women, and children. These people were odd-looking. Whereas the villagers were short and stocky with straight black hair and brown eyes, the strangers were tall and gangly, their skins as pale as a fish's belly. Their eyes were round and set deep in their sockets. Their hair was bushy—the color and texture of straw.

They were not walking but riding. The lead figure sat astride a long-necked, long-nosed beast which he controlled with leather straps fastened around the creature's mouth. The woman had seen a few of these animals before though large numbers of them were said to roam across the grasslands beyond the mountains. They were useless as livestock. Not placid like the pigs which her clan kept in pens. These long-necked creatures were easily frightened and, once startled, they ran like the wind. Sometimes her people would hunt them for their meat, but no one had ever tried to sit on one before.

Yet here was a band of humans astride the backs of these creatures as if it was the most natural thing in the world. Not all the strangers were riding the animals though. Several among them, mainly women and children, were traveling in even stranger fashion. They sat in square wooden boxes with round disks attached on either side. Long-necked beasts were tied to these boxes and pulled them forward, making the disks spin and leaving behind tracks in the grass.

The woman's son had wrapped his arms around her leg as if it were a tree trunk. He stared up at her, silently demanding to be carried. She hoisted him into her arms, so he could get a better view. He stuck his fist into his mouth, warily regarding the advancing procession.

The woman's eyes were drawn to a female figure seated in the foremost of the square boxes. A plank of wood was strapped to her back. On it rested an infant if the poor little thing could be said to rest at all. It was swathed in cloth strips that bound its tiny body to the plank. The infant was wrapped so firmly that it could move neither its arms nor its legs. Its forehead was held rigidly against the board to keep it from flopping to either side. For a moment, the woman wondered whether the baby was even alive. Perhaps this was the way these foreigners prepared their dead for burial. Then the baby's eyes blinked open lethargically. The pressure of the wrappings made the eyes seem to bulge from their sockets, but the infant remained mute. Perhaps it knew that no one would release it from its bindings, so there was no point in whimpering.

The woman's attention then traveled from the bound infant to its mother. Her hair was flame-colored. She wore an intricately stitched shawl—red and green thread had been worked into square shapes with straight lines shooting through them. The design was more complex than anything the clan weavers could produce.

This caravan was a peculiar sight to be sure. But of all the curiosities in this odd procession, there was one stranger than all the rest. It was a wooden platform, smaller than the boxes which held the women and children. It too had wooden disks attached to each side and was pulled by a long-necked animal. Beneath the platform were more disks with notched edges which seemed to interlock with one another. These all connected to a small pillar resting on top of the platform. The pillar was topped by an ornamental carving of the neck and head of one of the beasts these people used for conveyance. As this platform traveled forward, no matter which way it zigged and zagged down the hills, the nose of the carving always turned toward the same direction. The woman judged it to be pointing south. She couldn't imagine what purpose this device served.

Her silent speculation was cut short when the leader of the band raised his arm, commanding his followers to halt. They wordlessly obeyed. The man gave his beast a sharp kick in the ribs, and it ambled forward until he tugged on the strap in its mouth to make it stop a mere ten feet away from the assembled clan.

The farm folk gawked up at him. He impassively stared back at them. The woman took in every detail of his appearance. His yellow hair hung down his back. It was the color of ripe millet as was the color of the thick beard which flowed down his chest. His age was hard to guess. He was not a youth but not an elder either. His eyes were set so deeply that his eyelids folded over them like a hood. On his head, he wore some sort of metal bowl turned upside down. Horns had been affixed to either side of the bowl, giving him the fearsome aspect of a charging beast. A long knife hung from a leather belt at his waist.

The stranger made no threatening gesture despite his warlike attire. He merely sat on his animal and silently studied the people clustered below him. After a few moments, his gaze shifted from the crowd to the millet fields, the houses, the livestock pens and the river flowing endlessly off into the distance. A slight smile tugged at the corners of his mouth. The farmers continued to gape and point and whisper among themselves.

The woman felt a shadow cross the sun even though the sky was clear and bright. She didn't have the gift of second sight like the shamans of the clan. Her gift lay in making things grow. Still, she felt an unaccountable sense of despair welling up from the depths of her heart. Without being able to explain why she knew that her world was about to change—and not for the better.

2 – LEGAL THRESHOLD

Present Day, Western Suburbs of Chicago

"I think you've got OCD." Cassie climbed out of the driver's seat and slammed her car door for emphasis.

"Humor me," Griffin replied dryly as he exited his own vehicle.

They were standing in the parking lot of Cassie's apartment complex.

Leroy Hunt's persistent efforts to find her had caused the pythia to take shelter in the western suburbs—as far away from the vault and downtown Chicago as possible. Her housing development was a sprawling complex of modern three-story apartment buildings clustered artistically around a central retention pond whose fountain had been turned off for the winter. A thin glaze of ice still coated the water.

Cassie hugged herself to keep warm while she waited for Griffin to catch up with her. Even though spring was technically around the corner, the early evening temperature was barely above freezing. They scurried up the walk to her front door on the ground level.

"Look, I'm telling you," she continued. "I just cleaned my place two days ago, and I didn't see your missing field agent's journal anywhere."

"Really?" The scrivener sounded genuinely puzzled. "I could have sworn I left it here the last time I dropped by."

Cassie gave an exasperated sigh and fitted her key into the lock. "Go ahead and look but you won't find it."

She swung the door open to reveal a dark, quiet apartment. Without warning, the ceiling lights blazed on, and a chorus of voices shouted, "SURPRISE!"

"What the..." Cassie trailed off, blinking under the glare. She turned mutely to the scrivener.

Thirty people popped out from behind various pieces of furniture and came forward to greet her. She recognized them as co-workers from the Arkana. Her visitors must have been busy before her arrival because the dining room table was covered with an array of chips, dips, sandwiches, salads, and pastries. They had even gone to the trouble of decorating for the occasion. Helium balloons bobbed above the dining room chandelier, and the patio door valance was festooned with streamers.

The crowd launched into a boisterous rendition of "Happy Birthday."

By the time they finished, Cassie was blushing from the fuss everyone was making.

Maddie's tall form strode forward. She bent down to give Cassie a bear hug. "Happy birthday, kiddo. It's not every day that a pythia turns twenty-one."

"I guess that's because pythias usually don't live that long," Cassie retorted.

Maddie drew back. "Nonsense. Your sister Sybil was a lot older before she got murdered."

"Thanks, that's really comforting."

By this time, Faye had elbowed her way through the crowd to offer her own congratulations. "Never mind her, my dear. This day is a cause for celebration. You've officially come of age."

The pythia smiled ruefully. "After working for the Arkana for the past two years, I can honestly say I feel like I'm twenty-one going on forty-five."

"You don't look a day over forty-four." Griffin patted her consolingly on the shoulder.

She turned to face him. "So, your story about needing to find your missing journal was just a clever ruse to get me here?"

"That was only part of the ruse. I was charged with detaining you at the vault as late as possible until Maddie rang to tell me that all was ready. Then I was to lure you here at the proper moment."

"Good job on both counts." Cassie nodded approvingly.

At that moment, an unexpected guest walked up bearing a tray with several glasses of champagne.

"Oh, my goddess!" Cassie exclaimed. "Rhonda, what are you doing here?"

Her sister's former business partner handed the tray to Griffin, so she could enfold Cassie in an embrace. "It's so good to see you again, sweetie," she murmured, pressing her lips to the pythia's cheek.

Cassie held the woman at arm's length to study her. "You're looking tanned and rested. Last I heard you were on a world cruise courtesy of the Arkana."

Rhonda gave Maddie a sidelong glance. "I got back a few months ago. That's when your fearless leader set me up in an antique shop in San Francisco. Presumably, nobody's going to look for me there."

The pythia shook her head emphatically. "Absolutely not." She scowled as a new thought struck her. "Is it safe for you to be in Chicago?"

"Please," Rhonda protested. "If I were to miss your twenty-first birthday, Sybil's ghost would haunt me from beyond the grave. Besides, I'm not going anywhere near the city—just back to Midway to catch an early flight tomorrow morning. Don't you worry about me. I'm the one who should be worrying about my silent partner."

"You're still cutting me in on Sybil's share of the shop?" Cassie asked in surprise.

"The agreement stands," Rhonda affirmed, "no matter where the shop is located."

While Cassie gave Rhonda another hug for good measure, Maddie distributed champagne glasses to the group. Handing one to the pythia, she urged, "Your first drink. Take it."

"Oh, I've tasted alcohol before," Cassie hedged. "But this will be my first legal drink." She raised her glass. "To the Twenty-First Amendment!"

"To the Twenty-First Amendment," the others echoed and toasted her.

After a few sips, the pythia turned to survey the food and decorations and the sheer number of well-wishers. Her face must have betrayed her bafflement.

"Something the matter?" the scrivener asked cautiously.

Cassie shook her head in wonder. "No. Not at all. This is awesome. It's beyond awesome. It's the biggest birthday party I've had in my entire life." She hesitated. "I don't remember what birthdays were like while my parents were still alive. Later on, Sybil and I had an offhanded way of celebrating. She'd usually come home late from work, take one look at my face, smack herself on the forehead and say 'Oh, crap!' Then she'd rush out to the nearest convenience store and bring back a cupcake. I'd stick a candle in the middle, light it, and she'd sing me 'Happy Birthday.'"

Her story was met by an uncomfortable silence from her listeners.

Realizing how dismal her prior birthdays must have sounded to them, she tried to repair the damage. "Of course, at the time I didn't realize the kind of job Sybil was doing for the Arkana. I just thought she was being self-absorbed. Now that I know first-hand the number of knives she was juggling, I have to give her credit for remembering at all."

"How about we sample that spread," Maddie suggested, changing the subject. "My crew knocked themselves out to put it together."

In a loud voice, Cassie called out to the room in general, "I want to thank you all. You have no idea how much this means to me."

"Everybody dig in!" Maddie commanded in an even louder voice.

As the crowd moved toward the buffet, the chatelaine grabbed her coat and edged toward the front door.

In response to a quizzical look from Cassie, she explained, "Turns out party planning is even more stressful than running a covert global operation. I'm going to duck outside for a smoke to quiet my nerves."

***

Half an hour later, everyone was done milling around the table for seconds and thirds. Someone dimmed the lights and Griffin emerged from the kitchen carrying a birthday cake glowing with twenty-one candles.

After another rousing chorus of "Happy Birthday," Cassie blew them out, not missing a single one.

The scrivener leaned over and whispered, "What did you wish for?"

"I can't tell you that, or it won't come true," she protested. "Let's just say living long enough to snag the Sage Stone looms large in my plans."

As Rhonda and Faye busied themselves distributing slices of cake, the doorbell rang.

"Whoever that is, they're well beyond fashionably late," Griffin observed.

By the time Cassie reached the door, her visitor had already let himself in.

"Oh, it's you," she said in a small voice.

Erik seemed taken aback by the festivities. "What's going on here?"

"Shut the door, you're letting in a draft," Maddie commanded from the dining room.

As he entered the room, Erik confided to Cassie, "I just flew into O'Hare. When I called Maddie to check in, she told me to come straight here for a debriefing. She didn't mention anything about a party."

"Doesn't matter. Help yourself to some food," Cassie offered.

Erik shrugged pragmatically and headed for the buffet.

Griffin watched the interchange in silent disapproval. Under his breath, he muttered, "Not so much as a 'Happy Birthday'? That's a bit cheeky even for him."

"I thought you two made up after we got back from Tibet," Cassie remarked, walking back toward the dining room herself.

"We did. I'm merely offended that Erik continues to be Erik. His ubiquitous sense of entitlement never fails to appall."

The pythia grinned. "Can't help you with that. He is who he's always been." She handed Griffin a plate. "Here. Have some cake."

The scrivener smiled ruefully. "Very clever of you. If I'm eating I'm not sniping."

"I don't know what you're talking about," Cassie protested innocently.

***

Two hours later, Cassie stood in the doorway bidding goodnight to the last of her guests. Rhonda received a special caution to "watch her back." The kitchen had been tidied, and everyone sent home with containers of leftovers. Turning back into the apartment, the pythia was startled to realize that Faye, Maddie, Griffin, and Erik were all standing together waiting for her.

7

"Good," Maddie observed succinctly. "Now we can get down to business."

3 – FORMAL INVITATION

Zach surreptitiously checked his watch. It was almost nine PM. He glanced across the table at Hannah who was scanning a menu. The two sat in a booth at the village diner. They'd just walked over from the tiny local movie theater where they'd caught an early show. Unlike the multiplex at the mall, the town's lone theater stubbornly clung to the tradition of showing only one movie per week. Fortunately, it was a film that both Zach and Hannah had wanted to see. After sharing a tub of popcorn to stave off hunger for a few hours, they'd gone to the only restaurant on the green that was still open.

Much as Zach enjoyed having Hannah to himself for an entire evening, he was acting on Arkana orders. He'd leapt at the chance to be of service. As a tyro, the boy hadn't been trusted with anything more confidential than filing budget reports. This assignment was as close to top secret as he was likely to get for a while. Faye had told him to keep Hannah out until shortly before curfew. On Friday night, that meant eleven o'clock. His ancestor had been vague on the details but, apparently, she had some secret business to transact. Since Faye planned to return before their date was over, it would circumvent any awkward questions from Hannah about the old woman's whereabouts. The mission suited Zach perfectly. He had an agenda of his own to pursue with his girlfriend this evening.

The waitress returned to take their orders. Once she left, Zach leaned over the table and said, "Hannah, I'm a junior this year."

She gave him a quizzical look. "Yes, I know. And I'm a sophomore. Ever since school started last fall."

He smiled nervously. "Well, there's this thing. It's sort of like a rite of passage for guys my age."

She peered at him and whispered, "You haven't started drag racing, have you?"

"Drag racing!" His head jerked back in surprise. "Where'd you get an idea like that?"

"Well, I was watching an old movie last night called *Rebel Without a Cause*, and the high school boys in the movie were drag racing. Personally, I think you shouldn't try something like that. In fact, I don't think your car would hold together long enough to go over a cliff."

"Over a..." Zach's mouth hung open. "What?"

"It's very dangerous, and you shouldn't try it. I'm sure Granny Faye wouldn't want you to either."

The boy shook his head in disbelief. "What you're talking about isn't a drag race. It's a chicken race."

Hannah scowled. "There weren't any chickens in the movie. They were racing cars."

Zach gritted his teeth and tried again. "No, I mean what you described is called a chicken race. Usually, it's when two guys aim their cars straight at each other and whichever one swerves to the side first is the loser because he 'chickens out.' Get it?"

"Oh, I see." She nodded sagely. "Then what's a drag race?"

He shrugged. "That's just two guys racing against each other over a short distance. Whoever has the fastest car wins."

"So that's the kind of racing you do. Drag racing?"

"I don't drag race!" Zach exclaimed.

"Good." Hannah gave a relieved smile. "I'm glad I was able to talk you out of it in time."

"I never said..." Zach threw his hands up helplessly just as the waitress returned with their soft drinks. Removing the paper cover from his straw, the boy dipped it into his soda glass, eyeing his companion warily. "Can we get back to the topic?"

"I thought we were on the topic. I just convinced you to stop drag racing."

"How can somebody as smart as you be soooo linear?" he demanded loudly.

Hannah sat up straight in the booth, clearly offended. "You don't have to bite my head off, Zachary." She only used his full name when she was annoyed with him.

The boy moderated his pitch. "I was trying to explain about a rite of passage that happens to juniors in high school, and it's got nothing to do with poultry or engines."

The waitress came back with a tray and served them both veggie burgers and fries. She thumped down bottles of ketchup and mustard and then retreated back to the kitchen.

When they were alone, Zach tackled the subject once again. "This rite of passage that I was talking about is a school event that only kids in my class get to attend. Of course, they can bring whoever they want."

Hannah gulped down a mouthful of burger and stared at him. "Some of my friends were talking about that just the other day. It's a dance, isn't it? A special dance."

"That's right." Zach nodded with relief that he'd finally gotten her to focus. "We call it Junior Prom and I'd like you to be my date."

The girl gave a dreamy smile. "I would get to dress up, wouldn't I?"

"Sure." The boy warmed to the topic. "All the girls wear fancy dresses. Not long ones like for Senior Prom but fancier than regular clothes. The guys wear suits and ties."

"Oh, my." Hannah seemed flustered but excited by the prospect. "When Granny Faye took me shopping for school clothes we looked at dresses like the ones you're talking about. They were made of shiny, gauzy fabrics. In my whole life, I never saw anything as fine as that."

"Not likely." Zach snorted with derision. "When you were living with the Nephilim, they made you dress in old horse blankets."

She giggled self-consciously. "You're not wrong about that." Then her eyes glazed over as her imagination switched into overdrive. "And I would have to get my hair done in a salon. And wear evening makeup and maybe some jewelry. Granny Faye showed me a beautiful necklace of hers. She said I could borrow it if ever I went anyplace fancy."

Zach propped his hand under his chin, watching her make plans. It was nice to see her so happy. She'd come a long way from the scared runaway who'd taken refuge with his grandmother. Hannah kept up a steady stream of chatter for several more minutes. He wasn't really listening. He was just basking in the glow of her excitement. The way her eyes sparkled made his head spin.

Finally, she paused to catch her breath.

Taking advantage of the momentary lull, Zach grinned. "Should I take all of that as a 'yes'?"

"Oh, Zach!" She beamed at him. "I'll get to be a fairy tale princess for one night. Like Cinderella. Absolutely, I'll go with you." She paused. "There's just one thing..." Her tone was tentative. "Do you think you might be able to borrow your father's car that evening? Even though Cinderella rode to the ball in a pumpkin, it didn't have a bad muffler and polka dot spray paint on the doors."

"If I ask to borrow the sedan, you know he's gonna make me clean out the garage," the boy warned ominously.

"That doesn't sound so bad," Hannah countered.

"My family's garage hasn't been cleaned out in five years." Zach groaned at the prospect.

"Then I'll just have to ask my Fairy Godmother to help you out."

"Unless your Fairy Godmother has a wand that doubles as a grenade launcher, it's not gonna cut any ice with my dad."

Hannah giggled mischievously. "My Fairy Godmother's name is Granny Faye."

"Oh, that Fairy Godmother." Zach laughed. "Well, in that case, she'll get my dad to hand over the keys before you can say 'Bippity Boppity Boo.'"

"For such a tiny, soft-spoken lady, she certainly seems to have a lot of influence over people," Hannah observed.

Thinking of his ancestor's secret life as the leader of the Arkana, Zach cocked an amused eyebrow. "You've got no idea."

4 – GO WITH THE FLOW

Maddie motioned with her head. "Let's adjourn to the dining room, shall we?" By now the table had been cleared.

Faye took a chair at one end. "Would it be too much trouble to ask for another cup of coffee? I don't have as much energy as I once did for late night meetings."

"Oh, of course." Cassie darted into the kitchen and put on a fresh pot while Maddie took a seat at the end of the table opposite Faye.

Erik wandered to the refrigerator to grab a leftover sandwich. He silently returned to the dining room and sat down on Maddie's right.

Griffin retrieved cups and saucers and carried them to the table for Cassie to pour.

After gratefully receiving her beverage, Faye swept her gaze around the apartment. "I never got the opportunity to visit you in this place before. You've done a lovely job of decorating, my dear."

The pythia shrugged. "It's just your basic one-bedroom suburban apartment with post-modern decor. Big on the grey-and-chrome accents. I rented it furnished. All of Sybil's antiques are in storage. I figured if Leroy Hunt ever got a bead on me again I could decamp a lot quicker if a moving truck wasn't involved."

"A wise precaution, I'm sure." The old woman stirred cream into her coffee.

Cassie deposited the coffee pot in the center of the table and then sat down next to Griffin. Focusing on Maddie, she asked, "So what's this pow-wow all about?"

"First off, sorry to end your special day with a business meeting," the chatelaine began. "But this is probably the only chance we'll all have to talk face-to-face before you leave."

"You're leaving?" Erik asked sharply.

Cassie nodded. "Within the next couple of days, Griffin and I will be heading back to Asia to find that frozen river of ours. The Himalayas ought to be thawing out about now which means we can start hunting down the fifth relic."

"The final relic," Faye added quietly.

"You're right." The pythia felt startled. "I've been so focused on staying one step ahead of the Nephilim that I forgot. This is the last one. Once we get this artifact, we'll know where the Minoans hid the Sage Stone. And after we snag the Sage Stone, it'll be game over for the bad guys."

"Not exactly," Erik countered. "We still don't know how the Sage Stone fits into the Nephilim's grand plan."

"And just what is their plan?" Maddie directed her question to the paladin. "You've been overseas for two months now scoping out their satellite compound operations. Were you able to learn anything new?"

"Not as much as I wanted to find out," Erik admitted, "but enough to make me nervous. Tonight, I flew back from Spain and what I saw there is the same as everyplace else. It looks like the intel you got from Hannah when she first showed up didn't only apply to their headquarters."

"You mean to say they're setting up some sort of military operation at each of those far-flung locations?" Faye asked.

Noticing that the memory guardian's cup was empty, Cassie grabbed the coffee pot and poured a refill while the paladin continued.

"Yup. They've got armed guards posted at the entrance to each of those places with surveillance cameras mounted above the gates. Wherever I went, I made it a point to chat up the locals, and they all had the same story to tell. No weapons and no cameras at any of the compounds as recently as a year ago. Then two strangers showed up in the neighborhood. I was able to ID one of them as a Nephilim named Joshua Metcalf. The odds are pretty good that he's another of Abe's sons. The other guy is an outsider by the name of Orvis Bowdeen. I did some checking on the guy. His friends call him Chopper. He's ex-military and a crony of Leroy Hunt's."

"The Nephilim aren't known for fraternizing with anyone from the outside world," Griffin observed.

"I wouldn't exactly call it fraternizing," Erik said. "From what I was able to piece together, the Nephilim needed Bowdeen to provide weapons training to their own people. He also helped set up their surveillance systems at each satellite compound. After Bowdeen finished his part of the set-up, Joshua would show up to hand pick the best of the trainees for some kind of secret mission. Not sure what that is yet."

"Global weapons training, surveillance, covert ops," Cassie murmured. "It sounds like Metcalf is building an army."

"That's what worries me," the paladin agreed. "I know all this activity links back to Aboud and his secret lab, but I'm not sure how."

"Any progress on that front?" Maddie asked.

"Not much. Once my road construction gig ended, I didn't have an excuse to hang around that spot anymore. I picked up a stint as a sanitation worker, but the lab incinerates everything. There was nothing to sift through but ashes, so I still don't know what lethal concoction the good doctor is cooking up."

"You might not know what it is, but we all know who's gonna get it," Cassie noted gloomily.

"It's not the 'who' that bothers me," Erik objected. "It's the how and the when. Until we know that, we can't do anything to stop them."

"That's not entirely true," Faye interjected.

They all turned to look at her in surprise.

She continued. "I realize this hardly constitutes an action plan, but you must remember that Abraham Metcalf rules a religious cult. The bedrock of their organization rests on nothing more tangible than a set of bizarre beliefs. If you can shake those beliefs, you may yet succeed in dismantling their military plan."

Her listeners traded puzzled looks. Apparently, the memory guardian was still several steps ahead of them.

Faye gave a small smile and elaborated further. "I'm convinced that whatever nefarious scheme the diviner intends to launch won't begin until he has the Sage Stone in his possession. Although I'm at a total loss as to why our pagan artifact holds such sway over a fundamentalist Christian, we can be sure that it plays a major role in his plans. Otherwise, he wouldn't have gone to the trouble of chasing it halfway around the world."

"All the more reason for Griffin and me to get gone," Cassie said. "The sooner we find the fifth relic, the sooner we can claim the Sage Stone."

"Easier said than done, I fear," the scrivener retorted. "I still haven't completely solved the meaning of our latest riddle." Without being prompted, he repeated the clue. "'The kindred stir upon the high sharp peak where the river flows red to the serpent's heart. Under the lawgiver's glare, its coils tremble in the mirror at the lion's feet.'"

"Which means?" the paladin demanded.

"Something far more obscure than I've been able to comprehend. We have learned a few things, however. The first line refers to a river originating in the Himalayas which travels to a location called 'the serpent's heart.' The reference puzzled me until I remembered the Minoan fondness for astronomy. Our African relic contained an entire constellation map, and I thought the golden serpent we collected in India might be designed along the same lines. If you'll recall, the artifact was a rearing serpent with emeralds spaced at various intervals along its head and body. The center of the serpent's body featured a large ruby. After some digging, I was able to determine that the constellation in question is called 'Serpens.' It bears the distinction of being the only constellation which is divided into two parts: the serpent's head and the serpent's tail. The brightest star in the serpent's head constellation is a red giant known as 'Cor Serpentis' or 'the heart of the serpent.'"

"Makes sense." Erik nodded. "The emeralds in our snake artifact must have been positioned to match the other stars in the constellation. The ruby was supposed to stand for the serpent's heart."

"Quite right," the scrivener agreed. "The constellation itself has some unusual features. It's very faint. In fact, Cor Serpentis is the only star which can be easily seen and only during the summer in the northern hemisphere when one is facing south."

"We thought maybe the mention of the serpent's heart in the riddle was a directional pointer," Cassie chimed in. "In riddle speak, it's a sign that we should be following a river that runs south."

"This is all very promising," Faye said. "You know the origin point of the river and the direction it flows."

"But wait, there's more." Cassie nudged the scrivener. "Tell them, Griffin."

"I was able to partially solve the second line of the riddle as well," Griffin said.

"'Under the lawgiver's glare, its coils tremble in the mirror at the lion's feet,'" the pythia repeated helpfully.

"Yes, I believe both 'lawgiver' and 'lion's feet' refer to a second constellation – Leo the Lion. Alpha Leonis is the brightest star in Leo. It is commonly known by the name 'Regulus' which translates to mean 'lawgiver.' Depending on which graphical illustration of the star cluster one uses, Regulus is either depicted as the lion's heart or, more significantly for our purposes, as the lion's foot."

"So, you've got a snake, a lion and a river that runs south. If you put them all together, what does it mean?" Maddie urged, growing impatient.

"Unfortunately, the meaning of the riddle in its entirety continues to elude us," Griffin demurred. "The whole truly is greater than the sum of its parts. Briefly, we know that we are to search for a river that originates at approximately thirty-one degrees north latitude. We are instructed to follow this river southwards. The reference to the snake's coils trembling under the glare of the lawgiver seems to caution us to make this journey only during the summer months when Leo rules the sky and Serpens is most visible. Quite a sensible suggestion, I might add, given the climate of the Himalayas. The snake's trembling coils may also refer to the constellation's reflection in the river. Beyond that, we must speculate. The Minoans have consistently hidden their artifacts in sacred mountains, so we will need to find one in close proximity to our mysterious river."

"Why would the river be mysterious?" Erik challenged. "The Minoans practically gave you its GPS coordinates."

Griffin smiled thinly at the paladin's offhand remark. "In that respect, we are suffering from an embarrassment of riches. Sanjiangyuan Reserve in southeastern Tibet contains the headwaters of no less than three major Asian rivers. As ill luck would have it, they all begin in such close proximity to one another that the latitude offered in our clue could apply to any of them. We have the Yellow River flowing eastward across central China, the Yangtze which parallels its course further south, and the Mekong which flows through Cambodia and Vietnam all the way to the South China Sea."

"When Griffin showed me a map of eastern Tibet, I couldn't get a sense of which river it was," Cassie admitted. "For what it's worth, I did get a strong feeling that we'd found the right general vicinity. The Minoans were in the mountains of eastern Tibet, and they followed one of those river valleys to the spot where they hid the fifth relic."

"You aren't just going to cruise down those three rivers and trust to luck, are you?" Maddie asked skeptically. "You've got to have a systematic approach."

"We do have a tentative strategy," the scrivener assured her. "We'll begin with the northernmost of the three bodies of water – the Yellow River."

"We're going to target matristic archaeological sites that follow the course of the river," Cassie added. "Odds are the Minoans would have looked for a goddess-friendly place to stash their artifact."

"Because my knowledge of Asian culture and archaeology is sketchy at best," Griffin said, "we'll need to rely heavily on the expertise of local trove keepers to assist us."

"That sounds like a reasonable way to begin." Faye smiled approvingly. "I'd suggest you contact the Hongshan trove keeper first. He's been monitoring finds near the North Korean border. I realize that it's a bit far afield from the Yellow River, but he has an encyclopedic knowledge of Neolithic China and may be able to guide you to the right place."

"Ah, yes. The Hongshan keeper. I met with him a few times shortly after I was appointed chief scrivener. I'll contact him first thing tomorrow," Griffin said.

"I guess that means I'd better start packing." Cassie began clearing cups and plates.

"Gracious me! Look at the time." Faye consulted her wrist watch. "If I don't leave immediately, the young people will get home before I do. Hannah wasn't to know about my absence."

"Sounds like you're the one who's got a curfew, not them," Maddie said.

"Doesn't it though." Faye rose to depart.

Taking that as their cue, the others stood up, collected their coats and headed for the door.

Cassie received another round of birthday congratulations before bidding them all goodnight.

Erik lagged behind the rest. He stood hesitating in the living room. When Cassie shut the door and turned to him with a questioning gaze, he asked, "Can we talk?"

5 – FEATHERED FIEND

Abraham leaned back in his office chair and eyed the pendulum clock on the wall. It was late, and he'd already had a very taxing day. Early that same morning, he'd finally broken the news to Daniel that his wife Annabeth was dead. Of course, she'd died months earlier on his orders, but his son didn't know that. The scion must never know. Abraham explained to Daniel that Annabeth had succumbed while convalescing from mental collapse at a private hospital. Daniel hadn't taken the news well. He blamed himself for abandoning his wife when she needed him most. It did no good for Abraham to remonstrate that the relic hunt must always take priority over domestic concerns. The diviner consoled himself with the sure knowledge that time would make Daniel forget his distress. One day, his son would be reunited with his wife in the Celestial Kingdoms and Daniel would realize that his father had acted for the best. For his part, Abraham was glad to be done with Annabeth and the potentially awkward discussion of her demise. He could put all that behind him now.

The diviner stifled a yawn. He felt unbearably weary, but his workday wasn't over yet. He was scheduled to hold a meeting in ten minutes. For half a second he considered postponing it until the morning but then sternly reminded himself that duty mattered more than rest. Not that rest was likely to arrive after duty had been discharged. He could scarcely remember the last time he'd been able to sleep more than an hour or two a night. Abraham never woke refreshed. He dragged exhaustion around with him throughout the day like a ball and chain.

He blinked rapidly to fight the drowsiness that had lately begun to creep up on him at odd moments. A short nap never brought relief, only a distressing sense of disorientation when he awoke. No, he would not shut his eyes though they were burning with fatigue. Joshua was due to arrive shortly with half a dozen malefactors from the satellite compounds on the west coast. Abraham intended to dispatch them to perdition this very night—or rather dispatch them to Dr. Aboud's laboratory which amounted to much the same thing. Then perhaps he could rest. He could...

Abraham still sat in his office chair, but he felt strangely immobilized. He couldn't seem to move his arms or legs. A peculiar sense of lethargy had overtaken him. The lamp on his desk still burned dimly. The pendulum still swung monotonously below the clock face. His head was swimming. The familiar objects in his office melted into the background. The room seemed enveloped in fog. He saw an object far off in the distance. It appeared to emerge from a long tunnel and drift toward him. It was the figure of a woman. She drew nearer, but her feet weren't touching the floor. She floated in the air near where he judged the ceiling to his office had been just a moment before.

"Hello, Father," the woman said.

"I know you," he murmured.

She laughed mirthlessly. "I should hope so."

It was Annabeth—his son Daniel's dead wife. But this spectral version of Annabeth was different somehow. She didn't fidget or cower before his stern gaze.

"What do you want from me," he demanded petulantly. "It's late, and I have an appointment to keep."

She wafted nearer, perhaps ten feet away but still floating above him. "I don't want anything from you. I'm here to give you a message."

He noticed for the first time that she was dressed oddly. Instead of the grey garb of a consecrated bride, she wore a long white robe of a diaphanous material that drifted on invisible air currents. Her hair was no longer braided and coiled around her head. Rather it was unbound and rippled about her shoulders. Abraham noticed with a start that she now held an infant in her arms. The child hadn't been there a moment earlier.

Annabeth smiled down fondly at the child. Then she directed her gaze at the diviner. "As you can see, I found my son." She paused. "Where is yours?" A fleeting smirk crossed her face. "Oh, that's right. You lost him."

Abraham felt a pang of sadness at her mockery. Annabeth was referring to Hannah's child—the baby who had been born and died in the Fallen Lands.

The apparition spoke again. "Your boy was only the first to fall. Two more will follow." She counted on her fingers for emphasis. "One, two, three sons lost to you. How sad."

The diviner wanted to cry out in disbelief, but he couldn't seem to find his voice. He remained frozen, forced to listen mutely to the vile creature's predictions.

She advanced a few feet and regarded him dispassionately. Her child seemed to match her detached expression as he too gazed down at the diviner without a trace of anxiety or curiosity. "Three sons lost to you forever. Yet an even greater loss than all these three awaits."

"You lie!" he challenged, finding his voice at last. "You are the devil's instrument as you always were in life, sent to frighten me with your deceit."

"I do not come from the devil."

To Abraham's amazement, he saw huge white wings sprouting from her shoulder blades. It happened right before his eyes. They spread wide and lifted her higher in the air.

"My lady angel told me all these things would come to pass," she explained.

"How dare you presume to tell me the future? Your preposterous female angel is a false seer. I am the Lord's true prophet! I am the diviner!"

Annabeth raised a skeptical eyebrow at his posturing. "You are a frail, frightened old man. You grasp at straws while your house falls about your ears. Its cornerstone has crumbled."

"Begone, witch!" He could feel a sense of panic creeping into his throat. "Begone, demon!"

She shook her head and laughed lightly. "I am neither witch nor demon. Not enough power to be a witch. Not enough malice to be a demon. Goodbye, Father." Her voice held a hint of derision as it pronounced the last word. Her wings lifted her higher still, and she seemed to dissolve into the distance.

He felt his body being rocked from side to side. A hand was shaking him by the shoulder.

"Father, wake up!" The tone was urgent, worried.

In a flash, Abraham returned to wakefulness. His son Joshua was peering into his face.

The diviner shoved him away brusquely. "What do you want?"

His son hesitated. "I... uh... I'm sorry if I startled you. You were in a deep sleep. Your lips were moving. Your arms and legs were twitching. I feared you might be experiencing some kind of seizure."

"Seizure!" Abraham roared in disbelief. He raised himself to his feet. "I am sound in wind and limb. Don't be ridiculous!"

"Of course, Father." The spymaster backed away. "Just as you say."

With a start, Abraham realized that half a dozen men loitered awkwardly in the corners of the room. They had all witnessed this shocking display of his vulnerability. He needed to recover his composure. "I'll meet with you all in the morning. You have my leave to go."

"But Father," his son protested weakly.

A glare from the diviner silenced him.

"As you wish," Joshua murmured. He studied his father through narrowed eyes but made no further comment. Then he turned to his charges. "You men come with me. I'll arrange sleeping quarters for you."

They allowed themselves to be shepherded out of the diviner's presence though more than one looked askance at the old man before leaving.

"Joshua!" the diviner called after him.

"Sir?" The spymaster returned.

"Send Brother Andrew to me immediately. If he isn't in the infirmary, wake him. I have an urgent matter to discuss."

That look of calculating appraisal crossed Joshua's face once more, but he asked no further questions. Nodding his assent, he let himself out and closed the door.

***

Ten minutes later, a short, balding man in his sixties scurried into the diviner's office. He had obviously dressed in a hurry. His top shirt button was undone, his tie was knotted sloppily, and his sparse hair was uncombed. Brother Andrew constituted the Nephilim's sole resource for medical advice. An herbalist before he joined the brotherhood, he'd retained some fundamental knowledge of how to diagnose disease and could recommend a limited array of remedies.

Without preamble, the diviner commanded, "Sit down." He'd been pacing the office restlessly but resumed his seat at Brother Andrew's arrival.

The herbalist looked anxious. "Have I done something wrong, Father?"

"What?" Abraham asked sharply. Then softening his tone, he added, "No, of course not."

The man visibly relaxed.

"I've been having difficulty sleeping," the diviner explained.

Brother Andrew seemed perplexed. "Didn't the tincture I prepared for you help?"

Abraham thought back to his unnerving experience with the foul-tasting medicine. "No, it didn't. I poured it down the drain. It gave me bad dreams."

"Oh, I'm sorry to hear that."

The old man leaned forward over his desk and spoke in a confidential tone. "What we discuss here is to remain private. Is that understood?"

Brother Andres nodded vehemently.

"Good. I want you to prepare something potent enough to allow me to get to sleep and to stay asleep. Do you understand? I don't wish to dream at all!"

"Well, that's a bit difficult to control," the herbalist hedged. "I can't think of any plant that would suppress dreams completely."

"You must do something!" Abraham's fist landed on his desk with a thud. "This situation is unbearable. I can hardly sleep anymore, and when I do, I'm troubled by terrible nightmares. It's now gotten to the point that I'm having difficulty distinguishing dreams from reality."

"Hmmm," Brother Andrew said noncommittally. "Your condition indicates acute anxiety. There are substances that could help with that but..." he hesitated.

"Out with it, man!" Abraham commanded.

The herbalist continued warily. "I can make a tincture from the poppy plant, but it would need to be prepared with alcohol. The Nephilim are forbidden to drink."

"This isn't a drink, it's a medicine," the diviner retorted.

22

"That's very true," Brother Andrew agreed. "I'll need your permission to obtain the necessary ingredients."

Abraham waved his arm dismissively. "Of course."

"There's one more thing, Father." Again, Brother Andrew faltered. "This tincture is very strong and may cause you to become dependent on its use over time."

Abraham gave a bark of a laugh. "That's your concern? My sanity is hanging by a thread, and you cavil about dependency. Will this medicine of yours stop me from dreaming or not?"

The herbalist sighed. "It won't stop you from dreaming. No, it can't do that. But it will produce a profound sense of calm and replace your nightmares with sweet dreams. Very sweet dreams indeed. At least for a time."

"Well then, what are you waiting for," the diviner demanded tartly. "You'll begin immediately. I hope your remedy lives up to its promise."

Brother Andrew's face took on a troubled expression. "People have been using it for hundreds of years. It will do all I've said, but perhaps it will do more than you bargained for."

Abraham gave a thin smile. "For one good night's sleep, no price is too high to pay."

6 – TIME AND TIDE...

The paladin stood in the center of Cassie's living room jangling his car keys.

"What did you want to talk about?" the pythia prompted.

His eyes traveled around the room as if he were desperately searching for a way out. "I could use some fresh air," he said distractedly.

Cassie brightened. "I've got just the thing. Check this out." She opened a coat closet to display a standing infrared lamp. "Help me carry it out to the patio."

Erik hoisted the heavy lamp and brought it to the concrete slab outside the dining room that constituted Cassie's backyard.

She plugged the cord into an outdoor socket and switched it on. The light emitted a reddish glow, and gentle warmth immediately radiated around the small terrace. Cassie returned to the closet to retrieve two collapsible lawn chairs and brought those outside as well.

"It's been a long winter, and I was going stir-crazy being cooped up in the vault all day," she explained. "Once the snow melted, I got the brainstorm of treating myself to a heat lamp. That way I could get a little fresh air in the evenings without also getting frostbite."

Erik nodded approvingly. "Smart idea." He took a seat.

Cassie stood by the open patio door. "Hey, do you want a beer?"

The paladin grinned. "Look at you. All grown up and offering me a drink from your very own private stash."

"Don't get too excited. It was left over from the party. Somebody besides me needs to drink it."

After a few moments, she returned with two bottles and handed one to her guest.

He raised a questioning eyebrow when he noticed the second bottle still in her hand.

"Relax, pops. It's light beer." She settled into the other lawn chair.

The lights from the dormant fountain in the center of the frozen retention pond cast a pallid glow across the crust of ice.

"Another week and that'll be gone." Cassie tilted her head in the direction of the ice.

"You'll be gone by then too," Erik observed.

She stared at him in the dim light. "Yeah, that's true." Not wanting to hurry him, she waited in silence.

He began with a casual question. "So, are you and Griffin a couple now?"

"What!" she exclaimed in shock. "Where did you get a crazy idea like that?"

Erik put up his hands. "Whoa. I couldn't help noticing that you seemed pretty chummy at the party, that's all."

"And that's all we are. Chums. Teammates. Friends. BFFs as a matter of fact." She scowled at him. "And how is that your business anyway? You're the one who bailed, remember?"

"Yeah, I did," he admitted. "Like you said, it's none of my business. Just drop it, OK?"

She nodded curtly. "OK then." Settling back into her seat, she set her bottle on the concrete. In a calmer tone, she asked, "So what did you want to tell me?"

He didn't answer immediately. Instead, he took a long swig of beer and stared off into the darkness. "I thought I'd have more time," he remarked cryptically.

"For what?"

He sighed. "Time to figure out how to say what I want to say. As it is, I just flew back tonight, and here you are about to ship out. So, I guess it's now or never."

She made no comment.

Another half minute ticked by while he continued to gaze out at the frozen pond and gather his thoughts. Eventually, he said, "You weren't completely wrong. I mean, what you said while we were still in India."

"About what exactly?" she asked softly.

"About that wall you told me I'd built around my heart. About me being scared that you might break through it someday."

She nodded in silent acknowledgment but didn't push him further.

He continued. "Here's the thing. I'm really good at my job. It's not bragging. Just a fact. Over the years I've worked with dozens of field agents under some pretty dicey conditions. A handful of them didn't make it back home, but I always did. The main reason why I'm still breathing, and they're not is because I never let my guard down. Not ever. Keeping that wall up kept me alive. But then you came along and expected me to tear it down like it was the easiest thing in the world to do."

"I never thought it was going to be easy," she countered faintly.

He didn't seem to hear her. Forging on, he added, "Part of me wants to, but the bigger part of me doesn't."

Cassie registered surprise. She'd always thought he was unaware of his feelings. It had never occurred to her that he believed his defensiveness offered some kind of tactical advantage.

Erik was still speaking. "Blame it on force of habit or just pure stubbornness but, either way, I'm not ready to take that wall down. At least not today. I've got a feeling it won't be anytime soon either. Maybe never." He turned to face her, his tone earnest. "Cass, you need to know that I'm not that guy. The guy you need me to be."

She smiled wistfully, her eyes traveling toward the retention pond. "That water is so easy to freeze. Drop the temp twenty degrees, and it's solid. Not a ripple. If you kept the air cold enough, it could stay that way forever." She transferred her attention back to Erik. "I wish it was that easy to do with time. I appreciate the heads up you just gave me. I do. But there's something you need to realize about me too. Life keeps on remolding me like a lump of clay on a potter's wheel. Since I joined the Arkana, I've changed so much and so fast that I don't know who I'll be by the time this scavenger hunt is finished." She paused before adding gently, "You need to understand that by the time you get around to being that guy, if you ever do, I won't be this girl anymore."

"And here I thought love was supposed to last forever," the paladin joked.

"Is that what this is?" Cassie asked in mild surprise.

A fleeting look of panic crossed Erik's face. Then he shrugged helplessly. "I really can't say."

The pythia nodded, inwardly noting his choice of words.

Erik drained the rest of his beer. "I guess we'll have to take our chances on someday."

"I guess we will," she agreed in a half-hearted whisper.

He stood up abruptly. "It's time I let you get your beauty sleep."

She didn't protest. They unplugged the light and carried the lawn chairs back inside. Then she followed him silently to the front door. He stood framed against the night sky looking down at her.

"Whatever happens, I'm glad you told me where you stand," she said.

He smiled briefly and kissed her on the forehead. "Happy birthday, toots. Stay safe out there."

She regarded him gravely. "You too, dude."

Cassie shut the door and leaned her back against it. She listened to his engine growl to life and roar off toward the highway. "Happy birthday to me," she murmured ruefully.

7 – PAPER, AIRPLANES

Leroy Hunt entered his apartment around midnight and dropped his duffle bag unceremoniously on the floor. In a fit of peevishness, he gave it a well-aimed kick and sent it flying across the room. He slammed the door behind him, causing it to shudder in reply. He'd just returned from the latest of the many wild goose chases that had occupied his time over the course of the winter. As he well knew, each one had been cooked up by Mr. Big to keep him away from where Hannah Metcalf was actually hiding. This last junket had been the Mother Goose of them all. He'd flown to Minneapolis which still boasted a foot of snow on the ground. The only green things he saw in that Yankee icebox were the decorations for St. Patrick's Day!

A body would think that at least one of his fake leads would have taken him to Barbados or St. Kitts or even Miami. But no. In the dead of winter, he flew to every snowy hell hole in the sweet land of liberty. First, it was Billings, then Montpellier, then Boise, and finally Minneapolis—the land of ten thousand frozen lakes! Every place he'd visited, the story was the same from some flunky on the payroll of Mr. Big. Yes, Hannah had been there, Yes, Leroy had just missed her. Yes, he could have an address where she might be found.

As if the trips themselves weren't bad enough, dealing with the preacher afterward was worse. The old coot would work himself up into a lather waiting for Hunt's report. Once the bad news landed, he'd be madder than a snake on his wedding night who'd just married a garden hose. Metcalf even had the nerve to accuse Hunt of slacking off. If he only knew. The cowboy was pulling double shifts to carry out his own private investigation. While he was busy chasing down bogus leads for the preacher, he was also collecting a paper trail of the corporations that had leased the properties associated with those leads. He felt sure one of those companies would point back to the

Somebody who was hiding Metcalf's lost bride and the trio of relic thieves to boot.

He took off his hat and coat, hanging them on the rack by the door. No sense in calling the old man this late at night to tell him Minneapolis hadn't panned out. Leroy could easily postpone the wailing and gnashing of teeth til morning. He eyed his computer, sitting on a desk next to the window. He was itching to check out his latest bit of intel. First, he went to the kitchen cabinet and grabbed a bag of pork rinds. Airplane peanuts and tiny bottles of hooch were no substitute for down home comfort food—and drink. He retrieved a bottle of whiskey, poured a glassful and swallowed it down. Then he poured another and carried it back with him to the computer along with the bag of rinds.

Leroy consulted a note in his shirt pocket. Before he'd left Minnesota, he scribbled down the name of the corporation that had leased the property of his last fake lead. He typed it into the file he was keeping of all the shell companies that he'd encountered on his various jaunts. Then he did an online search to see if he could link this latest find to anything he'd come across before. He smiled to himself. The Minnesota lessee was an offshoot of a corporation that had made it onto his master list.

He thought he'd take a wild stab to see if the parent company owned any properties closer to home. He checked the online real estate tax records for Cook County and the counties nearest to the city proper. What he found made him blink. He checked the name twice. Sure enough, the corporation owned a house in McHenry County. That area would hardly count as suburban. It was mainly still rural. Leroy pulled up a map of the address. It looked to be part of a suburban tract housing development. Then he drilled down to a street level photo.

"Well, I'll be," he muttered in surprise. Gulping down the last of his whiskey, he went back to the kitchen to fetch the bottle. After pouring another glass, he set the bottle down on his computer desk and resumed his task. For several minutes, this consisted of nothing more than staring at the image on his computer screen. Leroy was in a brown study over that farmhouse sitting in the middle of a subdivision of raised ranches. It must have been the original homestead when that part of the state was all farmland which meant it was about a hundred years old. What would Mr. Big want with a place like that?

A lightbulb went off above Leroy's head. Maybe that old farm was a base of operations. It was owned outright by the corporation, not leased. Who knew how many burglars were working for Mr. Big besides the trio? Maybe he was running an entire ring. It wasn't all that far-fetched. Leroy already knew that little Hannah had wandered into this den of thieves when she went looking for Miss Cassie. What if Mr. Big decided to keep the gal as insurance just in case his own people got into trouble? No doubt, he'd heard what store the preacher set by her. She could be swapped for any one of the trio if the Nephilim ever snagged them.

Leroy scratched his head. This problem was taking a powerful lot of concentration, but he figured it might be worth a brain cramp to climb aboard this particular train of thought. Mr. Big had gone to a heap of trouble to send Leroy everyplace but northern Illinois. Maybe it wasn't simply to keep the cowboy away from Hannah. Who knew what else might be going on in that old farmhouse out in the middle of nowhere?

The cowboy printed out the address and directions to the place. He yawned and thought about hitting the hay. Not quite yet. He had to plan out his next move, and it was important for him to play it just right so as not to alert his quarry. Bright and early next morning, he'd call Metcalf on his bugged phone to tell him Minneapolis had been a wash. Of course, the stooge in the Twin Cities had given him a bum address to follow up in Buffalo. He'd tell the old man that he'd jump right on that lead. Once he was sure Mr. Big had got the message, Leroy figured he'd be watched til he drove to the airport. He'd park his truck in the long-term lot, enter the terminal and wait a couple of hours. Once he was sure nobody was on his tail, he'd change clothes, go to a rental agency and get a ride. Then he'd check out this farmhouse and see who lived there and what they might be up to.

He considered what to do if he found little Hannah. The gal still posed a threat to him. If he brought her back to Abe safe and sound, there was no telling if she'd keep her mouth shut. If Abe or one of his stooges pushed her hard enough, she might blab about who helped her to escape in the first place. She'd point the finger straight at Daniel, and Leroy's chances of grabbing all the doodads would go up in smoke. No, there was only one way this missing person's search was going to end. If Leroy found little Hannah at that farmhouse in the sticks, she wouldn't make it back to the preacher alive.

8 – VANISHING POINT

Chopper Bowdeen walked out to claim his rental car in the lot at the Melbourne Airport. He stopped himself. Force of habit had almost made him climb into the left front seat. Belatedly reminding himself of the right-side steering wheel, he walked to the other side of the car and climbed in. He also made a mental note to remember to drive on the left side of the road. It had been a while since he'd had to do that. Today he was heading to the end of the line, figuratively speaking. This would be his last training gig for the Nephilim. He'd worked his way through all the compounds in Europe, Asia, Africa, and the Americas. Now he was in Australia driving to the only foothold the brotherhood had been able to establish in the land down under.

The mercenary knew Australia well, so he'd opted to chauffeur himself to the compound, even renting a convertible in order to savor the sunshine which was sadly lacking back home. As he motored out of the metro area and into the countryside, he rubbed a trickle of sweat off his neck. While it was still the blustery tail end of winter in the States, March in Australia meant the end of summer and the beginning of autumn.

He took a brief moment to savor the feeling of fresh air on his skin, knowing the oppressive atmosphere that waited for him at the compound. It was situated in the Yarra Valley—a shrewd choice for a cult as secretive as the Nephilim. Even though the valley was only a short distance from the city of Melbourne, it was agricultural—mainly planted in vineyards. Despite its popularity as a tourist destination, the valley was sparsely populated so that a cinderblock fortress tucked away on a private road wouldn't attract too much notice.

Chopper headed toward his destination with a mixture of relief and paranoia. On the one hand, he would be glad to be finished with the cult once and for all. On the other hand, he couldn't help wondering whether the diviner could afford to let him walk away alive. He was one of the "Fallen" as the Nephilim liked to call everybody who wasn't them. Nobody from the outside world knew as much about the brotherhood's operation as he did. He'd seen the inside of every compound, trained every marksman and supervised the set-up of every surveillance camera around the globe. As a mercenary, it was his business to do his job and keep his mouth shut about the people he worked for. He hoped Metcalf would remember that when the time came to part ways.

During Chopper's employment with the Nephilim, he'd tried ten ways from Sunday to find out what they were really up to. He needed to know if his neck was in the noose, but nobody could offer any useful information. His old pal Leroy didn't sense any danger, and he'd been on the Nephilim's payroll even longer than Chopper. Then again, Leroy was an idiot when it came to seeing the big picture if it didn't affect him personally. The cowboy also had some private angle that involved a big payoff, so maybe he had an incentive to hang on.

Joshua, Metcalf's spymaster son, hadn't been of much use either in getting to the bottom of things. Bowdeen had put a flea in the kid's ear about a secret lab near the main compound. Despite digging for months, Joshua hadn't been able to find out squat about what was going on there.

Chopper knew there was more to Metcalf's plans than merely beefing up security at the satellite compounds. As far as the mercenary could tell, the diviner was preparing for war. Against whom he didn't know but he sure as hell didn't want to be around when it happened.

He only had one card left to play. Joshua was due to arrive in about a month. Before Chopper left Australia, he intended to worm out as much intel as he could from the kid. What he heard would be the deciding factor in whether he caught a plane back to the states to collect his final paycheck or slipped away and vanished himself off the Nephilim's radar for good. He'd prefer to disappear on his own terms if it came to that. He had a feeling that the disappearing act Metcalf had in mind for him might be a lot more painful.

9 – JADED TRAVELERS

Griffin looked anxiously at his watch. "I fear we'll be dreadfully late." He quickened his pace.

Cassie could barely keep up with his long stride given her fatigue from the grueling trip they'd just completed. The distance from Chicago to eastern China was 6,500 miles as the crow flies. The pythia doubted that any crow in its right mind would have attempted the journey in thirteen hours. That was how long their nonstop flight from the Windy City to Beijing had taken. Afterward, they'd boarded another plane for the hour and a half flight to Shenyang, the capital of Liaoning Province in northeastern China.

Liaoning skirted a region which bore the romantic name of Inner Mongolia. To Cassie, the phrase "Inner Mongolia" had always connoted the end of the world. Now that she'd personally traveled to Kathmandu and come within spitting distance of the equally exotic Timbuktu, Inner Mongolia didn't seem all that out-of-the-way anymore.

Feeling chilled, the pythia wrapped her scarf more tightly around her neck. The temperature was about forty degrees and windy. Turning to Griffin, she asked, "Is it my imagination or is the weather here exactly the same as Chicago?"

Never breaking stride, the scrivener replied, "It should be. We're at approximately the same latitude here as back in the Midwest which means a similar type of spring weather."

"I think we should have started our search in Cambodia where it's warm," Cassie muttered. She struggled to catch her breath while attempting to put on a burst of speed. "Are we there yet?"

They were en route to meet the Hongshan trove keeper at the Provincial Museum. Maddie had wisely booked them into a hotel which was walking distance from their rendezvous point. However, the chatelaine hadn't factored in Cassie's disorientation from the thirteen-hour time difference which made even a three-block walk to Government Square an ordeal.

"We'll be there in a moment." Griffin pointed directly ahead. "That's the museum across the street."

They paused at the curb for a red light. Cassie studied their destination—a massive concrete affair with angled corners and overhanging exposed steel beams surrounding a central glass-clad atrium. The patch of grass and small shrubs bordering the structure did nothing to soften its antiseptic appearance.

It occurred to the pythia that the design seemed consistent with the city's architecture as a whole. The impression she'd formed of Shenyang was of a bustling megalopolis complete with steel and glass skyscrapers, expressways, traffic lights, and eight million people going about their daily routines in the same way as any urban American. The street signs even bore English captions below the Chinese characters. Cassie thought wistfully of rickshaws and junks—those picture postcard symbols of the colorful Far East, but none were to be found hereabouts. Griffin had already told her that Shenyang was China's industrial capital. It had been Chairman Mao's model city of the future, complete with futuristic problems like smog thanks to its steel mills and coal-burning stoves. For decades, the air quality had been so bad that residents sometimes needed to wear face masks. Recognizing the necessity to go green, Shenyang had cleaned up its act about five years earlier by relocating its heavy industry to the outskirts and planting numerous parks within the city limits.

The light changed at last, and the duo hurried across the street and through the doors of the museum.

"Ah, there he is." The scrivener rushed eagerly toward an elderly man standing in the middle of the entrance hall.

Considering his wizened appearance and the grey streaks in his thinning hair, the trove keeper appeared to be in his late-sixties. The man advanced a few paces to clasp the scrivener's outstretched hand. Griffin seemed to tower over him, emphasizing the disparity in their heights. Cassie judged their guide to be no more than five-foot four.

"Zhang Jun, it's good to see you again." Griffin pumped his hand enthusiastically. "It's been a long time since you attended a meeting of the Concordance."

In a barely discernible accent, the old man joked, "It's a long trip to Chicago. I would need a good reason to fly that far." He enunciated every word precisely as if he'd taken time to consider the meaning of each. Giving Cassie a welcoming smile, he reached forward to take her hand. "I'm very pleased to meet the new pythia at last."

"Considering the miles I've logged since I started this job, I think the new has worn off," Cassie demurred. "It's very nice to meet you too, Mr. Jun."

In a low voice, Griffin said, "Jun is his first name. In this part of the world, surnames precede given names."

"Oh..." Cassie flushed at the realization of her gaffe.

The trove keeper waved his hand dismissively. "Please, call me Jun. It's what my friends call me, and I'd like us to be friends." His eyes twinkled warmly behind horn-rimmed glasses.

"Absolutely." Cassie bobbed her head in agreement, relieved that he wasn't offended.

"Allow me to introduce my granddaughter, Zhang Rou." The trove keeper turned from side to side as if he'd lost something. "Where did she go?"

A teenage girl hovered behind him. She was about Cassie's height with straight black hair cut into a short bob. Her jacket collar was zipped up so high that it covered her mouth. She darted an apprehensive glance at the two newcomers.

Jun reached for the girl's arm and guided her forward. "Rou is a tyro at the Hongshan trove, but her parents urged me to bring her on this field trip. They have great hopes she will follow in their footsteps someday and become a scout for the Arkana."

Zhang Rou blinked at the visitors. She reminded Cassie of a turtle ready to pull its head inside its shell at the first sign of trouble.

"Do you speak English?" Cassie asked cautiously.

The girl remained silent.

Zhang Jun smiled pointedly at his granddaughter. "She speaks English much better than she thinks she does. I keep telling her she is too self-conscious about her accent."

"Don't worry about that," the pythia reassured her. "Whether your accent is good or bad at least you can speak a second language. I can't speak Mandarin at all." She held out her hand to Rou. "It's very nice to meet you."

Rou stepped forward unwillingly. A muffled "Hello" emerged from her collar as she shook hands with Cassie and Griffin in turn. Apparently uncomfortable as the focus of everyone's attention, she immediately slipped back behind her grandfather.

Cassie deliberately shifted her attention away to ease Rou's discomfort. Her eyes swept the interior of the museum. "I expected we would meet you at a dig site," she remarked to Jun. "Not in the middle of a museum."

"Oh, there's nothing much to see at the site these days," Jun countered. "It's a three-hour drive to Chaoyang and another hour to the site, but digging has been suspended for a while. All the artifacts that have been found to-date are housed right here in this museum. Before the Iron Age and the Bronze Age, China had something called the 'Jade Age.' You'll soon see why." He motioned them toward an exhibit room on the first floor. The English lettering below the Chinese characters announced that they were entering the "Dawn of Chinese Culture" gallery.

Once they all filed into the exhibit, Jun explained, "Everything you see here originated with the Hongshan Culture. The artifacts have been found at numerous dig sites clustered around Chifeng and Chaoyang. The Hongshan were neolithic agriculturalists who thrived between 4700 and 2900 BCE. They fabricated stone tools and plows and lived in simple villages, but their ceremonial sites were much more elaborate. The largest temple complex we've discovered is called Niuheliang. It's fifty square kilometers around."

"What's that in miles?" Cassie murmured to Griffin.

"About nineteen," he whispered back helpfully.

Jun was still talking. "Excavations there have uncovered pottery, statues, jade carvings, and finely-crafted jewelry. There are also standing stones with carvings to mark astronomical events."

"Griffin and I have become experts on star-mapping the hard way." Cassie smiled ruefully. "Calendar stones in Turkey, more calendar stones in Africa, solar observatories in India. The list goes on."

"Then you can appreciate the level of astronomical sophistication the Hongshan possessed." Jun walked toward an aerial photograph on the wall of the exhibit room. The others followed.

He pointed to an image that looked like a long rectangular strip of furrowed earth on top of a hillside. Sprouting from the sides of the rectangle were asymmetrical lobes. "This is the dig site of the goddess temple."

"Why is it called that?" Cassie asked.

"Because numerous votive figurines were discovered inside—all of them female."

Jun turned toward a glass case on his right. "Here's an example."

They all studied a nude figure of a kneeling woman made from polished jade.

"Of course, this is a small specimen," Jun said. "Inside the temple itself were many oversized pottery figures of females, some of them three times life-size. Archaeologists assumed the statues were of the divinities which the Hongshan worshipped. The most striking image of a goddess is right here." He walked a few feet further down the gallery and paused before a life-size clay head of a woman.

"This was found in the underground temple. The body had been broken apart, but the head is still intact. It would have originally been painted red. Dated to 3000 BCE, it is the oldest known goddess figure ever discovered in China."

Cassie felt herself mesmerized by the face. The eyes were inlaid with two large globes of greenish jade. The full lips were curved into a Mona Lisa smile. The deity's features conveyed strength, unlike the prettified sculptures of overlord goddesses. The Hongshan goddess was mysterious and a trifle scary while being vaguely benevolent at the same time.

Griffin broke into her thoughts. "Doesn't all this remind you of something?"

She stared at him uncomprehendingly.

"Oversized female divinities. Underground temples. The lobed shape of the structure itself," he prompted.

Her eyes widened in recognition. "Malta. This is like the temples we found on Malta."

"Oh yes, it's quite possible," Jun chimed in.

Cassie whirled to look at him. "You mean Niuheliang was built by some Maltese goddess-worshippers?"

The trove keeper chuckled. "No, but the two cultures were roughly contemporary. Each flourished around 3000 BCE."

"But Malta is thousands of miles away," the pythia objected.

"You'd be surprised how far-ranging the trade routes were back then."

Griffin spoke. "Mainstream historians have fostered the belief that Stone Age cultures sprang up in isolation from one another. The kinds of trade goods that have been found in Turkey and in the Americas, originating from thousands of miles away, contradict conventional theories of an insular Neolithic world."

"Certainly, we have evidence that the Hongshan traded with nomads from the steppes." Jun gestured for the group to follow him past several more glass cases.

Rou stuck to him as persistently as a shadow and just as silently.

He paused before a case of Hongshan jewelry. "You see. Copper rings."

"Is that unusual?" Cassie asked warily.

"Indeed, it is." Jun chuckled. "The Hongshan did not produce these rings. At that point in time, the nearest copper-working people would have been the Afanasevo culture—Caucasian steppe nomads who ranged across central Asia."

"You mean overlords?" Cassie felt shocked. "They came this far east?"

"Most assuredly, though distinct proof of their presence is to be found centuries later and many miles away. Since the Hongshan Culture bears no other marks of overlord coercion, the Afanasevo may have merely traded with the inhabitants of this region. Copper rings aren't the only evidence of outside influence. Look at these." He gestured toward a case which contained small pieces of turquoise jewelry. "Though some turquoise has been found in Liaoning, it was more typically sourced from central Asia. That's the same area where the Afanasevo originated just as the Hongshan culture reached its peak. The Hongshan sites also disclose black-on-red painted pottery which was imported as well."

Out of the corner of her eye, Cassie watched as Rou quietly unzipped the collar of her jacket to reveal a perfectly normal mouth and chin. Given all the camouflage, the pythia had convinced herself that the girl might have some facial deformity she'd wanted to hide. However, Rou appeared to be suffering from nothing worse than a terminal case of shyness.

Taking no notice of his granddaughter's unveiling, Jun had already moved on to the next display. "As you look at these jade carvings, bear in mind that the raw material wasn't sourced locally. The jade itself came from mines far beyond China's borders."

The group made the rounds of the rest of the exhibit, pausing here and there to study items of interest.

"What are these?" Cassie pointed to a curious set of jade objects. Each one appeared to form a capital letter "C." The front of the C was shaped into a dragon's head, but the snout was squared off. It didn't look like any dragon the pythia had ever seen before.

"Those are pig-dragons," Jun explained. "You can tell why they're called that from the blunt shape of the nose. It's interesting when you think about the creatures the Hongshan chose to carve most often: turtles, birds, pig-dragons. All of them are symbolically associated with yin."

"As in the female principle of yin and yang?" Griffin asked.

"Yes, exactly. It's a further indication that we are dealing with a female-centric culture. Of course, we also know the Hongshan were matristic because they were a highly complex society with no evidence of warfare or oppression of any kind."

Cassie shook her head in disbelief. "Given how male-dominated Chinese society is today, nobody seems to realize there was an earlier stage of development that was a far cry from overlord."

"The truth has been buried for a very long time," Jun remarked sadly.

"Burning of books..."

The other three turned to look at Rou in surprise. They'd all but forgotten her presence. Her accent was thicker than her grandfather's though still understandable. Apparently realizing for the first time that she'd spoken out loud, Rou clapped both hands over her mouth in a frantic attempt to prevent any more words from escaping.

The pythia peered at her. "The what now?"

Rather than answering the question, the girl shook her head in panicky denial.

Her grandfather intervened. "That's a long story, and it's almost lunch time. I know a good noodle shop nearby. While we eat, Rou and I will tell you all about it."

His granddaughter ducked her head and scurried toward the exit ahead of the rest.

"Is Rou... ahem... is she... quite alright?" Griffin's tone was perplexed.

Jun sighed dolefully. "She's going through what you Westerners might call 'a phase.'"

10 – INCENDIARY PROSE

Cassie and Griffin trailed behind the Zhangs as they scurried up one street and down another in search of Jun's favorite noodle shop. After about ten minutes of walking, they arrived at a small restaurant with a red awning. There was a line out the door with ten people ahead of them.

Sensing Cassie's dismay, the trove keeper said, "Don't worry. This will move quickly."

The pythia studied the plate glass window facing the street. It was covered with pictures of various dishes. Although there were no helpful English subtitles, she could identify most of the food by the images—marinated salads, noodles, meat and vegetables combinations, dumplings, and soups. Taken aback by the sheer number of choices, Cassie asked hesitantly, "Can you recommend something?"

Jun chuckled. "I'll order four different items. That way we can share, and you can try a little of everything. You're sure to like the hand-pulled noodles."

"Hand-pulled?" the pythia asked suspiciously.

"You'll see in a minute." Jun gave a mysterious smile.

As the trove keeper had promised, the line moved briskly. In only moments, they were at the front counter where the cashier took their order.

While Jun spoke for the group, Cassie scanned the dim interior of the restaurant. It was minimalist—bare floors, no cloths on the tables, hard wooden chairs. The lack of upholstery served to amplify the noise inside. It made her think of bistros back home where the collective din meant you had to yell to be heard by the person sitting across from you. Waiters, oblivious to the racket, darted between tables and dodged patrons as they carried steaming platters of food.

Griffin and Cassie followed Jun and his granddaughter past the cashier. Cassie happened to glance to her left and stopped dead in her tracks. A clear plastic partition separated the kitchen area from the patrons. The pythia watched as one of the chefs lifted a ball of dough and began to pull it apart. He continued to stretch it, fold it and flip it around until the long strand of pasta resembled a lariat. Then he did something even more amazing. He stretched the rope of dough further and twirled it over his head and around his shoulders in ever-widening circles. Cassie hadn't seen a display like that since she'd watched a cowboy demonstrating lasso tricks at a rodeo. After several more minutes of pulling and twirling, the ball of dough had transformed itself into strands of spaghetti which the chef broke into segments and placed in a pot of boiling water.

Both the pythia and the scrivener stared goggle-eyed at the performance until Jun interrupted their trance.

"Just like Las Vegas," he quipped. "You get food and a floor show."

Both of them burst out laughing, as much at their own stunned reaction as at his joke.

Rou tugged insistently at her grandfather's sleeve to hurry him along. The girl motioned the trio to follow her through the narrow aisles of the restaurant toward an empty table for four. Rushing ahead, she commandeered the space just as a young couple was about to claim it. Shooing them off, she threw her jacket over one of the chairs and stood guard until Cassie, Griffin, and Jun caught up with her.

The little party had no sooner sat down and gotten settled than a waiter bustled over with their order. He set down platters of cucumber salad, pan-fried noodles with vegetables, pork dumplings, and cashew chicken over rice. Then he distributed plates and chopsticks, so they could all share the food.

"That was fast," Cassie observed in surprise.

"I imagine they must run a brisk business," Griffin said.

"Yes. Talk fast, eat faster, then leave," Jun cautioned.

"So much for ambience." The scrivener shrugged.

"Who cares about ambience when the food is so good." Cassie was already sampling the hand-pulled noodles. "This stuff is amazing. I've never tasted noodles like this before in the States."

They took turns passing around the platters, and after everyone had filled their plates, Cassie returned to the topic they'd abandoned when they left the museum.

"You were going to tell us something about China's buried past?" she suggested gently to Rou.

The girl slid her gaze toward the floor, refusing to make eye contact.

When it became obvious that she wasn't going to speak, her grandfather took over. Jun paused to swallow a dumpling and then launched into the tale. "It happened a long time ago when rival provinces were fighting for control of the whole country. The Qin ended the Warring States Period by conquering the other states and establishing imperial rule over all of China although their dynasty only lasted from 221 to 206 BCE. They wanted to solidify control of the entire country, and they did this by centralizing the government. Like many governments which followed, theirs was heavy-handed and bureaucratic. Not content to control the population through force of arms, the first Qin emperor wanted to control their thinking as well."

"That's rather a modern notion, isn't it?" Griffin asked.

"Oh no, a very old one in China," Jun countered. "Qin Shi Huang sought to purge ideas which ran contrary to his dynasty's official ideology. The texts that were considered most subversive were poetry, history, and philosophy. The emperor reasoned that if people read about better times in the past, they would become dissatisfied and wish to change the present state of affairs. Likewise, the philosophical treatises often expounded theories that contradicted the ideal totalitarian state the Qin wanted to maintain. All the books which contained subversive ideas were collected and burned. However, two copies of each were kept under lock and key by court scholars. The knowledge they contained became inaccessible to the public at large. Any citizen caught discussing these works risked execution."

"How awful." Cassie felt shocked.

Jun continued. "That era in Chinese history is commonly referred to as 'the burning of books and the burying of scholars.'"

"One hesitates to inquire about that second phrase," Griffin remarked dryly.

"Perhaps Rou should tell you what it means," Jun hinted.

Rather than reply, the girl stuffed her mouth so full of noodles that no words could emerge. Chewing energetically, she shook her head.

Her grandfather sighed and resumed the story. "Many scholars criticized the burning of books, and this provoked the emperor to take action against them. According to legend, 460 Confucian scholars were buried alive in Xianyang City. It is very possible that the number has been exaggerated."

"Still," Cassie objected. "That's a pretty horrible way to go."

"And that was precisely the point," Jun said. "An unpleasant death was the perfect way to discourage intellectual dissent. If even one scholar was buried alive, the others would think twice before spreading ideas than ran contrary to the imperial ideology."

"The concept of 'thought police' is much older than I estimated," the scrivener observed.

"I'm glad Rou brought up the subject," Jun said. "It explains why we have lost so much of China's matristic past. All the histories which documented the time of the Hongshan and other early cultures were destroyed during the Qin Dynasty purge. Even the two copies which would have been kept in the court library were lost to us in 206 BCE when the imperial palaces were burned by invading enemies. Now all that remains are the myths of Nu Kwa."

Taking another helping of sweet and sour cucumber salad, Cassied asked, "What's a 'Nu Kwa'?"

Rou giggled softly but offered no comment.

"Did I say something wrong?" Cassie gave the girl a curious glance.

Jun elaborated. "Rou is laughing because Nu Kwa isn't an 'it' but a 'she.' There are many different pronunciations of her name. Nu Kwa. Nuwa. Nugua. But they all refer to the same being. A female divinity who created the cosmos. Later historians saddled her with a male consort—her brother Fuxi."

Griffin raised a skeptical eyebrow. "Whenever we hear of brother-sister marriages, we're usually dealing with a transition from matrism to patriarchy, both in mythology and in actual social practice. Your fable of Nu Kwa hints at a time when China was matrilineal."

"Chinese names confirm that theory," Jun agreed. "The lettering of the most ancient surnames all contain a female root character. This would indicate a time in China's prehistory when lineage was traced through the mother's side of the family."

The trove keeper smiled self-consciously. "I seem to be straying from the topic. To return to the story of Nu Kwa. China's mythical past begins millennia ago under the rulership of three successive sovereigns followed by five emperors. You must understand that the terms 'sovereign' and 'emperor' are honorary titles since imperial China didn't exist until 221 BCE. The three sovereigns were: Nu Kwa—the Creator, Shen-Nung—the Divine Farmer, and Huang Di—the Yellow Emperor. Nu Kwa is the first, which makes her the primordial ancestress. As I said earlier, Chinese imperial historians married her to a brother-consort, but in the original myths, she reigned alone. Early records are vague on timing, but some say that Nu Kwa lived around 2900 BCE. That would make her contemporary with the Hongshan culture. In myths, she is often called the 'snake goddess.' The upper half of her body is human while the lower half is that of a snake."

Griffin nodded sagely. "Women and snakes have been mythologically connected since the beginning of time. The python seer in Botswana, the West African goddess Mawu, the Egyptian cobra goddess Wadjet, the pythia at Delphi, the Medusa, Minoan snake handlers, even Voodoo queen Marie Laveau and her python."

"There's a very simple explanation for that association," Jun said. "And it's not the silly phallic connection that overlord historians are so fond of making."

Both Griffin and Cassie gave him puzzled looks.

The trove keeper continued. "It all has to do with shamans—women who were the oldest spiritual guides of humankind. They existed in every culture around the world. In order to visit the phantom realms, they had to rely on substances to alter their states of consciousness. To this day in the Americas, shamans will ingest mushrooms or smoke peyote. Siberian shamans depend on repetitive drumming ceremonies to induce a hypnotic state. But the most ancient tactic used by shamans was snake venom."

"I never thought of that," the scrivener murmured in surprise.

"But snake venom is so toxic it would kill the shaman who used it," Cassie objected.

"That depends on the species of snake," Jun countered with a smile. "Not all are lethal. In fact, most produce the kind of venom that is a powerful hallucinogen. Shamans knew which snakes to use for their rituals. Have you never wondered why so many folk religions revere the wisdom of the snake?"

"It always seemed odd to me," the pythia commented. "There's nothing particularly brainy about reptiles."

"Not as such," Griffin said. "But the idea makes sense in light of Jun's explanation that their venom can induce paranormal states which impart wisdom to the shaman."

"Of course, shamans and their snakes were a threat to overlord religion and needed to be driven out," Jun added.

"Just like Catholic St. Patrick drove the pagan snakes out of Ireland," Cassie joked.

"Exactly so," Jun concurred in all seriousness. "There are many examples of serpents being destroyed by one overlord hero or another. The snake who caused all the trouble in the Garden of Eden was crushed under the foot of the Christian Virgin Mary. The Python who protected Delphi was slain by the Greek god Apollo. Tiamat was destroyed by Marduk in Babylonian origin stories. These are all examples of shamanic religion being eradicated to make way for overlord ideology."

"A bloodless form of religious genocide," Griffin noted sardonically. "I'm sure those myths correlated closely with the actual extermination of shamans living in the newly-conquered overlord territories."

"Speaking of which," the pythia said. "It's obvious that your Nu Kwa was based on some kind of matristic shaman until the overlords got hold of her story. So where did the overlords come from? Those barbarians on horseback couldn't have ridden all the way from the Caspian Sea to carve up China."

"Ah, but that's exactly what they did," Jun countered knowingly.

"But when?" Cassie persisted. "How?"

Without answering at first, Jun glanced around the restaurant. His listeners followed his gaze. Cassie noticed a group of people standing near the entrance and eyeing their table. She glanced down guiltily at their now-empty plates and remembered Jun's caution to talk fast, eat faster, then leave.

"Maybe we should continue this overlord discussion somewhere else," she suggested sheepishly.

"A very good idea," the trove keeper agreed. "We should go to Lanzhou."

"Lanzhou!" Griffin exclaimed. "Correct me if I'm wrong but that city is over a thousand miles away."

"Yes, it is," Jun agreed calmly. "But that is where your quest must begin. You wish to follow the Yellow River to pick up the trail of your Minoan relic, don't you? What better place to start than where the river itself starts. Lanzhou is near the headwaters, and it also happens to be the place where the overlords first entered China."

Griffin and Cassie exchanged dubious glances.

"Do you have a better idea of where we should start?" the pythia asked.

"Not at the moment, no." Turning to Jun, the scrivener said, "Right then. Tomorrow we fly to Lanzhou."

"Next time, remind me not to unpack my suitcase," Cassie murmured to her colleague. "I have a feeling Lanzhou won't be our final stop on this trip."

11 – INFORMED OBSERVER

Daniel's mind wandered while the sound of his father's voice droned on in the background. He was sitting in the Nephilim chapel enduring a memorial service for his departed wife, Annabeth. There was no casket as would have been customary. His father's explanation to the congregation was notably lacking in detail. According to the diviner, Annabeth had passed away unexpectedly at the hospital where she was recovering from mental exhaustion. Circumstances prevented her body from being returned for burial. Daniel eyed the center aisle of the chapel where an open coffin should have been placed. He felt a transitory sense of regret that he would never get the chance to look at her one last time and bid her farewell. He laughed grimly to himself. The phrase almost sounded romantic—bidding farewell to a lost love. But he had loved her, he protested fiercely. An inner twinge of guilt told him otherwise. His conscience couldn't be fooled. He relented. All right. Perhaps he hadn't loved her, but at the very least he never wished her any harm and certainly not a death as tragic as hers had been. Perhaps if he'd stayed behind. If he'd defied his father and refused to pursue the fourth relic he might have been able to prevent her collapse. Mere idle speculation, his conscience told him coldly.

He glanced surreptitiously around the chapel. The room could barely hold fifty people, so the event had been limited to close family. Some of his brothers and their principal wives were in attendance. A few of his father's own wives were there as well. Mother Rachel sat in the foremost pew, her eyes closed to prevent distraction as she drank in every word of the sermon.

The scion turned his attention to the small girl seated next to him. He gave her hand a soft squeeze. She looked up at him solemnly. Her expression showed less of a sense of loss than of confusion. Sarah was his youngest daughter. She'd just turned five and, earlier that day, Daniel had been forced to tell her that her mother was dead. He explained that Annabeth had gone to heaven and that they would all meet again someday. His words had little effect. Notions of heaven and hell meant nothing to a child that young. Sarah only knew that her mother was gone. Of course, Annabeth had been missing from the child's life for several months now. First, because of the birth and subsequent death of a baby brother and then because Annabeth had been taken away to a hospital. The diagnosis was nervous prostration. It was a dry, clinical description to cover his principal wife's embarrassing sleepwalking episodes and dramatic hallucinations.

Sarah squirmed on the hard bench and yawned unselfconsciously. Daniel made no move to correct her behavior. It seemed natural, unlike the masks worn by the adult members of the congregation. They might have been so many stone pillars, listening through deaf ears to his father's fevered exhortations. In a highly improper gesture by the standards of the Nephilim, Daniel put his arm around Sarah's shoulders and let her nestle against him. She closed her eyes and seemed to drop off to sleep. His other wives reported she was no longer crying in the middle of the night or waking them up calling for her mother. Daniel realized that while his other spouses tolerated her presence, they felt no urge to care for Sarah as her biological mother might have done. They had daughters of their own to consider. The scion felt remorse that he wasn't spending more time with the girl. Yes, he would make a point of doing that. He needed her to know that she hadn't been entirely abandoned.

The diviner fulminated for another ten minutes. It was nothing Daniel hadn't heard before, so he allowed his attention to drift to more immediate concerns. He knew he'd have to produce tangible results in the quest for the next artifact soon or face his father's wrath. Ostensibly, he still spent his days at the library researching the subject. In actuality, he'd spent the past four months accumulating a storehouse of knowledge about the outer world. Chris called him an information sponge because he absorbed it all so quickly. If there was one bright spot in Daniel's life, it was the hours he spent surrounded by books in the company of his beloved friend. He sighed inwardly at the realization that this pleasant interlude would soon come to an end.

The scion knew he must apply himself to the next riddle but balked at the prospect. Somehow, he had formed a mental association between Annabeth's death and the relic hunt. She might still be alive if he hadn't left to blindly follow his father's orders. Who knew if his next absence might not result in a worse catastrophe than a dead wife? He realized the notion was irrational, but the two events had become fused in his psyche and, try as he might, he couldn't separate them. The association had drained his enthusiasm for solving the next riddle.

He snapped to attention when he realized his father had finally finished speaking. People were standing up and filing out of the chapel. He woke Sarah and set her on her feet. Taking her by the hand, he led her through the gauntlet of congregation members who waited to offer them both condolences. She behaved patiently enough during the ordeal until the crowd dispersed. His other wives came up last of all with their daughters to claim Sarah.

He bent down and told her, "I'll come by to see you later this afternoon. Alright?"

She nodded without a murmur, looking back over her shoulder at him as she was led away by the rest of his small family.

He stood and straightened his coat, preparing to go back to the study room. As he turned, he realized a man blocked his path. It was his brother Joshua.

***

"Oh, it's you," Daniel observed without enthusiasm.

The spymaster barely noticed his brother's less than warm greeting. Joshua was too irritated by the inordinate fuss their father was making over Annabeth's death to register offense at this minor slight. One dead wife was hardly worth considering when one had so many others. No doubt, Abraham had already selected a younger and prettier woman as Annabeth's replacement—a reward which his brother scarcely deserved. Since Joshua was denied the pleasure of expressing any overt hostility toward the scion, he settled for rubbing salt in the wound of Daniel's grief.

"I'm very sorry for your loss," he began, his voice heavy with sympathy.

"Thank you." Daniel nodded curtly and started walking down the corridor.

Joshua joined him. "It was quite sudden, wasn't it?" he asked in hopes of churning up painful memories which his brother was probably doing his best to suppress.

"I couldn't say. I was out of the country at the time."

"But surely Father gave you some details," Joshua persisted, seeking to find a weak spot.

Daniel sighed. "He said she took a turn for the worse while I was gone and suffered a nervous collapse."

Joshua nodded gravely. "Yes, her behavior grew uncontrollable shortly after your departure. She needed to be sedated and confined to her room."

Daniel wheeled on him fiercely. "How do you know this?"

At last, Joshua had struck a nerve. Suppressing a sense of triumph, the spymaster innocently raised his eyebrows. "It was hardly a secret. Everyone knew. Father tasked me with posting guards in front of her room. No one was allowed to see her but the doctors from the hospital. Several of them came and went for a week or so. She was rambling much of the time, out of her head. Soon after that, she was taken away."

The spymaster watched Daniel's face contort with regret at the pitiful picture of Annabeth in her last days. Joshua drove the knife home. "Poor lost creature. I'm sure your presence would have made all the difference to her. She might still be alive today." He shook his head. "But you were thousands of miles away when she died all alone. How sad."

Daniel turned his back though Joshua was sure he'd seen his brother's eyes well up with tears.

The spymaster paused, choosing his next words carefully. "Did Father tell you anything more about the circumstances of her passing?"

Daniel's shoulders slumped in an attitude of defeat. He turned back around to face his brother's relentless cross-examination. "He said she contracted a highly contagious disease while she was at the hospital. It was so dangerous that her body had to be cremated afterward."

Joshua's sharp intake of breath sounded like a hiss. He felt genuinely startled. The spymaster had heard nothing of this, and it was his business to know everything that passed among the Nephilim. Quickly recovering his composure, he offered a bland smile of condolence. "What a tragedy."

Daniel was studying him intently.

Apparently, Joshua had betrayed himself. His desire for information had become too apparent. "It must have been a deadly disease to require such drastic measures," he observed, still hopeful that his brother might drop a few additional crumbs.

"Yes, well, everybody dies," Daniel countered acidly, not offering any further details.

"That's quite true," Joshua agreed. "But not everybody dies in such a way. What a misfortune for you."

Daniel barely heard him. They'd arrived at the reading room door, and the scion was on the point of entering. "I'll leave you here," he announced, obviously relieved to have arrived at his destination.

"Yes, goodbye." Joshua nodded pensively. Baiting his brother no longer held any interest for him. The scrap of information Daniel had unwittingly provided made the spymaster long for solitude. He needed to be alone with his thoughts because they were beckoning him down quite an unexpected path.

12 – IT'S HIP TO BE SQUARE

A mere two days after Cassie and Griffin had landed in Shenyang, they found themselves following Zhang Jun and Zhang Rou through another urban landscape a thousand miles to the west. This time they were trudging the streets of the equally modern city of Lanzhou, the capital of Gansu province in northwestern China.

Cassie's first impression, formed as their plane was descending, was that this city of four million was virtually indistinguishable from the city of eight million that they'd just left. Admittedly, Lanzhou did have one distinctive geographical feature. The Yellow River ran right through the middle of town.

Jun told them that Lanzhou had been an important trading center since ancient times. It was the largest urban area in the upper reaches of the Yellow River and had originally been one of the few towns with a bridge that allowed people to cross the river itself. During the first century BCE, it had been a major stop on the northern Silk Road which transported goods from China as far west as Rome and back again.

A Silk Road caravan was nowhere in evidence as the four made their way through the downtown section of Lanzhou which now consisted of block after block of retail space and high-rises. Although the city was still a mercantile hub, the fabrics on display in storefront windows weren't embroidered silk goods. Designer clothes and consumer electronics had taken their place.

Because the shopping district didn't allow motorized traffic, the center of the streets were used as pedestrian walkways. The Arkana group ambled down the broad promenade at a leisurely pace, passing quartets of people seated at card tables playing mahjong.

After strolling for several blocks, Cassie asked, "Where are we going exactly?"

"To the office of the Majiayao trove keeper," Jun replied. "She's off at a dig site for the rest of the week but said we could use the place while we're in town. It isn't much farther. Another block or two."

Cassie's attention was drawn to a gathering in the middle of the promenade just ahead of them. Two dozen middle-aged and elderly women appeared to be staging some kind of demonstration. When she paused to watch, her companions did the same.

Somebody switched on a boom box which blared out a peppy instrumental march. Once the music started, all the women picked up identical green volley balls and began going through a series of choreographed aerobic moves.

"What are they doing?" Cassie murmured in surprise.

"They're square dancing," Jun said.

The pythia squinted at him in disbelief. "Square dancing? But nobody's calling the steps."

"I don't believe he means an American-style square dance," Griffin remarked.

Jun chuckled when he realized Cassie's confusion. "It's called square dancing because they find a square and dance in it. This is a new fad in China these days. Every city has troupes of dancing grannies. They show up at all hours, from sunrise to sunset and go into their various routines."

Cassie was having trouble grasping the concept. "But why?"

Jun shrugged. "Exercise, companionship, patriotism. Not everyone thinks it's a good thing though. Some people who live near the favorite squares of these grannies complain about the loud music early in the morning or late at night."

Rou whispered in her grandfather's ear, and he laughed out loud. She nudged him to repeat her comment for the visitors.

"Rou wanted to remind me about the turf wars."

"I beg your pardon?" Griffin's eyebrows shot up.

"You mean to say these grannies slug it out over the best places to dance in?" Cassie asked.

Rou giggled and nodded.

Cassie turned to contemplate the energetic elderly ladies circling their green volley balls in synchronized arcs over their heads. "This is the hottest trend in China?" She rubbed her eyes in disbelief. "Now I really have seen everything."

Jun was already walking ahead. The rest followed him in silence until the echoes of the marching music had receded in the distance. He entered the lobby of a high-rise and made for the elevator where he pressed the button for the 20th floor. The little party was conveyed upwards in a matter of seconds.

When they exited, Jun went directly to a door in the middle of the corridor and unlocked it. "I know my way around, you see, because this used to be my office. My first assignment for the Arkana was to oversee the Majiayao trove."

"I suppose all the artifacts are stored somewhere else," Cassie speculated, secretly hoping to get a glimpse of the actual hiding place.

"Oh yes," Jun agreed. "Deep in the mountains and away from prying eyes."

He opened the door and switched on the lights. The office windows looked out over the business district.

Cassie peeped through the blinds and caught a glimpse of green volley balls a few blocks away below her. "They're still at it," she murmured with amusement.

Jun made no comment. He was reading a note that had been left on the desk. Smiling briefly, he turned to Cassie. "It would seem you'll get a glimpse of at least one artifact while you're here. The Majiayao trove keeper left me a message. Her people turned up an object which they can't identify. Since she knew the pythia would be coming to Lanzhou, she was hoping you might validate it for her."

Jun unlocked one of the desk drawers and removed a bundle wrapped in white cloth.

The other three drew up chairs around the desk. Jun sat down in the trove keeper's seat and placed the package before them. He carefully uncovered the object which was about a foot long.

"It's a horse's head," Cassie said matter-of-factly. She peered at it closely but couldn't see anything particularly unique—a rough wooden carving of the head and neck of a horse.

"I would guess that the mystery lies not in the shape of the object but in its function," Jun explained. He picked up the artifact and turned it on end to examine the base of the carving. "It looks to me as if this object sat on top of a pole of some sort."

"Perhaps it was the head of a scepter," Griffin suggested. "Or a staff?"

"If so, its design is quite different than any we've seen before," the trove keeper replied. "Such ornaments as you've mentioned are usually emblems of high rank and are made of more precious materials like gold or jade. They would be ornately carved and set with gems. This horse's head is crude by comparison."

"I see your point," the scrivener conceded.

"Perhaps the pythia would be kind enough to give us her impressions?" Jun slid the carving across the desk toward Cassie.

She took the precaution of sitting back in her chair and planting both feet firmly on the floor in case the object had any disorienting surprises in store for her. Then she took the horse's head and held it between her palms.

The sun was blindingly bright. She gazed off a hundred miles in every direction, but all she could see was a sea of dried yellow grass waving in a strong wind. She was seated on horseback. Or rather 'he' since she was inhabiting the consciousness of a man. Judging by his apparel, he was a warrior. He wore a helmet on his head, and a long knife was strapped to his leather belt. The wind blew his blond beard across his chest. He shielded his eyes and scanned the horizon for a few moments, considering whether it was time for a change of direction. He cast a glance behind him. There were several dozen people in his caravan. Some seated in horse-drawn carts. Some on horseback. All waiting for his decision.

"Bring me the south-pointing chariot," he commanded.

One of his followers rode forward, leading another horse which had been harnessed to a small two-wheeled cart. Resting on its platform was a collection of interlocking gears connecting to a pole surmounted by a carved horse's head.

The leader studied the motion of the cart as it drew up beside him. The horse's nose persisted in pointing off to his right. That meant they were still riding east. He squinted ahead in the glare of the overhead sun. The sea of grass was so vast and flat that it might as well have been an ocean. There were no mountains in sight. Not yet anyway.

"This way," he called to his followers. He flicked his horse's reins and advanced in the same direction they had been heading for weeks. Sooner or later, the dying grasslands would give way to mountains that gushed rivers. Then they would follow where the horse's head wanted to lead them.

Cassie blinked rapidly. The office seemed incredibly dim in comparison to her sunlit vision.

"What did you see?" Griffin's tone was worried.

She gave him a reassuring smile. "Nothing terrible, if that's what you're asking." Glancing down at the artifact, she laughed in wonder. "It's a compass."

"Aha, I knew it!" Jun clapped his hands in delight.

"I don't see any needle." Griffin picked up the carving and examined it closely.

"The horse's nose is the pointer, or needle, if you want to call it that," Cassie explained. "But from what I could see, it didn't work by magnets. It was driven by gears, and it always pointed south." She told them the details of her vision.

Jun's eyes were sparkling with excitement by the time she finished. "And you're sure this leader in your vision was Caucasian?"

"Well, I didn't have a mirror," Cassie demurred. "But the guy had a blond beard, he was dressed like an overlord barbarian, and his followers were a bunch of white people riding through steppe country. If it swims like a duck and it quacks like a duck..." She shrugged.

"Yes, I'm sure you're right." Jun traded a knowing glance with Rou.

Cassie scowled. "Wait a minute. The guy who owned this horse's head must have been somewhere a thousand miles away in the grasslands. Probably Kazakhstan. How did this artifact get to China?"

"It was found at a dig site only ten miles from here," Jun said. "The Majiayao culture inhabited the area around Lanzhou between 3100 and 2700 BCE. They were the earliest culture in China to show evidence of bronze weaponry."

"Weaponry?" Cassie asked. "I thought all the Neolithic tribes around here were peaceful agriculturalists."

"Oh, yes. They were."

"Then the weaponry must have been brought here by outsiders," Griffin speculated.

"Most certainly. Cassie's vision has offered us a missing link regarding the overlord migration to China."

"Then you're saying this warrior with the yellow beard and weird compass used it to find his way to Lanzhou?"

"That's right," Jun agreed, smiling broadly. "I believe this little carved horse's head pointed you directly to the Yellow Emperor."

"The Yellow Emperor!" Griffin exclaimed. "But that's impossible. He was Asian."

Cassie held up her hand. "It looks like I need some backstory here. I know you mentioned him as one of the three mythical sovereigns but who exactly is the Yellow Emperor?"

Rou leaned over and whispered in her grandfather's ear.

Jun nodded in agreement. Addressing the others, he said, "Rou wishes me to advise you that the answer to your question is far from simple. The true identity of the Yellow Emperor is cloaked in myth and legend. To unmask his face, we first need to separate fact from fable."

13 – DANCING AROUND THE PROBLEM

Dr. Rafi Aboud handed his ticket to the usher and accepted a program. He found his seat in the dress circle of the Auditorium Theater. After getting settled, he scanned his surroundings. The century-old theater had been a landmark of design in its day, credited with inspiring the Art Nouveau style in Europe. It boasted an elegance that the modern taste for curtain glass and bare metal had completely lost. Aboud decided he liked the excessive opulence of it all. Built in the 1890s, it still served as a major venue for the city's performing arts. The doctor glanced at his program. The Joffrey Ballet was dancing Stravinsky's *The Firebird* tonight. He, himself, wasn't an aficionado of ballet but his business associate was. He expected that Vlad had a particular fondness for this piece as it was scored by a Russian composer and based on a Russian folktale.

Aboud sighed at the thought that he had never had the time to cultivate his finer sensibilities. He expected that with the profit from his current venture, he could soon afford to be a patron of the arts as well as a man of leisure. He cast a glance at the theater-goers taking seats around him. They exuded a consciousness of privilege. He could tell by their familiar greetings that many were season ticket-holders. Their topic of choice seemed to be details of the resort locations they'd visited during the winter months. All of them were dressed expensively, as he himself was. Soon, he'd also be in a position to cultivate the acquaintance of the smart set.

A tall blond man took the aisle seat in Aboud's row. It was Vlad. The doctor and the weapons broker nodded at one another, but neither spoke. The doctor casually scanned the rows of seats behind him, now nearly filled with spectators. He didn't spy a black suit among them. That was good. In the event his benefactor was having him watched, Aboud knew a Nephilim would never cross the threshold of a theater. It was tantamount to passing through the gates of hell. The cult held a particular horror of public entertainments. It was laughable really that the same men who were commissioning him to develop a deadly plague could be routed so easily by a bevy of ballerinas. Aboud chuckled to himself at the paradox. The lights dimmed. The performance was about to begin.

***

When the house lights came up for intermission, Aboud followed Vlad out to the bar.

As they waited for their drink orders, Vlad asked, "How are you enjoying it so far?"

Aboud could offer no critique on the finer points of the performance. "This is the first ballet I've attended."

"Ah, this is nothing," Vlad waved his arm dismissively. "You haven't seen *The Firebird* until you've seen it performed by the Bolshoi. There are no words to describe it in any language. Pure poetry in motion."

"Perhaps one day I shall see a performance in Moscow," the doctor agreed noncommittally.

They took their glasses of champagne and wandered off to a quiet alcove on the mezzanine where they could speak more freely.

Vlad glanced at their champagne flutes ruefully. "Perhaps we ordered the wrong drinks. We have nothing to toast yet, do we?"

Aboud took a seat on an ornately carved sofa. "It would seem I was too thorough in my work," he remarked cryptically.

Vlad took a seat next to him. "Meaning?"

"My benefactor wanted the most virulent strain of pneumonic plague possible. One that could kill in a matter of hours." The doctor shrugged philosophically. "And that's what I created. I succeeded in developing a strain so lethal that even I can't stop it."

"So that means you haven't developed a vaccine yet?" Vlad sounded mildly annoyed.

"Oh, I have tried to develop a vaccine," the doctor countered. "A great number of them, in fact. I tested every conceivable type of vaccine on my last twenty subjects, and still they perished."

The Russian leaned in closer, his demeanor slightly menacing. "You need to appreciate my position. I have lined up half a dozen buyers, all eager to start bidding on your weaponized plague. I can only string them along for so long before they become impatient. Money is burning holes in their pockets, but that money will go elsewhere if you don't hurry up. And that is a best-case scenario. These men do not like to be disappointed. They have a very low tolerance for frustration and for those who are the cause of it."

"I am well aware of the need for haste," Aboud concurred dryly. "My benefactor reminds me of that fact every week."

Vlad took a sip of champagne, his attention temporarily diverted to another topic. "You still don't know who his target is?"

The doctor shook his head. "He's been very tight-lipped on that subject. He says he'll let me know when it's time to design a delivery device. Of course, I won't be ready to do that until the vaccine has been perfected."

The lights flashed, signaling that intermission was nearly over.

Vlad finished the rest of his champagne in a single gulp. "So what am I to tell our prospective buyers in order to hold their interest?"

Aboud pondered the question for a moment. "You may tell them that I'm very close to a breakthrough. I should have an effective vaccine within a month. Two months at the very most."

Vlad stood, towering over the little doctor. "For your sake, I hope you are right. When they run out of patience, we both will have run out of time."

14 – A JOURNEY OF A THOUSAND MILES BEGINS WITH A SINGLE STEPPE

Cassie and Griffin sat motionless in the trove keeper's office in Lanzhou eyeing the crude carving of the horse's head compass which lay in the middle of the desk. They were waiting for an explanation.

Zhang Jun leaned back in his chair. "It's a strange thing about archaeology," he mused. "Often a small, insignificant find can lead to something much bigger. In this case, a discarded piece of a mechanical compass brought us to our first physical trace of the Yellow Emperor. But let me begin at the beginning. Do you remember when we were in Shenyang I mentioned the original rulers of ancient China?"

"You told us about the three sovereigns and five emperors," Cassie replied readily.

"Quite so. As you'll recall, the serpent goddess Nu Kwa was the first sovereign. She created the universe. The second sovereign was Shen-Nung. He is called the Divine Farmer because he taught the people agriculture and the medicinal uses of plants. The third sovereign is known as the Yellow Emperor. He is credited with devising numerous inventions and has the dubious distinction of being named the inventor of warfare. All of the subsequent five emperors traced their lineage back to him. Of course, modern scholars dismiss all eight figures as mythical, but evidence has been coming to light about other legendary figures who have been proven to actually exist."

"Still," Griffin objected. "Do you seriously believe the man in Cassie's vision was your fabled Yellow Emperor?"

Rou nodded gravely.

Jun continued. "Asia is a huge land mass and not all its inhabitants are of Mongoloid ancestry. Some are Caucasian, but nobody seems to remember this. China has, for a long time, believed in its cultural isolation. Because the country is bounded on all sides by mountains and oceans, most current history books insist that no foreigners ever set foot here while the culture was in its infancy. As a result, China asserts that it developed its civilization without any stimulus from the rest of the world. We know this to be far from true. The influence of the west made itself felt from the very beginning."

Griffin stared at Jun with open skepticism.

Apparently interpreting the scrivener's reaction, Jun protested, "Please, allow me to elaborate. We have much more evidence than the pythia's vision for making such claims. One has only to look at the Tarim Basin mummies or the Beauty of Loulan."

"Oh yes," Griffin said. "I recall reading about those finds. It seems a large number of perfectly preserved specimens were discovered in the Tarim Basin in the northwestern part of China. They were very tall Caucasians, some wearing woven plaid cloth resembling Scottish tartans. The most ancient of the mummies are four thousand years old."

"The government resisted disclosing information about these mummies because they feared it would stir up controversy among the Uyghurs."

"Uyghurs?" Cassie asked cautiously.

"From Xinjiang," Rou mumbled under her breath.

Instantly everyone transferred their attention to her, and she blushed.

"You may as well continue," her grandfather prompted gently.

The girl tried to form a few words, but no sound came out. It seemed that the direct scrutiny of the group was too much for her. With a stricken look, Rou mutely appealed to Jun for rescue.

"Very well," the trove keeper conceded. "Xinjiang is in the northwest corner of China. The Uyghurs are a Turkic race who migrated there a long time ago. Many of them have light-colored eyes and hair. Some even have European features. The Uyghurs feel that their province shouldn't be part of China at all because the inhabitants are not ethnically Chinese. They've been staging government protests for years. Needless to say, the discovery of the Tarim Basin mummies wasn't widely publicized for fear of stirring up a furor in that region all over again. But the Uyghurs offer strong genetic proof that Caucasian tribes have existed along China's northern and western borders for the past four millennia or more."

Rou managed to squeak out a few audible words at last. "The Mongols."

"What have they got to do with this?" The pythia sat forward in her chair.

Jun replied. "As you know, the Great Wall was built to keep out barbarian raiders from the north. These raiders eventually coalesced into the Mongol Empire many centuries later. What most people don't know is that the Mongols were genetically quite diverse. Chinese historians of the time referred to them as 'the people with colorful eyes.'"

"That would mean they were Caucasian." Griffin sounded baffled.

"At least in part," Jun said. "In fact, Genghis Khan is described as having red hair and green eyes. His wife's name was Bourtai which means 'grey-eyed.' There are many people living in Mongolia today who have Asian features with light hair and eyes. It would appear that when the Caucasian tribes migrated eastward, they didn't stop in central Asia. They gradually extended their reach to encompass the northern and western borders of China. A smaller number continued southeastward into China itself. Gansu Province, where we are right now, is called the Gansu Corridor because it is the easiest way to reach the Yellow River Valley from central Asia."

"That means this province acted like a funnel to draw traffic from the steppes," the pythia concluded. "But I still don't understand why overlords would have traveled this far east. What was the attraction?"

Jun gave a humorless laugh. "They needed a new group of agriculturalists to exploit."

Cassie and Griffin exchanged troubled glances before turning their attention back to the trove keeper.

"Hold on," the pythia objected. "I was told the overlords left the steppes because the grasslands dried out and their herds needed greener pastures."

"That is only part of the story," Jun countered. "The grasslands dried out, but the livestock problem wasn't the main reason for their mass migration out of western Asia. As early as the fourth millennium BCE, the overlords had learned to prey upon the neighboring agricultural population."

"I never thought of that," Griffin interjected. "Of course, it makes sense. Before desiccation began, fertile farmland would have existed along the fringes of the steppes. Agricultural communities probably flourished side by side with the nomads."

"Sadly, the domestication of the horse gave an advantage to the nomads," Jun said. "Rather than trading peacefully with the farmers as they had done in the past, they swept in and raided the agricultural communities. On horseback, the nomads struck too quickly to be pursued."

"Nice people," Cassie said sarcastically. "Except that it's a bad long-term strategy. I mean, sooner or later the farmers must have gotten fed up with the chronic pillaging and moved away."

"I believe the nomads developed other tactics to control the farmers," Jun said. "Various tribes of horsemen would fight each other to claim control of a given agricultural area. The victors would offer to protect the farmers in their territory from other predators in exchange for a share of their crops and other goods."

"That's just great," the pythia remarked. "They invented the stone age version of a protection racket."

"And gave birth to the exploiter model of overlord culture which has plagued us ever since," Griffin concluded.

"This state of affairs existed for at least a thousand years before desiccation affected central Asia around 3500 BCE," Jun said. "Some of the farming communities would have died out from famine after their crops failed year upon year. Others would have moved their communities farther away from the dry grasslands into the mountains and river valleys. This would have made them inaccessible to the overlords whose principal tactic was a speedy attack over flat, open terrain."

"So, you're saying the overlords packed it in and went to look for easier targets?" Cassie asked.

"Yes, and this search led them very far from their homeland. We find evidence of their horse culture dispersing in all directions. The bulk of the nomads infested Europe, north Africa, and western Asia but other groups continued eastward. Their numbers were small, but they didn't need large armies to prevail over the resident agriculturalists. They brought with them the inventions of domesticated horses, spoke-wheeled chariots, and bronze weaponry. It has always been believed that these things were invented independently by the Chinese, but none of that is true."

"So, you're giving overlords the credit for all those inventions." Cassie's voice was doubtful.

"Not precisely." Jun balked. "The overlords were never any good at invention. Their only talent lay in exploitation. This is evident from the very start. There would be no overlord culture at all if they hadn't solved the puzzle of how to exploit horses as something more than a source of meat. From there, they learned to exploit other human beings."

"How do you mean?" Cassie asked.

"Consider the topic of metallurgy. History books frequently sing the praises of overlords for their invention of bronze weapons, but this is ridiculous when you think about it."

"Yes, I see your point." Griffin seemed to be turning over a new theory in his mind. "Mining metals requires a detailed knowledge of the local terrain. This could only be achieved by a sedentary population who worked the land and could identify ore deposits. Metal craft would also require a specialized labor force. A farming community with a dependable food supply could afford to support the efforts of miners and metalworkers. In contrast, nomads on horseback held only a superficial knowledge of the terrain through which they moved. They certainly had no specialized skills other than combat."

"But they could threaten and bully the people who did," Cassie observed. "Once an overlord gang was able to target a farming community that had its own miners and metalworkers, they could force them to make weapons to overlord specifications."

"I believe you're both right," Jun concurred. "The same principle would have been true in the invention of the spoke-wheeled chariot. Sedentary woodworkers and blacksmiths would have crafted the vehicles the overlords required to carry out their endless battles with one another."

"Because nomad populations were so mobile, I can see how they might have spread their extorted inventions all the way east to China. But what about horse domestication?" the pythia insisted. "I mean, there are wild horses in this part of Asia so that might have happened right here."

"DNA," Rou murmured cryptically.

Jun wisely decided not to remark on the fact that his granddaughter had finally found her voice. Apparently, he realized that doing so would only dampen her budding conversational skills. He proceeded as if she'd been actively conversing with the group all day. "Yes, you are correct. Until quite recently, horse domestication was believed to have developed in isolation in China. However, we now have DNA results which prove that theory to be false."

"How so?" Griffin asked.

"The yDNA of all the horses in China, in fact of all domesticated horses in the world, comes from a bloodline that originated in Kazakhstan. It would seem that domesticated male horses were brought into China by the overlord nomads and bred with wild mares who were caught locally and later domesticated."

"So, the overlords loaded up their horses and their war wagons and came to China looking for a new place to set up their extortion racket," Cassie said. "But that still doesn't connect all the dots for me. Why are you so sure that the man in my vision was your Yellow Emperor?"

Jun seemed to take no offense at her dogged persistence. "There are many stories associated with the man known as Huang Di—the Yellow Emperor. Some have been dismissed as pure myth when they should have been viewed as clues to his real identity. Let's start with the name itself, 'Yellow Emperor.'"

"Perhaps an association with the river of the same name?" Griffin suggested.

"Or quite literally a description of the coloring of the man," Jun countered. "Cassie said the man in her vision was blond. Myths tell us that the Yellow Emperor had four eyes. Two appeared shut at all times, but he could always see what people were doing."

"Now that has to be fiction," Cassie objected.

"No," Rou asserted quietly.

The two visitors glanced at her in puzzlement.

Jun smiled. "You need to consider how Caucasian eyes might appear to an Asian who had never seen such eyes before. The Caucasian eye is more deeply recessed in the skull than an Asian eye. It is the reason your eyelids have a fold, and ours do not."

Griffin peered at Cassie's face and then at Jun's, apparently noting the difference for the first time. "You're quite right, of course." His voice held a note of amazement.

"In Asia, there are women who have plastic surgery to create a double eyelid because this is considered more beautiful."

"Get out!" Cassie exclaimed. "It's the skin-bleaching issue from Africa and India all over again—everybody trying so hard not to look like themselves."

"I imagine because the Western standard of beauty dominated so many colonized countries," Griffin speculated. "A sad legacy of overlord values."

"Perhaps now you can understand why an ancient historian might have interpreted double eyelids as another pair of eyes," Jun continued. "A figurative way of saying that the Yellow Emperor had Caucasian eyes."

His listeners offered no contradiction.

"But there is more evidence," the trove keeper went on. "Much more. The Yellow Emperor is frequently credited with inventing the spoke-wheeled war chariot. As we have just discussed, this is an invention brought to China by overlords. Any sort of wheeled conveyance would have been far more useful on the open plains of the steppes than in the mountains of China.

"Aside from the war chariot itself, Huang Di supposedly invented the south-pointing chariot. He is said to have won a decisive victory over an enemy on a foggy battlefield using this device to find his way. The most interesting fact about a south-pointing chariot is that it only works over flat terrain. If the wheels are forced to travel over mountains, the gears will not function properly. To those who insist this was a Chinese invention, I must ask what possible use it could be in our rugged landscape. A south-pointing chariot is very helpful in steppe terrain because it lacks any sort of natural landmarks to guide travelers. Frequent dust storms in the region could cause disorientation which would also make such a device useful. There is no doubt the south-pointing chariot must have come from the steppes as did the man who first brought it here."

"Grandfather, tell them about his head," Rou hinted in a voice barely above a whisper. She had seemingly relaxed enough to form full sentences so long as no one was paying her any attention.

Both Griffin and Cassie had learned by now not to react every time she spoke. They kept their eyes firmly focused on the trove keeper.

"Ah, yes," Jun said. "In some accounts, the Yellow Emperor is said to have had a deformed cranium."

Cassie shrugged. "I couldn't tell from my vision since he was wearing a battle helmet."

"Deliberate cranial deformation was practiced by many overlord tribes," Jun said.

The pythia gasped in disbelief. "You mean they did that to themselves intentionally?"

"At first the result may have been accidental," the trove keeper explained. "Nomads swaddled their infants against a cradle board to keep them still during long migrations. The head, bound tightly to a board for hours on end, if not days, would eventually be remolded with a sloping forehead. Because the nomads became the ruling elite in whatever territories they conquered, a deformed cranium was viewed as a sign of high status."

"Yeesh!" Cassie exclaimed. "Any kid who spent the first year of its life in a straight-jacket would be likely to develop some serious psychological issues later on. Actually, swaddling might go a long way toward explaining why overlords were generally so bad-tempered."

"Have I convinced you yet that your blond man is the Yellow Emperor?" Jun teased.

"I'm coming around," Cassie joked back. "What else you got?"

Jun obliged by offering more evidence. "The Yellow Emperor engaged in warfare with other nomadic tribes like his own. There is a mention of a battle against 'the forces of the Nine Li under their bronze-headed leader Chi Yu and his eighty-one horned and four-eyed brothers.'"

"If we were to interpret that passage figuratively instead of mythologically," Griffin interjected, "'bronze-headed' might refer to a bronze war helmet like those worn by overlords. Similarly, the horned and four-eyed brothers might mean eighty-one warriors with Caucasian eyes who were wearing horned battle helmets."

"Very good." Jun nodded approvingly. "Now you're seeing the facts behind the flowery language. But the most telling evidence of all is a comment made by a much later historian. He said that the Lord of the Yellow Earth governed and protected the black-haired people and that they were happy under his rule." Jun raised his eyebrows quizzically, silently challenging Cassie to interpret.

"Black-haired," she echoed. "As opposed to what? Everybody in China has black hair." She paused to consider. "Unless, of course, the Yellow Emperor and his cronies weren't brunettes."

"Exactly," Jun concurred.

"But there should be some yDNA indicating a Caucasian influence here," the pythia insisted. "When we were in India, we found an overlord DNA signature all over the place."

"I don't believe the number of overlords who migrated to China was nearly as high," Jun said. "While we see the same general population-flow coming from the northwest and traveling to the southeast, a much larger number of overlords targeted India instead of China."

"It does make sense that there would be a very small genetic footprint this far east," Griffin agreed. "If the local farmers were peaceful and willing to tolerate the newcomers, the overlords might have set themselves up as the ruling elite with very little trouble. Jun's reference to the black-haired people being happy with the Yellow Emperor's rule implies as much. Over the centuries, the overlords would have intermarried and become assimilated into the Chinese population without much fuss."

Cassie threw her hands up in mock surrender. "OK, you win. I believe the Yellow Emperor was really a refugee from the steppes."

"Jun has certainly made a compelling case," Griffin agreed.

"Huang Di is credited with all sorts of inventions which set China on the path to advanced civilization. Of course, it's far more likely that he and his tribe acquired those inventions from the agriculturalists they conquered along their migration route: astronomy, writing, weights and measures, silk weaving courtesy of Huang Di's wife. All of these are inventions which would have been useful to a settled agricultural population, not to nomads."

"Apparently the overlord rolling stone gathered quite a bit of moss and spread it to the ends of the earth," the scrivener remarked.

"The Yellow emperor is said to have ruled the Yellow River valley for a hundred years from 2698 to 2598 BCE. That statement, I grant you, is most probably an exaggeration. The rest of what I've told you is fact rather than fiction." Jun carefully rewrapped the compass-head and slid it back into the desk drawer before locking it. Giving a little bow, he said, "Thank you, Right Honorable pythia, for providing us with this valuable bit of information."

Responding in kind, Cassie bobbed her head. "You're most welcome, Hongshan Trove keeper Zhang Jun. It was my pleasure to be of assistance."

The scrivener seemed amused by her rare attempt at formality.

"But this is not the reason you came here," Jun protested. "Considering the service you've just rendered to us, Rou and I must devote all our efforts to helping you find your missing Minoan relic."

The pythia glanced out the window worriedly. "Now that I've had a chance to absorb the vibe in Lanzhou, I'm fairly certain that the Minoans never stopped here at all."

"Then we must accompany you farther east along the river," Jun suggested. "There are other ancient sites you should examine."

"Erlitou?" Rou suggested tentatively.

"Early who?" Cassie asked.

Jun laughed. "Erlitou was the capital of the Xia dynasty around 2000 BCE. My granddaughter has offered a very good suggestion."

Rou silently beamed at his words of approval.

"How far is Erlitou from here?" Griffin asked.

"About six hundred miles. We can set out tomorrow morning."

"Great," Cassie said. "That will give me time to catch the evening show of the square-dancing grannies. I want to take some snapshots because nobody back home will believe me."

15 – WHAT DREAMS MAY COME

The diviner settled into the easy chair in his sleeping quarters. He gave a mirthless chuckle at its inappropriate name. Considering his chronic insomnia, there was nothing particularly easy or restful about this piece of furniture. He glanced at a tumbler of water placed on the table next to his chair. Beside it sat a small bottle containing the medicine that Brother Andrew had prepared for him.

Abraham thought about the previous concoction which the herbalist assured him would assist in sleep. It had failed miserably, only augmenting the nightmares from which he already suffered. He wondered if this new medicine would be any better. Could it be any worse? He sighed and carefully measured out the dose. The herbalist had been most insistent that Abraham take only the specified number of drops and no more. Apparently, this remedy was far more potent than the last.

He swirled the contents of the glass and drank it over the course of several minutes. Well, it didn't taste as bad as the other medicine had—perhaps because it was far more diluted. Abraham waited a few moments. Nothing happened. He fought the urge to double the dosage. Instead, he resigned himself to another failed experiment. Dimming the table lamp, he settled back and closed his eyes. Brother Andrew would certainly get an earful in the morning. He would...

***

Abraham was standing in a field of tall green grass that smelled of springtime. The sun was shining brightly overhead. He didn't know why, but he felt utterly free from care. All his worries, the burden of his position, fell away from him like a heavy overcoat on a summer's day. He felt a calm conviction that all was well. It was an utterly unknown sensation. Abraham couldn't recall a time, even as a little boy, when all had been supremely well. There had always been something to fear or someone. Above all else, he had lived his entire life in constant terror of displeasing the Lord. But at this moment, the diviner felt blameless in God's eyes. He knew he could do no wrong and that all his petty transgressions had been forgiven.

It was utterly baffling how he knew all these things, but he was convinced that they were true just the same. He walked up to the crest of a hill. The sight before him took his breath away. A quarter mile below, where the hillside sloped downward, stood a shining city. The buildings were all made of white marble, and the roofs of the buildings glinted of gold. A marble wall surrounded the city. The only opening was barred by a pair of tall golden gates. From inside the city walls, he could hear music—the sweetest sound he had ever heard or imagined. Voices endlessly raised in a chorus of praise. Abraham looked at the ground beneath his feet where a cobblestone path had sprung up out of the earth. It led from where he stood directly to the city's entrance.

A voice spoke beside him. "You are surely blessed among men, Abraham Metcalf."

He turned to see a being of surpassing beauty standing at his side. He was clothed in a shimmering white robe, and a golden glow radiated all around his form. Although the creature had no wings, Abraham was convinced he stood in the presence of an archangel.

"How are you called?" he asked timidly, stunned by the splendor of this divine entity.

"My name is Phanuel. I have come to show you the way to your celestial home."

"You mean there?" Abraham gestured to the gates which seemed to be slowly parting before him.

The archangel nodded.

"But it isn't my time yet," Abraham protested." I have much to do yet on earth."

"I understand," Phanuel replied without surprise. "This is merely a vision of the reward that awaits you at the end of your days."

The diviner was knocked speechless by this revelation. For months, even years, he had been plagued with visions of the fiery pit. He dreaded failing to do God's will. All of that seemed a foul illusion now, sent by the devil to frighten him. Only this moment was real. His heart felt so light that he imagined it was about to float free of his chest.

Phanuel continued. "The Lord knows of your plan to bring His kingdom to earth. He knows and is well-pleased. Remain faithful, stay the course and your reward shall be great in heaven. All the voices you now hear shall sing of your exploits. You shall be known as the Deliverer. You shall redeem the Blessed Nephilim and bring the Fallen World back to God."

Abraham closed his eyes and felt himself weightlessly flying through the air, borne on the chorus of celestial voices to the very throne of the Most High.

He blinked and opened his eyes. They were still standing on the hillside.

Phanuel placed a gentle hand on his shoulder. "In the days to come, remember all I have shown you. Stay the course, Abraham, and your reward shall be great indeed."

In a dazzling flash of light, the archangel disappeared. The diviner stood blinking in the sun until an overpowering sense of drowsiness overcame him. He sank down to the sweet green grass and fell into a deep repose.

***

A knocking sound intruded on his rest. Abraham shifted to resettle himself in a more comfortable position, but the knocking persisted. Then a door slammed, and a voice followed.

"Father Abraham, wake up."

Someone was tugging at his shirt sleeve.

"What?" He sat up groggily. It took several seconds for his eyes to focus. Much to his surprise, daylight was streaming through the drapes in his chamber. He rubbed his eyes with his fists. Sitting up straighter, he peered up at the owner of the voice. "What are you doing here?" he demanded.

Brother Andrew was at his elbow, helping him to rise. "I thought I should check on you after your first dose of medicine."

Abraham yawned and rubbed the back of his neck. "What time is it?"

"Seven o'clock in the morning, Father."

The diviner turned to stare at the herbalist in disbelief. "I took your medicine at eleven o'clock yesterday evening. Do you mean to tell me I slept through the night?"

Brother Andrew shrugged. "I wouldn't know. If you don't remember waking, then I suppose you did."

"The Lord be praised," Abraham murmured in wonderment. He felt better rested than he had ever done in his entire life.

"And did you dream?" Brother Andrew asked nervously.

Abraham treated him to a genuine smile of pleasure. "Oh, yes. Such dreams as I have never known. Visions of a city of God. Of a world reborn."

"You must remember that this medicine is strong," Brother Andrew cautioned. "It can spur the imagination to create all sorts of vivid fantasies."

Abraham scowled down at the herbalist in surprise. He ushered him out of the room. "You're wrong," he contradicted. "These were not fantasies. They were prophecies—a confirmation from heaven itself that I have chosen the right course."

He unceremoniously closed the door in Brother Andrew's face. Then he turned on his heel to prepare for the day ahead. "I have much to do before my time of glory arrives," he told himself. "Let the world tremble. I know beyond all doubt that the Lord is on my side. If God be for the Nephilim, who can stand against us?"

16 – THE WHEEL FACTS

Cassie stretched and gazed out the rear passenger window of the car.

"Before you even ask, 'are we there yet,'" Griffin cautioned, "I believe we are."

This was the second day of a two-stage journey by car. There were no direct flights from Lanzhou to their next destination of Luoyang which made a six-hundred-mile road trip the quickest way to get there. After spending the previous night in a hotel in Luoyang, they were now en route to the archaeological site of Erlitou which stood twenty-five miles outside the city.

During their trip, the landscape had changed from the mountains circling Lanzhou to green farmland. They were now traveling through the flat, fertile land along the lower reaches of the Yellow River which grew the crops that fed most of the nation.

Jun unexpectedly slowed the vehicle and pulled it over to the shoulder of the road next to what appeared to be farm acreage. Given the warmer climate of Henan, the cultivated furrows were already sending seedlings shooting toward the sun.

They all stepped out of the car and scanned the landscape. A series of plowed fields stretched in a level patchwork toward distant mountains.

"Where's the dig site?" Cassie asked in a baffled tone.

"Here," Jun replied matter-of-factly as he struck off across the field. "Follow me."

The three silently complied, treading carefully in an effort not to disturb the young plants. After about five minutes, Jun stopped in front of a rammed earth retaining wall.

"Careful," he cautioned, spreading his arms protectively to keep the rest from falling into a depression in the ground.

Cassie barely caught herself before taking a tumble. "You'd think somebody would put up a sign."

They all paused to stare at the excavation. As archaeological sites went, it wasn't particularly impressive. Piles of dirt were scattered around rectangular partition walls guarding a central depression which had been excavated a few feet below ground level.

"Isn't anyone working here now?" Griffin seemed mildly surprised.

"Off and on," Jun replied. "More off than on. The site is huge. It covers most of these surrounding fields. Objects have been found everywhere from here to the river." He gestured toward the nearby Luo, a tributary of the Yellow River. "This dig has been active for several decades. Any artifacts discovered here were immediately sent off to museums."

Cassie gave the excavation one more dubious glance. "Let's see if I can get a reading from something." She promptly crouched down beside the retaining wall and slid her fingers across its surface. Pictures flashed across her consciousness in rapid succession. She didn't even bother to close her eyes, aware of both the intent expressions on her companions' faces and the stream of images parading through her head.

A few seconds later, she smiled and stood up. "I got it."

"What? Just like that?" Griffin sounded disappointed.

"I don't know about you, but I can skip the bouts of nausea, dizziness, and pounding headaches," she countered.

"Sorry." His tone was mortified.

"What did you see?" Jun urged.

"Well, for starters, we're standing right in the middle of what used to be an enclosed courtyard. I'm pretty sure this was the center of town because I got the impression that the power elites hung out here. There were three or four buildings—one-story tall with steep roofs. I could tell that one was a temple and the biggest one was a palace. But there's a lot more." She gestured toward the innocent-looking fields all around them. "There were peasant shacks and grain fields. And over by the river, there was some kind of metal-working operation off in an enclosure of its own. Then on the other side of the walled palace grounds was another bunch of fancy houses that belonged to the aristocrats."

She frowned, concentrating. "The people who lived here weren't like the ones I channeled before. Not like in Mohenjo-Daro or Dholavira. They didn't pray to a goddess. They prayed to a human—the guy in charge. The ceremonies conducted in this courtyard were all about pleasing or placating whoever their king was. They were big on protocol and rituals. It was all very orderly and rigid and fearful." She laughed grimly. "I didn't like it."

Her listeners were silent for a few seconds causing her to question her findings. "How'd I do?" she asked Jun timidly.

The trove keeper seemed taken aback by the volume of data she'd collected in a matter of seconds. "Very impressive," he finally said. "Everything you say about life in Erlitou tallies with what we know of it. It was founded by the Xia Dynasty which came six hundred years after the Yellow Emperor and his five successors. During those six hundred years, more steppe barbarians arrived and brought more conflict with them. The Xia kings probably no longer appeared Caucasian, having been genetically assimilated, but the overlord culture of the steppes had taken firm hold by 2000 BCE when this city flourished.

"Unlike the Neolithic farming communities, Erlitou was socially-stratified. At the lowest level was a peasant class that worked the land and provided a labor force for overlord building projects. Above them was an artisan class, principally metal-workers, who created bronze weapons and ceremonial objects. On top of everybody else were the ruling elites. The city at its height may have contained twenty thousand inhabitants."

Griffin wheeled about to gaze at the surrounding farmland. "So, all of this was urban at one time."

"Yes," Jun agreed. "The peasant dwellings would have been placed outside the main enclosure but quite close to the farmland. Here in Erlitou, we see how the infiltration which began on such a small scale in the northwestern provinces intensified until it resulted in a rigid social hierarchy with overlords at the top and the indigenous farmers on the bottom."

"I'm sure traditional Chinese historians might disagree," Griffin countered.

Jun nodded philosophically. "I'm sure they would, but they would be wrong nonetheless."

"That's my hunch too," Cassie warily agreed. "But what proof do you have that everything here wasn't home-grown?"

Jun took a seat on the wall and indicated the others should join him. "There are objects and inventions discovered at Erlitou which have no native antecedents."

"Such as?" Griffin prompted.

"The wheel." As usual, Rou only spoke up when everybody had forgotten her presence. Cassie noticed that although the girl was seated right next to her grandfather, she hadn't whispered the information into his ear. The pythia considered this to be a sign of progress.

The trove keeper expanded on Rou's comment. "Here at Erlitou, archaeologists discovered the first set of wheel tracks found anywhere in China. Wheeled vehicles of any kind had not been seen before. These particular tracks may have been made by war chariots. Of course, traditional lore says that the war chariot was invented by an advisor to the first Xia emperor."

"Except that we know steppe nomads had been using them for a few thousand years," Cassie noted.

"That is correct," Jun affirmed. "Also, it goes without saying that if the Xia invented a war chariot, they would need horses to pull it."

"Steppe horses," Rou piped up. Her voice had grown a fraction less hesitant.

The others deliberately made no remark.

"Another oddity was the discovery of a turquoise dragon found in one of the excavated graves here."

"That doesn't strike me as too strange," Cassie objected. "Dragons are practically an international symbol of China."

"Yes, but did they originate here?" Jun smiled playfully. "Steppe mythology contains references to dragons going back thousands of years. Yet in China, dragons don't appear as a symbol of power until the one found at Erlitou. One might even argue that the pig-dragon figurines found at Hongshan might have been imported from the west. At the very least, their mythology might have been. The items I've mentioned aren't the only indicator of an overlord presence in Erlitou. Bronze-making techniques used by the Qijia Culture northwest of here are identical to those found among tribes in central Asia. Of course, the Xia refined those techniques."

"But I'm sure the original impetus to make bronze weaponry came from outside the country," the scrivener speculated.

Rou was gazing off into the distance, seemingly lost in thought. "So many things that don't belong here." Although she said the words aloud, she seemed unconscious of that fact.

"That is very true." Jun encouraged her. "We've already spoken at length about metalcraft, wheeled transport, and horses but there are other foreign items—sheep, cattle, barley, and even wheat. The excavation here revealed four-thousand-year-old wheat seeds. Wheat cultivation originated in central Asia. There is no form of the grain that is indigenous to China, yet the Xia cultivated it in these very fields."

"Speaking of things that don't belong here," Cassie said, "the overall sense I got was of order and control in Erlitou. Lots of rules and lots of punishments for breaking the rules. That sort of thing comes straight out of the overlord playbook."

"I don't suppose as you were forming impressions of this place, you came across any hint of our Minoan friends, did you?" Griffin regarded Cassie hopefully.

"Sorry, nothing even vaguely Minoan flashed across my radar."

Both Jun and Rou seemed crestfallen at the news.

"I am very sorry," the trove keeper said. "It appears we brought you here for no reason."

Cassie shrugged matter-of-factly. "At least we can check off another spot where the Minoans weren't." She smiled to try to cheer up their guides.

Rou seemed particularly distressed. She rose to her feet and paced back and forth before the retaining wall. Then she swung about to face her ancestor. "Grandfather, we must take them to Anyang." She sounded downright decisive for a change.

Jun gazed at her in baffled amusement at her vehemence. "Yes, no doubt we should."

"Anyang?" Griffin asked.

The trove keeper took a moment to let his eyes wander over the excavation site. "If Erlitou merely whispers of the overlords, Anyang shouts their exploits in blood."

17 – FLIGHT TO SUBURBIA

It was about three in the afternoon when Leroy Hunt parked half a block away from the farmhouse in the sticks. It had taken him all morning to play out the farce of driving to the airport for his imaginary flight to Buffalo. He'd seen a car tailing him from his apartment to O'Hare, but it didn't follow him into the parking garage. Leroy assumed his tail would report that the cowboy was on his way out of town. That suited him fine. Just as an added precaution, he had gone to the trouble of buying a ticket for Buffalo, so he could see if anybody else was lurking at the gate. He hung back after the last call to board, but nobody was loitering in the waiting area. When he had assured himself that the coast was clear, he ducked into a bathroom and changed out of his western attire into something nondescript. A baseball cap and dark sunglasses completed his look. He felt sure nobody would recognize him as he made a beeline for the rental car counters.

He selected a white cargo van with tinted windows which would make it easier for him to scope out the neighborhood without being observed. He also took the precaution of slapping magnetic logo signs on the side doors advertising that the van belonged to a building contractor. Quiet suburban neighborhoods might notice a strange car parked on the street. They tended to ignore tradespeople in vans.

It was a long drive from the airport to the address out in the boondocks, so he didn't arrive until mid-afternoon. He found the place as soon as he turned down the street. It stuck out like a sore thumb among the identical suburban prefabs. A blue stucco two-story farmhouse with a fenced backyard that sat on an acre of land. The street itself was quiet. Nobody was outside walking around. Leroy knew he couldn't dawdle on this stakeout because cars that weren't parked in driveways were an oddity.

He took out a laser microphone with a built-in spy glass and got down to work. For starters, there was an old station wagon parked in the farmhouse driveway. Hunt made a note of the license plate number. There was no way of telling how many people were inside, but the lone car was a good indicator. Then Leroy noticed the front door swing open. An old woman came out and stood on the porch.

For a minute Leroy thought this was a carbon copy of his first fake lead in Phoenix. Maybe this little old lady was another of Mr. Big's flunkies. For all he knew, she might be setting this place up as the next fake address he'd be sent to. Leroy ducked low in the front seat but kept his spy glass trained on her. She had white hair and was wearing a cotton dress with giant flowers splattered all over it—the kind women wore when his grandma was still in pigtails. She ambled down the front walk to the mailbox by the curb and took out some letters. She didn't look in his direction. Just sorted through the envelopes and went back inside the house. His microphone wasn't picking up the sound of any other voices inside, so she was obviously alone.

Hunt felt a sinking sensation. Maybe all the trouble he'd taken to find a paper trail had been useless. This place was going to prove to be just another dead end. He was on the point of starting up his engine and leaving when he saw a sight that changed his mind.

A school bus turned onto the street where he was parked. Again, he ducked low in the seat to watch. The bus stopped in front of the farmhouse, its flashers blinking red. A girl got out, and the bus drove away. Leroy glued his spyglass to his eye, so he could catch every detail of her appearance. He got a good look because she turned around to check the mailbox before going inside. He pulled the dog-eared photo of Metcalf's scared bride out of his pocket and compared it to the girl by the mailbox. Her hair was cut short, and she was wearing makeup, but she seemed to be about the right height and age. He glanced at the photo again. Yup, it was Hannah alright. Not scared anymore. She walked with her head up like she belonged here. When she reached the front door, she let herself in with a key.

Leroy used his laser microphone and listened in to the conversation that followed. It amounted to nothing more than "How was school?" Unless that was some kind of secret code for "the doodads are stashed in the basement" there was nothing fishy going on in that house.

The cowboy sat back to mull over what all of these facts meant. For starters, Hannah wasn't being held hostage as he'd originally thought. It seemed like she wanted to be right where she was—even had her own key to the place. It didn't sound like she had any notion that she was being sheltered by a band of thieves and their boss. And who was the old lady? She was probably another patsy who was even more in the dark about the real nature of Mr. Big's operation than little Hannah was.

Hunt sat there for another half hour waiting to spot any other activity around the farmhouse. At the end of that time, he concluded that unless there was a giant secret vault underneath the building, nobody else was using the place for any shady business. It clearly wasn't a base of operations for Mr. Big or his trio of artifact thieves. More likely it was a safe house for the little gal. That made good sense. A willing hostage was a lot easier to handle than an unwilling one. Hannah could still be used as a bargaining chip if need be, but for now she was just a normal kid going to high school.

The sound of a bad muffler cut into Hunt's thoughts. He craned his neck to see where the noise was coming from. An old junker had just turned the corner and was making straight for the farmhouse. Its driver pulled up into the driveway with no hesitation. Apparently, he was already familiar with the place. The engine died, and a runty kid with spikey hair climbed out of the driver's seat. Hunt put his spy glass to his eye, so he could get the kid's license plate number. He also cracked his van window open to catch any stray outdoor conversation.

Hannah poked her head out the front door. She called to the boy loud enough for Leroy to hear without his fancy spy equipment. "Zach, Granny Faye needs something from the grocery store. Would you mind driving me?"

"Sure thing," he called back. "And don't forget to remind Gamma that she needs to call my dad about the car for prom night."

"OK, I'll tell her right now." Hannah ducked back inside to transmit the message.

The boy leaned against the door of his car and waited for her.

A few minutes later, she ran out to meet him, giving him a quick kiss before climbing into the car.

Hunt raised his eyebrows in surprise. So that's how it was. Hannah had surely taken to the Fallen World in a big way. A boyfriend. Prom night. The preacher would fairly blow a gasket if he could see her now. The cowboy ducked down as the two of them tore off down the street. Then he sat up straight behind the steering wheel to assess everything that he'd learned. He knew all the players now. Little Hannah had a boyfriend named Zach. The old lady's name was Faye. She was probably the boyfriend's grandma since he'd called her Gamma. Hunt knew for a fact she wasn't related to Hannah even though the gal had called her Granny Faye.

It was pretty clear that nobody in that house knew squat about the doodads or the trio or Mr. Big. A kindly old lady looking after a teenager. A teenager with a boyfriend. It was about as vanilla as could be. He'd continue to scope out the place for a week or so just to be sure, but Hunt had seen enough for one day. He grinned at the thought that his long-standing loose end was about to be snipped off for good. He started his engine and drove off.

18 – THE PITS

One hundred and fifty miles to the east of the ruins at Erlitou, the Arkana group continued their search for a trace of the Minoans. After checking into a chain hotel in the contemporary city of Anyang, they took a short drive to the outskirts of town and stepped back three thousand years in history.

Jun steered their car into a gravel lot outside what appeared to be a public park. They walked through the gates and headed toward a long pagoda-roofed building surrounded by trees, grass and an enclosure wall. The layout was much like what Cassie had seen in her vision of Erlitou.

"The ruins of Yin," Jun announced. "This was once the palace grounds of the Shang Dynasty. They ruled this part of China from 1600 to 1300 BCE after taking control from the Xia."

"Another legend," his granddaughter mused softly. She glided toward the exhibit hall, leaving Griffin and Cassie to exchange puzzled looks.

Jun elucidated. "At one time, the Shang were also considered mythical— just like the Yellow Emperor and the Xia Dynasty. That is until this site was discovered in the early twentieth century. Farmers digging in their fields discovered turtle shell fragments strewn about in great numbers. These came to be known as 'oracle bones' because the shells were inscribed with writing for divination purposes. A priest would carve a question onto a shell and then the object would be heated. When heat caused the surface to crack, the priest would interpret the cracks in the carved letters to find an answer to the question. After archaeologists began digging in the area where the shells were unearthed, they realized that the original town stretched for eighteen square miles. It's the largest site found in China to-date. Aside from the palace and other aristocratic dwellings, other structures such as shrines, tombs and workshops were also revealed."

They reached the exhibit hall and walked inside.

"This is way beyond what I saw in my vision at Erlitou," Cassie remarked. "Within the space of a couple of hundred years, it looks like civilization took a huge leap forward."

"Backward." Rou's face was somber.

"What do you mean?" the pythia urged.

"You'll soon see," the girl warned gloomily.

Jun turned to the pythia. "Cassie, do you recall your impression of the culture that lived at Erlitou?"

"Sure," she replied. "Rigid, domineering. I didn't much like the feel of it."

"Then I imagine you'll like this far less." The trove keeper's tone was even darker than his granddaughter's.

The four clustered around an exhibit consisting of a deep pit in the floor which had been exposed so visitors could stand on an observation deck and view its contents from above.

"We're seeing a royal grave which, remarkably enough, escaped looting over the centuries," Jun explained.

Griffin pointed to an object standing in a corner of the grave. "A bronze battle-axe. The quintessential overlord weapon of choice."

"Yes, but observe the ornate design," the trove keeper noted. "You can see how far metal-working techniques progressed since the crude knives found in Gansu a thousand years earlier."

The scrivener transferred his attention to the plaque describing the grave's contents. "This pit originally contained the body of Lady Fu Hao. In addition to being the king's principal wife, she was also a military general and a high priestess."

"Who says you can't do it all," Cassie quipped. "That must mean the Shang were matristic."

"Hardly," Griffin countered. "From what little I know of the Shang Dynasty, they were decidedly overlord in their perspective. Fu Hao must have been an extraordinary woman to have achieved such distinction in her own right." He paused to read further. "In addition to the grave goods, the pit also originally contained the skeletons of six dogs and sixteen humans."

Cassie rolled her eyes. "Looks like blood sacrifice just reared its ugly head in China."

"And on a very big scale," Jun said. "Come this way."

They followed him to an exhibit of excavated chariots and animal skeletons in harness. Each chariot was meant to be drawn by a pair of horses.

The pythia couldn't believe her eyes. "You mean they dug a pit for the chariots and horses and then slaughtered and buried them?"

"It was a common practice among aristocrats of high prestige," Jun informed her.

"This isn't unlike what one might find in an Egyptian pharaoh's grave, and I imagine for much the same reason," the scrivener remarked. "The Shang must have also believed that the afterlife was a parallel to the physical world. An important person would want to be surrounded by the same possessions in the next world as in this."

"It's interesting that you would draw a comparison to the Egyptians," Jun observed. "We know that such burial customs only became common in Egypt after the overlords conquered North Africa. The same is true here. We are seeing displays of wealth and blood sacrifice in Shang graves that bear a strong resemblance to the kurgan pit graves of the steppes."

They proceeded in silence, walking past row after row of chariots and horses which had been interred with the dead.

The pythia felt appalled by the sheer volume of ritual slaughter on display. "I guess overlords didn't get the news that hearses don't come with luggage racks."

Once they exited the exhibit hall, Cassie's attention was drawn to plastic domes covering different plots of earth around the archaeological site. In an effort to distract herself from the unsettling displays she'd just witnessed, she darted forward. Stopping at the nearest dome, she leaned over to peer inside. "Oh!" She recoiled when she identified the contents.

The pit was filled with piles of bones—skulls, torsos, decapitated skeletons, all heaped together like scraps from a slaughterhouse.

The others caught up with her.

"Sacrificial pits." Rou sighed forlornly. "Murdered slaves."

"For major religious rites," Jun said, "the Shang would kill slaves or war captives. Some were decapitated. Some sliced in half. Then their remains were thrown into pits and buried. Perhaps the logic behind the mutilation had to do with the Shang's literal interpretation of the afterlife. One's enemies should never be sent to the next world intact where they might pose a future threat."

"The lesson here is never lose a war to the Shang," Cassie muttered.

"The dynasty was frequently in conflict with its neighbors who wanted to take over the territory," the trove keeper said. "By 1300 BCE, many more steppe nomads were migrating into northern China through Mongolia. The arrival of the Yellow Emperor a thousand years earlier had been relatively peaceful by comparison. He managed to stave off the competition because the number of other overlord bands was small. That state of affairs had changed by the time of the Shang."

"What we're seeing at this site is full-on overlord," the pythia observed. "There are chariots, horses, slaves, animal and human sacrifice, male dominance, and a rigid social order including a priest class to interpret omens."

"You forgot widow slaughter," Griffin added helpfully. "The Shang also practiced that delightful overlord custom."

"But where did it all come from?" Cassie asked. "Nothing we've seen so far leads up to this. It's like it happened overnight."

"Anyang may represent a tipping point of sorts," Jun speculated. "Over a span of two thousand years, a small influx of steppe nomads with superior weaponry and horses had set themselves up as the ruling elite, imposing their traditions on the native people wherever they settled in China. By the time of the Shang Dynasty, a fresh influx of nomads from Mongolia was eager to claim territory along the northern border. The rivalries and competition among them became more intense than ever before."

"Now I know why you warned me when we walked into this place." Cassie's tone was rueful. "Anyang is supposed to showcase the advance of Chinese civilization, but I think it's a huge step backward from the peaceful farm folk whose land this once was."

"And the march of progress didn't end here." Griffin gave sarcastic emphasis to the word "progress." "The overlord infection spread from agrarian China all the way to Korea and Japan. Japan, in particular, had enjoyed a gender-balanced society with many female leaders right up to the sixth century CE when patriarchal China first began meddling in the affairs of its neighbors. Little by little, Korea and Japan both became carbon copies of what we see here in Anyang."

By this time, the group had wandered across the park to another plastic-covered pit. Without thinking, Cassie rested her hands on the rammed earth wall surrounding the exhibit and immediately wished she hadn't.

She was an old man lying curled on his side. He rested on a pile of oracle bones. The pit was half filled with them. It was his duty to protect the prophecies. He was their keeper—a servant of the royal house. When his spirit traveled to the other world, he would resume his duty—faithful for all eternity to his master the king. Dirt began to tumble into the pit, across his body and across the prophecies he shielded. He could feel the weight of it gradually pressing down—surrounding and blanketing him. He watched patiently until the last shovelful fell across his face and eyes, blotting out the sky. After that, he saw no more. All he could feel was the earth mounding higher over his body, pressing down heavier and heavier until its weight crushed the life out of him.

The pythia was clutching at her throat, gasping for air. She had lost all sense of where she was, or even who she was. Time, space and identity had all condensed down to the single urgent need to breathe.

"Cassie!" Griffin gripped her by the shoulders and shook her, trying to break her trance.

It was as if she heard his voice calling her through dense fog. "Whe..." She tried to speak. "Where...?"

She could feel his hands gripping her arms now. The fog seemed less thick than it had a moment before. When she blinked, his face came into blurry focus. "Griffin?"

He threw his arms around her, hugging her fiercely. "Thank goddess, you're alright!"

Cassie realized that she had slumped to the ground next to the oracle pit. She could see other faces now. Jun and Rou were crouched on the grass beside her. They both looked apprehensive. She coughed, trying to clear imaginary dirt from her lungs. After several more gasps, her breathing returned to normal. Then she became aware that Griffin was still hugging her so tight it hurt.

"Uh, Griffin?" she croaked.

"Yes?" He was stroking her hair now. She could feel his lips lightly brush her forehead.

"Griffin?" she repeated a little more insistently this time.

"Yes, Cassie. I'm here." His fingers caressed her cheek.

"Watcha doin'?"

"Oh, dear!"

He recoiled so quickly that she fell backwards, hitting her head on the ground with a soft thump. "Oww!"

"Cassie!" He lunged back toward her. "How stupid of me!"

"I'm OK, really." She waved him back as she sat up, rubbing her head. "Don't help."

He leaped to his feet, obviously embarrassed by his display of emotion.

The pythia smiled shakily at the others. "I sure didn't see that flashback coming."

"Can you stand up?" The scrivener's voice was anxious. "It would be better if we could get you away from this spot."

She nodded.

Griffin pulled her to her feet and placed his arm tentatively around her waist, guiding her to a bench.

The Zhangs followed and sat down on either side of her. At first, they seemed afraid to speak.

"Water?" Rou quavered nervously.

The pythia patted her hand. "No, I'm fine. I just need a minute."

Griffin addressed the others. "I don't suppose you've been treated to the sight of a pythia who has just channeled a tainted artifact."

"I've heard stories..." Jun trailed off, his voice somber.

"Not a tainted artifact," the pythia corrected him. "I jumped into the consciousness of an old man who was being buried alive."

Rou clapped her hands over her mouth to muffle a gasp.

Cassie recounted her vision to the others. When she had finished the tale, she rubbed her temples distractedly. "What a useless waste of a life!"

"But you've seen many examples of blood sacrifice here." Jun sounded baffled. "I don't understand why this particular man's death would affect you so."

The pythia shook her head. "That isn't what I meant. It wasn't because the king used him as a sacrifice. It was because the old man just took it. He curled up on top of the oracle bones and let them pile dirt on him til he was dead." She paused to gather her thoughts. "It was a useless waste because he didn't believe his life was worth any more than that. To him, the king was a god, and he was nothing. It was his role in this life and for all eternity to serve the Shang, and he was OK with that."

"There are those who might applaud his self-sacrifice as a noble deed," Griffin remarked.

"Self-sacrifice is fine if there's a good reason for it," Cassie retorted angrily. "But this was all about serving the greed and ambition of a bunch of overlords who thought their lives mattered more than his." She faltered as a new thought struck her. "Why is that?" She peered at the scrivener. "I mean all the overlords, everywhere. They had the same entitled attitude. The ones who invaded India called themselves 'Arya'—the noble ones. Where does that come from? It can't simply be because they were better fighters. One guy trouncing another will say 'I'm a better fighter,' not 'I'm a god, and you're a worm.' Seriously, I want to know why they all believed that."

Griffin took a few moments to consider the question. "There are a number of contributing factors, but if I had to pick the most important one, I'd choose the horse."

"Really?" Cassie's tone was dubious. "That's the best you can come up with?"

"Hear me out," the scrivener protested. "Try to imagine how it felt to be the first nomad to ride. Previously this man, whoever he was, had lived his life on foot. He'd been forced to migrate immense distances carrying all his possessions on his own back and would have been lucky to travel twenty miles in a day. Now, for the first time, he could control a beast many times his own size. He could make it stop. He could make it turn. He could make it run as fast as the wind. He could use its speed to plunder unprotected villages. What a fatuous sense of omnipotence the horse must have conveyed to its rider. If he could impose his will so easily on an animal, why not a captured woman? Why not a neighboring tribe? Why not the entire world?"

"If you could bottle *Eau de Narcissism*, I'm pretty sure that's what it would stink like," the pythia remarked caustically.

"You're quite right," Griffin concurred. "It is a form of narcissism, isn't it? But, of course, the horse tempted its rider to overreach himself. The first opportunistic young male who formed a raiding party wanted dominance. Astride a horse, he could have it. Seated high above his fellow creatures, he could look down on the earth he'd once crawled across."

"Like a god," Rou murmured despondently. "It went to their heads."

"Exactly so!" Griffin exclaimed, regarding the girl with newfound respect. "In a very literal sense, it went to their heads because on horseback they were no longer grounded. Their mythology came to reflect that rootless perspective. Rather than worshipping earth goddesses who lived in nature, they adored sky gods ensconced above it all."

"OK, you've convinced me." Cassie sighed. "Wherever the horse goes, trouble follows."

"You're more right than you realize," the scrivener said. "The corrupting influence of the horse wasn't limited to the steppe nomads of Eurasia. The same phenomenon occurred in America. The Comanche were once a peaceful, gender-equal tribe of gatherer-hunters. A few generations after they acquired horses, they became a male-dominated, slave-owning, polygamous, warrior culture. Contrary to what you might expect, most of their aggression was directed toward other Native Americans. It is estimated that Comanche raiding parties abducted as many as twenty thousand women and children from neighboring tribes to be used as forced labor. Of course, the males on the losing side of the conflict were immediately massacred."

"I'm sorry I asked." Cassie's voice held a note of disgust.

Jun scowled as he surveyed the peaceful green park dotted with mass graves. "Considering Cassie's unfortunate reaction to the oracle pit, perhaps we shouldn't attempt to walk through the grounds any further."

"Too much death here," Rou agreed.

"You don't need to twist my arm," the pythia said. "I've felt enough for one day."

They rose and ambled back toward their car.

"I don't imagine this tour has brought us any closer to our Minoan friends," Griffin hinted.

Cassie paused, silently assessing something. "You know, it's funny. When we arrived in Lanzhou, I could hear a little voice in my head saying, 'You're getting warmer.' Now that we're here in Anyang, I feel as if we've overshot the mark."

"I'm sorry," Jun sounded deeply apologetic. "These are the major sites along the Yellow River. I can't think of any other places to show you."

"Just show me a map of China," the pythia suggested. "I think I've spent enough time absorbing the river vibe that I can finally figure out the right spot on my own."

19 – GETTING WARMER

Cassie stared moodily out the window of her Anyang hotel room at the lights of the city. She'd just returned from dinner with the group and was vainly trying to clear her head after the events of the day. Being buried alive was proving to be a persistently memorable experience. A gentle tap on the door interrupted her thoughts. She eyed the digital clock on the nightstand. It was 8 PM. With a weary groan, she answered the summons.

"May I come in?" Griffin asked.

She nodded and motioned him inside.

The scrivener carried his notebook computer under one arm. "I thought this might help."

Cassie glanced behind him after he entered. "Where are the Zhangs?"

He set up his PC on the table. "I convinced them that it might be better if you and I worked on our geographic problem alone."

"Good idea." Cassie pulled out one of the chairs and sat down next to him. "I'd prefer to do this techno-dowsing experiment without an audience. I hate the idea of letting them down again."

"They do seem to be taking our lack of progress quite personally," Griffin agreed. He waited for the computer to establish a WiFi connection.

"I wish I could convince them that it's not their fault." The pythia sighed.

The scrivener typed a few keystrokes, and a map of China popped up on his screen. He zeroed in on the northern section of the country. "This is where we are." He pointed to Anyang in Henan Province.

Cassie tapped her chin, considering. "Could you pan out a little?"

Griffin expanded the view to include the surrounding area.

The pythia scowled in concentration. "Show me the entire river."

Griffin typed in a new search criterion, and a map of the whole country appeared with two blue lines running parallel to one another on their way to the Pacific Ocean.

Cassie traced her finger along the course of the Yellow River from its headwaters in the Himalayas to its mouth at the Bohai Sea. She repeated the gesture, this time stopping at Lanzhou. "This is where we started to go off-course," she murmured half to herself. "It was the last place where I felt we were getting warmer. Now that we're in Anyang, the trail's gone completely cold." Her finger meandered down the page and hovered at a spot near the city of Chengdu. "What's here?" she asked.

"Not the Yellow River, I can assure you. That's the Yangtze."

"Hmmm." Cassie's index finger moved to the left of the spot she'd been pointing to. "Can you magnify this area instead?"

"Certainly."

The screen displayed the more southerly of China's two great rivers.

The pythia once more started tracing the river's route from its headwaters in the Himalayas very close to where the Yellow River began. The Yangtze, however, traveled directly south for half its length before veering sharply eastward and emptying into the ocean at Shanghai. Cassie's finger paused over the bend. "Zoom in here," she ordered.

Griffin silently complied.

The pythia pointed to a dot indicating the town of Lijiang. It appeared to be directly south of Lanzhou by about seven hundred miles. "I'm feeling a strong pull around this town. I'm pretty sure this is the way the Minoans went."

"I can't imagine why." Griffin's tone was perplexed. "The region's only distinguishing characteristic is that the Yangtze River makes a ninety degree turn and travels east near Lijiang."

The pythia stifled a yawn. "I'm not up to digging any farther into the town's lore tonight. Why don't we tell Jun about my hunch in the morning? He might be able to give us a quick rundown and save us hours of online searching."

Griffin studied her face intently. "You're utterly knackered, aren't you?"

"I guess so if knackered means I feel like I've been crunched in a carpet roller." She gave him a wan smile. "Being buried alive can sure take it out of a person."

His expression grew somber. "It was thoughtless of me to bother you with this nonsense right now. Sadly, not the first mistake I've made today." He rose and hurriedly packed up his computer.

Cassie followed him to the door. "Meet you in the dining room for breakfast?"

"What?" Lost in thought, Griffin seemed not to have heard her.

She repeated her question.

"Oh, yes. Absolutely. Eight sharp." He faltered, his hand hovering over the doorknob. Turning abruptly, he said, "Look. I'd like to apologize for my absurd conduct this afternoon." He was blushing to the roots of his hair.

Cassie stared at him through a fog of exhaustion. "What are you talking about?"

He opened his mouth several times, but no sound emerged.

The irony of Griffin being at a loss for words struck Cassie as funny until she realized the reason for his embarrassment. "Oh, that," she said in a small voice.

The scrivener's eyes darted toward the floor. "I'm afraid I behaved quite stupidly."

"No, you didn't," she protested gently. "You behaved like somebody who was worried about his friend."

He searched her eyes. "You really think so?"

She reached up to touch his cheek. "News flash. The world is full of selfish, stupid people who go through life trampling anybody who gets in their way. As of this afternoon, I literally know what being ground into the dirt feels like. So, when somebody acts like they care if I live or die, I don't find their concern stupid at all. I'm grateful."

For a brief instant, Griffin's eyes gleamed with something Cassie couldn't quite define. It was gone before she could decide what it meant.

He smiled with relief. "I'm glad." An awkward silence threatened to engulf them both until he rushed to add, "I really should let you get some rest."

As he turned to let himself out, she patted his shoulder. "I care about you too, you know. Don't ever forget that."

He paused, without turning. "You'll never know how much—" He broke off. "Well, good night." He slipped out the door and was gone.

Cassie collapsed on the bed fully clothed, asleep before her head hit the pillow.

20 – REASON TO RETRIEVE

Daniel felt his peaceful dream dissolve when someone rudely jostled his elbow.

"Daniel!" A voice whispered close to his ear.

"Just a few more minutes," he grumbled.

"Wake up!" The voice was insistent.

The scion yawned and opened his eyes. Chris's chiseled features came into focus. Daniel allowed himself a few seconds to furtively admire the view before raising his head. He wondered if his friend realized how handsome he was. Daniel frequently found himself so distracted by the librarian's good looks that he could barely form a sentence. He'd recently read an article about something called the golden ratio—an exact mathematical proportion among facial features which the eye perceived as beauty. Chris's face surely possessed that divine symmetry.

Daniel's musings came to an abrupt end when his arm slipped off a pile of books, causing them to tumble to the floor. It was then he made the embarrassing discovery that he'd nodded off while slumped over a stack of reference works in the Ancient History section of the Chicago Public Library.

"You did it again." The librarian's tone was mildly reproachful. He bent down to retrieve the fallen volumes.

Daniel sat up and massaged the back of his neck to relieve the stiffness. Still disoriented, he asked, "Is it lunch time already?"

Chris chuckled mirthlessly. "Hardly. It's only ten-thirty in the morning. Get up."

The scion obediently rose, closing the volume on Minoan Crete which he'd been reading, and followed the librarian to the elevator. "Where are we going?"

"Out for a walk." Chris punched the button for the lobby when the doors opened.

Daniel stepped into the elevator car after him. "But aren't you on duty? Won't your supervisor notice if you aren't staffing the Reference Desk?"

"So full of questions today, aren't we?" Chris shook his head in mock disapproval. "One of the new staffers agreed to cover for me. I did her a favor last week when she ducked out for a long lunch with her boyfriend."

Still having difficulty processing the reason for their walk, Daniel balked. "But I don't need any exercise."

The librarian snorted derisively as they exited the elevator and moved toward the revolving doors. "No, what you need is an intervention."

Once outside, Chris immediately headed east on Columbus Drive.

Daniel trailed him silently. As the stiff lake breeze hit him full in the face, the last of his sleepiness vanished. Turning up his jacket collar, he asked, "Intervention? What are you talking about?"

Chris paused at the next corner when the light turned red. "I'm talking about the fact that all you do these days is browse books and nap—mainly nap. What about your relic hunt? You've been back for almost five months without solving the next riddle. In fact, you haven't even told me what the next riddle is."

Daniel avoided his friend's eyes. "I'm having some difficulty getting motivated."

They crossed when the light turned green.

Chris's tone became gentler. "Look, I get it. I understand that your wife's death was a huge shock. It was bound to send you into a tailspin, but you have to pull out of it, buddy. You're missing the big picture here."

"What big picture?"

They ran across Michigan Avenue as the light turned yellow and entered Grant Park on the lakefront. It was too early in the season for Buckingham Fountain to be sending up jets of spray for the benefit of tourist photographers. In fact, there were no tourists at all. The two men had the plaza in front of the fountain all to themselves.

Chris didn't even pause. He veered south. "Let's keep walking."

"What big picture?" Daniel persisted.

The librarian gave an exasperated sigh. "Danny Boy, there's a lot more at stake here than finding another jewel-encrusted tchotchke for your dad's mantelpiece."

The comment brought Daniel up short. He'd never considered any other reason. "What do you mean?"

"Think about what might happen if you keep dragging your feet on this artifact quest."

The scion shrugged. "I don't know."

Chris tried a new approach. "I met your father once. He didn't strike me as a patient man."

"He likes to see results," Daniel agreed.

"And if you don't produce those results fast enough, what's he likely to do?"

The scion stared blankly at Chris, still at a loss.

"Don't you get it? He'll replace you with somebody who can give him what he wants." Chris cast him a sidelong glance. "Since I know the backstory on all the major players in your world, I'm guessing your psycho bodyguard, Leroy Hunt, would be next in line for the job."

Daniel stopped dead in his tracks. "My father would never do that! Hunt is incapable of rational thought."

"So, he'd have to send somebody with brains along." Chris smiled sardonically. "Maybe somebody like your shifty brother Joshua?"

The very sound of the name sent a chill down Daniel's spine. "No!"

"No?" Chris ambled forward. "Then who else? Your father trusts him, doesn't he?"

"But he's never trusted him with this secret. He... he... wouldn't!"

By this time, the pair had walked all the way to the Beaux Arts Garden at Eighth Street.

Chris abruptly took a seat on the low stone wall beside the dry fountain.

Daniel, half in shock, sank down next to him.

Chris studied the scion through narrowed eyes. "I see by your chalky complexion that I'm finally getting through but make no mistake. This isn't about sibling rivalry. Letting Joshua get the better of you isn't your biggest problem."

"It's a huge problem." Daniel's voice rose in pitch. "He's a terrible person. There's no telling what he would do if he gained our father's trust. He could hurt so many people."

The librarian nodded solemnly. "I agree. A guy like that could do a lot of damage. Even more than you realize." He paused to let the words sink in.

The scion frowned. "I don't understand. As terrible as that would be, Joshua could only harm members of our congregation. He has no control over anything else."

"Not even if he was put in charge of the artifact retrieval?" Chris's tone held a note of calculated innocence. "What do you think he'd do if he crossed paths with those three thieves you've told me so much about?"

The scion's eyes flew open in wild alarm. "He'd kill them. Even if he didn't murder them himself, he wouldn't hesitate to give the order."

"If you keep pulling a Rip Van Winkle, those three deaths will all be on you," the librarian concluded ominously.

Daniel slumped forward and sank his head into his hands. "Oh my God! It would be a disaster. For everyone."

Chris gave a thin smile of satisfaction. "I see the big picture has come into focus at last." He reached over and rubbed Daniel's shoulder. "Of course, none of that needs to happen if you'd get off your ass and do something about it."

The scion sat up abruptly. He turned sideways to face Chris. "You're absolutely right. I have to begin right now!"

"That's more like it." The librarian nodded approvingly. "I'll go so far as to spout a cliché and say, 'no time like the present.' I don't suppose you remember the riddle off the top of your head..."

Daniel paused to consider. "Yes, as a matter of fact, I do recall the words. Funny how often I've turned that puzzle over in my mind. Here it is: 'The kindred stir upon the high sharp peak where the river flows red to the serpent's heart. Under the lawgiver's glare, its coils tremble in the mirror at the lion's feet.'"

Chris wrinkled his forehead. "Wow, that's a heaping bowl full of alphabet soup."

"I did manage to figure out a few things," Daniel reassured him. "I know the first line refers to the doves from the previous riddle and I'm fairly certain the location in question is the eastern Himalayas. That region is the source of Asia's major rivers."

The librarian appeared lost in thought.

"Did you hear what I said?"

"Eastern Himalayas," Chris murmured. "Rivers with headwaters in the eastern Himalayas." He treated Daniel to one of his dazzling smiles. "I think I've got a shortcut to solving the first line."

"So quickly?"

The librarian shrugged. "If you'd bothered to share that riddle with me earlier, we could have cracked the whole clue by now."

"Sorry." Daniel ducked his head.

Chris ruffled his hair. "Cheer up, Danny Boy. That artifact's as good as found. It just so happens that the Reference Department received an interesting gift about a month ago. Around 1900, there was an explorer who came from a rich family on the North Shore. A hundred years ago, if you had a lot of money and a lot of time to kill, I guess you became an explorer. Anyway, he spent decades traveling through the Himalayas and kept detailed accounts of the places he visited. His family recently donated his journals to the library. They haven't been catalogued yet, but I can slip a few volumes out of storage when nobody is looking. Between the two of us, we ought to be able to find that river you're looking for."

Daniel stood up. "How wonderful. When can we start?"

Chris stood as well. "This afternoon."

"Why not now?" the scion insisted eagerly.

The librarian looked pointedly at his watch and then at Daniel. "Because now it really is lunch time."

21 – WHAT'S AROUND THE BEND

At eight o'clock the next morning, Cassie entered the hotel dining room where her three colleagues were already seated. She took a chair beside Rou.

The girl eyed her with concern. "Better now?"

"Way better." The pythia gave a bright smile. "Rested and ready for action."

The others relaxed visibly at her words. Her display the previous day must have worried them more than she'd realized.

Cassie was on the point of summoning a waitress when Griffin hastened to pour her a cup of strong black coffee.

"I took the liberty of ordering a pot for the two of us to share. The rest of the clientele seems to favor tea for some odd reason."

"Ah, java." She raised the cup gratefully to her lips. "What would I do without you?"

"Were you addressing that last comment to your beverage or to me?" the scrivener inquired playfully.

"A little bit of both, I guess," the pythia retorted slyly as she took another sip.

A few minutes later, a waitress arrived with what had become the group's standard breakfast order—baozi and congee. This consisted of steamed dumplings stuffed with sweet bean paste accompanied by bowls of rice porridge. Cassie had developed a fondness for both dishes during their stay.

After allowing them all a few moments to start their meal, Cassie broached the topic uppermost in her mind. "Has Griffin told you about my latest theory?"

"I thought I might let you do the honors." The scrivener passed her the coffee pot.

"OK then. Here it is." The pythia addressed her comments to the Zhangs as she refilled her cup. "Last night when I was scanning a map of China, I got a really strong hunch that the Minoans took a route along the Yangtze River and ended up around a place called Lijiang. Any reason why they might have gone there?"

At her words, Jun stopped chewing. He appeared thunderstruck. "Yes, of course. That makes perfect sense."

"It does?" Griffin sounded doubtful. "I couldn't find anything remarkable about the place."

"It's at the great bend of the river," Jun said. "The Yangtze travels for nine hundred miles in a southerly direction from its headwaters in the Himalayas and then turns abruptly east near Lijiang."

Griffin regarded the trove keeper blankly, apparently still not convinced of the location's significance.

Jun gave a slight smile. "Lijiang is very close to the land of the Mosuo. No doubt, you've heard of them."

"Of course, I've heard of them," the scrivener replied. "Maddie has been trying to set up a trove near Lugu Lake for several years now."

Cassie tentatively raised her hand. "Anybody want to fill me in about these Mosuo characters?"

Rou piped up. "Last matriarchy in China."

"Really?" The pythia turned to her with avid interest.

The girl withdrew immediately under Cassie's intense scrutiny and focused on picking apart her steamed dumpling.

Jun took up the explanation. "The Mosuo are a tribe living in a cluster of villages high in the mountains around Lugu Lake. They have managed to resist the influence of Han China and maintained their matriarchal customs to this very day. The eldest female is the supreme authority in the family. As you might expect, lineage is traced through the mothers. Their language has no word for 'father' or 'husband.' Men are responsible for the children of their sisters rather than their own biological sons and daughters since offspring never leave their maternal home. They don't marry in the sense that we understand marriage."

"No marriage?" Cassie's eyebrows shot up. "How do they pair off?"

"They have walking marriage," Rou said.

"Is that like walking pneumonia?" Cassie asked archly, trying to coax a smile.

The girl rewarded her with a soft giggle. "No. Not a disease."

The trove keeper continued. "When a young woman reaches a certain age, she's given her own bedroom where she can spend the night with a young man she likes. In the morning, the male partner returns to his own mother's house which is why the custom is called 'walking marriage.' Nobody frowns on this arrangement. Any children that result from such unions belong to the young woman's family."

"From what little I know of Mosuo customs," Griffin interjected, "these romantic alliances can last for years, sometimes even decades. At the very least, serial monogamy rather than rampant promiscuity seems to be the norm."

Jun nodded. "One might think that such an arrangement results in chaos but the Mosuo family structure is remarkably stable—far more so than the patriarchal nuclear family. Without divorce, there is no property division when a relationship ends. As for the children, their lives are not disrupted if their mother changes partners since Mosuo households contain large numbers of aunts and uncles. Children always have multiple adults looking after them. No one is ever an orphan. Aside from stability within the family, the culture as a whole is quite durable because there is no violence. The matriarchs manage to resolve conflicts without resorting to fistfights. There is no vicious competition for resources because nobody hordes wealth. All the members of each family receive a fair share. In local politics, the role of mayor is played by a man, but nobody pays him much attention. Everyone knows the real power is in the hands of the grandmothers."

Rou cleared her throat, a sure sign that she intended to complete an entire sentence. "Letting the grandmothers decide things is good for everyone in the clan."

The other three nodded their agreement with the wisdom of that phrase.

"So how did they manage to pull it off?" Cassie asked. "This Mosuo tribe must be surrounded on all sides by patriarchal Chinese."

"I imagine the same way the Basques did," Griffin speculated.

"You mean mountains," the pythia inferred.

"Yes, the area which the Mosuo inhabit is relatively inaccessible. It offers no resources which overlord armies might covet."

"There is no overlord genetic footprint around Lugu Lake," Jun said. "To this day, Mosuo DNA is distinct. The tribe is closely related to Tibetans with hardly any admixture from the ethnic majority Han DNA."

"It sure sounds like an interesting place to visit," Cassie ventured. "In terms of a likely hiding spot for a bunch of goddess-worshipping Minoans, it seems ideal." Eyeing Griffin, she asked, "So why don't you think this is where we should be looking?"

The scrivener gave an exasperated sigh. "Because it's nowhere near a major river."

"About one hundred and fifty miles from the Yangtze," the trove keeper corrected.

"The riddle explicitly mentions a river pointing to the whereabouts of our next artifact," Griffin insisted. "I'm sorry, but I don't see the connection."

"Tributaries," Rou whispered.

The scrivener looked startled. He stared at the girl. "I beg your pardon?"

Sensing that she was about to withdraw again, her grandfather intercepted the question. "All the Mosuo villages are built on the shores of Lugu Lake, and the lake itself is fed by small rivers which are tributaries of the Yangtze."

"You're saying that if the Minoans followed the Yangtze to the big bend, they would have been able to branch off along another river that would lead them to Lugu Lake?" Cassie clarified.

"Yes," Rou confirmed simply.

"Here is another fact which might be relevant to your search," Jun added. "Lugu Lake nestles close to Gemu Goddess Mountain."

"A goddess mountain?" Cassie repeated slowly. "That's practically a red flag for us! The Minoans love hiding stuff in mountains, especially if they're sacred to some goddess or other." She stared pointedly at Griffin, daring him to offer another objection.

Apparently conceding the argument, the scrivener threw his hands up. "What are we waiting for? Sichuan Province is a long way from here, and we have travel arrangements to make."

"Now why didn't I think of that?" Cassie asked wryly.

22 – POWER BEAUTY TIPS

"How does this one look?" Hannah emerged nervously to stand before Faye. The old woman had taken a seat in front of the fitting room doors and waited patiently as the girl tried on a dozen different prom dresses. They were shopping in a pricey boutique at the mall that catered to teenage girls whose parents had money. Considering that this was to be Hannah's first formal dance, Faye was determined to spare no expense.

"I think this one might be OK," the girl suggested diffidently, searching Faye's eyes for a confirmation.

The old woman smiled. She rose and walked over. Spinning the teenager around so she faced the triple mirror next to the fitting room, Faye answered her question with a question. "What do you think?"

Hannah gasped at the multiple images of herself reflecting the finery of a princess. The outfit was a pink skater dress. Its fitted bodice was spangled with rhinestones. The short skirt was made of ruffled chiffon and billowed around Hannah's legs as she spun around to get a better look. When she stopped spinning, she studied herself with a critical eye. "I think I look pretty." She uttered the statement with a note of shock in her voice.

"And that surprises you?" Faye asked gently.

The girl frowned. "It was a sin among the Nephilim to pay too much attention to appearance. We were told that vanity was the devil's favorite method to ensnare the female. Everybody knew that women who admired themselves were bound to go to hell."

The old woman chuckled mirthlessly. "A very effective strategy if one wishes to induce self-doubt in the fair sex."

Hannah whirled around to stare at her. "Why would somebody want to do that?"

"My dear, in the age-old battle between the sexes, women's trump card has always been physical attractiveness. In cultures where men make the rules, the irksome fact remains that the wealthiest and strongest man can easily be mastered by a pretty woman. I suspect the Nephilim brotherhood knows and deeply resents its vulnerability to female charms."

Hannah continued to stare at her uncomprehendingly.

Faye elaborated. "For women, beauty is power."

"So, a woman who knows she's beautiful..." Hannah trailed off.

"If she were unscrupulous enough, she could use it to her advantage and wreak havoc among the brotherhood. Possibly even destroy it."

"Do you suppose that's why we all wore grey dresses? And why our hair was bound around our heads?" Hannah asked the questions as if realizing the implication for the first time.

"Most assuredly," Faye agreed, returning to the cushioned seat before the mirrors.

The girl followed her and sat down, an anxious look still on her face. "So, you think this dress looks alright? That I look alright in it?"

Faye reached over and patted her hand. "Hannah, I've lived a very long time, and over the course of my life, I've learned a few things that have helped carry me through. The most useful lesson of all is never to place one's self-esteem in the hands of other people."

The girl still looked puzzled.

"How do YOU think you look?" Faye asked.

Glancing briefly at her reflection in the mirror, the girl replied hesitantly. "I think I actually look..." She faltered. "Beautiful."

Faye squeezed her arm encouragingly. "That's my girl. In the long run, your opinion of yourself is the only one that counts."

"There I said it," the teenager continued, gaining confidence. "I look beautiful. I am beautiful."

"I imagine that felt rather liberating," Faye observed.

Hannah's face appeared flushed, exhilarated. "A little scary actually," she admitted. "I never allowed myself to believe that before, much less say it out loud."

"No doubt, that's only one of many new concepts you've learned since you left the compound."

The girl gazed down at the floor pensively. "Living among the Nephilim seems like a bad dream to me now. The things they believe. The way they treat each other. Now that I can look at it from the outside, their ways are topsy-turvy. They stood the world on its head and tried to make everybody believe things were right-side-up."

"So, you're happy in this Fallen World, as the brotherhood calls it?"

"Happy?" Hannah repeated the word with incredulity in her voice. "There's no comparison. I never want to go back there. I'd die before I'd do that."

"Well, let's hope it doesn't come to that," Faye said dryly.

The girl scarcely heard her. She remained lost in her own past. "Even when I was at the compound in Missouri and my parents were there and my brothers and sisters, I don't think any of us were really happy. My parents always worried about whether they were doing the right things to please God. And then, when I was taken away from my family and brought to Illinois, everybody around me wasn't simply worried. They were all scared." She paused to consider. "Except Father Abraham. He never seemed to be afraid. I guess because he was too busy scaring everybody else."

"Oh, I think he was terrified too," Faye remarked quietly.

"You do?" Hannah turned to peer at the old woman.

Faye nodded. "Men who bluster and posture are trying to keep their own fears at bay and to keep everyone else from suspecting the truth. That they're the most frightened of all."

"But what could he have to be afraid of?" Hannah protested. "He made all the rules. He was in charge of everything."

The memory guardian paused to consider the question. "If he really believed the tenets of the Nephilim then he was accountable for everyone else. And if everything wasn't going well, who do you think God would blame? Mr. Metcalf must have lived in constant dread of divine retribution."

"Oh, my." Hannah's hand flew to her mouth as recognition dawned.

Faye continued. "I can't imagine a worse burden than holding oneself accountable for hundreds, if not thousands, of other souls. I find being accountable for my own is quite enough to manage."

"No wonder he was so crabby all the time," Hannah said.

Faye chuckled and stood up. "Enough gloom and doom. Why don't you change and we'll take your lovely new dress up to the counter and pay for it."

Hannah scurried to the fitting room door and returned five minutes later with the dress over her arm.

As the two walked toward the cashier, Faye said, "Now we'll have to find you some shoes to match."

"Glass slippers?" Hannah suggested with a grin on her face.

Playing along, Faye replied, "My dear child, they're very uncomfortable to dance in. Besides..." she added slyly. "I'm fairly certain your Prince Charming doesn't need a glass slipper to find you. He already knows where you live."

23 – LAME EXCUSES

Shortly after convincing Griffin to fly to Lijiang and search the vicinity of Lugu Lake, the Arkana group sprang into action. Although the actual flight time to their destination was only four hours, they were informed it could take a full day to get there. They would have to board a two-hour flight to Guangzhou that entailed an overnight layover. Since only four flights per week left from Anyang, they would have to hurry to catch a plane that very afternoon. They rushed off to pack and agreed to reconvene in the hotel lobby at noon.

Griffin and Cassie were the first to arrive. They went to the registration desk to complete their check-out. About five minutes later, Rou came downstairs and did the same. The three of them, trailing their luggage behind, took a seat on one of the lobby's couches to await the trove keeper.

The scrivener checked his watch. "I do hope nothing's amiss."

All three of them kept their eyes trained on the elevators, but Jun never appeared. Just as they were all growing restive, one of the desk clerks called them over. The trove keeper had phoned downstairs to request them to come to his room. They crowded back into the elevator, luggage and all. A few minutes later, they were tapping at his door.

A muffled voice inside said, "It's open."

Griffin entered cautiously followed by the others. They were greeted by the sight of the old man lying in bed with his left leg propped up on a pillow, an elastic bandage wrapped around his foot.

"Grandfather!" Rou rushed to his side.

"Good grief, what's happened to you?" the scrivener cried.

The old man chuckled ruefully. "A clumsy accident. I was hurrying to pack and had taken off my shoes. Before I could change to another pair, I accidentally struck the bottom of the dresser with my foot. When you get old, your bones become as thin as egg shells and just as easy to crack. I've had enough such injuries over the course of a lifetime to know that I fractured a metatarsal." He winced, obviously in pain, as he shifted his weight.

"Have you seen a doctor?" Cassie asked.

Jun shrugged. "There's little they can do for a hairline fracture. The doctor's standard advice would be to apply ice to bring down the swelling, wrap the foot, keep pressure off the limb, and wait for it to heal. All these things I've already done."

"You certainly can't go with us in this condition," the pythia objected. "You need to stay off your feet and rest."

"I quite agree," Jun said. "I'll have to remain here for a few days until I can walk with a crutch. Then I'll fly back to Liaoning. My granddaughter will take over as your guide."

His proposal was met by a shocked silence.

"But she's just a kid." Cassie wanted to bite her tongue the second she uttered that phrase, remembering the number of times Erik had used those same insulting words about her when she first became pythia. "Uh... I mean... if she's never been there before it would be..." she trailed off.

Jun gave an airy wave. "Rou has been to Lugu Lake many times. Her parents were the first Arkana scouts sent there to assess its suitability as a trove site. She knows the region quite well."

"I'm sure she would be an asset to us," Griffin parried tactfully. "However, you must realize that if the artifact is hidden there, our assignment could become quite dangerous. We wouldn't wish to put a member of your family in harm's way."

The old man maintained his composure in the face of this additional objection. "I spoke to the chatelaine just before I called you all in here. She assures me that your adversary Daniel is still immersed in research at the library. She will inform you when he's ready to depart. Maddie will also alert the operatives you used in Tibet. They will fly out to meet you and arrange to transport the artifact out of the country if you find it."

Griffin and Cassie exchanged resigned looks. The pythia shrugged.

"It seems you've thought of everything," the scrivener concluded.

Rou, who had remained silent during this interchange, spoke for the first time. "No, no, no!" She shook her head violently. Then she launched into a rapid stream of verbiage in Mandarin proving just how fluent Rou could be in a crisis. The torrent of chatter continued for a full two minutes without a break.

Jun regarded his granddaughter placidly as the pitch of her voice rose to a shrill squeak, and her hands gesticulated wildly. He was apparently waiting for her to take a breath.

When Rou's verbal storm had spent itself, the trove keeper reached out and took the girl's hand. "My child," he murmured, "I know you."

This comment brought her up short. She blinked in surprise.

He continued. "I have watched you grow from a tiny baby into a young woman. All that time I could see your clever and resourceful nature, even if you failed to notice it yourself." He gave her hand a gentle squeeze. "Little sparrow, how will you ever know you can fly if you never trust your own wings?"

Jun turned his attention to the others. "Rou will be able to help you find your artifact. I'm only sorry I won't be there to see her do so."

The girl gave her grandfather a stricken look but remained silent.

The trove keeper shifted the pillow behind his back. "Might we have a few moments alone to say goodbye? Rou will meet you in the lobby. I wish you every success on the next stage of your journey."

Cassie and Griffin awkwardly made their farewells and let themselves out.

As they traveled down the hotel hallway toward the elevator, the pythia grumbled, "This retrieval just got interesting."

"Quite," Griffin concurred ominously.

24 – HIGH WAY TO HEAVEN

The diviner tapped his foot impatiently, waiting for a response to his rap. The door remained closed. He pounded more insistently. "Brother Andrew!" His voice echoed down the silent corridor.

A few minutes later, the herbalist opened his chamber door. "Oh, I'm sorry, Father. I was at the back of the infirmary. I didn't hear you."

"Never mind." Abraham swept in and surveyed the waiting room—three or four empty chairs in the front alcove, then a short corridor which led back to a consulting room and the herbalist's store of supplies.

The diviner held up an empty bottle and gave Brother Andrew an accusatory stare. "You aren't making this preparation properly anymore."

"Father?" the herbalist asked weakly.

"As you can see, the bottle is empty. You gave me a full supply less than a week ago."

Brother Andrew's eyes darted nervously toward the door. "Please come through to the back room, and we'll discuss the matter."

Metcalf followed him and was led to a large open area at the rear of his chambers fitted with shelves and bookcases built into the walls. The shelves held bottles and jars, the bookcases various medical reference texts.

"Please sit down." The herbalist indicated a chair in front of his desk.

The diviner sat and placed the empty bottle on the desk in wordless reproach.

Brother Andrew scrutinized the label and instructions. Then he looked up. "This quantity should have lasted you for several more days."

"I suppose it might have done if you'd made it correctly," Metcalf sniffed.

"I—"

"You obviously didn't concoct as strong a mixture as the first bottle. I had to take twice the dosage you prescribed in order to sleep as deeply—to dream as sweetly."

"Twice!" The herbalist registered shock at his own exclamation. He tried in a softer voice. "Father, I warned you that this medicine is very powerful."

"Not nearly as powerful as it was at first. You must have diluted it."

Brother Andrew's face took on an expression of owlish concern. "The second bottle was filled from the same batch as the first. In fact, I shelved it the same day I delivered the first bottle to you."

This information gave Abraham pause. He sat back in his chair and crossed his arms defensively. "Well, something is clearly amiss here."

The herbalist sighed and tried again. "This medicine has certain properties which you need to be aware of. Over time the body will build up a tolerance to it. If you continue to take it every night, then you will need to increase the dosage to achieve the same effect."

Abraham narrowed his eyes. "How much more will I need to take?"

"That is a very individual matter. Sometimes twice as much. Sometimes less. Of course, if you could do without it for a day or two, you won't build up a tolerance as quickly."

"Impossible!" The diviner rejected the idea out of hand. "I have never slept this well before in my entire life. As my responsibilities increase so does my need for rest. I cannot direct an organization of this size without proper rest!"

"Yes, of course." Brother Andrew retreated.

"And far more than rest, I need to maintain my connection to the Lord."

"I don't understand." The herbalist peered at him quizzically.

Abraham allowed his gaze to drift off into space. "This medicine has granted me visions of the world beyond. It has given me the power to discern things to come, to discourse with angels. I am the Lord's chosen prophet. With this medicine I can, at last, hear His voice perfectly. I know His will with absolute certainty. I can execute his plan for the Nephilim with no hesitation." Abraham trailed off, noticing the frightened look on Brother Andrew's face. "You'll simply have to make more," he concluded awkwardly.

The herbalist said nothing at first, apparently weighing how much he wished to offend his leader. "There may come a time when you've built up an extreme tolerance..." He hesitated. "There may come a time when the medicine won't work as you expect it to."

"What do you mean?" The diviner felt a sense of panic rising. To have finally found a solution to his problem and then have it snatched away was worse than never experiencing these sublime visions at all.

"It occasionally happens that the pleasant dreams are replaced by others."

Metcalf raised a skeptical eyebrow.

"Other not so pleasant dreams. And not merely dreams. You may begin to see... things... Strange shapes, phantasms during your waking hours."

"Nonsense!" The diviner waved his hand as if he were swatting a fly. "Until that day comes, you will supply me with as much of this medicine as I require. Is that understood?"

Brother Andrew gulped and nodded. "If the nightmares should return, you may wish to break off using the medicine. I feel obligated to warn you that stopping is far harder than starting was." He stood and walked to a shelf near the window. Selecting a small brown bottle, he handed it to the diviner. "This should last for about a week. In the meantime, I'll distill more."

Metcalf took the bottle and rose to leave. "Double the quantity you prepared last time. I don't wish to run out."

Brother Andrew scurried around the desk and blocked his path. "Please, sir, remember what I said. Even a prophet of the Lord is not immune to the effects of too much medicine."

The diviner laughed humorlessly. "I'm sure if that were true, the Lord Himself would give his prophet ample warning."

25 – UPON REFLECTION

Cassie walked along the shoreline looking into the depths of the clearest lake she'd ever seen in her life. According to rumor, the water was even safe to drink. Lugu Lake was classified as "alpine" despite the fact that it was a continent away from Switzerland. The designation was most likely due to the lake's nine-thousand-foot altitude. Lugu's daunting elevation didn't trouble the pythia though. Thanks to her stint in Tibet she'd learned how to cope with thin air. The same locale had taught her another useful skill—how to drink yak butter tea without gagging. The beverage was as popular around Lugu Lake as in the Himalayas.

The three Arkana agents had just finished checking into their hotel in Luoshui – one of the many villages that rimmed the lake. Despite Cassie's misgivings about Rou, the girl had proven herself an able travel guide. She had taken charge of booking their accommodations and gotten them on the right airplane to Lijiang and the right bus to the lake. At the moment, she was in the hotel lobby haggling over their bill with the proprietor. It seemed that Rou's self-consciousness disappeared whenever she was speaking her own language.

Cassie scanned the architectural style of the buildings surrounding the lake and let out a soft chuckle. Given the evergreens and mountains, the hostelries in the area looked like Rocky Mountain ski lodges complete with knotty pine paneling in the guest rooms. The pagoda roofs offered the only hint that this wasn't Colorado. The parallel to the Wild West was further emphasized by the cowboy hats and blue jeans that Mosuo men wore.

In contrast, Mosuo women were more likely to be seen in traditional attire—long white cotton skirts covered with elaborately embroidered jackets and sashes. Their headdresses were even more intricate than their clothing, consisting of thick black turbans festooned with beadwork, flowers, and ropes of pearls.

The pythia glanced at a group of Europeans avidly snapping photos of the lake, the surrounding mountains and a costumed villager posing in the foreground. Tourist season was just beginning to gear up, and tourism was booming for the Mosuo. The anthropological oddity of a "Kingdom of Women" advertised in travel brochures was an irresistible draw to both Asians and Westerners alike. It had transformed the previously obscure location of Lugu Lake into a must-see attraction. The natives were happy to oblige since tourist money had given them a prosperous lifestyle beyond the reach of most rural Chinese.

The Mosuo didn't seem to mind that some visitors came to the lake in search of lax moral conduct. Han Chinese sex workers, dressed in Mosuo costume, had been imported to fulfill male tourist fantasies in a small red-light district. The local women, as a rule, were more selective in their romantic partners than outsiders anticipated.

Lugu Lake had other attractions to offer besides the lurid prospect of nightly orgies. Nature buffs were drawn to its picturesque beauty, and the best way to see that beauty was via pig-trough boat. The shallow-bottomed, square-ended skiffs were so named because they looked like feeding containers for swine. At the moment, several oarsmen sat at anchor waiting to row tourists across the water to get a closer view of the islands dotting the lake and the mountain beyond.

Griffin walked up beside Cassie, interrupting her reverie. "Amazing view, isn't it?"

She turned. "Where's Rou?"

The scrivener laughed. "She's still involved in a heated dispute with the innkeeper over the rate we're being charged. I didn't catch what she was saying, but I suspect she'll prevail in the end."

"I think we underestimated her." Cassie's tone was rueful.

"She's certainly proven her worth in getting us to this rather out-of-the-way speck on the map." Griffin looked behind him. "Ah, here she is now. Is everything sorted out?"

Rou scurried up to them, looking flushed and mildly irritated. "The bill was wrong."

"Thanks for straightening things out for us." The pythia gave an encouraging smile.

Rou bobbed her head in acknowledgment. Ill at ease with the direct compliment, she immediately changed the subject. Pointing straight across the lake from where they were standing, she announced, "Gemu Goddess Mountain."

"I can see why somebody would have picked that mountain as the home of a goddess," Cassie observed. "The shape is really unusual."

Rising on the opposite side of the lake was a long flat-topped mountain. It's upper half, devoid of trees, appeared golden brown in the afternoon light.

"It almost looks like an animal crouching," the pythia observed. "A tiger or maybe a lion stalking its prey."

"It was once called 'Lion Mountain,'" the girl informed them.

Griffin, who had been casually gazing at the scenery, swung abruptly to face Rou. "What did you say?"

She took a frightened step backward.

"Griffin!" Cassie warned. "Ease off."

Recovering, the scrivener apologized. "I'm terribly sorry, Rou. I didn't mean to alarm you. You said that the peak across the lake was once known as 'Lion Mountain'?"

The girl nodded warily. "In ancient times."

"Good grief! I'm a complete idiot." Griffin sloped off to a bench next to the water. Puzzled, his two companions followed him and sat down.

"You want to explain why?" Cassie prompted.

He sighed and raked his hands through his hair. "The riddle. It all makes sense now."

"Riddle?" Rou ventured uncertainly.

Cassie took up the explanation. "Each of the artifacts we're trying to find is inscribed with a riddle to help us locate the next one. The current clue stumped us both. It says: 'The kindred stir upon the high sharp peak where the river flows red to the serpent's heart. Under the lawgiver's glare, its coils tremble in the mirror at the lion's feet.'"

The girl seemed no less baffled by the attempt at clarification. "Lion's feet?"

"Yes, Rou, lion!" Griffin announced triumphantly. "As in Lion Mountain. I feel confident that I can decipher the clue completely now." The scrivener's eyes had taken on a feverish glow which Cassie interpreted as a good sign. It usually meant he was on the verge of making an important discovery.

"So, spill already!" the pythia commanded.

He grinned happily. "The confusion arose because we both thought the lion's feet of the riddle referred to Regulus in the constellation of Leo. Though Regulus does factor into the time of year for our search, quite a different lion points to the location of the artifact. We are being instructed to look near the foot of Lion Mountain. And what do we find there? A lake. All lakes are reflective surfaces or mirrors if you will. So, the mirror in which the serpent's coils tremble is the lake itself. It reflects a shimmering image of the constellation Serpens in the night sky which makes the great snake appear to tremble."

"Oh." Rou sat forward, gazing with newfound interest at the body of water before her.

"If the Minoans are running true to form, then I'll bet they hid the artifact in a cave on the mountain." Cassie groaned. "That's a lot of real estate to cover."

"I believe I can cut our search by three-quarters," Griffin countered.

Her eyes narrowed as she studied him. "You're being oddly precise with that estimate."

"I'm quite convinced that the specific constellations named in the riddle can tell us which side of the mountain to search. Both Leo and Serpens are prominent in the southern sky during the summer months."

"I'll take a wild guess and say we search the south side of the mountain," Cassie ventured.

"And I would heartily concur." Griffin scowled as he contemplated the mountain. "Which way are we facing now?"

"North," Rou piped up helpfully. "We are viewing the south side of the mountain."

"Excellent." Griffin rubbed his hands together with glee.

"Gemu Goddess Cave is facing us," the girl added.

Both Griffin's and Cassie's smiles faded.

The pythia said, "Just to be clear. You mean the tourist cave that's listed in the brochure? The one with a cable car that drops dozens of people right at the entrance. That cave?"

"That cave." Rou seemed mystified by their reaction. "Good, right?"

"Not good," the pythia retorted. "So not good!" She turned to her colleague. "Griffin, it'll be a repeat of Kailash all over again. Honestly, I don't think I can take another night of flashlights, and frostbite, and being kidnapped."

Rou looked from one to the other in helpless distress.

"Cassie, do calm down. We don't know with certainty that the Minoans hid anything in that particular cave. Let's investigate first, shall we?"

The pythia stood up and dusted off her jeans. "OK, but we both already know how Murphy's Law works. I'll wait til we get up there to say, 'I told you so.'"

26 – ANTIPODAL ALLIANCE

Joshua Metcalf stowed his gear in the back seat of Chopper Bowdeen's rental car. The mercenary had come to pick him up personally at the Melbourne Airport. The spymaster climbed into the left front seat and Chopper darted away from the curb.

As the breeze ruffled his hair, Joshua made a vain attempt to smooth it down. "I've never ridden in a convertible before."

Chopper couldn't tell from his tone whether he was offended or simply making conversation. "Nothing like it in the world, son. We both spend too many hours cooped up indoors. You need to breathe in some fresh air."

Joshua gave a noncommittal smile.

They rode in silence through the suburban area that surrounded the airport and then onward to the valley. Although the airport was far removed from the center of town, it still looked like an extension of the city. This urban feel eventually gave way to acres of vineyards and rolling green fields encircled by mountains.

The spymaster took note of the changing landscape. "I'm surprised that the brotherhood succeeded in finding such a remote location. We aren't that far from Melbourne, are we?"

"No, not too far," Bowdeen agreed. "But we're in the Yarra Valley which is mainly agricultural. It's far enough from the big city to give some privacy to what goes on here."

They drove in silence until the car approached a narrow dirt lane branching off from the main highway on the right. Instead of turning into the lane, Chopper pulled onto the shoulder across the way and parked the car near a row of gum trees for shade.

The spymaster turned quizzically toward his companion.

"Let's get out and stretch our legs here," Chopper suggested. "There are a few things I wanted to talk over with you before we go inside."

Joshua nodded and complied.

The two men strolled along the shoulder of the road and took up a position near the trunk of a tree.

"Well, this is it," Chopper began conversationally. "The last compound on the last continent. My work for the Nephilim is done. You can take it from here with my blessing."

"What will you do now?" Joshua asked casually.

The mercenary hesitated. "That all depends."

"On what?"

He stared the spymaster directly in the eye. "On whether your father will let me go or not."

Surprisingly, Joshua didn't try to reassure him of the diviner's good intentions.

That fact alone gave Chopper a sense of foreboding. "Son, is there something you should be telling me?"

Joshua sighed and cast a furtive glance toward his colleague. "I don't know. I just don't know. There are things..." he trailed off and seemed on the point of walking back toward the car.

Bowdeen stepped between him and the vehicle. "What things?" he urged.

Joshua appeared unwilling to meet his gaze. He turned aside but murmured, "I've recently discovered some facts that are upsetting, to say the least."

"Something that concerns me?"

"It might," the spymaster hedged. He retraced his steps and leaned against the tree trunk. Folding his arms across his chest, he asked, "Do you remember when you asked me to look into a secret lab several miles away from the main compound?"

The hair stood up on the back of Chopper's neck. Despite his original intention to uncover Metcalf's master plan, he felt he was on the brink of finding out something he really didn't want to know. "Sure do."

"It seems the foreign doctor running that lab has been tasked with developing some kind of lethal substance. I don't know what it is or what its intended purpose may be."

"Way back when we talked about this last, you mentioned that the diviner was having you round up ne'er-do-wells in the congregation. Did they end up in that lab?"

Joshua nodded. "Yes, I was able to confirm that much. The doctor who runs the lab would send a driver to the collection point to take them away."

"And what happened to them after that?" Bowdeen feared he already knew the answer.

"They were never seen again," Joshua murmured furtively.

"Seems the diviner found some use for them after all."

"That isn't what worries me." The spymaster started pacing around the base of the tree.

Bowdeen stood back and watched him for a few minutes, waiting for an explanation.

Finally, Joshua wheeled around and said, "My father is no longer distinguishing between the evil and the innocent."

Chopper blinked. He didn't know what to make of that statement. "Come again?"

"Let me go back to the beginning." Joshua took a deep breath. "Last fall, my Brother Daniel's principal wife suffered a mental collapse. She had just lost a baby and became emotionally unstable. Her behavior couldn't be controlled. Ordinarily, we send disruptive wives to hospitals where they can be sedated. Some can be rehabilitated. The ones who can't be are shut away, but they aren't physically harmed. This month, my father announced that Annabeth had died of a contagious disease while at the hospital. Her body was cremated to avoid infecting the Nephilim."

Chopper shrugged, not seeing how these facts pertained to him. "Sounds like a tragic accident to me."

Joshua slid down against the tree trunk and sat unceremoniously on the ground.

The mercenary crouched down beside him, wishing the spymaster would come to the point.

"I decided to do some checking on the circumstances surrounding Annabeth's death. She never went to the usual hospital we use for such cases. The diviner privately arranged for a hired car to deliver her to the collection point. I was taken out of the loop entirely."

Bowdeen gave a low whistle. "Your father sure didn't want you to know about this."

Joshua laughed bitterly. "He didn't want anyone to know about it. Even Daniel, her husband, has been kept in the dark as to the circumstances of her death." He paused, weighing his next words. "Once I'd discovered that the malefactors I had collected were being sentenced to death, I still believed my father's actions were just. Their punishment was merited. But Annabeth's sin was nothing more than immoderate grief at the death of her son. There was no justice in sentencing her to such a fate."

"Yeah, that's messed up," Bowdeen agreed warily.

In an unexpected move, Joshua grabbed Bowdeen by the shirt collar and shook him lightly, almost knocking him off balance. "You're missing the point. Annabeth was my sister-in-law. A member of the diviner's own family."

Chopper extricated himself gently. "Alright, son. Calm down now."

Joshua barely heard him. "It's a very short step from murdering a daughter-in-law to killing a son."

Those words brought the mercenary to attention. "So, you think he might—"

The spymaster cut him off. "Kill me or one of my brothers. Yes, I do. My father grows more irascible with each passing month. It takes very little to offend him these days. One mistake and I could be sent to the lab." He paused and gave the mercenary a shrewd look. "Or perhaps you."

Chopper blanched at those words, finally realizing where this conversation was tending.

"I'm sure you've thought about it," Joshua challenged. "What my father would do once you'd completed all your tasks. You're in a unique position, Mr. Bowdeen."

"Don't I know it," Chopper agreed ruefully.

"A man from the Fallen World who is privy to the most confidential details of the Nephilim's defenses. You know who the trained marksmen are. You know where the surveillance cameras are positioned. And you know those facts about every compound in every corner of the world." Joshua gave him a sardonic smile. "It would be a tactical error on my father's part to let you walk away from us."

Bowdeen sprang to his feet, running distracted fingers through his cropped hair. "I been worried about this since Day One. It's time I made myself scarce."

Joshua stood up as well, giving a short bitter laugh. "My father can be a relentless foe. I doubt he would settle for your absence when your death could make him feel so much more secure. The brotherhood would hunt you to the ends of the earth."

Chopper felt his heart skip a beat as Joshua voiced his own worst fears.

The spymaster placed his hands on Chopper's shoulders and stared him directly in the face. "I can think of a better solution to your problem. In fact, it's something that will solve both our difficulties at the same time."

Chopper watched the spymaster's expression. Those dark eyes didn't blink. He was dead serious.

Joshua continued. "I'm sure you've contemplated this possibility from the beginning as well. You had to. As things stand now, my father hasn't left either one of us any choice in the matter. There's only one way to assure our own survival." He held out his right hand. "Are we agreed?"

Dazedly, Chopper took the offered hand and shook it. Deep down, maybe he'd always known this gig wasn't going to end any other way.

27 – PSYCHIC FRIENDS NETWORK

The morning after they arrived at Lugu Lake, the Arkana operatives took the cableway to Gemu Goddess Cave to see if the Minoans had hidden their artifact there. Tourist traffic was light, partly because it was early in the season and partly because it was early in the day. The three wanted to get a head start to avoid attracting attention while conducting their search. They hired a pig-trough boat to row them across the water from Luoshui to Nisai Village which was situated right at the foot of the mountain.

In Nisai, they boarded the cableway which would carry them to the cave. The transportation system was unpopular with some locals who had once earned a living guiding tourists up the mountain on horseback. Although a few visitors still opted for the equine experience, most people preferred the convenience of the cableway. The foot of the mountain was traversed via an alpine slide. The steeper slopes were navigated by chair-lift. Each of the green metal cars could carry two passengers. Cassie and Rou took one car with Griffin following behind. The lift carried them slowly to their destination 11,000 feet above sea level with the apex of the peak a thousand feet higher still.

When they arrived, the chairs deposited them right in front of a Buddhist temple festooned with colorful Tibetan prayer flags. The entrance had been positioned in such a way that it offered a picture-perfect view of the lake and several quaint villages dotting the shoreline. Griffin informed them that the temple was a recent addition by the Han developer who had built the cableway. It was just as unpopular with the locals as his cable scheme had been. Traditionally, the Mosuo used the cave itself as their place of worship and saw the Buddhist temple as nothing more than a tourist attraction. Bypassing the shrine interior, the three followed the steep stone stairway which led directly to the cave entrance.

Cassie nudged Griffin as they climbed. "Erik would go nuts if he could see this."

The scrivener treated her to a puzzled glance until he noticed a gang of monkeys hanging from nearby trees and railings to watch their approach.

"Guard your valuables, Rou," he cautioned. "One of our associates came to grief in India during an altercation with furry bandits much like these."

Rou smiled and nodded politely, not understanding the joke.

Their climb ended at a square doorway chiseled out of the surrounding rock and reinforced by massive wooden beams. A sign above the lintel announced this to be the entrance to Gemu Goddess Cave. Once past the threshold, they were greeted by the sight of thousands of stalactites suspended above their heads. Colored lights had been positioned to reflect upwards, highlighting the cavern icicles like so many crystal chandeliers.

"This cave is huge!" Cassie exclaimed in wonder.

"And so deep." Rou pointed off into the darkness beyond the entrance.

"Oh, dear." The scrivener sounded dismayed. "Given the scale of this cavern, our search will take hours." He glanced cautiously toward the doorway to detect any activity outside, but all was quiet.

"Wait a minute." Cassie held up her hand. "I'm picking up a vibe. The Minoans have been here for sure!" She closed her eyes briefly to get a sense of which direction held the strongest pull. "There!" She pointed off to the right. Heading without hesitation toward the side wall, she placed her palm flat against a spot about six feet off the ground. "Anybody got a flashlight?"

Rou dove into her backpack and produced one.

"Aim the beam at the wall where my hand is," Cassie instructed.

Rou's flashlight revealed a flower emblem chiseled into the rock.

"The Minoan lily," Griffin whispered in awe. "In spite of all our false starts and wrong turns, we actually found it."

"Finding the lily is only half the battle," the pythia cautioned. "Now we have to find the thing it's pointing to."

Griffin dug a torch out of his pack and joined Rou in searching the area near the chiseled symbol.

Cassie had moved out of the range of their lights, allowing her hand to trail along the wall. "Uh oh!"

"What!" Griffin sent his beam in the direction of the pythia's voice. He gave an involuntary gasp. His light revealed a niche hollowed into the rock wall. A thin layer of stone must once have concealed the cavity, but it had been shattered. The niche was empty. "I'm beginning to wish this retrieval had been a repeat of Kailash after all. At least we'd have something to show for it! As it is..." the scrivener trailed off despondently.

At that moment, a scuffling sound could be heard emerging from the depths of the cave. All three of them froze.

"You're breaking up." A woman's voice echoed, coming closer. "Can you hear me now?"

She walked into the range of their flashlights—an attractive Asian woman in her late-30s with high cheekbones suggesting Tibetan ancestry. Her long black hair was styled with artfully chopped bangs and side fringes. She was dressed in skinny jeans, knee high boots with stiletto heels and a leather jacket. A hand-dyed gauze scarf was knotted casually around her neck, and a designer messenger bag hung from her shoulder.

Holding up her cell phone by way of explanation, she shook it for emphasis. In a perfect American accent, she remarked, "Don't you just hate that? I swear I can't keep a signal in this place to save my life." She pocketed the phone and held out her hand toward Cassie, causing a diamond tennis bracelet to flash in the dim light. "Hi, my name's Elle."

Concluding she was a tourist who'd wandered off the beaten path and gotten lost, the pythia smiled nervously. "Nice to meet you. Is Elle a Chinese name?"

The woman gave a snort of derision. "No, but it's the name I would have chosen if anybody had bothered to ask me."

Cassie returned the handshake. "I'm—"

Elle cut her off. "I know who you are." She gave a slight smile. "Let me rephrase that. I know what you are."

Cassie's eyes grew wide with alarm. "But—"

Elle continued. "And I know why you're here."

Tensely, the scrivener asked," Did the Nephilim send you? Do you have the artifact?"

To everyone's surprise, Elle laughed. Her eyes raked Griffin from top to bottom. "Well, hello there." She stepped forward. "What's your name?"

Cassie blocked the move. "He's with me. He's my partner."

"Is he now?" The smile never left Elle's face. "For business or pleasure?"

The pythia was struck speechless by the question.

Never missing a beat, Elle forged ahead. "Business it is then." She reached around Cassie to take Griffin's hand. "Nice to meet you, whoever you are."

"I'm... er... ahem. That is... My name is... um... Griffin." He returned the handshake.

"You sure about that?" Elle teased.

"Yes, quite."

Rou had sunk into the shadows along the wall, trying to remain invisible.

Her tactic apparently failed because without even glancing in the girl's direction, Elle asked, "Is she with you?"

"Yes, of course," Griffin affirmed. "This is Rou. She's our guide."

The girl folded her arms across her chest in a refusal to shake hands.

"I get that a lot around here," Elle observed dryly.

"You still didn't answer Griffin's question." Cassie's tone was insistent. "How do you know about the artifact?"

The woman paused a moment to consider the question. "That's a long story, children." She wandered over to an outcropping of rock and hopped up to take a seat on it. "The short version is that I lost a game of tag with my grandmother."

The others gathered around though Rou chose to lag behind them a few feet.

In a rush of comprehension, Cassie understood. "You're the sentinel."

"Lucky me."

"You mean you're the individual chosen to guard the artifact?" Griffin sounded skeptical. "You don't look like—" He broke off.

"You mean there's an official costume?" Elle's hand flew to her heart in mock surprise. "I never got the memo." She settled herself more comfortably on her rocky perch. "Once upon a time, my ancestors came across a bunch of strangers asking for directions. The strangers were looking for a special place to hide a relic of their goddess. My ancestors, being goddess worshippers themselves, knew the spot they were trying to find and brought them here. This mountain has been sacred for a lot longer than anybody suspects. Your Minoan friends would have made good used car salesmen because they even convinced one of my ancestors to stick around and guard the place until the right person came to claim the artifact." She stared pointedly at Cassie. "That would be you, sweetie. They said a seer with 'eyes the color of rain' would come for it someday."

Elle paused in her narrative to give a sardonic chuckle. "'Someday.' That's such a vague word, isn't it? It can mean a week, or it can mean three thousand years. So, from one generation to the next, my ancestors appointed a member of the family to keep watch over the cave until 'someday' arrived."

"Then you're Mosuo?" Griffin asked.

"Partly. My ancestors crossed paths with your Minoans in the Himalayas but the sentinel at that time settled down here. My family considers itself Mosuo now. Not me though. Like the song says, I was born in the USA. When my mom was young, she wanted to see the world, so she bolted from here decades ago. Moved to New York. Became a cab driver. She never looked back, and neither did I."

"You looked back!" Rou countered. "You are here."

The sentinel cocked an amused eyebrow. "So, she can speak after all." Turning her attention to the other two, she added, "And she's not wrong. Family has a way of roping you back in. Try arguing with a Mosuo matriarch, and you'll know what I mean. Ancestral honor, sacred trust, yaddy yaddy. You get the picture. My grandmother was the sentinel until she decided about ten years ago that she'd gotten too old for the job. She needed to figure out who was destined to replace her, so she consulted one of the local crackpots who put the sham in the word 'shaman.'" Elle gritted her teeth. "If I ever catch up with that snake charmer..."

"So, you moved back once you were named the sentinel," Griffin concluded.

"Hardly! I didn't bust my butt to create a fabulous life for myself in New York just so I could spend the rest of my days lurking in a bat cave!" She glared at the scrivener. "There are other ways."

"Such as?" he prompted.

"Such as psychics."

"You mean you relied on paranormal advice to predict when we would arrive?" He sounded incredulous.

"Really? You want to go there?" Her voice dripped with sarcasm. "This whole gig has woo-woo written all over it. A seer is hardly mainstream. After the exhibition I saw when you first came in, I'd say your girlfriend doesn't just ride the astral plane. She could pilot it solo."

"G... girlfriend." Griffin seemed flustered, but he didn't contradict Elle's assessment of their relationship. "I suppose we do rely on the paranormal in our line of work as well."

"Anyway," Elle continued. "At first, I checked with a couple of psychics to see just how long I was going to be tied to this legacy gig. After all, I had no reason to assume the chick with the grey eyes was going to show up during my lifetime. You could have knocked me over with a powder puff when they all told me it would happen soon. Yet another vague word I dislike—'soon.' That's when I decided to go on the offensive and track down the seer myself. I put every big-name New York psychic on retainer. Each month they'd give me their predictions about her whereabouts. Most of the time they contradicted one other, so I waited until I hit the paranormal equivalent of a trifecta." She paused for emphasis. "Every single one of them independently confirmed that this month, 'soon' would turn into 'now.' The seer would show up at Lugu Lake."

"A month is a pretty big window of time," Cassie noted.

"Yeah, it is. Try sitting in this cave for a single hour, and you'll understand the meaning of the word 'excruciating.' So, I phoned an astrologer I know. She specializes in precision timing, and she was able to narrow your ETA down to today."

"It seems you made quite a leap of faith," Griffin said.

"She charges big bucks because she's dead-on accurate when it comes to timing an event. I figured she could be trusted." She jumped off her perch. "Speaking of leaps of faith, you three took a huge jump yourselves by showing up in this cave. You had no way of knowing your precious relic was hidden here at all, much less whether it would still be around after three thousand years."

"Obviously, it isn't," the scrivener retorted.

"She knows where it is," Rou growled from behind them.

"Ooh, your little shih tzu is getting snappish," Elle commented archly.

"Rou's right," Cassie said. "You wouldn't have bothered to hang out here to meet us if you didn't know where the artifact is."

Elle inclined her head. "Fair enough. I do know where it is. But first, some standard boilerplate. The original sentinel was given a mandate that's been passed down through the ages. He was supposed to ask the seer one question before surrendering the relic. If she couldn't answer it, then the artifact was to stay under wraps." In an unexpected move, the sentinel reached into her shoulder bag and pulled out a small handgun. She pointed it directly at Cassie's chest. "OK, grey eyes. Time to find out if you're the real deal."

"Whoa, hang on there," the pythia protested.

All three of the Arkana operatives raised their hands above their heads.

"What do you intend to do? Shoot her if she gives an incorrect answer?" Griffin cried in disbelief.

"No, I'll split, and you'll never see me again," Elle replied. "This gun is for my protection. Who's to say you aren't imposters? One of me, three of you. You might force me to take you to the artifact using unpleasant means of persuasion."

"We'd never do such a thing!" Griffin protested hotly.

"I've known you for all of fifteen minutes, so you'll excuse me if I don't take your word as gospel." Elle's tone was grim.

"Ask your question," Cassie commanded flatly.

Elle transferred her attention back to the pythia. "Here goes. You need to give me a physical description of the person who hid the artifact in this cave."

"What?" The scrivener's voice echoed into the darkness. "That's absurd! How is she supposed to know that?"

"Griffin, it's alright. I got this." Cassie lowered her arms cautiously. "I have to walk back to the niche to pick up a vibe about what happened here."

"Knock yourself out." Elle kept the pistol trained on her as Cassie moved toward the shadows blanketing the side wall.

The pythia contemplated the now empty niche. She tried to ignore the butterflies in her stomach. So much was riding on this moment. If she couldn't get a vision on cue, the sentinel would vanish forever. Elle would take with her the Arkana's only hope of finding the Sage Stone. The quest that had led them across four continents could end in the next five minutes depending on the answer Cassie gave. She smiled wryly to herself. No pressure there. She uttered a silent prayer to the Minoans. "OK, you guys. If you really want me to find your precious relic, then you better step up. Show me what happened in this cave three thousand years ago." She closed her eyes and placed her hand inside the niche. Immediately, the scene sprang to life in vivid detail. Cassie waited until she was sure there was no more left to see.

Then, giving a sigh of relief and a whispered "thank you," she turned to face Elle.

"There were only four of them left by the time they got here. It was a larger group when they first started out from Crete. A few must have died along the way. I saw the priestess. She was the one who placed the artifact in the niche. She's an old woman with long white hair. I've had visions of her before. She's always dressed in a white robe. When she was here, she was wearing a white hooded cloak too. It must have been cold that day."

"Congratulations." Elle nodded with grudging respect. "You've just won our stupendous grand prize along with a six-month supply of carnauba wax." Treating Griffin to a scornful glance, she added, "And I'm the one who's crazy for trusting East Coast psychics."

He shuffled his feet in embarrassment. "I withdraw the observation."

"No hard feelings, I hope." The sentinel slipped the gun back into her bag. "Dealing in lost treasure is a dangerous business. A girl can't be too careful."

Cutting to the chase, Rou demanded, "Where is the artifact?"

Elle raised her arms expressively. "Not here, lemon drop. The cave isn't safe anymore which is so ironic when you come to think about it. This was a secure hiding place for three thousand years. The locals were never a threat. It would have been sacrilegious for them to touch, much less remove, anything from the cave. Nope, the locals were OK. Even the first wave of tourists was OK since the only way to get here was on foot or by horse. Right up through my grandmother's time, sentinels could keep tabs on strangers in the area by simply using the village grapevine.

"But that was the end of an era. When the cableway was built in 2005, it could haul droves of people to the top of the mountain in a matter of minutes. What used to be a handful turned into hundreds and then thousands. When I became sentinel, I knew I had to move the damn relic or lose it." She shrugged philosophically. "That turned out to be a blessing in disguise since it meant I wouldn't have to hang out here full-time. I could stash the artifact someplace else where nobody but me could find it."

"So where is it now?" Cassie asked.

"The safest place in all of Asia to hide a goddess artifact." The sentinel gave a knowing smile.

"And that would be?" The pythia was growing impatient.

"Indonesia, of course."

"I beg your pardon," Griffin squinted at her.

'Did I mumble?" Elle challenged.

"Right then." The scrivener sighed helplessly. "Ours is not to reason why. Cassie, pack your bags. We're off to Indonesia."

28 – ABOMINABLE WRITING

"Are you done with these?" Chris leaned over the pile of journals Daniel had been perusing.

The scion rubbed his eyes wearily. "This man may have been a competent explorer, but it's obvious he was no writer!"

"He is kind of long-winded." Chris slid three slim volumes under a stack of reference books. He placed all of them on a cart to be wheeled back to storage.

For the past week, the pair had combed through the explorer's journals searching for something that might help them find their mysterious Himalayan river. They worked on a few volumes at a time so that the full collection wouldn't be missed.

Chris took a seat beside Daniel and lowered his voice. "We need to pick up the pace. I just heard the entire set might be moved to a branch library next week."

"How many more books do we have to go through?" Daniel's tone was bleak.

"About ten volumes."

The scion slumped over the reading room table. "I don't think I can stand any more. The man is a complete barbarian. If he isn't writing about what he slaughtered for breakfast, he's writing about what he intends to massacre for supper. It makes you wonder if he ever digested a vegetable in his entire life. And when he isn't writing about murdering his food, he writes about animals he intends to assassinate for sport. The wildlife of the Himalayas wasn't safe with him in the region. Do you know he scribbled two entire volumes reporting his interviews with sherpas who thought they'd seen yetis? He said he wanted to shoot one and stuff it. A yeti, that is, not a sherpa."

The librarian grinned. "The quest for the Abominable Snowman, huh? At least it's a diversion."

"Diversion?" Daniel's tone was shocked. "His descriptions are mind-numbing. Listen to this passage: 'Although none of the guides I have employed heretofore were able to produce tangible evidence of a yeti footprint, I continue to be sanguine in my hopes. My persistence shall be rewarded. We have now traveled to the foothills of the Tanggula Mountain Range in the central portion of the Tibetan plateau. A profusion of yeti footprints, if not the creatures themselves, have supposedly been found near the top of Mount Geladaindong. At twenty-two-thousand feet above sea level, it is the tallest summit in the range. My sherpa is adamant that the elusive creatures live upon the high sharp peak, for that is what the mountain's name means in Tibetan. I have further been informed by the same reliable source that the area also boasts a colony of snow leopards. I should very much like to bag one during my stay. Its head would make a fine addition to my trophy room and—'"

"Stop!" Chris commanded, gripping Daniel's arm.

The scion peered at his friend. "I know. I can't bear it either. It's awful stuff. Aside from the writing itself, aren't snow leopards endangered?"

"No, that isn't what I meant." Chris cast a wary glance around the reading room. Its two other occupants were immersed in their own studies. He lowered his voice. "Go back to the explorer's description of the mountain. Read that part again."

Daniel scanned the page, finding the relevant passage. "Here it is. 'A profusion of yeti footprints, if not the creatures themselves, have supposedly been found near the top of Mount Geladaindong. At twenty-two-thousand feet above sea level, it is the tallest summit in the range.'" The scion looked inquisitively at the librarian.

Chris was frowning in concentration. "No, that's not it. Read the next sentence."

"'My sherpa is adamant that the elusive creatures live upon the high sharp peak, for that is what the mountain's name means in Tibetan.'" Daniel stopped abruptly and turned to Chris.

Both men smiled simultaneously.

"High sharp peak," the librarian repeated in an elated tone.

"That's it!" Daniel exclaimed. "We found it!"

"Shhhh!" A warning shush came from one of the reading room's occupants.

"Very sorry," the scion murmured.

"Let's go back to my desk," Chris urged. "I want to check something on the computer. And bring that book with you."

They hastened back to the Reference Desk, and Chris darted behind the counter. "The whole point of mentioning the 'high sharp peak' in the riddle was to get a fix on a river, right?"

Daniel stood in front of the counter. He nodded solemnly. "A river that runs red to the serpent's heart. I'm not sure what that part means."

"One thing at a time." Chris studied his monitor intently. He typed a few keystrokes. "I'm trying to find out if the headwaters of any major river start at that peak. What was it again?"

Daniel spelled the name.

"Jackpot!" Chris turned the monitor so Daniel could see it.

"The glacial meltwaters beside Mount Geladaindong give rise to the Yangtze River." The scion read the words in a disbelieving tone. "We solved part of the riddle by stumbling on an obscure reference in an obscure journal purely by accident."

"There are no accidents, my friend." Chris retorted.

Daniel squinted at him.

"Never mind. That's a much longer conversation." The librarian began typing again. "I want to test a theory about your riddle. What was the name of that mountain you climbed in Nepal?"

"It was called Kailash."

Chris typed again. "Latitude thirty-one degrees north." He typed another string of characters then turned triumphantly to the scion. "The headwaters of the Yangtze are also located at thirty-one degrees north."

"So that's what the first line of the riddle meant. I finally understand it." Daniel was speaking more to himself than to the librarian. "The flock of doves originated on Kailash and flew in a straight line toward sunrise—east. They perched on the high sharp peak where the river begins. It's all so obvious."

Chris was only partially listening, intent on a new search. "Ha!" he exclaimed. "And here's another piece of your jigsaw puzzle. When the Yangtze flows from the mountain, it starts out as a smaller river."

"The Ulan Moron," Daniel read aloud. "That's a funny name for a river."

"Not Moron, you adorable wingnut. It's pronounced 'Mor-AHN.'" Chris turned his gaze fully on Daniel. "In English, Ulan Moron means 'Red River.'"

"'Where the river flows red to the serpent's heart.'" Daniel repeated the clue. "The Red River."

Chris leaned his elbow on the counter and propped his chin in his hand. "You'd better start packing, Danny Boy."

"But we've only solved the first line," Daniel protested.

"One down, one to go." The librarian's eyes were twinkling. "Between the two of us, I'll bet we can crack the rest of that riddle before the week is out."

The scion gave a grateful smile. "I'll dust off my suitcase tonight."

29 – LOCATION, LOCATION, LOCATION

Griffin, Cassie, and Elle handed their boarding passes to the gate attendant and found their row on the plane. It held three seats across. Elle chose the center, Cassie the window and Griffin the aisle for more leg room.

Cassie leaned back against the cushioned headrest, breathed a sigh of relief, and closed her eyes. It had been a hectic few days. When they'd first come down the mountain, Elle insisted that they go to her grandmother's house, so the matriarch could meet the seer who had come to claim the artifact at last. The old woman, sturdy in spite of her eighty-odd years, immediately announced a feast to celebrate the occasion. None of the rest of Elle's extended family had been let in on the sentinel secret. They were told that the celebration was to welcome Elle and her Western friends.

Aside from yak butter tea, fried pancakes, seasonal vegetables, and Guangdang wine, the guests were offered slices of pork from a pig which had been pressed and aged for seven years. When Elle explained to the visitors that seven-year-old pig meat was the equivalent of uncorking a bottle of 1921 Dom Perignon, they were suitably impressed.

While the festivities continued on into the night, Griffin slipped away to call Maddie with an update. When he reported back to his colleagues, he said the chatelaine would contact the Tibetan twins immediately. Rinchen was to fly to Lugu Lake to help Rou keep watch just in case the Nephilim arrived sooner than expected. Rabten was to fly to Indonesia where he would meet Cassie and Griffin to arrange transport for the real artifact. Rou seemed anxious about being left behind until she was told her role as lookout was critical to the success of their quest.

Once the party broke up, Elle made their complicated travel arrangements as Cassie and Griffin packed. They left early the next morning to catch the first bus back to Lijiang. The ride itself took seven hours over hazardous mountain roads. Once in Lijiang, they headed for the airport and a two-and-a-half-hour flight to Guangzhou on China's southeast coast. The following day they boarded a five-hour flight to Jakarta in Indonesia. This stop included an overnight stay. Given their grueling travel schedule, the layover was not unwelcome. The next morning, they boarded a plane for their final destination—Padang City—the provincial capital of West Sumatra.

Cassie's musings ended abruptly when she felt the plane jolt into motion as it taxied to the runway. She opened her eyes and sat up to watch the takeoff through her tiny window.

Once they were airborne, Griffin turned toward Elle with a quizzical expression on his face. "You still haven't explained your choice of hiding place for the artifact. I'm sure Cassie is as curious as I am to know why you selected Sumatra."

The pythia immediately switched her attention from the scenery to the sentinel. "He's right. I am. Why Sumatra?"

"I suppose you've both noticed that Asia isn't the most female-friendly of continents." Elle grimaced. "In these parts, women are treated like second class citizens when they aren't being treated like annoyingly verbal livestock. My Mosuo mother grew up in a completely different atmosphere where women were respected and had a lot of self-esteem. She raised me that way too. Life in the Big Apple isn't so different from life around Lugu Lake. Pushy New Yorkers respect anybody who can shove back, so my mom and I fit in pretty easily there. My life would have been a lot simpler if your artifact was hidden in a cave in the States or even Europe. But no. I was stuck guarding a goddess artifact hidden in the global epicenter of patriarchy. Since I didn't want to take the relic out of Asia, I had to find a pocket of matriarchy somewhere other than Lugu Lake."

She paused in her explanation while the stewardess came through with refreshments. During their travels, Elle's frosty attitude had thawed considerably. It must have dawned on her that Griffin and Cassie were rescuing her from the irksome duties of sentinel. In consequence, she became as cordial toward them as her abrasive nature would allow.

Once the attendant was out of earshot, the sentinel continued. "At first I considered Taiwan as a possible location."

"Taiwan?" Cassie asked in surprise. "Why there?"

"Because it's an island and islands seem pretty good at resisting the march of 'progress.'" Elle made air quotes to emphasize her point. "Even after the Han Chinese took over, most of the local tribes remained matriarchal. To this day, some of the aborigines still follow the old ways."

"Sounds ideal," Griffin observed. "And yet we aren't flying there today."

"That's because it belongs to patriarchal China," Elle countered. "Who knows when some crazy new government program is going to mess with Taiwanese culture on a local level? I mean, look what happened to the

Buddhists when China first invaded Tibet. I figured I was better off taking the artifact out of the country entirely."

She paused for a sip of bottled water. "So, I had to broaden my search. At first, I struck out. The farther north I looked, the more male-dominated the culture seemed to get."

"That's because the overlords infiltrated China from the northwest," Cassie informed her.

"Overlords?"

Griffin intercepted the question. "The less you know about our overall mission, the better. Suffice it to say that patriarchy was transmitted to Asia from the northwestern corner of the country to the southeast."

"Hmm." Elle pondered the comment. "You know that actually might explain a lot. Once I changed course and focused on the south, my luck improved. Thailand, Cambodia, Laos, and Vietnam were once completely matriarchal."

"We've been throwing the term 'matriarchy' around quite freely today," the scrivener remarked. "Yet there are scholars who will adamantly insist that such a form of social organization doesn't exist. Of course, they've defined the term so narrowly that it allows them to dismiss the phenomenon as a myth. They wish to classify matriarchy as the mirror image of patriarchy—a society in which women dominate and oppress men. Of course, that has never been the case. Female-centric societies tend to practice gender equality.

"Mainstream anthropologists have parsed the social structure of such cultures using a variety of terms to describe separate practices. When inheritance is traced through the female line, they call it 'matrilineal.' In cultures where the husband moves in with the wife's family, they call it 'matrilocal.' If women in a particular culture are given more rights than men, it's called 'matrifocal.' However, these same anthropologists would never use the dreaded word 'matriarchy' to describe a culture which might possess all the features I've just discussed."

Elle glanced at the scrivener dispassionately. "Scholars can slice and dice it any way they want, but if the key decision-maker in a family is the mother, then I say it's a matriarchy."

"I'm with her," Cassie agreed.

The sentinel continued. "I found matriarchies everywhere I looked south of China. Among the traditional cultures of southeast Asia, the ladies were in charge. In some places they still are. In Thailand, there are more female construction workers than male."

"Then why are we flying over Thailand rather than landing there?" Griffin asked impishly.

Elle shrugged. "For the same reason that I rejected Taiwan as a possible hidey-hole. All the countries I mentioned are too close to the Chinese border. In the bad old days, imperial China invaded Vietnam and Burma on a regular basis. Even the countries next door had their cultural values warped by those conflicts."

"So, you wanted to put a big body of water between our artifact and Han China," the pythia concluded. "That's why we're going to Indonesia?"

"Only partly." Elle gave a mysterious smile. "We're also going to Indonesia because it contains the largest remaining matriarchal society on the planet. Four million women walking around like they own the place because they do. We're going to visit the Minangkabau."

"Of course!" Griffin exclaimed. "It's an obvious choice."

Cassie leaned over and squinted at him. "To you maybe. Care to fill me in?"

The scrivener apologized. "I'm sorry for not mentioning them sooner, but the thought didn't occur to me. It's no secret that I've had very little active involvement with the Asian troves. The only reason I have any knowledge of the Minangkabau at all is because we are in the early stages of setting up a trove there."

Elle interrupted. "What's a trove?"

Griffin hesitated.

Cassie cut in. "That also falls into the category of things we shouldn't talk about. If you know too much about our operation, it might put you at risk."

The sentinel eyed her skeptically. "And here I thought you guys were just on a scavenger hunt."

"More like a scavenger hunt with flying bullets." The pythia grinned ruefully. "There are some very bad people who want to get their hands on the Minoan relics. Let's just say it would be better for the world if they didn't."

"Relics plural?" Elle's eyebrows shot up. "You mean there's more than one?"

"Like I said, the less you know—"

Elle put up her hands in resignation. "Forget I asked. The last thing I want is to be caught in the middle of your private war." She shifted slightly in her seat, turning her attention back to Griffin. "You were saying something about the Minangkabau people?"

Griffin hastened to elaborate. "Yes, the Minangkabau hold the distinction of being the largest remaining matriarchy in the world. Even the most dyed-in-wool mainstream anthropologists can't deny it since the people describe their own society as a matriarchy."

"I've never heard of them," Cassie murmured.

"They are quite a fascinating culture," Griffin continued. "As you might expect, property is passed to female descendants under the rationale that women need a home to provide for their offspring while men have the luxury of living anywhere. When a woman marries, her husband moves in with her family and is guided by their decisions."

The sentinel chimed in. "The Minangkabau believe that undirected male energy is chaotic. It disrupts the harmony of the family if left unchecked by the wisdom of the elders, both male and female." She smiled wryly. "Given the guys I've dated over the past decade, I'd say the Minangkabau got it right—at least about men under fifty anyway."

Griffin forged ahead, trying to ignore the unintended insult. "Though their village headmen are male, they are elected by the property owners."

"Who all happen to be female," Cassie stated.

"Correct."

"That's exactly like the Iroquois," she added.

"It's like most other matriarchal societies around the world," Griffin countered. "Women control the resources and men manage political affairs with their consent. Even if that division hadn't originally been part of their culture, the patriarchal societies surrounding the Minangkabau would have eventually pressured them to appoint a male authority to represent them in the outside world. The most curious trait of these people is that they are all staunch Muslims."

"What?" Cassie registered disbelief. "How is that even possible?"

Elle laughed at her reaction. "Islam in Sumatra is an entirely different animal than in Saudi Arabia. Just to give you an example, a lot of women in Sumatra wear the hijab. That's the traditional headscarf worn by Muslim women. To people who live in the West, the hijab is a symbol of Islamic male oppression. But that isn't how the Minangkabau view it. The women have managed to hang onto their power, headscarves and all."

"I suspect that many of the traits which we define as Islamic are merely Arabic," Griffin said. "Culture frequently shapes religion rather than the other way round. The Minangkabau have a fluid and adaptive way of dealing with the outside world. Assimilation and compromise are excellent strategies to guarantee social stability. Of course, it also helps that Indonesian Muslims weren't converted at the point of a sword. The spread of the religion was entirely peaceful. Islamic traders from India first began to appear in the area in the 14th century. Their beliefs became fashionable with the rulers of various principalities and some converted. Over time, the rest of the population followed suit. However, the Minangkabau appear to have adopted some Islamic ideas and discarded those which were at odds with their culture, such as the notion of male superiority."

"They have this thing called *adat*," said Elle. "It's hard to translate, but it means something like 'custom' or 'tradition' or even 'cosmic balance.' They live their lives by it. It's just as important to them as Islam. Maybe more so since it's been around longer."

"Still I have to wonder." Cassie frowned as a new thought struck her. "If they are Islamic then I don't think they would take kindly to graven goddess images of any kind. How did you manage to convince them to protect the relic for you?"

"I had to find some common ground. After a little digging, I learned that the Minangkabau believe in a semi-mythical queen mother who founded their culture along with her sons. They think they're all descended from her, and she's still venerated in songs and stories. All I had to do was tap into that."

Given the puzzled reaction of her listeners, Elle elaborated. "I asked around until I found the most influential matriarch in one of the hill villages outside Padang. I explained to her that I had a cherished relic which had belonged to the queen mother of my own people. I told her that it was no longer safe to keep it in my homeland because the men there had forgotten how to respect their mothers and they might destroy it. I asked her to hide the artifact for me until I came back to claim it and she agreed."

"Very clever." Griffin nodded his approval.

"I didn't build a career in marketing for nothing," Elle retorted. "It also helped that I took the time to learn their language. Let me tell you, there aren't any Rosetta Stone courses in Baso Padang."

The pilot came on the intercom at that moment to announce their descent. They all dutifully adjusted their seats and refolded their tray tables.

"When we land, we're going straight to the hotel to check in," Elle informed them. "After that, we're off to a little village in the highlands where you'll get your precious artifact, and I can be on my merry way."

Griffin studied her for a moment. "I must say, despite your personal objections to the role, you've proven yourself to be an able custodian of our priceless relic. I'm sure your sentinel ancestors would be very proud of you."

"Sentinel," Elle echoed. "Yet another word I don't like." She folded her arms decisively. "After today, nobody better call me that again. Ever!"

30 – DEAD ZONE

Leroy killed his van's lights and turned onto a dirt lane that ran next to the back fence of the farmhouse property. His surveillance had shown that nobody used this road, so it was the perfect place to lay low for a couple of hours. He wanted to wait til everybody in the neighborhood had turned in for the night before he made his move. Yup, tonight was the night. He'd been staking out the place for nearly two weeks now. That was longer than he'd originally intended but he wanted to make absolutely sure he knew the schedule of everything that happened in that house.

The additional time spent in surveillance contradicted his pet theory that the farmhouse was a front for Mr. Big's operation. Even though the trio and Mr. Big were somehow connected to the place, Hunt figured that both Hannah and the old lady were in the dark about the doodads. Nothing in their monotonous daily routine betrayed anything remotely shady.

After little Hannah left for school, the old lady would pile into her station wagon and do errands. She'd be gone for hours during the middle of the day, but Leroy didn't trouble himself about what she was up to. Probably stocking up on more flowered housedresses. Once the gal got back from school in the afternoon, she helped the old lady with cooking and chores, did her homework, and went to sleep. On weekends, her boyfriend showed up to take her out to dinner or a movie and always got her home before curfew. Everything was as humdrum as could be. Of course, after tonight nobody in the neighborhood would ever be able to say that again.

The cowboy had thought long and hard about how he wanted to play this scene. His main objective was to eliminate Hannah. He couldn't have her ratting out Daniel and gumming up the works for him with the old man. Teenage girls generally had a tendency to blab too much. They couldn't help themselves. It was in their natures. Unfortunately, killing Hannah outright might rile the preacher, so Hunt had to make it look like an accident.

For starters, Leroy planned to break into the back of the house around 3 AM. He'd go upstairs to the old lady's room and smother her with a pillow before she knew what hit her. A nice quiet way to take her out. Then he'd tiptoe down the hall to the little gal's room. She was maybe a hundred pounds soaking wet, so she wouldn't put up much of a fight. Leroy could snap her neck like a dried twig. Then he'd drag the two bodies to the top of the stairs and roll the old lady down first. The body would get banged up enough to make it seem she'd died from the fall. Then he'd drop the gal from the railing. Same result.

Of course, he planned to tell the grief-stricken preacher a whole different version of how things went down. With a catch in his voice, he'd explain that his plan had gone horribly wrong. He'd broken in with the intention of grabbing Hannah, but the old lady woke up and got in the way. While he was struggling with her, Hannah lunged at him, missed and went over the railing, breaking her neck. The old lady squirmed free and tried to run down the stairs but tripped and took a tumble herself. Before Leroy could do any damage-control, somebody had called 911, and the sirens told him he needed to high tail it out of there. With no fingerprints at the scene of the crime and a pane of broken glass in the kitchen door, the cops would naturally assume it was a burglary gone wrong.

Leroy leaned back against the headrest and took a minute to admire the elegance of his plan. With Hannah gone, the treasure hunt could stay on track. And, as an added bonus, tonight's raid might send a message to Mr. Big. He would know that Leroy was on his trail. Maybe that would rattle him enough to call the trio off for good, leaving the field clear for Daniel to collect the rest of the doodads. No doubt about it. Everything was coming up roses for a change. The cowboy consulted his watch. Plenty of time to get some shut-eye. He had a late night ahead of him. Tipping the brim of his baseball cap over his eyes, he nodded off to sleep.

***

Hunt snorted into wakefulness. The alarm on his wrist watch was chirping at him. He checked the time. It was 3 AM. He yawned, stretched and then scanned the backs of the houses in the subdivision. Not a single light was on. Clearly, nobody in the neighborhood suffered from insomnia. It was show time. He grabbed a pair of black leather gloves sitting on the passenger seat. When he lifted them up, he noticed a cell phone lying beneath. It was the tapped line that he used for calls to the preacher. Leroy made it a rule never to turn that phone on while he was conducting his private surveillance operation because whoever was monitoring his calls to old Abe might also be tracking his physical location. If Mr. Big's flunkies were to pinpoint his coordinates a hundred feet from the farmhouse, all kinds of bells and whistles would go off. He stared at the phone with a sense of foreboding. The cowboy already knew whenever that phone had been shut off for long periods the preacher would find a reason to call him. He couldn't help feeling that his wise precaution of staying off the grid was just about to jump up and bite him in the ass.

Leroy tried to dismiss the urge to listen to his messages. After all, he had big party plans for tonight and didn't want to be distracted. On the other hand, the cowboy usually operated on instinct and that method had always served him well. As a tracker, he knew that good instincts spelled the difference between a dead animal and a live one. That rule applied to two-legged critters as well as four-legged ones. Try as he might, he couldn't quell the impulse to check that phone right away.

Of course, he couldn't power it on from this location. Swearing under his breath, he switched on the ignition and drove off. About ten miles down the road, he pulled into a gas station parking lot. That should be far enough away from the farmhouse so as not to attract Mr. Big's attention. Leroy had already disabled the GPS tracking feature on his phone but whoever was dogging him could still triangulate a signal if he stayed on the line too long. He'd have to make this quick. He parked and switched the phone on. Sure enough, there were half a dozen voice mail messages waiting for him. The first one was time-stamped early that evening. It was businesslike. The preacher's voice was cut and dried. "Mr. Hunt, please phone me immediately." Click. By the time Leroy reached the sixth, he had to turn the volume down. It was time-stamped at 11 PM, and the old man was spitting brimstone. He wanted the cowboy to drop whatever he was doing and call back ASAP, no matter how late.

Leroy cursed his luck and switched the phone off again. Those calls needed to be answered but not from here. The cowboy's only option was to drive back to his apartment in order to have his late-night chat with the preacher. He was already certain he knew the reason for all those messages. The old man wanted him to saddle up and hit the trail with Daniel, most likely at the crack of dawn.

If that was the case, then Leroy couldn't afford to start something tonight that he couldn't finish. If he went ahead and snuffed Hannah right now, the days after her unfortunate demise would be critical. He would need to hover at Abe's elbow to maneuver him into the right frame of mind over his dearly-departed—to steer the preacher away from any suspicion of foul play. He couldn't manage Abe from overseas, so it was either one thing or the other. Kill Hannah tonight or follow Daniel tomorrow. The competing ideas tussled inside his head for priority. He let out a frustrated growl, feeling as frazzled as a two-dollar whore on nickel night.

After some serious internal struggle, Leroy decided it was best to follow the money. His staged break-in would have to keep til he got back. He shrugged philosophically. After watching Hannah and the old lady go through their boring routine for two solid weeks, it was obvious nothing earth-shattering was going to happen before he returned. Muttering a final curse, he started his engine and drove back to the city to place his call.

31 – CROWNING MOMENT

The airplane touched down smoothly and on schedule in Padang City. Immediately after they retrieved their luggage, Griffin, Cassie, and Elle took a taxi to their high-rise hotel in the downtown district.

The island on which the city sat had once been part of the Dutch West Indies. In modern times, Sumatra was a big draw for surfers who could find immense waves on the island's western shore. As a result, tourism had become a major industry, and beach resorts weren't hard to find. Though the 2009 earthquake had demolished many of the older inns, ultra-modern replacements quickly rose to take their place.

When the three arrived at their hotel, they checked in and separated briefly to unpack. After reconvening in the lobby, Elle led them outside to a waiting car.

"No taxi?" Cassie asked.

"It's quite a distance out to the village, so I hired a car and driver for the afternoon. Get in," she directed them.

Elle sat up front while the other two slid into the back. Once the doors were shut, the driver screeched away from the curb. The sentinel shifted in her seat to speak to them. "You don't want to take the wheel yourself in this part of the world, trust me, and it isn't simply because there's a left-hand traffic pattern. Indonesians have a very unusual take on the whole driving experience."

Their chauffeur slapped on the brakes to avoid hitting a pedestrian, causing his passengers to lurch forward.

Unfazed, Elle continued, "They carry a set of Rules of the Road in their heads, but sometimes their intuition is off the mark. Do you know there's no such thing as vehicular manslaughter here?"

Griffin squinted at her in disbelief. "Really?"

131

"I swear. If somebody gets killed accidentally in a car accident, the person responsible just pays compensation to the victim's family, and they all walk away. In fact, the person driving the biggest car usually gets stuck with the bill because everybody assumes he can afford it."

"You're kidding!" Cassie gasped.

"I wish I was," Elle countered. "Driving here would scare the hell out of my mother—the New York cabbie." She shook her head in wonder. "Indonesians. They're the nicest people on the planet, but they drive like maniacs."

As if to punctuate her comment, the driver slapped on the brakes again, almost sending the sentinel through the windshield. This time, a motorcycle had cut directly in front of their car to make an unsignaled right turn.

"Need I say more?" Elle turned to face forward and cinched her seatbelt.

They traveled in silence for nearly half an hour. Once out of the city traffic, they passed coffee and rubber plantations on a flat plain which separated the sea from the mountains to the east. The driver took a road leading upward toward the hills. After days spent in the cool mountain air of Lugu Lake, the humid tropical climate took some getting used to.

Fortunately, the higher the car climbed, the cooler the air became. The road grew narrower, and the vegetation became so dense that it qualified as a jungle. The car followed one bend after another in a series of disorienting curves until it brought them into a clearing. A jumble of houses of varying sizes sprouted from the undergrowth. They were constructed of wood and bamboo on pilings raised about ten feet off the ground. Some houses had horn-shaped gables of woven palm fronds which were so sharply pitched they resembled steeples. Elle informed them that this design was meant to mimic the horns of a water buffalo. The driver stopped in front of the biggest house in the village. Its proportions suggested it might be the town hall rather than a dwelling.

They all got out.

"We're here," Elle announced. "I sent word ahead, and she's expecting us."

A woman less than five-feet tall emerged at the top of the front stairs to greet them. She was dressed in a floral batik mumu dress. In her sixties, the matriarch was portly with short gray hair and a good-humored face.

Elle rushed up the stairs ahead of the rest. The sentinel and the matriarch exchanged greetings in the local language. Then Elle gestured for Griffin and Cassie to join them.

"I'd like you to meet..." Elle rattled off a name several syllables long.

Griffin and Cassie eyed one another, silently trying to decide whether they should be rude enough to ask the sentinel to repeat the name.

Cassie whispered, "I don't think we'd be able to catch that even if you repeated it a dozen times." She stepped forward and took the woman's hand. "Very nice to meet you." She gave a little bow.

Griffin did the same.

The matriarch gestured them inside. The interior of the huge house offered what appeared to be a long, covered verandah at the front where guests were received. The floors, walls, and support beams were made of varnished wood. Pendant lamps hung at intervals from the ceiling. Every five feet, window openings had been cut into the walls though they contained no glass. Given the tropical climate, this seemed a practical design. Moveable shutters could be lowered to keep out the rain. The matriarch motioned for them to take seats. There were four bentwood chairs with cloth seat covers and backrests arranged around a small tea table. This furniture grouping was repeated all along the length of the fifty-foot parlor. Despite the immense size of the building, nobody else appeared to be in residence.

"These ancestral houses are built on a big scale," Elle explained. "Some of them go back centuries. Think of this more like the rec center of a housing development. Aside from this being the home of the women of the family, various functions and ceremonies are held here too."

The guests nodded and took chairs around the table.

Elle directed her next question to their hostess. Griffin and Cassie inferred she was asking about the whereabouts of the artifact.

The matriarch's face lit up with a smile, and she raised her hand in a gesture which obviously meant they should wait while she retrieved it.

Scanning the interior, Cassie said to Elle, "You picked a good hiding place. This house is so huge there must be dozens of nooks and crannies where nobody would think to look."

"Just between you and me, I think our hostess is relieved that I came to claim it so soon. She probably felt it was a big responsibility, but she was too polite to tell me so."

A few moments later, the tiny woman shuffled back to the parlor bearing a bundle wrapped in brightly colored cloth. She laid it on the table and Elle did the honors of unwrapping it.

Cassie and Griffin rose to stand behind her as she completed the operation. When they saw what the bundle contained, they traded looks of triumphant recognition.

Elle gazed upward at them "Is this what you came to find?"

Griffin traced the Minoan glyphs carved into the object with his index finger. "Without a doubt. These symbols look quite familiar."

The sentinel gave a nod of confirmation and rewrapped the object. Smiling at the matriarch, she spoke at length. Apparently, expressing gratitude in Baso Padang was a very complicated process. Then she opened her messenger bag, deposited the artifact inside, and pulled out a rectangular velvet box which she handed to their hostess.

"It's a thank you gift for acting as caretaker," she explained to the other two.

At that moment a younger woman appeared from the opposite side of the house carrying a tray.

"That's her youngest daughter," Elle said.

The girl set down chilled glasses of a frothy white beverage.

Handing them around, the sentinel said, "This is called *dadiah*. Fermented water buffalo milk. Think of it as Sumatran yogurt. I'll warn you it's an acquired taste."

"After yak butter tea, I don't think I'll have too much trouble adapting," Cassie mumbled under her breath.

The matriarch's daughter also set out small dishes of what appeared to be fruit covered by scoops of a frozen white substance.

"That's *es campur*," Elle explained. "It's a coconut slushie with chunks of fruit. They eat it for dessert here."

The visitors sampled the refreshments and gave wide smiles to indicate their pleasure.

Their hostess beamed at them, clearly delighted by their reaction. Once they had all finished and the dishes were cleared away, the matriarch picked up the box Elle had given her. When she raised the lid to view the contents, a string of phrases erupted from her mouth that continued for a full minute. It didn't take a translator to understand that she was impressed by the gift.

She called her daughter back into the room and held the object up for her to see.

Both Griffin and Cassie gasped audibly when they saw it too.

"It's a crown," the pythia blurted out.

"More like a tiara," Elle corrected. "It's part of the traditional Minangkabau ceremonial headdress."

Unlike a circular crown or a tiara, the headpiece was flat. It was held in place by a gold headband which fitted the wearer's temples. The design was an ornate gold filigree of flowers and leaves. The scalloped edges rose to a peak half a foot high. At its apex, the headdress contained a large jewel.

"That can't be a diamond," Cassie whispered to Griffin. "It's huge!"

"Given the value of the rest of the crown, I hardly think it's cubic zirconia," the scrivener retorted dryly.

The matriarch and her daughter avidly examined the gift, making comments to one another as they pointed to various features of its design.

Elle leaned over to say, "It's meant to be a family heirloom. When the next daughter gets married, she'll wear this."

Griffin remarked, "It must have cost you a fortune."

"Not me, sport," she retorted archly. "I'm sticking you with the bill. All part of my master plan. I set this in motion the minute I knew our rendezvous at Lugu Lake was in the stars."

The scrivener blinked once in shock before he immediately conceded. "Very well." Reaching into his shirt pocket, he removed a business card. Handing it to the sentinel, he said, "You may send an invoice to this address. I assure you, it will be paid promptly."

Elle gave a satisfied nod. "A pleasure doing business with you."

The matriarch directed several questions to Elle and continued to exclaim over the beauty and expense of the gift.

While the others were speaking, Griffin leaned over and whispered in Cassie's ear, "We shall be very lucky if Maddie doesn't have a seizure over our expense report for this trip."

Cassie smiled brightly so as not to give her hostess cause for concern. "Maybe we can slip some tranquilizers into her coffee before you show her the bill for the crown."

Small talk continued until the two main participants had chatted for a suitable interval. After that, Elle rose signaling the visit was over.

The matriarch escorted them to the door, bowing with great ceremony and once more expressing her thanks.

The three climbed back into their hired car. The trip back to their hotel seemed much shorter than the outbound journey.

As they stood in the hallway in front of their rooms, Elle reached into her messenger bag and handed the artifact to Griffin. "Well, it's been a slice. See you guys around."

"Are you leaving?" the scrivener asked in surprise.

"I'm out of here on the first flight that will get me to New York. I did my part. You two are on your own."

As Elle turned to go, Cassie called out, "We owe you a lot. Thanks for everything."

"Absolutely," Griffin concurred.

The sentinel wavered and then spun around to face them. Her typically fierce expression softened. "You helped me out too, so I guess we're even." Then, with a wry smile, she added, "I hope those bad guys with guns are terrible shots. I'd hate to see three thousand years of sentinel work go down the drain. You two watch your backs." She gave a small wave, swiped her key card and was gone.

32 – TERMINATION BENEFITS

Joshua Metcalf and Chopper Bowdeen waited in the darkened corridor outside Abraham Metcalf's office. Both men were armed with pistols and silencers. It was nearly midnight. A light glowed through the crack at the bottom of the door, indicating that the diviner was still busy doing paperwork. With the exception of the guards at the front gates, the rest of the brotherhood and their families had retired for the night. No one disobeyed the ten-thirty curfew without express permission from the diviner.

Bowdeen glanced nervously at the surveillance camera suspended from a corner of the hallway ceiling.

Noting his gaze, Joshua whispered, "Don't worry. I disabled it. The guards are watching looped footage of an empty corridor. I also disabled the cameras in my father's office." Warily, he added, "Are you clear on what needs to happen tonight?"

The mercenary nodded. "I'll go in first and take the shot. You back me up in case anything goes wrong."

The spymaster added, "You understand why, don't you? I can't be the one to kill my own father. If one of my brothers should ask, I couldn't lie about a thing like that."

Bowdeen placed a reassuring hand on Joshua's shoulder. "I understand, son. You just make sure you get me out of here, OK?"

"Of course. I'll sneak you out of the compound before I raise the cry that my father's been murdered. I'll have no difficulty shifting blame to one of the malefactors who were brought here for chastisement. Be assured, nobody will ever suspect it was you."

"Sounds better than any other option I had going for me," Chopper muttered ruefully. "I'll be damn glad to be done with the Nephilim once and for all."

"I give you my word," Joshua said solemnly. "You'll never have to see any of us again after tonight."

The mercenary checked the magazine of his pistol. "Let's do this." He quietly turned the handle of the office door and stepped inside.

Joshua hung back in the shadows.

Abraham looked up from the documents he'd been inspecting. Narrowing his gaze when he recognized his visitor, he demanded, "What do you want?"

"My severance pay," Bowdeen remarked coldly.

Abraham rose to his feet to face the intruder. The expression of disbelief on his face proved that he'd noticed the gun in the mercenary's hand. "What do you think you're doing?"

"I'm making sure I don't have to spend the rest of my life looking over my shoulder." Chopper shrugged. "Nothing personal." He raised his pistol, aiming it at the old man's chest.

Before he could fire, a dull thud sounded. Bowdeen grabbed his own chest and whirled around. "Joshua?" He gasped in disbelief before crumpling to the floor in a heap.

The spymaster emerged from the darkened corridor. Stepping over the mercenary's lifeless body, he grabbed the diviner by the arm to steady him.

The old man listed to one side.

"Father, are you alright?"

"I... I..." Metcalf stuttered.

"Here, sit down." Joshua helped him back into his chair.

The diviner rubbed his forehead, confused. "I don't understand. Why did he try to shoot me?"

Joshua poured his father a glass of water from the carafe on the desk. "Please, drink this."

The old man silently obeyed.

"I was afraid something like this might happen. In Australia, Mr. Bowdeen was talking wildly. He had convinced himself that the Nephilim would never let him leave because he knew too much. He suspected you would have him killed once he'd outlived his usefulness."

"I would do what?" Metcalf's eyes grew wide with surprise.

"Of course, I told him his fears were groundless, but he wouldn't believe me," Joshua protested. "That's when I decided to keep tabs on him personally. Tonight, I saw him disable the surveillance cameras in the guard shack. Realizing his intentions, I armed myself and followed him. When I saw him approaching your door, there could be no doubt that he planned to kill you. I did what was necessary to stop him."

Metcalf's eyes never left his son's face as the younger man spoke. It was as if the diviner had never truly seen him before. "Joshua, you certainly have a cool head in a crisis."

"Thank you, Father," the spymaster replied modestly.

"You just saved my life," the old man added in wonderment.

"As head of the Order of Argus, it's my duty to protect you at all times."

Abraham rose shakily. "Yes, but you did more than that. You not only saved your father's life, but you preserved the glorious destiny of the Nephilim. If I had died, all my plans and hopes for the brotherhood would have died with me."

"Then perhaps you need to confide in someone to make sure that doesn't happen," Joshua suggested softly. "Daniel ought to be party to whatever—"

Abraham cut him off. "No, not Daniel. He hasn't the temperament. Perhaps..." The old man hesitated. "Perhaps, I was hasty in naming my successor. I must pray on the matter further." He glanced at the spymaster. "I shall reveal the full nature of my plans to you, my son. In due time, when the day of reckoning draws near."

Joshua adopted a solicitous manner. "We must not talk of such things now, Father. There will be time enough once you've recovered. Sit down and let me attend to the intruder."

He settled Abraham comfortably.

"Thank you, my boy." The diviner took another sip of water.

Joshua smiled. "I'll always be here for you, Father. You can depend on me."

The old man, weakened by shock, sank his head back against the cushions and closed his eyes.

The spymaster went to the desk phone and called the guard shack. "Send a detail to the diviner's office immediately. Mr. Bowdeen has just tried to kill my father." He paused to listen to the question coming from the other end of the line. "Yes, that's right. He's dead. We'll need to dispose of the body tonight."

33 – KEYLESS ENTRY

Cassie paced to-and-fro beside the window in Griffin's hotel room.

The scrivener sat hunched over the desk scribbling notes and referring to his computer screen. "You're going to wear out the carpet if you continue at that rate," he commented without turning around.

She wheeled toward him. "Are you done yet?"

"Very nearly." He consulted the display again and made a few more notes. "Yes, I believe I've got it."

At that moment, a knock was heard at the door.

"That's got to be him." Cassie rushed to answer.

Their visitor was a muscular Asian man in his mid-twenties.

"Rabten! You made it in record time." She gave him an enthusiastic hug.

The field agent dropped his duffel bag and returned the greeting. "It's good to see you again, Cassie."

Griffin rose to shake hands. "So glad you arrived quickly."

"I was waiting for your call," the agent confessed. "Hopped on the first flight I could get out of O'Hare."

"How's life in the States?" the pythia asked.

"A lot duller than what's going on around here, that's for sure. By the way, Rinchen sends his regards. He called me to say he met Zhang Rou today." Rabten gave a knowing grin. "That sort of assignment is right up my brother's alley."

"What do you mean?"

"He likes rescuing damsels in distress. You have to keep an eye on him. He's a heartbreaker."

"Good to know," the pythia murmured, now worried on Rou's behalf.

The agent's gaze swept the room. "Did you snag the artifact already?"

"There it is." Cassie gestured toward the desk where the Minoan relic lay next to the scrivener's computer and notes.

"May I?" The Arkana agent hesitated before picking up the find.

Griffin handed it to him. "Please."

The artifact stood about a foot high and a foot wide. It was a Minoan labrys—a double-headed axe—made entirely of gold.

"It's pretty unusual for the haft of a labrys to be shaped like the figure of a woman," Rabten observed.

"A goddess actually," Griffin corrected him. "The goddess with upraised hands—an image of benediction which predates the Minoans by forty thousand years. There are cave paintings in France showing female divinities in this exact posture."

"She looks like she's giving the hand signal for a touchdown in American football," Rabten joked.

"I think she looks like a butterfly with the axe blades as her wings," Cassie remarked.

All three of them paused to study the elongated figure of the goddess. She wasn't dressed in the typical Minoan costume of bare bodice and ornate flounced skirt. Only the outline of her form and skirt were represented. Her arms were raised at right angles to her body and pressed against the axe blades in bas-relief. She wore a crown of rubies on her head.

"Why rubies?" Rabten asked.

"In all likelihood, they're meant to represent poppies," Griffin replied. "That was a typical Minoan motif. Opium poppies have been cultivated as far back as the Neolithic period. The drug was used in religious rituals as a means of communicating with the goddess through altered states of consciousness."

"Like shamans used snake venom," Cassie said helpfully.

"Exactly," the scrivener concurred.

Rabten ran his finger across the axe. "What do you think these are supposed to mean?" He pointed to four gems affixed to the blades—two on each side and spaced equidistantly from one other. In the upper left quadrant was a topaz, beneath it an emerald. The opposite blade held a sapphire and below it a ruby.

"We're not sure yet," the pythia said. "One thing is certain. They don't stand for constellations like the gems on the other artifacts we found."

Rabten frowned in bewilderment. "Does the riddle help explain what they mean?"

"I wouldn't know." Cassie stared pointedly at the scrivener. "Griffin was still translating it when you got here."

"Correction, I finished translating it." The scrivener picked up his notes and read from them. "'Past the golden road of Boreas, where his islands kill the sea, seek the great river's mother. Her reliquary holds the key.'"

"Hey, you made it rhyme," Rabten noted appreciatively.

"Reliquary?" the pythia echoed with suspicion. "Your secret Minoan decoder ring came up with a word like 'reliquary'?"

"Not precisely. It was the closest word in English which matched the intent of the riddle. A reliquary is a container or depository for sacred objects. During the Middle Ages, reliquaries were used to house the bones of saints."

"Or, in our case, the Bones of the Mother?"

"Yes, I think that's what the Minoans were implying."

"So maybe all five artifacts have to be collected together in the same place before we can get to the Sage Stone," the pythia speculated.

"The riddle does say 'the reliquary holds the key,'" Griffin concurred.

"But the riddle doesn't help explain the gems," Rabten noted.

"It doesn't help explain much of anything." Cassie tried not to sound too crestfallen.

"I understood only one word—*Boreas*." Griffin tossed his legal pad back on the desk.

"You mean like the north wind?" the pythia asked.

The scrivener nodded. "I see you remember." Turning to Rabten, he said, "In a previous riddle, the Minoans made reference to the *anemoi*—deities who control winds which blow from the four cardinal directions. *Boreas* is the god in charge of the north wind. In terms of our current riddle, the allusion to *Boreas* may simply mean that we must search north of our current position."

"There isn't too much real estate south of where we are now," Cassie said.

"But the clue refers to the original location of the artifact at Lugu Lake," the scrivener pointed out.

Cassie raised her eyebrows skeptically. "I don't think that helps. Even if we travel north from Lugu, that still leaves Europe, North America, most of Asia and the top half of Africa."

"Obviously, a large area to cover," Griffin agreed.

"This is kind of odd." Rabten was once more scrutinizing the artifact.

The bottom of the goddess statue wasn't flat. Instead, it terminated in a series of five rectangular prisms of a grayish cast. They were all bundled together though each one was a different length.

The agent studied the relic intently. "Aside from the weird shape, the base is made of a different metal."

"It's an alloy of some sort," the scrivener explained. "I suspect it's much harder than gold."

"The first time I picked that artifact up, I got a vision," Cassie elaborated. "I knew that the bottom of the statue was meant to be a pressure point key. When we get to the right location, the key slides into a recessed lock. That's how we open the secret compartment where the Sage Stone is hidden." She sighed regretfully. "I tried half a dozen times to get more information by reading the artifact, but this little butterfly goddess doesn't believe in oversharing."

"Even though we only have a limited understanding of the artifact itself, the first step is to get a duplicate made." Griffin's voice took on a note of concern. "The latest communication from Maddie tells us that the Nephilim will soon be on their way. We have very little time." Turning to the agent, he asked, "Can you help us?"

Rabten smiled. "It's what I do. The minute I knew I was coming here to meet you, I started lining up resources. I found somebody in Padang City who can turn the job around in less than a week."

"Excellent! That is good news indeed." The scrivener looked toward Cassie for confirmation, but she was staring at the artifact and scowling. "Cassie, did you hear? Less than a week."

"What?" She gaped at him blankly. "Oh, jeez, I'm sorry. I was just thinking about something." She transferred her attention to Rabten. "Could you make one modification to the copy?" She picked it up. "Cut off the bottom."

Both men registered surprise.

"You mean lop off the key?" Griffin sounded appalled.

"Exactly. I mean duplicate the artifact down to the last detail but make it stand upright so it looks like a statue."

"Why?" Rabten still seemed puzzled.

"Guys, think about it. This isn't just another artifact. It's the artifact that will take us to the Sage Stone. The Nephilim have been hot on our heels since Day One which means we've never gotten a comfortable lead in this race. Do you really want to take the chance that they beat us to the finish line?"

"But surely tampering with the artifact will arouse their suspicions," the scrivener objected.

"How?" the pythia challenged. "None of the other relics had keys attached. The Nephilim won't think something is missing when they get this one."

"She has a point," Rabten admitted.

"At the very least, this will buy us a little time. I don't even like to think about the possibility that they get to the right spot before we do but Murphy's Law—"

"Yes, yes, I'm well acquainted with your views on Mr. Murphy, his laws, and their various codicils." Griffin rolled his eyes. "You've certainly been living up to your namesake quite a lot lately."

"Huh?" The field agent looked from one to the other.

"The Cassandra of Greek mythology after whom Cassie is named," the scrivener explained. "Apollo, captivated by her beauty, gave her the gift of prophecy. When she rejected his advances, he cursed her so that no one would believe her dire predictions."

"Yeah, but the takeaway is that even with zero cred she was usually right," Cassie countered. "All I'm saying is that we're better off preparing for a worst-case scenario. If the Nephilim don't have the key, it will take them time to figure out how the lock works and how to pick it. Maybe long enough for us to swoop in and grab the Sage Stone." She glanced questioningly at Griffin.

The scrivener still appeared unconvinced. "Very well, but I do hope you're right."

Cassie handed the artifact to Rabten. "Have it made just like I said."

The agent opened his duffel bag and deposited the relic inside. "I'll get on this right away."

"And hurry!" both Cassie and Griffin shouted as he slipped from the room.

34 – PHOTO OPPORTUNITY

Joshua looked up from the surveillance monitor on his desk in time to see his father entering the spymaster's office. He immediately switched off the screen and rose to greet the diviner. "Is there something I can help you with, sir?"

"Yes, indeed." Abraham smiled at him warmly, an unknown experience in Joshua's memory.

The younger man pulled out a chair and placed it beside the desk. "Please, have a seat."

Metcalf settled himself and gazed at his son. The smile disappeared as quickly as it had come. "I have a matter of deep concern to discuss with you."

"Sir?" Joshua felt a mild sense of alarm. "Do you not find the performance of the Order of Argus satisfactory?"

Barely registering the question, the diviner shook his head. "My visit has nothing to do with that." He stared vaguely off into space. "I've grown concerned of late with the outsiders that have been employed to help the Nephilim."

"Considering Mr. Bowdeen's appalling behavior, you certainly have reason to be," the spymaster agreed. "How can I be of service?"

The diviner rubbed his jaw, gathering his thoughts. "I'd like you to investigate the activities of Mr. Leroy Hunt."

"Who?" Joshua asked blankly.

Abraham raised his eyebrows in surprise, finally focusing all his attention on his son. "You aren't acquainted with Mr. Hunt?"

Joshua belatedly realized who his father meant. "Oh. Is that the Fallen man who is helping Daniel with the tasks you assigned him?"

"Yes, that's right. However, Mr. Hunt also has other duties. When he isn't safeguarding Daniel, he is charged with finding my missing wife, Hannah."

"But Father," Joshua protested. "You should have trusted me with a matter like that."

The diviner sighed heavily. "Ordinarily that would be true, but Hannah has taken refuge among the Fallen. I assumed that one of their kind could find her more easily than a Nephilim might."

"I see." The spymaster paused. "But now you have reason to doubt this Mr. Hunt's abilities?"

"I have reason to doubt his truthfulness," the old man replied acerbically. "After months of following one lead after another, he's produced no tangible results at all. It makes me wonder if he's taking my money under false pretenses. Aside from that, he's been difficult to reach of late. I don't know what else he could possibly be doing with his time. He assured me he has no other clients but the Nephilim at the moment."

"Do you want me to question him?" Joshua asked in surprise. He'd never interrogated one of the Fallen before.

"I want you to search his apartment," Metcalf said flatly. "To find out if he's withholding information from me. Let me know what he's been up to. He's out of the country with Daniel at the moment. This is the perfect chance to put my mind at ease about his integrity. You are to take charge of this matter personally."

Joshua nodded. Handling this particular task suited his purposes as well as his father's. He wished to become indispensable to the diviner. Bowdeen's death had been a good start. This new assignment would further solidify his position.

The diviner slid a piece of paper across the desk toward his son. "This is Mr. Hunt's address in the city. He lives in an apartment building. I'm sure you can find a way to let yourself in."

Joshua gave a slight smile. "Of course, sir. I'll look into this immediately."

***

The spymaster wasted no time in carrying out his father's orders. First, he ran a quick background check on Leroy Hunt. Then he changed his Nephilim garb for blue jeans, a sweater, and a light spring jacket so that he might blend in easily with the Fallen. An hour later, he pulled his car into a parking space on the quiet block where Hunt lived. He'd had no trouble finding the place. The spymaster took a few moments to study the exterior of the building. It was an older four-story walk-up. The age and size meant there wouldn't be a doorman or any security cameras to contend with. That was all to the good.

Joshua's familiarity with the outside world was proving to be surprisingly useful. Much as he despised time spent in the company of the Fallen, he had observed their ways and knew how to mimic their behavior. When he got out of his car and casually strolled through the building lobby, he seemed like any other resident of the area. It was the middle of the day, and nobody was around. Presumably, the people who lived here were all away at work.

Without hesitation, he climbed the stairs to the top floor, scanned the hallway and then picked the lock to Hunt's apartment.

What he found when he entered the unit took him by surprise. It was neat as a pin. Hunt's profile had suggested a man of slovenly personal habits. Perhaps all those years spent in the army had given the fellow a sense of discipline. The spymaster wasn't entirely sure what he was looking for, but he instinctively gravitated toward the desk near the living room window. While he waited for Hunt's computer to power on, he checked through the desk drawers.

Inside he discovered cameras, a laser microphone, recording equipment and monocular spyglasses. Obviously, Hunt had been watching someone or possibly several people. When Joshua opened the shallow center drawer, it revealed photos of the subjects of that surveillance. Sitting down in the desk chair, he rifled through the images. The pictures were of a farmhouse in the suburbs and an old woman who presumably lived there. Those images held no meaning for the spymaster, but the next one did. It was a picture of his father's youngest wife, Hannah, looking into the mailbox of that same farmhouse. She was almost unrecognizable with her make-up and cropped hair—both abominations in the eyes of the Nephilim. She was dressed in a skirt much too short for a modest consecrated bride to wear. Joshua's eyes narrowed in disapproval. She had clearly embraced the ways of the Fallen and taken refuge with an old woman out in the countryside where she thought nobody would find her.

The next photo showed her descending from a school bus. A school bus! As if the wearing apparel and customs of the Fallen weren't bad enough, Hannah was imbibing the corrupt notions that passed for knowledge in their world. He was appalled. His father would be speechless with rage when he saw these images.

There was one more picture beneath. It caused Joshua to gasp audibly. He always prided himself on maintaining his composure, but this image shocked him to the core. In the final photo, Hannah was kissing a boy—a youth of about her own age. They were standing beside an old car. As if her other sins weren't bad enough, she had completely forgotten her marriage vows. How could she be so lost to heaven that she could forget being sealed to the diviner as his spouse for all eternity?

Joshua leaned forward over the desk and rubbed his forehead. What did all of this mean? Hunt was plainly aware of the spot where she was hiding. Why hadn't he given that information to the diviner? What game was he playing at? The spymaster briefly entertained the notion that Hunt might be blackmailing Hannah in exchange for keeping silent about her whereabouts. Then he dismissed the idea. The old woman in the first picture didn't look prosperous enough to buy the Fallen man's cooperation.

He turned his attention to the computer screen. He needed to find out where this farmhouse was located. Opening a browser window, he checked the sites Hunt had visited last. The Fallen man had been looking up an address and map directions to find it. When Joshua checked a street view photo of the location, he knew he'd found the right house. He wrote down the address.

Then he stood and paced around the room, considering how he might best use these facts to his own advantage. While the spymaster would certainly disclose what he'd found to his father, he might also be able to shake his father's belief that this Fallen man could be trusted. If Hunt were out of the picture, Abraham would have no choice but to send Joshua on these mysterious missions with Daniel in order to protect him. Joshua would become even more central to the plans of the diviner. Perhaps, if he handled the situation correctly, he could eclipse Daniel entirely in his father's affections. Then, who knew? The title of scion might yet be his.

35 – LEROY AND THE BANDITS

Cassie and Griffin marked time fretfully in Padang City while the duplicate artifact was being fabricated. The minute it was ready, they headed back to Lugu Lake to rejoin Rou and Rabten's twin brother Rinchen. It took several flights and a bus ride over winding mountain roads before they once more found themselves in Luoshui Village. Much to their surprise, Rou and Rinchen were waiting at the bus stop to meet them.

"Hey, guys. What are you doing here?" the pythia asked.

"No time to talk now." Rou glanced nervously over her shoulder.

In a low voice, Rinchen said, "I just got word from Maddie. Your friends arrived a couple of hours ago. They've got a Chinese Nephilim guide with them who knows the mountain roads, and he drove them here. That's how they shaved a few hours off the travel time from Lijiang. Hunt phoned Metcalf to say they were going to check out the cave this afternoon. For all we know, they might already be on their way there."

"Holy cats!" Cassie exclaimed. "We need to get there first."

"Yes, we must find a boat right now!" Rou tore off toward the town dock, expecting the others to follow.

"They aren't staying in this village, are they?" Griffin scanned the surrounding hotels warily.

"Nope," Rinchen reassured him. "We caught a break. They're at a place on the northeast shore."

The scrivener checked his watch. "Nearly three o'clock. Even though we took the early bus from Lijiang, it may not prove to be early enough."

"Hurry!" Rou was shouting and waving at them from the stern of a pig-trough boat. Its owner was untying the mooring line.

The other three ran to catch up and climb aboard. Since the boat was long and narrow, only one person could fit on each bench. The boatman took the

148

prow. Rou sat on the bench after him, followed by Cassie, Griffin, and Rinchen.

In a few moments, they were en route to the cableway across the lake.

Rou dug into her backpack and produced a set of binoculars. "I thought we would need these." She immediately began scanning the opposite shore.

Cassie turned to face Griffin. "Is it my imagination or did she get amazingly fluent in English since we've been gone?"

The scrivener regarded their guide with a baffled air. "Her language skills do seem to have improved immensely."

The pythia called out, "Rou, your English is really good now."

The girl beamed at Cassie. "Rinchen said I have no need to be embarrassed. He told me my English is perfect."

"Did he indeed?" Griffin swiveled his head toward the Arkana agent.

Rinchen blushed. "Well, it is," he protested awkwardly. "She talks better than some American-born Asians I know."

Griffin shifted forward to whisper in Cassie's ear. "Apparently, she only needed the proper encouragement to come out of her shell."

"Such as the brave young Arkana agent sent to protect her?" the pythia murmured archly.

The two lapsed into amused silence.

"*Aiya!*" Rou gasped.

"What!" the other three demanded at once.

She put down the binoculars. "Two men climbed into a boat across the lake. One is wearing a cowboy hat."

"That's not so unusual around here," Rinchen countered.

"He is also wearing a denim jacket and a piece of string tied around his neck."

"You mean a bolo tie?" Cassie asked tensely.

"Perhaps that is what you call it. See for yourself." The girl pointed across the broad expanse of water toward a speck of a boat just leaving the dock.

Cassie raised the field glasses, scanning the distance until she brought the object into focus. "Rats! It's Daniel and his evil sidekick."

"Is anyone else with them?" Griffin asked.

"Just the two of them and the boatman."

"We must go faster," Rou muttered. She crept toward the prow to have a discussion in the local dialect with the man rowing their boat. It went on for several minutes.

Cassie watched the boatman's expression. He seemed mildly surprised and made protests, but eventually gave a nod of grudging consent.

Rou moved back toward the others. "Rinchen, you row too."

The agent carefully balanced his weight as he stepped over Griffin and Cassie to change seats with Rou. The boatman handed him an oar. It took a few minutes for the two men to synchronize their movements, but soon their craft began to gain speed.

"Too bad there's not a second set of oars," Griffin remarked. "I could have lent a hand as well."

"I promised the owner we would pay double to get across the lake fast," Rou informed them. "At first, he said we are on vacation and should relax. Then I told him we are meeting friends at the Goddess Cave and must not be late."

Griffin's startled expression mirrored Cassie's own surprise at Rou's resourcefulness. The pythia said, "You really do think fast on your feet. Your grandfather was right."

The girl appeared not to have heard her. She'd reclaimed the binoculars and was keeping tabs on their enemies. After a few moments, she concluded, "I do not think they have seen us. They would need spy glasses for that."

The combined rowing power of the boatman and Rinchen allowed them to pull ahead of the other skiff. As a result, they arrived in Nisai Village first. The minute the boat touched the dock, they all clambered off while Rou handed the owner a wad of bills. They didn't wait to receive his thanks as they dashed off toward the cableway.

All the way up the mountain, they uneasily charted their enemies' progress across the water. When they disembarked at the Buddhist temple, Rou used her binoculars to scan the area below.

"They are on the chair lift now," she reported.

"We won't have enough time!" Griffin exclaimed in dismay.

"Guys, we have to try anyway. If they see that hole in the wall, we're done for." Cassie made a dash up the stairs to the cave entrance with the others following.

***

Daniel trudged up the stone stairway leading to Gemu Goddess Cave.

Ahead of him, Leroy Hunt was voicing a steady stream of complaints. "'Kingdom of Women,' my ass! There ain't no truth in advertisin'. Where's all the loose females who live in these parts? That's what I'd like to know. Ever since I got here, I been waitin' for a proposition to do the horizontal bop with somebody of the feminine persuasion. And I'm still waitin'!" He paused to curse under his breath and kick a rock out of his path. "And here's another thing. It sure would be nice for a change to go on a junket that don't wreck my boots."

"Shhh!" Daniel cautioned.

"Look around, son. Ain't nobody hereabouts for miles."

The scion paused to listen. "I don't like this. I can't help feeling that someone is watching us. Perhaps we should have brought Brother Yu along with us to the cave."

The cowboy swung around on the stairs to stare down at him. "Brother Yu drove us here. He's got his orders to sit tight at the hotel and watch out for them three suspicious characters in case they're followin' us. That's as much as he needs to know about this salvage operation. The less folks that know, the less I'll have to kill later."

Daniel solemnly regarded his companion. "I wish I could believe you were joking."

The cowboy resumed his upward march. "It's bad enough we had a third party drive us here at all."

"Do you really think you could have managed some of those hairpin curves yourself?" the scion challenged.

"I reckon not," the cowboy admitted. "Between loose gravel and switchback trails for hours on end, it was like to make a feller dizzy. All I can say is Yu better be keepin' a sharp eye for them three thieves in case they're down in the village."

Daniel, who hadn't been listening closely to Hunt's rant, paused in bafflement. "How am I supposed to do that when I'm up here on the mountain?"

Hunt stopped cold, trying to process the question. Once more he turned toward Daniel. "Not you. I said Yu!"

"What?"

The cowboy rubbed the back of his neck in irritation. "Lord Almighty! This ain't no time to play 'Who's on First.'"

Daniel squinted up at him uncomprehendingly.

"Never mind, son." Hunt waved his arm wearily. "Tryin' to explain would only give me a worse brain cramp than I already got."

The two climbed onward in silence until they reached the cave entrance. Once there, they paused just inside the doorway to catch their breaths. Without warning, a dark shape hurtled forward, attempting to dart between them and escape.

Daniel was caught off guard, but Hunt's reflexes were lightning-quick. He grabbed the runner by the shoulders.

"Now hold on there. It ain't polite to shove folks. Where I come from a body says, 'Excuse me' when they—" The rest of the sentence died in his throat.

The light streaming in from the cave entrance revealed a face that Daniel knew all too well. "Great God in heaven!" he exclaimed.

"Well, well." Hunt chuckled and tightened his grip. "If it ain't little Miss Cassie."

"Oh crap!" the female thief muttered.

The cowboy drew one arm across her windpipe and pulled out his pistol with the other. Then he pressed the gun against her temple. "Brother Dan'l, would you kindly search this gal for bug zappers? I ain't fallin' for one of her tricks again."

The scion complied. "Sorry," he whispered apologetically as he patted her down. He then made a thorough search of her backpack. "She isn't carrying a stun gun, Mr. Hunt. No weapons of any kind."

"Gettin' cocky, ain't we?" the cowboy remarked to his captive. "You figure I'm so toothless that you don't need to pack no heat? Pride surely goeth before a fall."

"You ought to know considering the number of times I've dropped you like a sack of dirt!" Cassie grumbled.

Ignoring the comment, Hunt continued. "Where's your friends? Blondie and the Limey."

"They're not here. I'm working this job alone," the young woman replied sullenly.

"Now how come I got trouble believin' that?" The cowboy's tone was sarcastic.

"I told you, I'm alone!"

"No, she isn't." Another voice emerged from the shadows along the side wall of the cave.

"Well, well. If it ain't the Limey." Hunt's voice held a note of wonder. "This surely is my lucky day."

"The name is Griffin actually. Please do try to remember it in future." Although he advanced forward a few feet, he took care to remain blanketed in shadow.

"So, where's Blondie?"

"Otherwise occupied," came the impassive reply. "Only two of us will be pummeling you today."

Daniel fancied he could see the glint of a gold object in the thief's hand.

"Let her go," Griffin commanded.

"Boy, I tell you what. If brains was leather, you ain't got enough to make a saddle for a junebug. Can't you see my gun pointed at her head?"

Griffin allowed his hands to emerge briefly into the light. "And can't you see my gun pointed at your artifact?"

Daniel gasped.

Hunt guffawed. "What you fixin' to do? Kill it deader?"

"I intend to kill your quest. Right here. Right now. Gold is a surprisingly soft metal. A bullet fired at close range will obliterate the inscription entirely."

"Mr. Hunt!" Daniel thundered, sounding very much like the diviner himself. "Lower your weapon this instant. Don't you understand? We need the lettering on that artifact to find the Sage Stone. Without it, we're finished."

The cowboy remained motionless, apparently judging whether he had a clear enough shot to dispatch the thief before the relic could be destroyed.

"I'm prepared to offer you a trade," Griffin continued. "You may have the artifact if you let Cassie go."

"Griffin, no!" she shouted. "We worked so hard to find it!"

"Hush, love," he replied softly. "It's nothing compared to your life. Let them have it."

Daniel noticed the female thief's eyebrows shoot upward in surprise, but she lapsed into silence.

"Your terms are acceptable," the scion concurred.

"Like hell they are!" Hunt objected.

"Mr. Hunt, if you refuse to obey me, be assured this will be the last job you ever do for the Nephilim." Daniel's voice contained a steely resolve that brooked no opposition.

His words had a curious effect on the cowboy. For whatever reason, Hunt flinched as if he'd been struck. His hand wavered, and he lowered the gun.

"Release my associate and give her your pistol," Griffin ordered, still keeping to the shadows so Hunt couldn't get a bead on him.

"I ain't givin' her the chance to shoot me with my own gun," the cowboy protested.

"Unlike you, Cassie and I aren't murderers. We simply want your weapon to guarantee that you don't shoot us in the back as we make our escape."

"Do as he says," the scion ordered.

Hunt remained frozen.

"Now!"

The cowboy grudgingly released his stranglehold on Cassie and handed her his gun.

Griffin finally stepped into the light.

Cassie retrieved her backpack and ran to stand beside him, taking care to keep the gun pointed at Hunt.

"You'll have to allow us twenty minutes' head start," Griffin told Daniel. "Agreed?"

"You have my word," the scion assented. "We won't leave this place for twenty minutes."

Hunt snorted in disgust but held his tongue.

Griffin handed Cassie the artifact and, with a look of deep regret, she brought it to Daniel. "What a waste," she murmured dolefully.

Giving the cowboy a wide berth, the two thieves scuttled out of the cave.

"See you at the finish line," Cassie called back before darting out of sight.

Hunt made a move toward the entrance. "What you waitin' for, boy?"

Daniel hastily put the artifact on the ground and rushed forward to block his exit. "Didn't you hear me promise them twenty minutes' head start?"

"I don't recollect hearin' no such thing. Feller stole my pistol, and I mean to get it back." Hunt was on the point of shoving Daniel aside when a noise made him freeze in his tracks.

Voices were approaching rapidly. It sounded like a heated conversation in Chinese between two people.

The men exchanged baffled looks.

"Must be tourists," Hunt speculated.

Before they could decide what to do, a young couple entered the cave arguing vehemently. They paused, silhouetted in the doorway. The male pointed at what appeared to be a map. The female shook her head and uttered a string of protests.

They both ended their conversation abruptly when they noticed the Westerners.

"Harro." The young woman smiled cheerfully. Her accent was very thick.

The young man bobbed his head and murmured, "*Ni hao.*"

Daniel assumed this must be a greeting in Chinese. "Hello," he responded awkwardly.

"Howdy," Hunt said, tipping his hat.

The newcomers were instantly attracted to the cowboy's Stetson. They flanked him, pointing and smiling at his head, all the while chattering rapidly in their native language.

Hunt seemed pleased by the stir he was creating. He smiled down at them benevolently.

"Prease?" The young woman peered up at him beseechingly. "You show us." She said several more words to her companion in Chinese, and he unfolded the map he was carrying.

Thrusting it in front of Hunt's face, he asked, "Where we?"

The cowboy squinted at it, trying to get his bearings. "OK, my little yella buddy. Let's see what you got here." He took the map with both hands, scrutinizing it intently.

In a motion so quick that Daniel could barely register what had happened, the young woman jammed a small object against Hunt's leg. He convulsed and immediately collapsed in a heap on the ground.

The scion gaped in shock. The young man whipped a gun out of his jacket. In an accent even thicker than the woman's, he said, "Money! You give!"

Daniel had no difficulty translating that these were bandits who preyed on tourists. This isolated cave was the perfect location for a hold-up. He took out his wallet and handed it over.

The young man rifled through the contents, taking only the cash and leaving the credit cards. Daniel hoped the bandit wouldn't look deeper into the cave and notice the gold statue lying on the ground a few feet behind him. He moved slightly to block the bandit's view. He needn't have worried. The man was intent on counting the cash.

Meanwhile, the female bandit was rooting through Hunt's wallet. The cowboy had been reduced to an inert lump on the floor of the cave. He twitched periodically. She too removed only the cash, taking nothing else. Then she stood up and said something to her companion in Chinese.

The two of them advanced toward Daniel. He warily stepped back a few paces.

The woman lunged in close to his face and spoke in a tense whisper. "You go to porice?" She made a slashing motion across her throat and gave a wicked grin. "You dead men!"

Still pointing his gun at Daniel, the male bandit backed toward the entrance. The female ducked behind him.

The scion could hear their triumphant laughter as they ran down the stairway, presumably to some secret lair on the mountainside. Daniel dropped to the ground in a stupor, almost afraid to breathe while he waited for Hunt to recover.

***

Half an hour later, the cowboy stirred to life. He sat up, rubbing his head. "What the hell happened?"

Daniel regarded him gloomily. "We were robbed. They took all our cash."

Hunt cursed loudly. "Goddam it! If'n I get bug-zapped by one more tiny female, I'm swearin' off women for life!" He crawled on all fours to retrieve his hat then, swaying slightly, he stood upright. "When I catch up with them bandits," he snarled ominously.

"They threatened to kill us if we notify the police or try to pursue them."

"That don't scare me none." Hunt dusted off his jacket with offended dignity.

"We have no time for vengeance, Mr. Hunt. Our mission has been accomplished."

The cowboy seemed perplexed. "You mean they didn't grab the doodad?"

"I don't think they saw it." Daniel rose and retrieved the artifact.

Hunt walked over to study their latest find. "Well, ain't that somethin.'" His tone bordered on reverence. "You think it might fetch a good price?"

"My father has no interest in selling it," Daniel replied inexpressively. "Still, it would be worth a king's ransom if he did."

"I'll surely bear that in mind."

Daniel peeped anxiously at the cave entrance. "Given the value of the artifact we're carrying, I don't believe it's safe for us to linger here. This region is obviously infested with scoundrels."

Surprisingly, Hunt didn't contradict him. "We best saddle up and hit the dusty trail before sundown. We need to get this little dingus locked up someplace safe."

The scion treated him to a puzzled look. "So, you've lost interest in pursuing the bandits?"

Hunt shrugged. "All they got is chump change. We're walkin' away with the jackpot."

"True enough."

The two men exited the cave and made for the chair lift station.

"We still have a few hours of daylight left," Daniel remarked distractedly while scanning the path ahead for lurking assailants.

"I bet Yu can get us back to the big city in two shakes."

"No, I can't. I wouldn't try driving these treacherous mountain roads during the day much less after dark," the scion objected.

Hunt groaned. "This day ain't never gonna end!"

36 – SCENE STEALERS

Cassie and Griffin stared worriedly across the table at one another in Cassie's hotel room.

"I hope they're alright," the pythia remarked. "It's been hours."

A quiet tap on the door made them both jump.

Griffin rose to answer.

Rou and Rinchen entered the room exuberantly.

"All is well!" the girl announced.

Cassie stood up and let out a deep sigh. "Don't scare us like that. We've been biting our nails about you ever since we left the mountain."

"Rou and I wanted to make sure they got on the road," Rinchen explained. "We rented an electric scooter in Nisai and rode over to the village where they're staying. Then we staked out their hotel." He chuckled. "Just like you thought, their driver loaded up their bags and off they went."

Rou giggled as well. "The one you call Daniel seemed nervous as he got into the car. The one called Hunt looked very sour."

"We must have really thrown a scare into them."

"This is hardly a laughing matter," Griffin rebuked them solemnly.

"Why didn't you call?" Cassie demanded. "It's not like the villages don't have cell service."

Rinchen regarded them both with wry amusement. "You do realize we're all about the same age, give or take five years, but you two are carrying on like fretful parents."

"That's because when it comes to the Nephilim, we've got what amounts to decades of experience over you both," Cassie retorted.

"You truly have no idea what they're capable of," the scrivener added. "We've seen things..."

"I get it." Rinchen raised his hands in surrender.

In a chastened tone, Rou said, "We are sorry to have upset you."

"Apology accepted." Griffin's stern expression softened.

The pythia smiled. "OK, guys. Lecture over."

Relieved to be off the hook, Rou immediately changed the subject. "You must tell us what happened when you were inside the cave with them."

Griffin moved toward the door. "Since it's well past dinnertime, I suggest we postpone that discussion until we've found a place to eat. Now that the Nephilim have left the area, we are at liberty to move about the village."

"Sounds like a plan," Rinchen eagerly approved.

***

Ten minutes later, the four Arkana operatives were wandering down the main street of Luoshui Village to find a restaurant. This wasn't hard to do since the entire Lugu Lake district seemed to specialize in outdoor barbecues. They found an open-air eatery and seated themselves. Rou and Rinchen claimed a wooden bench together while Cassie and Griffin took the bench opposite. Between them sat a rectangular stone table with a recessed charcoal grill in the middle. A waiter provided them with plates, chopsticks, sauces, and food on skewers to cook and eat. Their meal consisted of pressed chicken and assorted chunks of vegetable including mushrooms and eggplant. They were also given yak butter tea and Sulima beer to wash it all down. As one or another of them turned the skewers and tended the food, they caught up on the events of the afternoon.

"Now you have to say what happened after the Nephilim entered the cave," Rou urged.

"They totally bought it." Cassie smiled triumphantly. "I took a run at the door like I was trying to escape. It's a good thing I gave you my stun gun because they searched me."

"Just as you thought they would," the girl noted.

"That was a pretty big risk," Rinchen said. "I mean, to dangle yourself as bait. That cowboy might have shot you point blank."

"Oh, he wouldn't do that," the pythia countered. "Leroy hates me too much to kill me outright. He'd want to taunt me first. Besides, Griffin and I have run into them often enough to know what makes them tick. Daniel needs us to get his artifacts, and Hunt needs Daniel to stay employed. I figured we'd be OK."

"It was a clever plan if I do say so myself," Griffin interjected. "We knew we wouldn't have enough time to hide the artifact."

Cassie flipped a skewer of vegetables to brown them evenly. "Which turned out to be a good thing since there was no guarantee those nimrods would manage to find it even if we did have time to hide it."

The scrivener handed plates and chopsticks across the table. "So, we needed to stage a scene to make it look as if we'd been caught in the act of taking the relic."

"Stage a scene is right." Cassie picked up the narrative. "You should have heard Griffin. He really sold it. Called me 'love' and everything."

"Why would he do that?" Rou squinted in puzzlement.

"The reason seemed pretty obvious to me," Cassie replied casually.

Griffin abruptly dropped a bowl of dipping sauce with a clatter.

"Careful, butterfingers, or you'll be wearing your food." Cassie absent-mindedly righted the dish before resuming her explanation. "Griffin called me 'love' because it made our story more convincing. It would seem far less suspicious that he'd surrender the relic without a fight if the Nephilim thought we were involved. Right?" She turned to the scrivener for confirmation. "That is why you said it."

Griffin stared at her open-mouthed. After a few seconds, he rallied. "Yes... um... Of course. That's why I said it. 'Love' is a common endearment among the British. We apply it to everyone. Greengrocers, postmen. I thought it lent a certain verisimilitude."

"And you should have seen Daniel's face when Griffin threatened to destroy the inscription." Cassie laughed.

"I wish we had a video." Rinchen sounded wistful.

"And by the bye, thank you for lending me your pistol. It came in quite handy," Griffin said to the agent.

"No problem. Good thing you remembered to hand it back to me on your way down the mountain. I wouldn't have been a very convincing bandit without it."

"Speaking of which," Cassie prompted. "How did your part of the act go? Give us details."

Rinchen slid a cooked piece of chicken onto a platter. "First off, Rou can mimic the worst Chinese accent I ever heard. 'Harro?'" He turned to the girl with mock surprise. "Since when did you forget how to pronounce an *L*?"

Rou laughed softly. "You are a fine one to point a finger at me when you say things like 'Where we?'"

Noting the puzzled faces of his listeners, the agent explained. "I needed to distract the cowboy with something, so I pulled out a map and asked him for directions."

"And while he read the map, I stunned him," Rou summed up proudly.

"He never saw it coming?" Cassie asked.

"Nope." Rinchen winked at Rou. "I have to say, this girl has a great future as a field agent. Cool as a cucumber in a crisis. It's hard to believe she hasn't had any training yet."

Rou blushed with pleasure at the compliment.

Sensing how close the two had become, Cassie cautioned, "You'd better not be toying with this young lady's affections, Rinchen. Your brother warned me about you. He said you're a real heartbreaker."

"What?" The agent gasped. "He's one to talk. Rabten is the player in the family. I think he's overcompensating."

"What on earth for?" the scrivener asked.

"Because Rinchen received the good looks," Rou concluded sagely. "Rabten only received the brains."

Cassie and Griffin traded baffled glances at the observation.

"Rou, surely you realize that Rabten and Rinchen are identical twins," the scrivener ventured.

The girl remained unfazed. "Oh no. Rinchen showed me pictures. I can tell the difference."

"You see," Rinchen agreed without a hint of irony. "She can tell."

"Let it go," Cassie mumbled under her breath to Griffin.

"Here is your stun gun." Rou presented the object to the pythia with both hands as if she were handing over a samurai sword.

Cassie pocketed it. "I'm going to send you one of these engraved with your name on it."

Rinchen scratched his chin. "I know we had only minutes to put this plan together before the Nephilim got to the cave but here's something I don't understand. Why the bandit ruse? If all you wanted to do was put Hunt out of commission long enough to escape, you could have pistol-whipped him when you left."

"Ah, there was more to the scheme than that, my friend," Griffin retorted. "If I had dispatched him, he would have turned these villages upside down trying to find us and take revenge. We needed to make his departure a matter of some urgency."

"That's where you guys came in," Cassie continued. "Luckily for us, you're both Asian, so you could pose as locals."

"Bloodthirsty local bandits," Rou piped up gleefully.

"If Daniel was convinced that the area is crawling with desperados, he would have believed the artifact was at risk here," Griffin concluded. "Even Hunt would have to agree that their top priority would be to get the relic to a safe location."

"And I think we guessed right." The pythia poured herself a cup of tea. "You two saw their getaway with your own eyes."

Griffin leaned back in his chair, lacing his fingers behind his head. "All things considered, our plan went swimmingly."

"Oh, I forgot to tell you," Cassie confided. "Maddie texted me that the real artifact arrived at the vault today."

"Speaking of all's well that ends well." Griffin treated Rinchen to a quizzical look. "You'll be escorting Rou back to Liaoning tomorrow, yes?"

"I'll make sure she gets home safe and sound."

Rou beamed at him adoringly.

The pythia nudged Griffin. "It's time we booked a flight home too."

"After our assorted trials during the past few weeks, I must say I'm looking forward to a quiet, predictable environment. Thank heaven nothing eventful ever happens at HQ."

Cassie's gaze narrowed as she regarded her partner. "You know you're just asking for trouble when you say stuff like that."

"Are we about to have another dire prediction from Mr. Murphy?" Griffin's eyes twinkled with mischief.

The pythia sighed and gave a lazy smile. "Nope. I can't bring myself to harsh your mellow on a night when the stars are this bright."

Griffin looked upward. "They are indeed."

Both Cassie and Griffin pretended not to notice when Rinchen slipped his arm around Rou's shoulder as they too gazed up at the night sky.

37 – NEPHILIM NINJAS

Joshua sat in the front seat of a black van parked in the dirt lane behind the farmhouse. It was still quite dark out—two hours before dawn. A week earlier he'd acquainted his father with Hunt's surveillance activities. As the Fallen man was still out of the country with Daniel and his trustworthiness in retrieving Hannah remained open to question, the diviner decided to delegate the recovery operation to the spymaster. Joshua was to observe the activities of the household. When he was sure the time was right, he was to strike quickly to reclaim Hannah. No one was to be harmed in the process. This was less an indication of his father's merciful nature than it was an attempt to avoid complications with the police.

Joshua stepped out of the van and went around to the back doors. He opened them. Three armed men wearing ski masks and black flight suits confronted him. "You know what to do," he said curtly, pulling a ski mask down over his own face.

They all nodded silently and got out. Each one held a set of night vision goggles which they donned over their ski masks. The four men then climbed over the privacy fence into the garden and headed for the kitchen door.

***

Faye awoke from a sound sleep. She blinked several times, trying to orient herself. Checking the digital alarm, she saw it was four AM. Her heart was beating quickly with an unaccountable sense of anxiety. She didn't know why but she could feel something wasn't quite right. Then she heard a faint sound coming from downstairs. Had Hannah gotten up to find a snack in the refrigerator? She lifted herself out of bed and put on a bathrobe and slippers. Cracking her bedroom door open, she peeped around the edge. There were no lights on downstairs. Surely, if the girl was in the kitchen, the light would be on. Then she heard the faint tinkle of glass falling. Someone was breaking in. She seriously doubted that this was a random burglary. It wasn't a matter for the police. It was a matter for the Arkana.

Scurrying to her dresser, she slid open the middle drawer and pulled out a cell phone. It was the one she used only to communicate with Arkana personnel. Maddie's number was on speed dial. She waited tensely for a groggy voice to answer. When it did, Faye's words were succinct. "Maddie," she whispered urgently. "Someone's trying to break into the house. I believe it might be Leroy Hunt come for Hannah. Send help right away."

She shut the phone off and hid it back inside the drawer. Rubbing her head distractedly, she tried to think of a strategy. At least Faye still had the element of surprise on her side. She cast around the dark bedroom, not seeing anything she could use as a weapon. In all likelihood, Hunt had come alone. Perhaps she could create a loud enough disturbance to scare him away. All she needed to do was buy ten minutes, and Maddie's team would be there. Her eyes settled on her purse, sitting on the highboy. She ran to it and dug into the front compartment for her car keys. Zachery had insisted on fitting out her old station wagon with an electronic security system. She found the key fob and hit the panic button. Immediately, her car horn blared. She looked through the blinds and saw the flashers blinking madly as well. The commotion would continue until she shut the alarm off or somebody came to see what the noise was all about.

"Granny Faye!"

She could hear Hannah shouting from down the hallway, her voice becoming louder as the girl ran toward her room. "Are you alright?"

Faye scurried out to meet her, keeping the key fob in her hand.

"It's alright, child. I thought I heard a burglar."

Out of the corner of her eye, she saw two dark shapes running up the staircase. The old woman barely had time to react before they gained the second-floor landing. Darting past her, they lunged for Hannah as a third man charged the old woman. He grabbed her, but Faye put up a fight. She managed to knock his goggles askew, gouging him in the eye with her thumb. He reached for her arm, but she squirmed out of his grasp. Losing her balance at the top of the stairs, she could feel herself twisting in the air. Falling backwards. Tumbling downwards. And then... nothing.

***

Joshua rushed to assist his men with Hannah. He darted past the body of the old woman, now lying motionless at the bottom of the stairs. The girl was screaming as his Argus agents tried to subdue her. The spymaster had come prepared for this. He held a chloroform-soaked handkerchief over the girl's mouth until she stopped struggling.

Then he found the key fob which the old woman had dropped at the top of the staircase. He pressed the button and the noise outside instantly ceased.

By this time, every dog in the neighborhood was barking. He peered out the front windows to see lights flickering on in several houses.

"We need to get out of here!" he commanded.

"But sir," objected one of his agents. "What about that one?" He pointed down the stairs toward the old woman.

"Not our concern," Joshua said coldly. "She probably broke her neck in the fall."

"But if she lives, she might identify us," another agent hissed.

Joshua wheeled on him. "And what could she tell the police?" he challenged. "That she caught a glimpse of four men wearing ski masks and night vision goggles in an utterly dark house? I think adding murder to our list of tasks tonight might invite more attention from the authorities than the diviner would wish."

At the mention of his father's name, his men immediately stopped protesting.

"We need to get my father's wife out of here. Now!" Joshua led the way down the stairs.

Two of his men carried Hannah's limp body between them. A third man went ahead to climb the garden fence and receive the girl as she was lifted over by the first two. Joshua left the house last, closing the kitchen door behind him. In the distance, he could hear a siren's wail. The sound grew louder. Presumably, it was the police. He loped to the back fence and clambered over. His men were waiting in the back of the van. Hannah was unconscious, but she'd been gagged and bound for good measure. The spymaster nodded and shut the doors on his crew. He climbed into the driver's seat and pulled out of the lane, his headlights off. As he turned down a different side street, he saw an unmarked car pull into the farmhouse driveway—its red beacon flashing and siren howling. Even if the old woman was still alive, there was little enough she could tell anyone. Hannah's abduction would be treated as most such events were treated in the Fallen World. Her face would eventually appear on a milk carton, and her whereabouts would never be discovered. Joshua removed his ski mask and gave a satisfied smile. His father would be well-pleased with him this night.

38 – PLANNED AGGRESSION

Zach pulled into the driveway of the farmhouse shortly before 8 AM. Maddie had called him an hour earlier to give him the shocking news—somebody had abducted Hannah and injured Faye. When he heard those words, he felt as if he'd been punched in the stomach and an hour later he still couldn't catch his breath. The chatelaine said that the attacker might come back to search the place. She wanted Zach to go to there and collect Faye's cell phone and computer as well as anything else that might link the memory guardian to the Arkana.

The tyro was out the door before Maddie had time to hang up. By ignoring the speed limit and barely slowing down for stop signs, he cut his usual travel time to the farmhouse in half. As he parked the car, he noticed a neighbor hovering nearby. Groaning to himself, he climbed out of the driver's seat. "Hello, Mrs. Martin," he said as he darted for the front door.

The neighbor intercepted him. "Oh, Zach! I'm so sorry to hear about your grandmother."

He felt a catch in his throat. "Thank you."

"What happened? We heard the car alarm from the station wagon go off. It must have been around four o'clock. It woke up the whole neighborhood. Somebody even called the police. A squad car got here, but there was already a car from Faye's security company. Then an ambulance arrived, and the driver explained that it was a medical emergency. The police left and the next thing I knew Faye was being carried out on a stretcher."

Maddie had coached Zach on what to say in case anybody asked. He went into his story. "Gamma woke up with chest pains. I guess she must have known she was having a heart attack. She couldn't walk so she grabbed her car keys and pressed the panic button to wake somebody up."

"Thank goodness Ashley had the presence of mind to call for an ambulance."

Zach had to stop and think for a minute. Ashley was the name Hannah used around outsiders. "Yeah, that's what she did. After taking one look at Gamma, she saw what was happening and called for an ambulance. Then she... uh... rode to the hospital with her."

"What hospital is Faye at? I'd like to visit her when she's feeling better."

Zach realized that whatever he told Mrs. Martin would be telegraphed around the subdivision in a matter of minutes. "She's at a private hospital. No visitors allowed except for family. Please don't worry." He swallowed hard. "She's doing fine. I just came to pick up a few things that she'll need."

"Poor Ashley," Mrs. Martin continued. "She can't stay here all alone with your grandmother away."

The teenager paused. Maddie's coaching hadn't covered this particular question. He thought fast. "She won't be. My folks offered to look after her until Gamma gets back on her feet."

"Well, if nobody's staying in the house for a while you should probably clean out the refrigerator," the neighbor advised. "You don't want food spoiling, do you?"

That issue had already been anticipated. An Arkana sweeper team would swing by to secure the place after he was gone. To Mrs. Martin, Zach replied, "We have some family friends who are going to come over later and straighten the place out since we don't know how long she'll be gone."

"It's nice that you all pull together to help out such a sweet old lady."

Zach could feel tears forming in his eyes. He looked away. "Yeah, we all do our part. I'm sorry, Mrs. Martin, but I really have to be going."

"Oh, of course." She gave his shoulder a sympathetic pat. "You take care and give my best wishes to your grandmother for a speedy recovery."

"Thank you. I'll do that," he murmured as he ducked his head and hurried inside.

The parlor seemed eerily quiet. He'd never entered that room in the past year without feeling elated at the prospect of seeing Hannah. Now she was gone. Just like that. He didn't want to think about how scared she was. He shoved away darker thoughts that hinted she might not even be alive at all. Instead, he focused on the task at hand. He wanted to know how somebody had gotten inside. Scanning the front of the house, he couldn't see anything out of place.

Fortunately, the Arkana paramedics had sidestepped a police investigation that morning with the story of Faye's heart attack. The authorities never came inside to investigate which made Zach the first person to inspect the crime scene. Once he walked into the kitchen, he immediately noticed that a panel of glass in the back door had been broken. That meant the intruder had come in through the garden. The tyro walked out into the yard. The ground was still too hard to show footprints though it looked as if one of the withered flower beds by the fence had been trampled. He guessed that whoever abducted Hannah had exited that way. His eyes narrowed as he considered the escape route. The privacy fence was six feet high. Even if Hannah had been drugged, it was hard to imagine somebody scaling that fence with a girl slung over his shoulder. Zach concluded that more than one person was involved in the abduction.

He walked back inside the house, making a mental note to have Maddie tell the sweepers to repair the window. Unplugging the monitor from Hannah's PC, the tyro carried the computer out to his car. There was no telling if the hard drive might offer a clue about the Arkana, so he figured he'd better take it. Then he found Faye's laptop and carried that out as well. The sweepers would go through all her papers to remove anything incriminating. Zach's only other task was to find his Gamma's cell phone. He knew she'd called Maddie from upstairs. He ran up to her bedroom but didn't see it. Then he rifled through the dresser drawers and found it under a pile of handkerchiefs. Pocketing the phone, he was on the point of leaving when he paused and turned his head.

For no good reason, he walked to Hannah's room and stood in the doorway for a moment. The air smelled like the cologne she favored. It reminded him of lilies. Was it lily-of-the-valley? He hadn't been paying attention when she told him what it was. In the middle of her bed, propped against the pillows, was the plush stuffed cat he'd given her long ago. It reminded her of her pet kitten—shot on the crazy preacher's orders. She'd started to cry when she first saw the fake feline. He hadn't realized she still had it, much less valued it enough to keep it near her when she slept.

His eyes traveled to her closet. A hanger was hooked over the top of the door displaying a fancy pink dress. He ran his fingers across the soft fabric. She'd told him about the outfit, but he hadn't seen it before. She said it was supposed to be a surprise, that he'd see it on prom night. Every time she mentioned this dress her eyes would light up. She was so excited to be going to a formal dance. And now...

He felt himself choking up. Fleeing the room, he ran back downstairs, slammed the door, and jumped into his car. There was nothing left to see. And too many things he wanted to forget.

***

Maddie stood in a patient's room in the vault infirmary watching Faye's monitor. The blips on the screen were steady. The memory guardian's heart was beating normally. She was in a deep sleep.

The door behind her opened, and Zach slipped in. "How's she doing?" the boy asked.

The chatelaine shrugged. "As well as can be expected after tumbling down a flight of stairs."

He came to stand beside her, staring down at his ancestor. In a nervous voice, he asked, "When is she going to wake up?"

"We don't know, kiddo," Maddie replied gently. "There was a lot of swelling around the brain. The doctors had to induce a coma. Until the swelling goes down, she'll have to stay this way." Changing the subject to take his mind off the problem, she asked, "Did you get the stuff?"

"Yeah, the two computers and her cell phone." Turning to look Maddie in the eye, he asked, "Who did this?"

"If I had to guess, it was Leroy Hunt. He's Abraham Metcalf's hired gun." She laughed bitterly. "All the time, I thought I knew what he was up to. I guess I made the biggest mistake a person can make. I underestimated my enemy. Turns out he wasn't such a dufus after all. Somehow, he found a way to throw my people off his trail."

"I don't think it was one guy who pulled this off," Zach said. He explained what he'd found in the backyard.

"Maybe Metcalf sent a few other lackeys along to help out." Maddie shrugged.

Zach's temper flared. "How can you be so calm about this?"

"Hey, kiddo, pipe down. Even if Faye can't hear you there are other sick people in the vicinity." She grabbed him by the elbow and steered him out of the infirmary and back across the Central Catalog to her office. Once there, she closed the door. "Have a seat," she ordered.

He sullenly dropped into a chair.

Settling behind her desk, she said, "You've obviously got something on your chest, so let's hear it."

For once, Zach didn't seem worried about the war club propped in the corner. He stared at the chatelaine angrily. "Gamma's in a coma. Hannah's been carried off, and you're acting like it's business as usual instead of grabbing every gun in this place and storming the Nephilim compound to get her back!"

"You think I don't care?" Maddie challenged. "I think the problem is that loss is a new experience for you."

The boy refused to back down. He returned her glare. "So, you're saying that once I've lost as many people as you have, I'll learn to shrug it off?"

Maddie enunciated her reply through gritted teeth. "I'm saying that I've learned not to bleed until I'm cut. Kid, try to remember. Faye is still alive. She might pull through this. Hannah is still alive too."

"You don't know that for sure!" he cast back fiercely.

"Yes, I do," she retorted with conviction.

Zach paused in his tirade, stunned enough to look her in the eye. "How?"

"From what I've observed and what Faye has told me about her, Hannah is a very smart girl."

"Yeah, she is," the tyro agreed, softening.

"But she's something a lot more important than smart. She's determined and resourceful. When she was fourteen, she figured out a way to escape a compound protected by armed guards and razor wire. She's got a powerful will to live and to live life on her own terms."

The boy wasn't entirely convinced. "But it's not up to her, is it!" he challenged. "That old weirdo she was married to probably wants her dead."

Maddie laughed outright at his statement. "Metcalf? Please. He dotes on her. He's the last person on earth who wants to see her dead. Trust me on this. She'll find a way to stay alive."

The tyro lapsed into silence.

The chatelaine tapped her long fingernails on the desk blotter, considering. "My biggest problem, at the moment, isn't what to do about Faye or Hannah. It's what to do about you."

A stunned look crossed the boy's face. "Me? I didn't cause this mess."

"No, you didn't." Maddie cast an appraising look at him. "But you've got an overwhelming urge to finish it. And to finish it right now."

"Yeah, I guess that's true," he admitted.

"You're so angry that you're itching for payback."

"Is that so wrong?"

Maddie smiled. "No, it makes sense given how much they both mean to you. But as it stands now, the only thing you'd accomplish by going off half-cocked is to get yourself killed."

Zach jumped out of his chair. "So, what am I supposed to do? Sit and twiddle my thumbs while you and the rest of the Arkana bigwigs discuss strategy?"

Refusing to be offended, the chatelaine replied smoothly. "Aside from lots of experience with loss, I've had even more experience dealing with reckless young hotheads."

"Don't tell me," he raised his hands in protest. "You're going to assign me some more filing as penance for going off on you."

"Nope. I'm going to give you something to hit."

Zach was so surprised by her words that he sank back down into his chair and gawked at her. "Huh?"

"You're a little young for this kind of training. I ordinarily don't approve it til a candidate is at least eighteen, but this is a special circumstance. Tomorrow you'll report to the Security Division. You'll be taught hand-to-hand combat and how to use weapons."

"And what am I supposed to do with all that?" Zach asked helplessly.

"In the short term, it'll satisfy your need to pummel somebody, and you'll learn how to do it properly. It will also tire you out enough so that you don't get into mischief during your downtime. While you're busy with that, me and the rest of the old fogies will have that strategy session you mentioned earlier.

Once we figure out how to handle the situation, we'll give you what you want most."

"And what's that?"

Maddie smiled sardonically. "A way to get your girlfriend back."

39 – ARRIVALS AND DEPARTURES

Leroy listened to the click of his boot heels echo down the marble corridor. He hated coming to the compound. The place always gave him the heebie-jeebies. Daniel slouched along at his side. The runt's shoes didn't make any noise at all. They'd just returned from overseas, and Leroy hadn't expected to be summoned to a debriefing with the old man. Usually, Daniel handled that part of the operation. The cowboy could sense that something was off, but he didn't know what. They reached the preacher's office, and Daniel knocked. There was no answer. He tried again with the same result.

Finally, he cracked the door open. "Father?"

Leroy could see the preacher sitting at his desk staring off into space. The old man had certainly slid downhill since their last meeting. Abe seemed to be shriveling up like a maple leaf ready to fall off the tree—all crinkly and brittle around the edges.

Daniel entered the office, followed closely by Leroy. He stopped directly in front of the desk. "Father, we've returned," he announced in a louder voice.

That seemed to snap Metcalf out of his trance. "What?" he barked, looking around the room half-blindly.

At close range, Leroy could tell that there was something wrong with the old man's eyes too. They were glazed over, and the pupils were so big they looked like black train tunnels in the middle of his face.

"We're back," Daniel repeated. "You wanted to see both of us."

Abe blinked several times, trying to bring his eyes back into focus. Staring down his nose at the two of them, he said, "Oh yes. That's right." He must have realized he'd been caught napping, so he tried to seem dignified and in charge. Standing up, he straightened his tie and commanded them both to sit.

171

The visitors dropped into the bucket-bottomed chairs that forced them to look upwards at the preacher—bully-pulpit style.

Metcalf didn't take a seat himself. He leaned against his desk and eyeballed them critically. "First things first," he began. "I trust your mission was successful."

"Yessir, boss," Leroy hurried to reassure him. "Got your doodad right here." He set a metal box on the desk beside the old man.

Metcalf took a few moments to unpack and examine the artifact. "Some heathen goddess, no doubt," he murmured, not expecting an answer. He set the statue down. Transferring his attention to Daniel, he asked, "Did you have any trouble?"

"None," Daniel answered smoothly.

Hunt did a double-take. The kid had become a seasoned liar during the time they'd been working together. Daniel wasn't planning to say diddly about the two thieves or the two bandits who came after. Well, maybe he was right not to. There was no sense in ruffling the old man's feathers for no reason.

Without smiling, Metcalf said, "You are both to be congratulated."

"We aim to please, boss." Hunt felt even more certain that something wasn't right.

"There have been a few developments since you left," Metcalf continued. "I chose to wait until your return to inform you." He shifted his position and fixed the cowboy with a baleful glare. "I'll begin with the news that your friend Mr. Bowdeen attempted to kill me."

"What?" Leroy stared up at him in disbelief.

Daniel looked from one to the other. "Who's Mr. Bowdeen?"

Metcalf waved his hand dismissively. "An acquaintance of Mr. Hunt's who has been working on several projects for me. Projects which don't concern you."

"When did all this go down?" Hunt was genuinely flummoxed, and Metcalf must have realized that he wasn't faking surprise.

"Shortly after your departure. He entered my office late at night with a pistol. He would have murdered me if not for Joshua."

"Joshua!" Daniel yelped.

"Yes, your brother had the presence of mind to follow Bowdeen and dispatch him before he could pull the trigger."

Leroy let out a low whistle. "If that don't tear the rag off the bush..."

"You had no idea Bowdeen was planning to assassinate me?" Metcalf challenged.

The cowboy was the picture of injured innocence. "Boss, I ain't seen Chopper for more'n six months. Ain't talked to him either. If a feller is too dumb to know his own luck, then he gets what he deserves. That's all I gotta say."

The preacher's eyes narrowed. He studied Hunt in silence for several seconds. Apparently satisfied that the cowboy wasn't involved, he changed the subject. "To offset that unpleasant business, we've had a triumph of sorts. You'll both be pleased to know that Hannah has been safely returned to the Nephilim."

Daniel gulped. "H... H... Hannah is back here?"

"Indeed." The old man gave a satisfied smile. "Of course, she remains traumatized by her ordeal in the Fallen World. She won't speak to anyone. I trust, over time, we can undo the damage. She'll remember where she belongs—and to whom she belongs."

Leroy was too stunned to open his mouth for several seconds. He gave a shaky smile. "How'd you manage to get her back, boss?"

Metcalf scowled at Hunt. "No thanks to you, that's how. I had my son Joshua search your apartment while you were out of the country. I wanted to see what sort of progress you'd made in tracking her. I must say I'm very disappointed, Mr. Hunt. Joshua found photos indicating you'd been following my wife for quite some time. He took the necessary steps to recover her. Why wasn't I kept informed of your findings?" He leaned over the cowboy. "Did somebody pay you to keep her whereabouts from me?"

Leroy felt seriously rattled by this unexpected turn of events. He had to think fast. "You got it all wrong, boss."

The preacher folded his arms across his chest. Some of his old arrogance had returned. "Enlighten me," he demanded.

"You settled for hookin' a minnow when I was fixin' to land you a whale."

The analogy was lost on the old man. "What?"

"It was like this, Mr. Metcalf. I tracked the gal to where she was hidin' and what do you think I found? The house she's stayin' at is connected to them thieves."

"That's impossible!" Daniel exclaimed. His complexion had gone dead pale. "How could she possibly be involved with them?"

"You mean the three devils who have been interfering with your artifact search?" Metcalf asked.

"Yessir. I'm pretty sure little Hannah had no notion what was goin' on. She was just a lost lamb out in the big bad world who fell in with the wrong crowd. Miss Cassie found her and took her in, near as I can figure out."

The preacher rubbed his head, trying to follow Hunt's narrative. "Who is Miss Cassie?"

"The deadliest female ever to pack a bug-zapper east of the Pecos, that's who."

Metcalf stared at him blankly.

"She's one of the three thieves, Father," Daniel chimed in to clarify. He turned toward Hunt. "You're saying that Hannah somehow became mixed up with those people?"

"The little gal couldn't of known the score. See, she was livin' in that house with a kindly old lady. I don't think the granny had any notion who she was workin' for either. But them three did. I figure they planned to keep Hannah as their ace in the hole in case they ever got into a tight spot with y'all."

"Yes, that makes sense." Metcalf agreed, softening toward Leroy. "So, you were trying to set a trap for the entire crew?"

"I was tryin' to set a trap for more than them three," Leroy demurred. "When I was in the middle of trackin' your little bride, it come to me that somebody was feedin' me false leads. That somebody had a whole bunch of people on his payroll. I expect this Mr. Big has got himself a set-up the size of yours with pockets just as deep."

"I find your story hard to believe." Daniel peered at his bodyguard intently. "You're saying the three thieves are taking their orders from some mastermind who heads a secret organization that rivals the Nephilim?"

"Believe it, son. It's all true."

The old man raked his fingers through his hair. "This is very troubling news, Mr. Hunt. Why didn't you inform me of the depth of this conspiracy?"

"Cuz they bugged my phone, that's why," the cowboy retorted. "Had me followed too."

The preacher cleared his throat self-consciously. "It would appear I owe you an apology."

"No need, boss," the cowboy protested magnanimously. "Course now that your son Joshua jumped the gun and queered my chances of nailin' the whole crew, they're all in the wind again."

"So, you don't think the thieves and their leader will return to the house you had under surveillance?"

Leroy snorted. "Not likely. I'll have to track 'em another way. Boss, we need to shut their operation down or else they're bound to show up when we go lookin' for you last doodad."

"I believe you're right, Mr. Hunt." The preacher nodded solemnly. "We must take every precaution to prevent the final artifact from falling into the hands of this Mr. Big and his minions."

"Father, may I see Hannah?"

The question came out of nowhere.

Both Hunt and Metcalf turned to Daniel in surprise.

It occurred to Leroy that Daniel had as much reason to want Hannah to keep her mouth shut as he did himself. If the little weasel had helped her escape in the first place, he'd try to persuade her to stay quiet. Leroy took some comfort from the notion that somebody inside the Nephilim was accidentally furthering his own interests.

Metcalf was speaking again. He seemed downright cordial now. "In due time you may see her, my son. But be warned. She hasn't said a word to anybody since she returned. Poor child. It may be a long time before she finds her voice again."

"Better and better," Leroy thought to himself. He put on his hat and rose to go. "I guess if you got no more use for me today, I'll be on my way, boss."

"Yes, of course, Mr. Hunt. I'll make sure you're generously compensated for a job well done."

"A pleasure doin' business with you, sir." Leroy tipped his hat.

The cowboy and Daniel silently exchanged glances. Each wondered what the other was thinking but, like Hannah, they seemed inclined to keep their secrets to themselves.

40 – AN ENEMY IN NEED

Cassie sat listlessly on the camelback sofa in Faye's vault parlor with Maddie beside her. Griffin stared unseeing through one of the faux windows against the side wall. All three of them were doing their best to avoid glancing at the empty purple armchair in the corner near the fireplace. It had been the memory guardian's favorite spot.

The pythia slumped forward and rubbed her eyes wearily. She and Griffin had just returned from China. Instead of Faye's usual warm greeting, they had been welcomed by the sight of her comatose body in the vault infirmary. Cassie found herself reliving Sybil's death in an infinitely more painful way. As the pythia stood beside the old woman's bed and watched her breathe, she expected Faye to blink and sit up at any second, but the memory guardian never did. Periodically, Cassie would glance at the clock on the wall and then back at the body on the bed, expecting a miraculous change for the better which never came. That hope, endlessly revived and then disappointed with every sweep of the second hand, was far crueler than the finality of death itself.

Eventually, Cassie and her colleagues left the infirmary and tried to talk of other things. The chatelaine filled them in on the details of the break-in. Much to Cassie's surprise, Leroy Hunt had played no part in the abduction. Metcalf must have trained his homegrown security forces well. They had been skillful enough to strike the farmhouse and get away without being spotted. The idea of what the Nephilim might do next with those expert capabilities sent chills down Cassie's spine. The pythia shook herself out of her reverie when she became vaguely aware that Maddie was speaking.

"Zach is a basket case." The chatelaine toyed with her cigarette lighter. "And who can blame him? His great-great-grandmother is in a coma. His girlfriend has been carried off to face goddess knows what."

Her comments were met by a dull silence from her listeners.

"Any thoughts on a plan?"

Neither Cassie nor Griffin answered immediately.

The pythia made a supreme effort to focus on the question that hung unanswered in the air rather than on the tragedies of the past week. She raised her head. "For starters, we have to get Hannah back. The day I met her, I promised her a brand-new life, and I mean to keep that promise."

Griffin turned from the window to regard his associates. "We can't very well lay siege to the compound and demand the girl's release."

Cassie felt taken aback. "Are you saying you won't help?"

"Not at all. I'm simply saying we have to find a less direct means of accomplishing our goal."

"Erik came up with an idea," the chatelaine offered.

The other two traded surprised glances.

"Erik?" Cassie echoed. She'd forgotten that the paladin was still engaged in spying on the Nephilim.

"He thought we should start with Daniel."

"You mean the guy we just robbed in China?" Cassie didn't attempt to mask her sarcasm. "Yeah, I'm sure he'll cooperate."

"Erik's approach may have merit, much as I hate to admit it," Griffin countered archly. "You'll recall that Daniel helped Hannah escape in the first place. It would be dangerous for him if she were to remain in the clutches of the Nephilim."

"How do you mean?" The chatelaine squinted at him.

"If Metcalf is determined to discover the specifics of his wife's original escape, who knows what methods the Nephilim might employ in an effort to obtain answers."

"You think Hannah would admit Daniel helped her," the pythia concluded.

"Under extreme duress, she may very well give him up."

"And he couldn't afford that," Maddie completed the thought. "I think we can make this situation work to our advantage. It isn't hard for us to get to Daniel. My intel says Metcalf's favorite son had gotten pretty chummy with one of the librarians at the Main Branch. He hangs out there every day."

"What about Hunt?" Griffin objected. "Isn't he Daniel's bodyguard?"

"Leroy likes libraries about as much as vampires like garlic. When they aren't on a field mission, the cowboy stays as far away from his charge as possible."

"So Daniel will be unprotected if we try to talk to him," Cassie speculated.

"Erik said he wanted to make the initial contact." Maddie rose to leave, pulling a pack of cigarettes out of her pocket. "Now that I've run this plan past you two, I'll give him the green light to go ahead. The next time Daniel comes out of the library, Erik will be there to meet him. Then our paladin will make him an offer I'm pretty sure he won't refuse."

41 – SILENCE IS GOLDEN

Hannah's feet dangled over the side of her bed. She swung them idly back and forth to mark the time. There was really nothing else to do. Her captors might at least have given her a book to read. The random wish struck her as oddly funny. The concept of reading for entertainment was completely foreign to the Nephilim. She'd never realized that before she left. The only books to be found at the compound were scripture or commentaries on scripture. Instruction manuals for how to get to heaven weren't supposed to be amusing. She smiled gloomily to herself. Everybody here was trying so hard to please an invisible, ill-tempered god that they feared to take pleasure in anything else.

The girl cast a glance around her chintz-upholstered prison. These had been her quarters a lifetime ago, but everything looked so much smaller now. As the wife of the diviner, she was entitled to a room with a private bath and a small sitting area. These luxuries were a sign of Father Abraham's favor. She eyed the barred window skeptically. Was that a sign of his favor too? But then all the windows were barred. She wondered how many members of the congregation might choose to walk away if their path wasn't blocked by iron bars, fences, and men with guns.

She smoothed the fabric of her plain gray smock. It felt scratchy. The white starched apron covering it was no better. After the chloroform had worn off, she'd awakened to find herself dressed in the stiff garb of a consecrated bride. She didn't know who had switched her clothing but that someone had also given her a bath. Her skin had been scrubbed so hard that there were raw patches on her arms and legs. Did they think they could erase the influence of the outer world as easily as that? She touched her hair which had been cut to chin length. At least the Nephilim couldn't alter that aspect of her appearance. She still looked like one of the Fallen. The thought gave her a perverse sense of triumph.

After her initial escape, she had ceased to think of the outer world as Fallen at all. It had become the real world to her. The beliefs of the Nephilim, once the bedrock of her existence, now seemed like the fevered dreams of a lunatic. Hannah concluded that the cult's founder, Jedediah Proctor, must have been mentally disturbed. She'd learned about other religions at school. While some of them practiced odd rituals, none of them felt compelled to protect their faith at gunpoint the way the Nephilim did. Perhaps it was because Nephilim ideals were so contrary to human nature that they couldn't survive in the real world. They would evaporate in the light of common sense like all nightmares must. That was why it took a ten-foot fence guarded by soldiers to separate the believers from the sane people outside.

She anxiously twisted the fabric of her apron, wondering what had become of Granny Faye the night of her abduction. Hannah hadn't dared to ask in case the diviner might want to destroy anyone she cared about. He had once slaughtered all the children's pets because the animals inspired a love not directed at God. What might he do to Granny Faye, or Cassie, or Zach if he knew the affection Hannah felt for them?

The girl hadn't spoken since she'd been brought back. It wasn't because she was sulking. It was because she needed the silence to figure out how to respond if they questioned her. She had been living under the roof of a woman who was secretly engaged in the artifact quest and was committed to thwarting the diviner's plans. Even though Hannah didn't know much, it would be better to pretend she knew nothing.

The girl jumped slightly at the sound of a knock on her door. What was the point of knocking, she wondered bitterly? A polite attempt not to intrude on her privacy? She'd been dragged from her place of refuge and carried off in the middle of the night. How much greater a violation of privacy could there be than that? Another knock came, and then the doorknob turned. Since the door was locked from the outside, she knew her prospective visitor already had the key.

"Hannah, my dear?" The diviner entered.

She cringed inwardly as his eyes devoured her. Obviously, his lust hadn't diminished during the time she was gone. However, his appearance had altered dramatically. His skin was now shriveled, giving his face the appearance of a mummified skull. His entire physique had shrunken to the point that his body appeared to be nothing more than a huddled bundle of bones beneath his black suit.

Hannah flashed back to the nights she'd been forced to spend in his bed. It now seemed like being trapped in the embrace of a rotting corpse.

"How are we feeling today?" His speech sounded slurred. He gave a fleeting smile and advanced tentatively into the room.

The girl regarded him with a blank expression.

He sat down on the bed beside her though, thankfully, not too near. "I know, my little one. You have suffered a great shock. It will take time." His voice was uncharacteristically soft. "It will take time to restore you to us."

Apparently, he was attributing her unresponsiveness to the trauma of the kidnapping. She turned her face away. The sight of him was too unnerving.

He took no offense. "My son has shown me pictures of the place you were being held. There was an old woman and a boy."

She felt her heart skip a beat. He already knew about Granny Faye and Zach? Fighting an urge to ask about their welfare, she commanded herself to keep still.

He continued. "The Fallen can be very beguiling when they want to corrupt a pure soul. They can seem friendly and kind in order to persuade one of the blessed to succumb to their godless ways. You are a mere child." He reached out to stroke her hair then caught himself.

She stifled a grimace of disgust.

"It's alright. I understand. You are an innocent in all this. You couldn't have known. Someday you will tell me who they are but not now. This is not the time." He stopped speaking abruptly as if he had lost his train of thought. Then he nodded, seemingly listening to a voice only he could hear. "Yes, yes. I will tell her."

The old man rose heavily to his feet. He fixed his attention on the opposite wall. "I have had such visions, Hannah. The angel of the Lord has shown me wonders. A bright future lies in store for us both. As I foresaw long ago, you shall rise to the rank of my principal wife. The angel has prophesied you will bear me a dozen sons. More sons than any of my other wives have borne—even Mother Rachel. Male issue is a sure sign of God's favor. You shall occupy a place of honor beside my throne when we ascend to my celestial kingdom together." He clasped his hands, swept away by his rapturous vision. "Oh, how beautiful our life will be!"

As Hannah listened to his ramblings, she recalled that the diviner used to frighten her. Before her escape, she had been intimidated because he spoke to God. Everyone said he was the voice of God on earth. Now, he frightened her for an entirely different reason. She realized he was a madman.

Once more he halted unexpectedly in his monologue and turned around to peer at Hannah through bleary eyes. Transferring his attention from his dazzling revelation to the girl who was his captive audience, he said, "But I speak of things that are yet to come. In the present moment, you must think only of regaining your strength. Once you have rested for a time, you will remember who you are. Then we shall be reunited to live again as man and wife." He lapsed into a vague silence and drifted toward the door without bidding her goodbye.

The minute he was gone, Hannah sprang up and followed him. She twisted the doorknob on the off chance that, in his addled state, he had forgotten to lock her in. Unfortunately, he hadn't. What was she going to do? The diviner's grand plan hinged on her becoming his sweet little wife again— innocent, timid, compliant. She was none of those things now. The real world had given her a dangerous taste of freedom. She meant to choose her own path in life no matter what Father Abraham wanted her future to be. She needed to escape. If only she could get word to Daniel. He had helped her once. He might be willing to try again.

The sound of the door opening once more made her jump. Whoever wanted access to her now wasn't even pretending to be polite. She backed away toward the window. Her latest visitor was one of Daniel's brothers. The one called Joshua. She hardly knew him at all, but there were rumors that he had an uncanny knack for ferreting out secrets. Hannah found him unnerving and not simply because of his formidable reputation. It was his eyes. They were cold and dead as a shark's. In the real world, it was said that the eyes were the windows to the soul. She sensed that this man didn't have one.

"Hello, Sister Hannah," he began. "I trust you're feeling better these days."

A bizarre thought flashed through Hannah's brain. This man was her step-son by marriage. What should she call him? Brother Joshua? Son? She chose not to call him anything at all.

"I see you aren't in the mood to speak. Perhaps, over time, I can do something to loosen your tongue." The observation wasn't menacing. It was a mere statement of fact. He didn't wait for her to resume her seat. Instead, he drew up a chair and sat down.

She pointedly turned away from him and stared out the window. Hannah had formed the disturbing impression that he might be able to read her thoughts or, at the very least, her facial expressions. Best not to give him that advantage.

He directed his comments to her back. "I'm sure you're aware that my father dotes on you. I showed him some provocative pictures of you in your new life among the Fallen. Dressing indecently. Painting your face. Courting the lustful attentions of men. Kissing that Fallen boy."

Hannah let out an audible gasp but kept her posture rigid.

"Incredibly enough, the diviner cannot see your corrupt nature. But I can." He paused for emphasis. "You are a true daughter of Eve—the serpent's first ally. A scheming adulteress who forgot your marriage vows the minute you doffed the attire of a consecrated bride. If your punishment were left up to me, you would suffer the same fate meted out in the Bible to women of your sort. You would be stoned to death." He sighed regretfully. "Sadly, your destiny remains in the hands of my father, and he continues to see you as a lost innocent. But you and I know better."

Hannah was trembling. She folded her arms across her chest in an effort to control her shaking limbs. It was critical that he not see the destructive effect his words were having. Mustering all her self-command, she turned to face him aloofly.

Joshua returned her stare impassively. He stood up. "Sooner or later you will tell me how you escaped from here. You will tell me who you consorted with in the Fallen World and why. You will tell me everything I want to know so that I can make my father see the truth about you." He gave a fleeting smile of triumph. "Like everything else, time is on my side. We'll chat again soon. Next time, you'll do all the talking." He turned and let himself out.

Hannah could hear the click of the lock. She collapsed onto the bed, muffling her sobs in the coverlet as she allowed suppressed waves of terror to crash over her. Beneath the surface turmoil, a rock-hard conviction was forming. With Daniel's help or without it, she was going to find a way out of here. Once and for all.

42 – EMBRACING TRUTH

Daniel dashed through the library lobby and ran up the escalator to the Reference Department.

Chris smiled a greeting when he saw the scion arrive breathlessly at his desk. "Danny Boy! How was your trip? Successful, I hope."

The scion cast an anxious glance around the empty reading room. "I need to speak to you privately. Can you get away for a few minutes?"

The look on Daniel's face must have convinced the librarian of the urgency of the matter. He briefly poked his head through the swinging doors leading to the staff area, presumably asking to take a break. When he re-emerged, he said, "Let's go upstairs."

They took the elevator to the Rare Book Exhibit.

Daniel found himself breathing easier the minute Chris was beside him. He relaxed further still when they entered his favorite room in the building. He immediately walked to the back wall to study the glass-encased illuminated manuscripts. He thought about the monks who had toiled for years on end to create such works of visual and spiritual beauty. He would give anything to be one of them right now, immersed in scholarship and meditation, a world away from his own troubled life.

Chris walked up beside him. "I know you didn't want to come up here just to look at the pretty picture books."

They both retreated to the circular bench in the center of the room and sat down facing one another.

"I'm dying of curiosity. How did your retrieval go?" the librarian urged.

"All things considered, it went well," Daniel replied distractedly.

"All things considered?"

"The thieves I've told you about very nearly made off with the artifact, but we stopped them."

Chris leaned forward. "How? Tell me everything."

"Mr. Hunt caught one of them and held her at gunpoint. The second thief offered to let us have the artifact if we would spare his partner's life."

Chris knit his eyebrows. "I don't get it. Why wouldn't the second thief just take off with the relic?"

"Because they care about each other, of course."

"But they're thieves."

The scion failed to grasp the objection.

"If these thieves are such badass relic hunters, why would they look out for each other?"

"Because they're good people," Daniel concluded simply.

This bit of news brought Chris up short. "Huh?"

Daniel waved his hand dismissively. "That isn't why I needed to talk to you today. I have a much bigger problem. Hannah has been recaptured."

"Get out!" Chris exclaimed. "This just keeps getting better and better."

"You've got an odd notion of 'better,'" the scion retorted bitterly.

"Sorry. Go on."

"While Mr. Hunt and I were away in China, my brother Joshua raided the house where Hannah was staying and brought her back."

"So, where was she?" The librarian, caught up in the story, leaned even farther forward.

"She had taken shelter with the thieves."

Chris shot out of his seat. "What?"

"She asked for refuge, and they gave it. Mr. Hunt seems to think they planned to keep her as a hostage."

"She was locked up?"

"No, she stayed with them willingly. She went to school like any other teenager in the outer world."

Chris rubbed his chin reflectively. He began to pace back and forth in front of the bench, frowning in deep concentration. Eventually, he turned to address his friend. "I'm going to ask you a strange question but bear with me. You'll see where I'm going with this in a minute." He paused, choosing his words carefully. "What would have happened if the tables were turned? What if those thieves had thrown themselves on your father's mercy and asked for asylum? What would he have done?"

"He would have had them killed," Daniel answered simply without reflection.

"That's what I thought you'd say." Chris walked toward the illuminated manuscripts and faced the wall, not speaking.

Daniel craned his neck. "You said you were going to explain?"

"I'm just having a hard time sorting out the bad guys from the good guys." Chris continued to gaze at the manuscripts. "And I'm feeling colossally dense right now."

"Why?" The scion peered up at him.

The librarian reclaimed his place on the bench. "Danny Boy, I got so caught up in the thrill of helping you solve your real-life Raiders riddles that I forgot to ask the most important question of all."

The scion stared at Chris in mute bafflement.

"I forgot to ask whether it's a good thing to give your father what he wants. Once they're all assembled, what's he going to use these artifacts for?"

Daniel shrugged helplessly. "He won't tell me."

"That, all by itself, is suspicious. A person who's starting an art collection usually wants the world to know about it. A person who's building a nuclear bomb usually doesn't."

"What nuclear bomb? You're being absurd."

"OK, maybe that's a bad example but have you noticed anything strange going on with the brotherhood since your father first sent you chasing these relics?"

The scion paused to consider the question. "There are rumors. Nothing that pertains to what I'm doing."

The librarian crossed his legs, interlacing his fingers around one knee. "So tell me about the rumors."

"It's said that my father has ordered secret facilities to be built near the main compound and at all the satellites where hand-picked men are given weapons and combat training. And then there's the lab."

"The lab?" Chris's eyebrows shot up in surprise.

"Again, it's nothing but hearsay," Daniel demurred. "A secret lab was supposedly built several miles from the main compound. A foreign doctor works there on a project for my father. Some of the rumors have grown to ludicrous proportions—that this doctor is creating a lethal substance and that my father is sending malefactors to the lab to be used as test subjects. They're never seen again."

The librarian studied his friend in stunned silence. "Danny Boy, connecting the dots isn't your strong suit, is it?"

"You think all these facts are related?"

"Like a polygamist who marries his first cousin," Chris countered scornfully. "I can't believe you don't see it."

The scion's gaze slid away. "You have to understand the way I was raised. Among the Nephilim, the greatest sin is disobedience. From the time we're small, we're taught to follow the commands of our parents without question. And that rule applies even more strictly when one's father is the diviner—God's voice on earth."

Chris didn't seem swayed by Daniel's explanation. "I thought you dropped all that nonsense when you dropped your black suit and tie."

The scion shook his head sadly. "Those beliefs run deep. Lately, I've been studying the subject of psychology, and I've learned about a hidden part of the mind called the unconscious. Maybe that's where my compulsion to do as I'm told is lurking. Even if I don't rationally think that blind obedience is a virtue, the urge to please my heavenly father and my earthly father is still alive at the core of my being." He rubbed his eyes tiredly. "Maybe that impulse forced me to suppress glaring evidence that my own flesh-and-blood could be guilty of horrible crimes. And yet..." He trailed off as he contemplated a new idea. "Some part of me knew and resisted. I've been waging a war with myself ever since this dismal relic quest began." He laughed sardonically. "The thief named Cassie told me so a year ago. She said I had to get off the fence and pick a side."

"And this woman is your enemy?" Chris's tone was incredulous. "She sounds more like a friend offering you a piece of good advice."

Daniel gave him a stricken look. "What do you think my father's goal is?"

Chris raked his fingers through his hair. "I don't know how the artifact hunt factors into it, but I think your father wants to start a war. Maybe he's waiting to collect the last relic before he fires the first shot."

"But the Nephilim are a peaceful sect. Our scriptures instruct us to bear up patiently under the corruption of the Fallen World until the Final Judgment is at hand."

Chris smiled wryly. "As I've observed before, your father isn't the patient sort. He probably got tired of waiting and decided to bump up the schedule on Judgment Day."

"And you think he'll launch some sort of attack once the Sage Stone is in his possession?"

The librarian nodded somberly.

Daniel leaped to his feet. "I can't allow that! Innocent people would die. Not just the Nephilim. Thousands among the Fallen." He could feel a wave of panic rising in his throat.

"Whoa, hold on there." Chris's tone was soothing. "You can't quit cold turkey. Do you remember what we discussed that day we took our walk in Grant Park?"

The question curbed Daniel's dark imaginings. He temporarily switched his focus from bloody visions of Armageddon to the peaceful stroll with his friend in the Beaux Arts Garden. "We were talking about the big picture," he murmured, recalling the scene.

"Right." The librarian stood and placed a hand on Daniel's shoulder. In a gentle tone, he continued. "You remember I told you it would be worse if you didn't continue the quest. That if it wasn't you, your father would pick somebody more ruthless to take your place."

"What am I supposed to do?" Daniel asked helplessly.

"You'll play along. Pretend to cooperate. Maybe you can form an alliance with those thieves. You have to keep your father from getting the Sage Stone but not let him know he's not going to get it."

The prospect of such a scheme accelerated the scion's panic attack. "It's too much! It's all too much! First, Hannah comes back, and I could be exposed as her accomplice any second. My brother watches me constantly, looking for a weakness, waiting for his chance to strike. And now this! Pretending to search for the Sage Stone and sabotaging my father's plans while Leroy Hunt tracks my every move. I can't do this alone." He was nearly hysterical. Throwing himself into Chris's arms, he began to sob.

The librarian held him until the fear subsided. He stroked his hair. "It's OK, don't worry. Everything is going to be alright. You're not alone."

Daniel raised his eyes to meet Chris's. "Really? You'll help me?"

"Every step of the way. We'll plan this together."

The scion smiled tremulously. "I'm so grateful to have a friend like you, Chris."

The librarian's eyes glowed softly. He held Daniel's face between his hands. "Oh, Danny Boy. After all this time in my world, you're still just a babe in the woods." He leaned in gently and kissed Daniel on the lips.

For a few seconds, the scion fell into that kiss and, for the first time in his life, basked in the sensation of being cherished. Then his eyes widened in shock. He pulled back abruptly. "What are you doing?"

Chris smiled sheepishly. "Taking a shot."

Daniel shoved him away and ran toward the door. "I have to go. Right now!"

"Wait!" the librarian shouted after him.

The scion pelted down the stairs and into the lobby, all the while wondering if it was Chris he was running from or yet another unconscious part of himself.

43 – AFTERSHOCK

Even after he left the library and fled down the street, Daniel was still reeling from his encounter in the Rare Book Room. It had never once crossed the scion's mind that his beloved friend might be a sodomite. Even more shocking was the notion that Chris considered him one too. Such an abomination was strictly forbidden among the Nephilim. An offender would be banished from the brotherhood and cast out of the celestial kingdoms for all eternity. It was unthinkable that one guilty of such a sin could ever be the son of a diviner. God would surely never allow it. Had Chris forgotten that the scion was a married man who had sired four children? Daniel brushed aside the contradictory memory of his own unwillingness to consummate his marriages and quickened his pace.

His car was parked in the garage of an office building two blocks away. It was dark and quiet in there—the perfect refuge. His thoughts still churning, he ran toward the underground lot like a fox diving for its burrow. Once past the dim entryway, he spotted his car and immediately made a beeline for it. Fumbling for his keys, he managed to drop them on the ground beside the driver's door. Only when he stooped to pick them up did he realize someone had glided up directly behind him.

"Hey, buddy. Long time no see."

Daniel jumped up and wheeled about. The face that confronted him almost made him faint dead away. "You!" He backed up and bumped into the side view mirror.

"The name's Erik." The blond thief had the audacity to extend his hand.

Daniel didn't return the greeting. Instead, he asked, "What do you mean to do? Kill me?"

Erik chuckled. "Now why would I want to do a crazy thing like that?"

"Because you ARE crazy!" the scion retorted. "You and your two friends. Why won't you leave me in peace?"

"Your life is anything but peaceful. Besides, we have mutual interests that I'd like to discuss with you."

Erik took the car key out of Daniel's limp hand. He pressed the fob and unlocked the doors. "Get in," he commanded as he walked around to the front passenger side of the vehicle.

Daniel mutely complied even though he wondered at his own willingness to cooperate. If Erik was going to kill him, the thief would surely want to stage the attack inside Daniel's car where the garage's security cameras couldn't detect the crime. Nevertheless, the scion obediently slid behind the wheel and closed the door.

Erik climbed into the passenger seat and did likewise. He turned to face Daniel. "The Nephilim must be slaying a whole herd of fatted calves this week."

Daniel squinted at him uncomprehendingly.

"You know. The return of the prodigal daughter and all that jazz?"

"H... Hannah. You mean Hannah."

"Yup. I bet your father is jumping for joy." Erik studied Daniel's face appraisingly. "You don't look too happy about the reunion though. What gives?"

Daniel hesitated before answering. He had to get his thoughts off of Chris and onto what was happening in the present moment. The thief was asking him about Hannah. He needed to make sure he didn't betray too much information. "It's obvious she left because she was discontented with the Nephilim—discontented with her marriage to the diviner. She should have been allowed to go her own way. My father is interfering with her happiness by bringing her back."

Erik folded his arms and cocked his head to the side, considering. "So, you're not even a little bit worried that she'll rat you out?"

The scion gulped. "What?" He forced a laugh. "What could she possibly have to say about me?"

The thief shrugged casually. "Oh, I don't know. Maybe that you helped her escape in the first place?"

"You couldn't possibly know that unless—"

Erik cut in. "Unless she'd told us so herself."

"Then it's true." Daniel let out a gasp. "She was being held by you three. I thought Mr. Hunt was lying."

"Hey, she wasn't being 'held' by us." Erik made air quotes. "She found Cassie on her own and asked for shelter. We simply provided it."

"I see." Daniel grew somber. "I wish I'd known."

"If she'd tried to contact you, Hunt would have found her in a matter of weeks."

The scion frowned in concentration. "He said it wasn't just the three of you who helped her."

"Huh?"

"Mr. Hunt said you're part of a much larger operation. Are you?"

Erik faltered, obviously taken aback by the question.

Daniel pounced. "Then it really is true! Who are you people?"

The thief darted him a wary glance. "Better if you don't know. We like to fly under everybody's radar—especially the Nephilim's."

"It's too late for that." Daniel shook his head regretfully. "My father knows about you now. He's ordered Mr. Hunt to find your leader and to destroy your organization, so you can't interfere with the quest for the Sage Stone."

"That's just great!" Erik threw his hands up in disgust. "Like we didn't have enough plates to spin already."

"You should protect yourselves. Go into hiding," the scion urged.

"It's not your concern," Erik retorted dismissively. "You and I have got other things to discuss today."

Daniel rubbed his head distractedly. Chris was intruding on his thoughts again as if this day weren't already bad enough. "What do you want from me?" he asked in resignation.

"A little information. A little help. We want to rescue Hannah."

The scion sat up straight and turned to stare at the thief. "Are you insane?"

Erik smiled derisively. "You already called me crazy so why would you even be surprised?"

"The Nephilim compound is run like a prison these days. There are guards at the gates. Guards with guns."

"I'm well aware of that, chum," Erik countered.

"There are also security cameras set up around the outer walls and inside the hallways of the main building. It would be impossible to get Hannah out of there."

"By yourself maybe," the thief retorted. "But with a little help from us..." He trailed off.

The scion still couldn't follow Erik's train of thought. "What are you saying?"

"I'm saying that if we join forces, we might be able to pull it off."

The thought had never occurred to Daniel before, but these thieves had shown remarkable ingenuity in the past. Knowing that they had a pool of resources from which to draw actually gave him some comfort. Perhaps they and their associates could find a way where he could see none. He permitted himself a faint glimmer of hope. For the first time that afternoon, his attention was entirely riveted on Hannah's escape. "How would we go about it?"

Erik grinned triumphantly. "I knew you'd see things my way. What I need from you is some information. You'll have to stroll around the grounds of the compound and note the location and angle of every surveillance camera on the outside wall. You'll also need to check the cams around Hannah's room. I'll want schematics of all that stuff."

"What possible good would that do?"

"It will help me pinpoint blind spots. There are bound to be sections along the fence line that can't be seen by one or more of those cameras. The same rule applies to the corridors inside the building. I should be able to map a path to get her out of there without anybody noticing."

Erik paused as another thought struck him. "I assume she's got somebody guarding her room?"

"Actually, no. She's locked inside her chamber, but several people have the key. I'm sure I can get a copy myself."

"Hmmm," Erik rubbed his chin. "That's a break for us. How long will it take you to pull the information together about the cameras?"

"A few days, I suppose. How will I get in touch with you?"

Without replying, Erik handed him a cell phone. "It's a burner. My number's already programmed. When you have the intel I need, call. I'll meet you here."

"Don't expect to hear from me for at least two days."

"Fair enough." Erik handed the car keys back to Daniel and opened the passenger door.

"One final question before you go."

Erik was already outside the car, but he leaned back in. "What is it?"

Daniel wavered. "I know my reasons for wanting Hannah to escape. Her return could create some difficulties for me personally." He eyed the thief skeptically. "But why on earth would you go to all this trouble to help her?"

Without even pausing to consider his answer, Erik replied, "Because everybody should have the right to be free." He slammed the door and disappeared.

44 – CHOOSING UP SIDES

The pythia sat behind her obsidian desk with the chatelaine and the scrivener opposite. They'd chosen this venue for their strategy sessions since it was larger than either Maddie's or Griffin's offices. Cassie also found she could think more clearly surrounded by lighted waterfalls and the grounding stone of the desk itself.

"Hey." Erik strode into the room carrying a roll of papers under his arm.

"Um, how are you?" Cassie asked tentatively. It was the first time the two had met since their conversation on her birthday.

"Fine." The paladin shrugged. "I hear your retrieval went well."

"Who told you that?" Griffin sounded surprised.

"Rinchen. I've been getting an earful from him about the Dynamic Duo. That's his new name for you and Cassie. He can't seem to talk about anything else." For some reason, Erik appeared mildly irritated by their success.

"We were rather brilliant." Griffin gave Cassie a conspiratorial wink.

She laughed.

"So I've heard," the paladin said testily. "Again and again and again. The only time Rinchen isn't singing your praises is when he's skyping with his new girlfriend in China." He abruptly threw his stack of papers onto Cassie's desk. "How about we skip the chit-chat and get down to business?"

"What put you into such a foul mood?" Maddie asked.

"Something a little birdie told me. Daniel says Hunt knows about the Arkana."

His listeners exchanged shocked looks.

The chatelaine pursed her lips. "I guess I gave that hayseed one too many breadcrumbs to follow. Who would have thought he could put it together on his own?"

"He doesn't know where we are, just that we exist," the paladin added. "Daniel says the diviner ordered Hunt to find us and shut us down so we can't get to the Sage Stone before he does."

Maddie shrugged. "He's welcome to try."

Erik unrolled the sheaf of papers he'd brought. "We can talk about that another time. Right now, we've got an extraction to plan."

The other three stood up to get a better look at the diagrams.

Erik went straight to the point. "This is what Daniel was able to map out about the security set-up." The top page contained a rough sketch of the perimeter of the compound with markers to indicate the location of each camera. "He gave me enough intel about the types of cameras and lenses they're using for me to be able to calculate the angle of coverage." He traced his finger over green lines which had been drawn across the map. "You can see the gaps. There are blind spots along the fence line, especially at the back of the property. As long as I stick to those, the Nephilim will never see me."

Erik selected another schematic and placed it on the top of the pile. "This is the corridor outside Hannah's room. The camera is mounted up high, and her door is right next to an intersecting hallway, so the cam doesn't quite cover it. I guess when it was first installed she'd already flown the coop and nobody cared about an empty room. There should be enough of a blind spot for her to slip out." He leafed through the pile of papers and extracted another map. "This is the corridor layout for the main compound. We can thank Metcalf for his paranoia. Some spots have too much coverage like he was targeting specific individuals. Other spots have no coverage at all. As long as Daniel follows the route I mapped out, he should be able to get Hannah out of the building via a service door. I'll be waiting outside to take her the rest of the way through the grounds."

"What do you want us to do?" Cassie asked.

"Us?" Erik's eyes narrowed at her choice of words.

"Yeah, us," the pythia repeated in annoyance. "Griffin and me."

"So, are you two joined at the hip now?" the paladin asked sarcastically.

Griffin turned on him. "And how is our relationship your business?"

"It's not," Erik admitted off-handedly.

The scrivener warily returned to studying the diagram.

"How do we fit into your plan?" Cassie persisted.

"You don't," Erik said. "This is a one-man operation, not a three-ring circus."

"But you'll need some kind of backup," Maddie objected.

"Why?" the paladin challenged. "I think I can fetch one little girl all by myself."

"That's crazy!" the pythia exclaimed.

Griffin laid a restraining hand on her arm. "You're wasting your breath, Cassie. Clearly, a superhero like Erik doesn't require the assistance of mere mortals."

"You're going to take at least one person with you." The chatelaine's tone was menacing. "And make no mistake. That's not a request."

"It has to be someone who has some context and knows Hannah's story," Cassie said. "Preferably somebody she trusts. Your choices are pretty limited. It'll have to be me. She's never met you or Griffin."

"Not you, toots," the paladin countered. "If I'm gonna be forced to take somebody, I'll take Zach."

"Zach!" the other three shouted in unison.

"You have got to be joking!" Maddie snapped.

"The kid has a bigger stake in this than anybody," Erik retorted. "It's his girlfriend who's being held captive."

Cassie shook her head vehemently. "That's all the more reason to keep him out of it. He's too emotionally involved."

"Being emotionally involved never stopped you from going on a mission," Erik grumbled in a low voice.

The pythia walked around the desk until they were standing nose to nose. "If you've got something to say to me, then say it!"

The paladin's eyebrows shot up in mock surprise.

"What is going on with you?" she demanded. "The three of us used to be a team."

"You and I used to be a lot of things." His tone was cynical.

"And if we're not anymore, whose fault is that?" the pythia shot back.

"Shut up!" Maddie stamped her foot. "And I mean all of you! This sniping is getting us nowhere. Cassie, sit down! You too, Griffin! Erik, cut the snark! If you three want to stage a brawl, do it on your own time. Right now, there's a girl whose life might be in danger. I need you people to check your personal baggage at the door and get it together! Alright?"

Cassie and Griffin resumed their places. Erik folded his arms truculently. They all lapsed into a mutinous silence.

"That's better." The chatelaine settled into her own chair and turned toward Erik. "Now explain to me why Zach is your pick to go on this mission. The kid has barely finished his first round of self-defense training."

Erik rolled his eyes at having to justify his choice. "Hey, I'm just trying to cooperate. You tell me I can't make this a solo mission, so I agree to take backup. Cassie says I have to take somebody Hannah already knows. Who's a better choice than her boyfriend?"

"I don't like this," Maddie said ominously. "The kid might be reckless."

"He won't be involved in anything dangerous," Erik protested. "All Zach has to do is hook a ladder over the wall, act as lookout and drive the getaway car. I'm pretty sure any tyro on his first day could manage that."

"When?" Maddie asked simply.

"I'll need a couple more nights to coordinate everything. I have to notify Daniel and get Zach on board."

The chatelaine remained silent for several seconds, tapping her long fingernails on the arm of her chair. Finally, she said, "This plan has disaster written all over it. Ordinarily, I wouldn't approve, but I've seen you pull crazier stunts than this and come home without a scratch." She studied Erik intently. "Don't make me regret my decision."

"Trust me, chief. It'll be a walk in the park."

"Yeah, with snipers," Cassie murmured.

45 – CAGE FIGHTERS

Daniel knocked lightly on the door to Hannah's chamber. It was a polite formality. He had already made a copy of the key for himself. After waiting a few seconds, he let himself in. He hadn't seen the girl since he'd helped her originally escape from the Nephilim. She was standing in the middle of the room when he entered as if poised for flight.

"Daniel!" She ran into his arms and buried her head against his chest. "I'm so glad it's you. I thought it was your father. He's the only one who knocks. The rest just let themselves in whenever they want. I feel like an animal in a zoo cage—a specimen on display that people come to stare at."

He hugged her for a few seconds. With a growing sense of alarm, he realized she was shaking. "Are you alright?" He held her at arm's length to study her face. She'd changed so much during her time in the outer world. When she left, she'd been little more than a frightened child. She was still frightened but definitely no longer a child. Her short-cropped hair made her look like one of the so-called Fallen, as did the expression in her eyes. There was a keen spark of awareness which hadn't been there before. He'd grown used to the dull submissiveness of most consecrated brides. Hannah no longer belonged among them.

He led her to a seat on the bed and drew up a chair facing her.

She laughed a trifle hysterically. "It feels so good to hear my own voice again. I haven't spoken to anybody since they brought me back."

"Why not?" Daniel registered puzzlement.

She dropped her voice to a whisper. "I don't want them to know anything about the people I was with. Not about Granny Faye or Zach or Cassie."

"Cassie!" The scion flinched at the name. It brought back a memory of her last ominous words to him. "See you at the finish line." He switched his attention back to Hannah. "I was told you were being sheltered by Cassie, but I didn't believe it. How on earth did she find you?"

"She didn't." Hannah shrugged simply. "I went looking for her. I thought I'd be safest staying with an enemy of the diviner."

Daniel smiled in spite of himself. "That was a very clever thing to do. I don't know the Zach or Faye you mentioned. Only Cassie, Griffin and Erik."

The girl looked confused. "Who are they?"

"The three people who are making it extremely hard for the diviner to get the artifacts he wants."

"Good!" she exclaimed decisively. Her mood shifted immediately to one of concern. "Is Cassie alright?"

"Oh yes, quite well," Daniel replied dryly. "I recently crossed paths with Cassie and Griffin in China. They very nearly stole the relic I was sent to retrieve. As for Erik, he stalked me at the library last week."

"Why would he do that?"

Daniel patted her hand. "Because he and his friends want to get you out of here. He asked me to help."

Contrary to his expectations, Hannah didn't receive the news gladly. She sank her head into her hands and began to sob.

"Oh, my goodness, Hannah. What is it?"

She raised her tear-stained face and smiled. "Not what you think. I'm crying because I'm so relieved. It all came out in a rush. I've been walking a tightrope ever since I was brought back. Not talking to anybody. Your brother Joshua coming to visit every day—trying to force me to give him information."

"Joshua?" Daniel's heart sank at the name. "He's been bothering you?"

"He keeps questioning me, trying to break me down. He wants to know how I got out, details about the people I stayed with, all of it. I haven't said a word though. I promise I won't."

"He'll try to find your weaknesses. Hannah, he can be relentless. I ought to know. I grew up with him. Be on your guard around him, always."

"I'm trying." Tears streamed down her cheeks. "I think I can take anything knowing there are people who care about me. People who want to get me out of here."

"You do! Absolutely." Daniel came to sit beside her on the bed. He placed his arm comfortingly around her shoulder. "Erik and I are putting together a plan. It won't be more than a week. You just have to stay strong til then."

She nodded vehemently. "I will. I promise. Joshua can't lay a hand on me as long as your father still thinks..." she trailed off with a grimace.

"So long as my father still thinks you'll share his bed again soon." Daniel completed the thought.

She nodded and wiped away her tears. "That's never going to happen, but he doesn't need to know that."

Daniel gave her arm a reassuring squeeze and then rose to go. "I'll come back to see you as soon as we have our escape route finalized. Hannah, don't ever forget. You're not alone."

She flashed a grateful smile. "I'll remember. Thank you, Daniel!"

***

The scion backed out of the girl's room as quietly as possible. He didn't want his visits to be noted by anybody in the community. Sliding the door shut noiselessly, he turned, almost jumping out of his skin at the sight confronting him.

"Hello, brother." Joshua gave a triumphant smirk.

"Where did you come from?" Daniel demanded angrily. "You nearly scared me half to death."

"Only half?" the spymaster asked dryly. "You look pale as a ghost."

"I just went to visit Hannah," Daniel stated the obvious.

"So I see. I suppose it's only natural. She was your wife before she was reassigned to our father." He eyed his brother slyly. "I do hope you're not asserting any conjugal rights. She isn't your wife anymore, you know."

Daniel flushed angrily. "What a despicable thought!"

Joshua shrugged. "In any case, I don't imagine you would experience much success in gaining her favor. The girl has been uncommunicative ever since her return."

The scion took a moment to remind himself to keep up the pretense. "She wouldn't talk to me either. I just wanted to make sure that she was being treated well."

"In my opinion, she's being treated far better than she deserves," Joshua commented.

"Since she isn't your wife any more than she is mine, her treatment remains our father's concern." Daniel moved away from the door. "Are you walking this way? I'm going toward the study room myself."

Without replying, Joshua fell in step with him. "Her silence may indicate a darker problem than simple female perversity."

"What are you talking about?" Daniel asked impatiently.

"Being forcibly removed from the Fallen home may have seemed a traumatic experience to the girl. I've heard there's a medical term for it."

"You mean post-traumatic stress disorder?"

"Yes, that's it. You were always so knowledgeable when it comes to trivia. I believe mutism is one of the characteristics of this condition."

"Your point being?" Daniel nudged the conversation forward.

"Perhaps she requires professional help like your wife Annabeth did."

The scion stopped dead in his tracks and swung to face his brother. "You mean you want to have her institutionalized."

199

Joshua adopted a disingenuous expression. "It seems to me the girl needs professional care. I'm sure I could prevail upon Father to see things my way—for Hannah's welfare, of course."

Daniel was speechless. A horrifying vision of history repeating itself shot through his brain. He turned and marched forward again, but his brother hung back.

"I forgot something in my office," Joshua explained. "I need to go the other way to retrieve it."

"You do that," Daniel cast back over his shoulder. He suspected Joshua had retreated because he'd lost interest in baiting him further. Or perhaps he'd gleaned whatever inscrutable tidbit of information he'd hoped to find. As the scion walked on alone, he knew one thing for certain. Getting Hannah out of the compound had now been escalated to an immediate priority.

46 – ONE STEP BEYOND

Erik and Zach skirted the side fence of the Nephilim compound. They had parked their SUV a half mile away and trudged the rest of the way on foot. They wanted the sound of their car engine to be well out of Nephilim earshot and out of the range of their bullets. To make sure they remained unseen as well as unheard, they were both dressed completely in black. Erik also wore a black sock cap to cover his light hair.

"Are you ready, kid?"

"Ready as I'll ever be," the boy replied shakily. If Erik only knew how unready Zach was despite his swagger when he'd charged into Maddie's office and demanded that the Arkana do exactly this—storm the gates of the compound and get Hannah back. Like Gamma once told him, "Be careful what you wish for."

Despite Maddie's assurance that they would find a way to save Hannah, Zach had never dreamed he would be included in the rescue party. He was painfully aware of his inexperience, but the paladin had insisted on somebody who knew Hannah personally. That requirement made Zach the obvious choice. Nobody knew Hannah better than he did except maybe for Gamma. His thoughts strayed to a hospital bed in the vault infirmary. He immediately suppressed the image. That was one place he didn't want to visit right now, mentally or otherwise. Instead, he shifted his focus to the object that stood between Hannah and her rescuers—a ten-foot chain link fence topped with razor wire.

"That's new." Erik pointed toward the privacy slats interwoven through the links. From the outside, it looked like an AstroTurf hedge. "Score another point for us because of Metcalf's paranoia," the paladin remarked. "The slats were added so nobody on the outside could look in. It also means nobody on the inside can see what we're doing out here."

Zach studied the wall of fake pine needles doubtfully. "How are we supposed to get over that?"

"Not we," Erik corrected. "Me." He removed his backpack and took out a lightweight assault ladder. Fastened to one end was a metal grappling hook. The paladin extended a telescopic pole which fit into a hollow tube on the side of the grappler. He guided the hook over the top of the fence and secured it. "Once I'm up, you put together the ladder in your pack just like you saw me do this one. OK?"

Zach nodded.

"I'm going to swing my ladder over to the other side of the fence to climb down. I want you to set up the second ladder on this side, climb to the top and haul up my ladder. The last thing we need is for the Nephilim to notice something dangling from their fence inside the compound. After you do that, stand at the top and keep watch. When I bring Hannah back to the fence, throw my ladder back down so we can climb over. Have you got your night vision glasses?"

"Right here." Zach produced the binoculars.

"Good. You keep scanning the yard and the guard tower by the front gates. If you see anything moving besides me, you send a signal. Got it?"

"Got it," the tyro echoed.

They each held small two-way radios. All the boy had to do was send a call to the other unit and Erik's radio would receive a silent alert.

Apparently noting Zach's worried expression, the paladin said, "Relax, kid. She'll be back on this side of the fence before the hour is up."

"Thanks, man," the tyro mumbled gratefully. "I'm gonna owe you bigtime."

"You can thank me now by watching my back."

"Absolutely. I'm on it!"

Erik removed the contents of his pockets and crouched down to stow them in his pack which lay on the ground.

The boy scrutinized his odd behavior. "What are you doing?"

The paladin paused. "Rule one. On a mission like this, you never take anything with you that can connect you to the Arkana."

"So, you've done this before." Zach chuckled nervously. "Someday you'll have to tell me about your adventures."

"I could, but I'd have to cut out your tongue afterward." Erik grinned sardonically.

Zach winced. He was fairly certain the agent was kidding, but he decided not to press the matter.

The paladin drew a pistol out of his pack and stuck it into the waistband of his pants.

"Don't guns have serial numbers?" the boy asked cautiously.

"Not this one. It's homemade. We've got people in the Arkana who specialize in making weapons—serial-number-free and completely legal."

Erik clamped the two-way radio to his belt.

"What about that. Isn't that traceable?"

The paladin gave an exasperated sigh. "If things head south, I'll ditch the radio where the Nephilim won't find it. Now hand me the rug."

Zach pulled a small piece of carpet out of his backpack and gave it to his colleague. He had no idea why the paladin had told him to bring it but was reluctant to test the senior agent's patience by asking for an explanation.

Erik stood up and walked toward the fence. After climbing the ladder, he scanned the grounds on the other side. Apparently satisfied that all was quiet, he folded the carpet in half and threw it over the barbed wire before straddling the top of the barrier. Pulling the ladder up after him, he reversed the grappling hook so it hugged the opposite side. As he stepped onto the ladder, he threw the carpet back down to Zach. Then he lowered himself into the compound.

Zach immediately assembled his own set of stairs and clambered up to the top. He hoisted Erik's ladder back outside the fence and then adjusted the range of his binoculars to check the guard tower at the front of the property. Its floor-to-ceiling windows made it easy to see what its occupants were doing. There were two men seated in front of surveillance consoles. Two others were standing and talking. Each of them carried assault rifles slung over their shoulders. Zach gulped. He scanned the woods at the back of the property but couldn't detect anything moving, not even Erik. The tyro sighed, hoping that Daniel and Hannah would be able to slip out unnoticed. He knew the next ten minutes were going to be the longest of his life.

***

Hannah could hear the lock on her prison door give a small click.

A shadowy figure slipped inside and a voice barely above a whisper announced, "It's time."

She looked at the clock. Three in the morning. Well past the point when members of the congregation should have fallen asleep. Only a handful of security personnel at the main gate would be awake. She bit her lip apprehensively, scarcely believing that this was actually going to happen. It was a miracle. Although Zach and Granny Faye cared about her, she hadn't thought they could do anything to solve her predicament. Apparently, they knew people who could. The ones Daniel called "the three thieves" clearly had some experience with Hannah's type of problem. That Daniel had agreed to help his enemies secure her freedom was the biggest miracle of all.

The scion, who was dressed entirely in black and wearing a baseball cap, handed a sack of clothing to Hannah. "Put these on."

She ducked into the bathroom to change. He had brought her jeans, a turtleneck, sneakers, and socks—all black. She almost wept with joy at the feel of normal clothing from the real world against her skin. She reached into the sack one more time to retrieve a final item. It was a black baseball cap like the one Daniel wore. The front had been fitted with two rows of what looked like small Christmas tree lights above the visor. She had been told that these battery-powered LED lights would temporarily blind the cameras. If they chanced to catch her on their surveillance feeds, the guards wouldn't be able to identify her. The lights would create a sunburst effect around her head and shoulders even more effective than a mask. Tucking her blond hair under the cap, she studied the effect in the mirror. Not a trace of the Nephilim remained.

"Hannah!" Daniel's voice hissed through the door. "We must leave now."

She snapped out of her reverie and joined him. "I'm ready."

They cautiously exited her room, taking care to press themselves against the wall.

"Keep low," Daniel advised.

She sank down and inched along a few feet, finally standing upright when she was slightly behind the camera which guarded her hallway.

Daniel peeked around the wall of the intersecting corridor then motioned her to follow him. His co-conspirators had identified a way to get out of the building without being detected by the monitors. Hannah followed Daniel and mimicked his posture, first crouching, then pressing herself against the wall to stay out of the range of the cameras. After several tense minutes, they finally arrived at a service door leading to the utility buildings at the rear of the property. They slipped through soundlessly. The cool night air brought welcome relief. Hannah's nerves were stretched to the breaking point.

"We need to stop here," Daniel instructed. "Erik knows the blind spots of the perimeter cameras. He'll guide you the rest of the way."

They waited for five minutes, but nobody appeared.

"Are you sure he's coming?" she whispered.

Daniel nodded.

They both squinted anxiously into the darkness but saw and heard nothing.

Hannah happened to glance toward the compound fence off in the distance directly across from her. She saw something gleam. It was an object reflected by the yard lights. The girl kept her eyes fastened to the spot. It was too far away for her to make out the shape of the object, but she knew it must be near the top of the fence. She had been told Zach would be acting as Erik's lookout. It had to be him. His binoculars must be the glint she'd seen. She was filled with a flood of relief. She had truly thought she'd never see him again. Surely, he'd seen her as well. She wondered why he didn't give her a signal that he was waiting to take her home. "Zachary!" she murmured. Without thinking, she took a step forward.

"Hannah, no!" Daniel gasped. He jerked her back against the side of the building and put a hand over her mouth.

They waited. It only took a minute before they both heard the sound of boots clattering down the metal stairs of the guard tower by the front gates.

"You must have been caught on-camera," the scion whispered. "They can't see your face, but they know somebody is out here who shouldn't be. We need to go back. If they find us here, they'll shoot to kill."

Hannah remained frozen with horror at what she had done. The next thing she knew, Daniel was dragging her inside the building. She followed numbly, allowing him to guide her back to her own room and lock her inside as if nothing had happened. She prayed Zach would be alright.

***

The tyro could hear men shouting near the front of the compound. He trained his binoculars on the guard tower which was now buzzing with activity. Something had gone wrong. He ducked below the razor wire and immediately sent a call to Erik. Where was he? How fast could he get back to the ladder? Trying to stay out of camera range now was the least of his worries. Zach saw a small object fly over the fence directly above his head. With a sense of dread, he realized it was Erik's radio. The agent said he'd ditch it if things went wrong. Apparently, things were going very wrong. Raised voices were rapidly approaching the section of the fence where Zach stood on his perch.

A gunshot erupted from somewhere off in the woods. Erik must be trying to draw their attention away from his rendezvous point. Then he would circle around to reach it before the guards realized he was no longer near the back fence.

"Over there," one of the sentries cried.

Four armed men ran in the direction where the shot had been heard. Without hesitation and without taking aim, they fired wildly into the thicket. Bullets went whizzing everywhere. The noise they made sounded like dull pops instead of explosions. Zach was surprised that the guards were using silencers, but he had no time to ponder why. He covered his head even though he realized that a turf-covered fence offered no protection at all. He couldn't leave because Erik would need him to throw down the second ladder when he circled back. The tyro had no choice but to stay glued to the spot and hope that a stray bullet wouldn't strike him.

"We got him, sir!" one of the guards shouted in triumph.

A man who was clearly in charge was striding across the open field from the main building.

Two other guards were dragging a body out of the brush.

With a sickening sense of dread, Zach forced himself to look. He trained his binoculars on the group of men and the object they were hauling between them. There could be no mistake. It was Erik. Even though they stood some distance away, they spoke loudly enough for Zach to catch every word.

"He's dead, sir," a fourth guard called proudly to his superior.

"Well, that's inconvenient," the man in charge said. "I would have liked to question him."

"What should we do with the body?" the leader of the night patrol asked.

Zach had heard enough. As silently as he could, he clambered down the ladder, retrieved Erik's belongings including the two-way radio and ran back to the SUV. He didn't want to think about how he would break the news to the others.

***

Joshua stared down at the dead intruder, puzzling over his identity. His sentries clustered around, waiting for further orders. He turned to his lieutenant. "Did this disturbance awaken any of the community?"

"No sir," the lieutenant replied. "As you ordered, all the men on the night watch use weapons fitted with silencers. There was only one shot that might have been heard as far away as the main building. If the brethren are at rest as they should be, no one will know."

The spymaster nodded. "Very good."

"Sir, look." His second-in-command directed his attention to someone emerging from a service door at the side of the building.

It was the diviner. He was wandering aimlessly across the grass like a man who had lost something.

Joshua needed to think quickly. In a low tone, he commanded, "Stay here and say nothing. I'll handle this."

The spymaster hastily ran across the field to intercept the diviner. "Father, what are you doing out of bed at this hour?"

Abraham passed a weary hand across his forehead. "I have had a restless night." His voice sounded thick, almost as if he were in some kind of stupor. "I rose to take another sleeping draught when I thought I heard a commotion outside." His face bore a baffled expression. "It sounded like gunshots. Has someone tried to escape?" He squinted hazily in the direction of the sentries.

The spymaster immediately stepped into his sightline. "No, Father. Nothing you need to be concerned about. A wild animal was rummaging through the garbage dumpsters, that's all. My men detected activity around the back fence. It sometimes happens with security equipment as sensitive as ours is. Unfortunately, the guards grew overzealous and began shooting before they'd identified the threat. It was nothing more serious than a raccoon."

Abraham searched his son's face.

Joshua tensed. His father could usually tell when a person was lying, but the diviner's perceptions had been impaired of late. The spymaster didn't know the reason, but he was grateful for these recent vagaries. He smiled blandly and touched Abraham's shoulder, gently turning him in the opposite direction. "Father, please go back inside. You need your rest. It was a trivial matter. I'm sorry it disturbed you."

"A trivial matter," Abraham echoed dreamily. "Very well. Carry on." Without protest, he did as he was bidden and tottered back toward the building.

Joshua remained stock-still until he was sure the diviner was safely inside. Then he motioned his lieutenant forward.

The man registered confusion. "Sir, why didn't you bring your father to view the body? It would surely have pleased our diviner to see the prowler we apprehended."

"Would it?" the spymaster asked coldly. "If you think that, you don't know my father very well. It's far more likely that he would berate us for having allowed anyone to infiltrate our property. Given the sums he has spent on security equipment and training, he might feel that his money was wasted. He might even wish to vent his spleen on the men he'd appointed to protect the Nephilim. I don't know about you, but I don't much care for the idea of being demoted."

The lieutenant appeared mortified. "I never thought of that." In a wary tone, he asked, "Is that the reason why the night guards have standing orders to use silencers on their weapons?"

Joshua smiled wryly. "Given tonight's incident, I would say those measures were justified, wouldn't you?"

"Yes, sir," the lieutenant readily agreed. "I will direct my men to say nothing about what happened." He cast a glance toward the body lying on the grass. "Who do you suppose he is?"

Joshua ambled back to examine the remains at close range. "I have no idea. I'm sure my father has made many enemies amongst the Fallen. Have you searched him yet?"

One of the guards bent down to turn out the dead man's pockets. He looked up helplessly at his superior. "Nothing here, sir. No identification at all."

Joshua sighed. Once again, he turned toward his lieutenant. "You say you caught him on a security camera by the side entrance?"

"Yes, sir. We couldn't identify his face. Only a figure dressed in black, but we're quite sure it was him."

"I see." The spymaster silently contemplated the corpse for a while longer. "If I were to posit a theory, I would say this intruder was employed by the Fallen boy that Sister Hannah seduced while living in the outer world. He must have been hired to steal the girl away from her lawful husband. Given our trespasser's demise, we'll never know for sure. Since he is one of the godless, a missing person's report might be filed with the Fallen authorities.

That's just the sort of pretext that would allow the local police to meddle in our affairs. We can't give them a reason to suspect our involvement."

In a louder voice, Joshua instructed his men, "Search the perimeter. If you find a vehicle, dispose of it immediately. And remember that all of this must be done with absolute secrecy."

"Yes, sir." They all saluted.

His lieutenant asked, "How do you want to get rid of the body? The same procedure as the mercenary who tried to kill our diviner?"

Joshua gave a slight nod. "Yes, that method will do quite nicely."

47 – BAD NEWS BEARER

Cassie drummed her fingers fretfully on the cushions of her living room sofa. Griffin, no less tense, was seated beside her and making a supreme effort not to tap his foot. Maddie had taken up a position by the front window, peering through the side of the curtains. It was almost five o'clock in the morning. Something had gone terribly wrong. The pythia could feel it, but she didn't want to alarm the others by saying so out loud. Erik and Zach were supposed to bring Hannah straight to her apartment. After the attack on the farmhouse, Faye's home was no longer considered safe. Taking Hannah to the vault was out of the question because it would make her privy to all sorts of information she was better off not knowing. Since the Nephilim hadn't been able to track Cassie to her new place, this was the best location they could find on short notice.

The pythia stiffened at the sound of a car pulling up.

"They're here," Maddie announced. She immediately swung the door open.

A few minutes later, Zach entered sheepishly.

"Where's Hannah?" Cassie asked.

"Where's Erik?" demanded Maddie.

"Can I sit down?" the tyro asked in a weak voice. Without waiting for permission, he sank into an armchair.

Maddie closed the door but remained standing.

"This is bad, isn't it?" the pythia asked in a small voice.

The boy nodded, afraid to meet her eyes. "I was waiting on the ladder at the top of the fence. I had night vision binoculars, so I could keep tabs on what was happening. I saw Daniel and Hannah come out of a side door. They stood there for a while, waiting for Erik to show up. I could tell Hannah was getting antsy. Then, for some reason, she looked in my direction. I don't know how she knew I was there. It was too far for her to be able to see me in the dark from that distance. Maybe my spy glasses reflected off the yard lights. I don't know, but I swear she looked straight at me. I saw her lips move. It seemed like she was saying 'Zachary' and then she took a step toward where I was hiding."

Zachary raked his hands through his hair distractedly. "One step. That's all it took. She must have moved out of a blind spot, and one of the cameras caught her. Right after she took that step, I could hear a commotion in the guard tower by the front gates. I still had my glasses trained on Hannah, and I could see Daniel pulling her back inside the building. He must have realized what happened and I guess he figured they couldn't make it. If they tried to run for the fence, the guards would have cut them off before they got halfway there. Their best bet was to go back the way they came and get her into her room before anybody noticed she was missing. I sent an alarm call to Erik on the two-way radio, but I couldn't track him. Next thing I knew, his radio came sailing over the fence and almost hit me in the head."

"In an emergency, ditch anything that can connect you to the Arkana," the chatelaine said mechanically.

"Yeah," Zach agreed feebly. "That's what he did. Then I heard his gun go off somewhere in the woods at the back of the property. I guess he was trying to draw the sentries away from the spot where I was waiting. Then he was going to double-back. Four guards went charging for the place where they'd heard the shot. They all had assault rifles with silencers, and they just started spraying bullets everywhere—not even aiming, just shooting into the trees. Erik didn't stand a chance. I'm so sorry!" Zach groaned and sank his head into his hands.

"He's dead?" Maddie sounded baffled as if the words made no sense.

Cassie and Griffin were too shocked to speak.

"Yeah, he's dead." The tyro glanced at the chatelaine regretfully. "I heard one of the guards yell that they'd got him. Then their security chief showed up. Two of the sentries dragged Erik out of the woods. Another one of the guards called out that he was dead. Then I heard them ask their boss what to do about the body. After that, I had to clear out of there, or they might have gotten me too."

Cassie turned toward Griffin and buried her head against his shoulder. He wrapped his arms around her and bent his head over hers.

"This can't be," he whispered in disbelief.

To her own amazement, Cassie didn't cry. She was too stunned by the news to feel anything at all.

The four of them remained frozen in place for what seemed like hours. The only sound was the ticking of the wall clock.

Maddie broke the stillness by walking to the dining room to retrieve her purse. Then, without saying a word, she drifted back toward the door in a kind of stupor and let herself out.

"Maddie!" the pythia called after her.

They all heard the sound of her engine as she drove away.

Zach seemed frightened and confused. Looking from Cassie to Griffin, he asked, "So what do we do now?"

His question was met by bleak silence.

48 – PHANTOM PAINS

Cassie sat on the top step of the schoolhouse in the glade. Afternoon sunlight was slanting through the canopy of budding trees, forming bright patches on the grass. It had been over a week since Zach had returned from the failed attempt to rescue Hannah—a week since the night Erik had died. The last seven days had passed in a kind of blur as the pythia and her colleagues mechanically performed their duties.

Shock hadn't quite dissolved into acceptance yet. They all felt the loss, but Maddie had taken it hardest of all. She'd grown very subdued, reminding Cassie of the chatelaine's meltdown when she'd tried to quit smoking. The pythia allowed herself a brief smile of irony. Everybody knew Maddie was alright when she was yelling, but during the past week, she'd barely spoken a sentence to any of them. For the most part, she'd spent the interval locked in her office. Cassie didn't need to be a psychic to predict that this behavior didn't bode well for Maddie or for anybody else.

All further attempts to rescue Hannah had been placed on hold until Maddie showed some inclination to tackle the problem once more. Zach was understandably anxious about his girlfriend's plight, but he knew better than to pester the chatelaine before she was herself again. Like Cassie and Griffin, Zach kept out of her way. The tyro went back to combat training and filing, the pythia returned to validating artifacts, and the scrivener resumed management of the Central Catalog.

Cassie drew in a deep breath of soft spring air. She'd hoped to shake off her lethargic mood outdoors, but the strategy didn't seem to be working.

At that moment, Griffin emerged from the schoolhouse and stood on the platform. Gazing down at the pythia with a troubled expression, he asked, "How are you today?"

Cassie glanced up at him. "I came out here to clear my head. So far, no luck."

The scrivener took a seat beside her on the stairs.

The pythia scowled pensively. "Griffin, do I strike you as a cold person?"

He stared at her in confusion. "I beg your pardon?"

"I mean do I seem uncaring?"

"That's ridiculous! Given your sensitivity and your empathy, coldness would be impossible for you. Why would you ask such a question?"

She swiveled to face him directly. "Then why can't I cry?"

"You mean about Erik?"

She nodded.

"I imagine people have different ways of handling their grief."

Unconvinced by his theory, she knit her brows. "Maybe it's because we ended things between us for good last month."

Griffin seemed taken aback. "Why didn't you tell me?"

"Didn't I?" Cassie registered confusion.

He drew himself up. "I'm quite sure if you had, it's the sort of thing I would have remembered."

"That's funny. I could have sworn I told you." Her voice took on a faraway quality as she recalled the scene. "It was the night of my birthday."

"Pillock!" Griffin muttered. "Although one shouldn't speak ill of the dead, I must say Erik couldn't have chosen a more inappropriate time to terminate your relationship."

Cassie laid a restraining hand on his arm. "Hey, it wasn't his fault. He'd just come back from Spain, and you and I were about to leave for China. There wasn't going to be another chance."

Griffin relented slightly. "Perhaps I overreacted."

"Ya think?"

"If I'm not being presumptuous, would you mind giving me the details of your conversation?"

"Sure, why not." Cassie shrugged in resignation. "For starters, he admitted that I'd been right about him in India."

"Very magnanimous of him, I'm sure."

"Do you want to hear this or not?"

"You're quite right. Please proceed."

The pythia stared off toward the tree line at the edge of the clearing. "He said that he didn't think he could be the guy I needed. At least not now anyway."

Griffin's eyes narrowed. "Let me guess. Like most women who have fallen under Erik's spell, you forgave his weakness and promised to carry a torch for him indefinitely."

"You're automatically assuming I cut him some slack because he's so pretty?" Cassie asked in an annoyed tone.

"Reductive but accurate," the scrivener admitted.

"Please! Give me a little credit!" she protested. "Since when have I ever been like most women? I told him that by the time he got around to being the kind of guy I needed, I wouldn't still be the kind of girl who needed that kind of guy."

"I see." The scrivener pondered her comment. "It sounds as if you made a clean break and parted ways with no further expectations from one another." He raised a skeptical eyebrow as a new thought struck him. "But then again, people's words are frequently at odds with their emotions."

"I'd be lying if I said there wasn't some feeling left." Cassie's voice was regretful.

"Especially now," Griffin agreed.

She did a double-take. "What do you mean?"

The scrivener's mood seemed to darken. "I don't wish to seem callous, but I believe a certain glamor attaches to a demise as tragic as Erik's. I doubt any fellow of flesh and blood could strive for your affections against a slain hero's ghost and hope to win."

"Are you moonlighting as a matchmaker or something?" Cassie asked suspiciously. "Don't be in such a hurry to hook me up with anybody new. I haven't even processed what just happened. It'll be a long, long time before I get emotionally involved again."

She paused to consider another idea. "Maybe I can't cry because I feel guilty."

"About what?" Griffin asked absently, apparently lost in thoughts of his own.

"About the fact that the last memory I have of Erik is an argument."

The scrivener chuckled grimly. "I have more reason to feel guilty on that score than you do. I once punched our paladin in the jaw."

Cassie sat bolt upright and peered at the scrivener. "When did this happen?"

He seemed baffled by the question. "I'm sure I told you."

Mimicking his accent, the pythia retorted, "I'm quite sure if you had, it's the sort of thing I would have remembered."

"Sorry." He winced sheepishly. "It was the night Erik left us high and dry in India. I had a row with him in the parking lot afterwards. Certain accusations were flung and, suffice it to say, I lost my temper."

"I can't see Erik letting you clock him," she countered.

"I caught him off-guard. He did say that if I ever repeated that action, and I quote, they'd be scraping me off the sidewalk for days."

"That sure sounds like Erik." Cassie chuckled. "But why would you pick a fight with him in the first place?"

The scrivener faltered, casting an apprehensive glance toward the pythia. "I thought he didn't know how to value you properly. I'm sure any decent man would have counted himself the luckiest chap alive to be romantically involved with you. Yet Erik treated that immense gift as if it were commonplace. I thought someone should teach him a lesson, that's all."

The pythia studied him with wry amusement. "Look at you, resorting to fisticuffs to defend a lady's honor. You really are an old-fashioned kind of guy; you know that?"

"I'm feeling positively ancient at the moment," Griffin murmured under his breath.

Cassie's face took on an earnest expression. "Given everything that's happened in the last couple of weeks, promise me you won't get yourself killed or fall into a coma or let the Nephilim kidnap you. I'm not ready to lose somebody as special as you."

"I'll always be near, Cassie." The scrivener squeezed her hand reassuringly and gave a bleak smile. "Even though I might occasionally wish that my heart had a stronger sense of self-preservation."

Cassie knit her brows and was on the point of asking what he meant when Zach came bursting through the schoolhouse doors.

"There you are!" the tyro exclaimed. "I've been looking all over for you two. Something's up."

They both rose and turned to him in puzzlement.

He continued. "I went to Maddie's office to see if she was ready to talk about Hannah again. When I got to the door, I overheard her on the phone. She's calling for a blackout. I don't exactly know what that means, but I'm guessing it's a bad thing."

"A very bad thing indeed!" Griffin blanched.

"So, I'm also guessing you're gonna want to stop her," the tyro added. "She's arranging a meeting of the Circle for tonight."

Cassie and Griffin traded stricken looks and ran up the stairs.

Trailing after them, Zach asked, "But what does it mean?"

"The end, that's what!" Cassie exclaimed.

49 – GOING DARK

Cassie and Griffin warily entered the main hall of the old schoolhouse. In the hours since Zach had made his alarming announcement, they'd been unable to discover anything specific about Maddie's plan or how to counter it. Now they'd run out of time. The sun had set, and the Circle was beginning to assemble. For once, the overhead lights weren't blazing. A single pendant lamp had been lowered above the center of the table. It cast immense shadows against the walls, obliterating the stained-glass birds and flowers which decorated the windows. Faye's throne rested forlornly in a corner. There would be no need to carry it forward. The memory guardian would not be in attendance. Thirty-four chairs had been arranged around the vast circular table. Many were already occupied by representatives from the troves of Asia, Europe, Africa, Australia and the Americas. No one had worn a mash-up of their national costume tonight. The topic under discussion was much too serious to allow for any fashion frivolities.

As the pythia searched for empty seats, she noticed an unoccupied chair draped in black bunting. With a start, she realized it was meant to be a memorial to Erik. Feeling a lump forming in her throat, Cassie hastily looked away. "C'mon," she urged Griffin. "Over this way."

They found two seats together on the opposite side of the table.

Once they'd settled themselves, a familiar voice piped up. "It's nice to see you both again."

"Jun!" Cassie exclaimed. In the dim light, she hadn't noticed that they'd taken seats beside the Hongshan trove keeper. "What are you doing here?"

The old man shrugged. "I thought this meeting was important enough for me to fly to Chicago."

"How is your foot?" Griffin asked.

"It still hurts, but I've graduated from a crutch to a cane." Jun smiled ruefully. He pointed to the walking stick hooked to the back of his chair. "My granddaughter sends her regards."

"Rou was a big help to us," Cassie assured him. "I don't think we would have been able to pull off the relic switch if not for her quick thinking."

"Ever since her return, she's become very..." The old man paused to select the right word. "Chatty."

All three of them laughed knowingly.

"I'm sure Rinchen had something to do with that," Griffin noted.

"Yes, they speak all the time. In English. Full sentences."

While Griffin continued to converse with Jun, Cassie scanned the Circle. Much to her surprise, the pythia recognized several other attendees because they had assisted her team in the quest for the Sage Stone. Michel Khatabi, the Berber trove keeper from North Africa, sat three chairs away. She smiled at him, and he inclined his head to acknowledge the greeting. Since this was a closed session for voting members only, his daughter Fifi was nowhere to be seen. Cassie gave a mental sigh of relief. The meeting was bound to be stressful enough without the added annoyance of Erik's former hookup lamenting theatrically over his crepe-draped chair.

The pythia allowed her gaze to wander further until she spotted Stefan Kasprczyk, the Kurgan trove keeper from the Kazakh steppes. She was unlikely to ever forget the tainted artifact he had brought for her to validate. Stefan waved when he saw her looking in his direction.

Toward the opposite end of the table, the pythia also spied Aydin Ozgur from the Anatolian trove in Turkey. He didn't see her because he was conferring with yet another familiar face—Grace Littlefield of the Haudenosaunee trove in upstate New York.

The murmur of small talk died abruptly when everyone felt a blast of cold air emanating from the front doors. The chatelaine strode into the hall. Taken aback by the sight of Cassie and Griffin, she faltered for a second but recovered quickly. It was obvious she hadn't meant for them to know about this gathering. She moved forward to claim the remaining empty seat at the table. "The Circle is now complete," she announced authoritatively. "I call this meeting to order."

An expectant hush fell over the group. Several people leaned forward in anticipation.

Maddie settled herself and began. "I want to thank you all for attending on such short notice. I wouldn't have summoned you unless there was an emergency and, in my opinion, what we have is a full-blown crisis on our hands. As you all know, the Arkana's search to recover the Sage Stone has forced us to cross paths repeatedly with the Blessed Nephilim. We did more than cross paths with them when one of their own ran away from the cult and took refuge with our memory guardian Faye. The girl's name is Hannah, and she's the youngest wife of the Nephilim's diviner. Needless to say, he made her recovery a high priority. I seriously underestimated the measures he would take to get her back. Abraham Metcalf went so far as to send a raiding party to Faye's house. In the process, his thugs put our memory guardian in a coma."

A gasp was heard from several quarters. Apparently, not all the trove keepers had been kept in the loop.

"Last week during a failed attempt to rescue Hannah from the Nephilim compound, our paladin Erik was shot and killed." Maddie's eyes strayed unwillingly to the empty chair draped in black. Her face expressed a mixture of sorrow and desperation. "Shortly before his passing, Erik found out that the Arkana has officially made the Nephilim's hit list."

A burst of exclamations followed this announcement.

Grace Littlefield asked tensely, "Do they know the location of the vault?"

The chatelaine shook her head. "Not yet. They only know that we played a role in sheltering Hannah and that three of our agents have been obstructing their artifact search." She paused and added heavily, "Correction—two agents now. Because of our interference, the diviner has targeted our entire organization for destruction."

She solemnly regarded the troubled faces around the table. "Things have taken a bad turn for us, but we've been in tight places before. The Arkana has been around for a long, long time and we've managed to weather witch hunts, the Spanish Inquisition, Communist purges, and two world wars. Every time the planet faced a new crisis, we declared a blackout and shut ourselves down temporarily. I believe we need to apply the same measures now. That's why I propose we end the quest for the Sage Stone immediately, dismantle the Central Catalog, and suspend operations."

"For how long?" Michel Khatabi asked in a concerned tone.

Maddie shrugged. "Who can say how long it will take for the cult to forget about us. A year? Five years? A decade? I only know one thing for sure. The price of fighting the Nephilim has gotten too steep to pay. Faye was like a mother to me. I'm sure many of you felt that way about her. Now she's in a coma. Erik was the son I never had, and he's dead. I'll never—" She cut herself off abruptly as her voice threatened to crack. Mastering her emotions, she sighed wearily. "We've lost too many good people already. We can't afford to lose any more. Before I call for a vote on my proposal, the floor is open for discussion."

Worried voices surged as people turned to their neighbors and debated the situation. Nobody appeared to dispute Maddie's assessment of the need for a shutdown.

Cassie stood up. "I have something to say," she declared.

The buzz ceased immediately.

Maddie folded her arms truculently across her chest. "Of course, you do." She looked annoyed but knew she couldn't stop the pythia.

All faces turned toward Cassie. She took a deep breath. "I don't think everybody here realizes how close we are to the finish line. We just returned from China with the final clue that points to the hiding place of the Sage Stone. Now that we're only one step away from retrieving it, you want us to back off and call it quits?"

Aydin Ozgur cleared his throat to speak. "I have been a trove keeper for many decades now. Perhaps more than most, I understand the symbolic importance of the Sage Stone. It is the matristic equivalent of the Holy Grail. But what is that when weighed in the balance against the survival of the Arkana itself? It seems to me the wisest course of action would be to terminate the quest."

The pythia shook her head. "This isn't about us nabbing the Sage Stone. It's about keeping that rock out of the hands of the Nephilim. Their diviner has been assembling global death squads ever since this quest started. He's planning to arm those guys with some kind of biological or chemical weapon and turn them loose on the world. I don't know why the Sage Stone is important to him, but Faye believed that his whole plan hinges on it. I believe it too. He won't give the order to attack til he has it. We can stop him cold by snagging the artifact before he does."

"But what if your theory doesn't hold up?" Grace Littlefield challenged. "Say you prevent Metcalf from capturing the Sage Stone, what's to keep him from unleashing his army without it?"

"He won't," Griffin remarked quietly. "You must remember that the brotherhood of the Nephilim owes its very existence to nothing more substantial than a mad set of religious beliefs. The god they serve is exacting and prone to wrath which makes cult members anxious to please him. Their diviner has apparently decided that the best way to gratify his lord is by starting a holy war—a war which he is convinced he cannot win without the Sage Stone. If we deprive him of the artifact, he will interpret his loss as a sign of divine disapproval of his military ambitions. Such an ill omen will immobilize him with fear."

Grace remained unconvinced. "Even if you're right, it would still be a good idea to hedge our bets. In the past, whenever soldiers started marching, the Arkana went dark and waited til the smoke cleared."

Several members of the Circle nodded vigorously in agreement. Half a dozen voices chimed in with comments like "Yes, absolutely" and "We need to lay low."

Cassie raised her hands for silence. "You're forgetting one major difference. Every time the Arkana used that strategy in the past, we were spectators. We could afford to sit back and watch while the rest of the world slugged it out. Now that Abraham Metcalf has tagged us for extermination, we don't have seats in the second balcony anymore."

Her listeners looked stunned as the implication struck them.

The pythia continued. "None of you have been up close and personal with the Nephilim the way Erik and Griffin and I have. The cult has a zero-tolerance policy for anybody who doesn't drink their flavor of Kool-Aid. You can't simply stick your heads in the sand and wait for this thing to blow over because it never will. We're the Nephilim's Number One Enemy now which means they'll be coming after us bigtime. You might as well paint a giant red bull's eye on the roof of the schoolhouse because they won't quit til they've wiped us out."

"All the more reason to dismantle the Central Catalog," Stefan Kasprczyk objected vehemently. "Above all else, we have a sacred duty to protect the troves, no? We have guarded them for centuries, and they must remain our chief concern."

Cassie nodded. "You're right. The troves are your top priority, but I think you've lost sight of what the troves really are."

Several attendees exchanged puzzled glances.

"The troves aren't just collections of cracked pottery and broken statues. You've preserved them because of what they stand for. They prove there was a time long ago when we knew how to live in peace with each other. We created entire civilizations that weren't fueled by invasion and slavery and murder. The troves prove that the world was a decent place before overlords slaughtered their way across the globe and almost destroyed it with their endless warmongering."

She eyed her listeners intently.

"If you hide and don't lift a finger to stop them, the Nephilim will root out every single trove and burn it to the ground. They won't simply destroy the Arkana, they'll destroy the only proof that a better way of life ever existed and the hope that it could ever exist again."

She paused to let her words sink in before continuing. "And it won't end with us either. After we're out of the picture, Metcalf's death squads will keep killing until civilization as we know it is gone. In its place, the Nephilim will set up a world where women are traded around like herds of cattle. Where families are broken apart and reassembled like Legos at the whim of the guy in charge. Too many good people in the Arkana gave their lives to keep that kind of world from becoming our only option."

"You just proved my point, kiddo," Maddie remarked acidly. "We've had too many losses already."

"You want to talk about loss?" Cassie wheeled on her. "I've lost everybody I ever cared about because of the Arkana. My parents, my only sister, Faye, Erik."

She stared at the chatelaine accusingly. "If Erik were standing here right now, what do you think he'd say to your proposal?"

Maddie glowered back, refusing to answer.

"He'd ask you why he died for nothing. He went down fighting, and he expects us to do the same—to keep on fighting til we win or die trying."

Despite Maddie's stubborn silence, she forged on relentlessly. "Well? He's waiting for your answer, and so am I. You say he was the son you never had. If you really loved him as much as you claim, then you couldn't use his death as an excuse to take the coward's way out. He would never have stood for that!"

The chatelaine leaped from her chair, overturning it in the process. She towered over the pythia.

Cassie fought the instinctive urge to take a step back. Instead, she stood her ground, wordlessly daring the Amazon to strike her.

Maddie drew herself up. Her eyes were burning with fury and grief. Tears streamed down her face unchecked. In mute rage, she turned and stormed out of the hall. The doors slammed behind her with a decisive bang.

During the stunned silence that followed her departure, Cassie walked around to the other side of the table. She rested her hands on the back of the paladin's empty chair as she searched the faces of her colleagues. "Erik would ask all of you the same question. Did he really die for nothing? The only way you can honor his sacrifice is by seeing this mission through—by rescuing Hannah and recovering the Sage Stone and shutting the Nephilim down for good. That's the answer the Arkana owes him."

The pythia stopped abruptly. "I don't have anything else to say." Without another word, she returned to her seat.

Just as the chorus of voices resumed its chaotic rumble, Griffin stood up. "I'd like to add a comment or two, if I may."

In an instant, the chatter ceased.

"Although Cassie has ably addressed all your concerns, there's one topic we haven't touched upon yet—the divergence between the collective and the individual."

This comment spurred a flurry of confused speculation.

The scrivener elaborated. "All of you are aware of the brutal methods which the Nephilim employ to achieve their ends. Kidnapping, murder, and potentially even global terrorism. From birth onward, members of the cult are taught that obedience is the highest virtue. In consequence, they are willing to commit innumerable atrocities at the behest of the deranged fellow who calls himself their diviner. Such is the damage that can ensue when unquestioning obedience supersedes personal conviction of right and wrong."

"I'm not sure what your point is," Michel Khatabi interjected testily. "But stooping to fear tactics to sway our decision is beneath you."

"That wasn't my intention at all," the scrivener countered. "I simply wanted to clarify my motives for tendering my resignation as chief scrivener."

Cries of disbelief erupted from around the table.

"Please." Griffin raised his hand. "Allow me to finish. Collectively, we are bound by the decisions of the Circle. As individuals, we must consult our own best judgment when deciding upon a course of action. Without that necessary counterbalance, we would follow authority as blindly as the Nephilim, no matter how misguided that authority might be. Personally, I am convinced that the Sage Stone is Abraham Metcalf's Achilles heel. If we deprive him of it, all his schemes will collapse like a house of cards. Therefore, should the Circle decide to terminate the relic hunt and declare a blackout, I will dissociate myself from the organization and pursue the Minoan relic alone."

The assembly fell still. Shock had evidently taken the place of protest.

The scrivener gazed around at his flabbergasted audience. "Of course, I would welcome the support and assistance of the Arkana but, either way, I intend to see this quest through." He glanced down at Cassie. "I haven't discussed my decision with our pythia yet, so I can only speak for myself."

Cassie jumped up beside him and took his hand. "Griffin speaks for me too. We didn't battle our way this far to fail in the end. Trust me when I tell you that we mean to finish what we started."

The scrivener gave a slight smile. "It would appear the two of us are in accord as to our future plans. The direction the Arkana chooses to take now rests with you, but I would hope that you understand the necessity of standing with us in this fight. The survival of the troves depends upon it."

They both sat down.

Jun looked around at his fellow members. "Does anyone wish to offer any final comments?"

No one spoke.

The old man nodded. "Very well. I will officially close discussion of this topic. Since the chatelaine is unlikely to return, I suggest we now take a vote on her proposal."

Cassie reached for the scrivener's hand once more and gripped it tightly.

"All those in favor?" Jun announced. He waited several seconds, but there were no votes to count. "All those opposed?" Thirty-two hands shot up in the air including his own.

"Brilliant!" Griffin exclaimed.

"The Nephilim wanted a war." Cassie's tone was ominous. "They just got their wish."

50 – RECYCLABLES

Dr. Rafi Aboud sat in the office of his underground laboratory reviewing a batch of test results. For the past two months, he had tried, with only limited success, to develop a vaccine which would quell the strain of pneumonic plague he had created. He was running out of patience with himself. His own mild disappointment was nothing compared to the vocal displeasure of both his benefactor and his business associate Vlad. Their demands for immediate results grew more strident with each passing day.

He scanned the data before him. The last test subject had taken days to succumb. At least Aboud had succeeded in slowing the advance of the bacteria. He'd made some additional adjustments to the vaccine formulation and was hopeful that the next test might produce a better outcome. He smiled morosely. When he first began the testing process, he'd been worried about how to obtain human subjects. Much to his own amazement, his benefactor possessed an inexhaustible supply of people he wanted to get rid of. The trait seemed to run in the family.

A month earlier, Aboud had been surprised by a visit from one of his benefactor's many sons. The young man introduced himself as Joshua and explained that he was the head of security for his father's organization. He told the doctor that he was tangentially involved in the supply chain insofar as he was the man responsible for identifying malcontents who were then sent to Aboud's laboratory. Although Joshua wasn't privy to what went on inside, he did know that those who entered never returned. Given that fact, he was wondering if the doctor might help him with an awkward situation.

When Aboud followed Joshua out to the reception area, he was confronted by the sight of two of Joshua's men carrying what appeared to be a body bag. They placed it on the floor. Joshua explained that his father had nearly been assassinated by the person now lying within said body bag. Joshua was aware that the doctor's laboratory contained an incinerator and he wondered if the doctor might do him the favor of disposing of the remains. Considering the circumstances, Aboud felt it in his best interests to comply. He instructed the security team to leave the corpse and gave his assurances that he would take care of the problem. Joshua left satisfied, presumably never to bother the good doctor again.

Since Aboud was a practical man, he saw no point in destroying something he might be able to use later. The body was still fresh enough to harvest odds and ends. He extracted the organs and removed slabs of tissue to culture several new batches of vaccine. After he had finished salvaging what he needed, the scraps were incinerated along with the most recent test subject. The matter should have ended then and there. Aboud shook his head.

When Joshua showed up with four sentries carrying another body bag two weeks earlier, the doctor began to think he'd gone into the waste management business. His benefactor's son didn't bother to explain how this latest subject had come to his untimely end. The chief of security quite literally dropped the remains on Aboud's doorstep and presumed the doctor would know what to do.

Aboud sighed philosophically and prepared for another salvage operation. Once the body had been placed on his dissection table, he performed a cursory inspection to determine if it was still fresh enough to harvest. Aboud drew back in surprise when he realized that this particular body was quite fresh—in fact, it was still alive. He found himself wondering if Joshua and his men had even bothered to check for a pulse. As things stood, it would have taken more than a simple carotid artery test to discover the feeble heartbeat that remained. The man might not be dead, but he was hovering dangerously close to that point.

The doctor immediately performed a thorough examination of the subject and concluded that it might be possible to save him. Of course, he had lost a significant amount of blood from several bullet wounds. Aboud called in his team, and they all went to work. The irony of the situation wasn't lost on the doctor. His staff had spent months inventing ever more efficient ways of extinguishing life from the human body. They soon proved to be equally adept at forcing life to remain, no matter how unwillingly. The bullet wounds were cleaned and disinfected. Several blood transfusions later, it became obvious the patient would survive. Aboud dismissed his team and took charge of the subject from there. When the man eventually showed signs of regaining consciousness, Aboud sedated him. Less trouble that way.

The doctor finished checking his test results and rose from his desk. He whistled an old tune from his homeland as he walked into the decontamination chamber where his hazmat suit hung on a peg. There he methodically donned his coverall, helmet, and gloves as a prelude to conducting yet another experiment. After he had taken care to cover every square inch of his body, he moved on to the testing area.

His technicians had already strapped the unconscious blond man into the plastic chair. Aboud attached an oxymeter to the man's finger. Then he gave a signal to his assistants on the other side of the glass wall. One of them waved back to indicate that the vital signs were being transmitted properly.

The doctor retrieved a gas canister from a corner of the room. Then he placed a breathing apparatus over the man's nose and mouth. The subject twitched briefly. Aboud attached the tube from the canister to the mask over the man's face. Then, he turned the valve on the gas canister to release its deadly contents through the breathing tube.

The man was returning to consciousness. He blinked and struggled to sit up. His eyes opened wide with alarm when he realized his predicament.

"Welcome back to the land of the living," Aboud said. "No matter how brief your stay may be."

ABOUT THE AUTHOR

"There's a 52% chance that the next Dan Brown will be a woman ... or should we just make that 100% now?" --Kindle Nation Daily

Nancy Wikarski is a fugitive from academia. After earning her Ph.D. from the University of Chicago, she became a computer consultant and then turned to historical mystery and adventure fiction writing.

She is a member of Mystery Writers of America, the Society of Midland Authors, and has served as vice president of Sisters in Crime - Twin Cities and on the programming board of the Chicago chapter. Her short stories have appeared in *Futures Magazine* and *DIME Anthology*, while her book reviews have been featured in *Murder: Past Tense* and *Deadly Pleasures*.

Her novels include the Victorian Chicago Mysteries set in 1890s Chicago. The series has received People's Choice Award nominations for best first novel and best historical. The seven-volume Arkana Archaeology Adventure Series is an Amazon bestseller.

VICTORIAN CHICAGO MYSTERIES

The Fall of White City (2002)
Shrouded in Thought (2005)

ARKANA ARCHAEOLOGY ADVENTURES

The Granite Key (2011)
The Mountain Mother Cipher (2011)
The Dragon's Wing Enigma (2012)
Riddle of the Diamond Dove (2013)
Into the Jaws of the Lion (2014)
Secrets of the Serpent's Heart (2015)
The Sage Stone Prophecy (2016)

Made in the USA
Coppell, TX
23 June 2020